The Travels of Lao Ts'an

老殘游記 By Liu T'ieh-yün (Liu E)

TRANSLATED FROM THE CHINESE AND ANNOTATED BY

Harold Shadick

Columbia University Press

NEW YORK

Columbia University Press Morningside Edition 1990

Columbia University Press
New York   Chichester, West Sussex

Library of Congress Cataloging-in-Publication Data
Liu, E, 1857–1909.
  [Lao ts'an yu chi. English]
  The travels of Lao Ts'an / Liu T'ieh-yün (Liu E) ;
  translated and annotated by Harold Shadick.
  — Morningside ed.
      p.   cm. — (Modern Asian literature series)
  Translation of: Lao ts'an yu chi.
  Includes bibliographical references.
  ISBN 0-231-07255-4
  I. Shadick, Harold.   II. Title.   III. Series.
[PL2718.I8L313   1990]   895.1'348—dc20   89-25421
                                                CIP

⊗
Printed in the United States of America

p 10 9 8 7 6 5 4 3

Contents

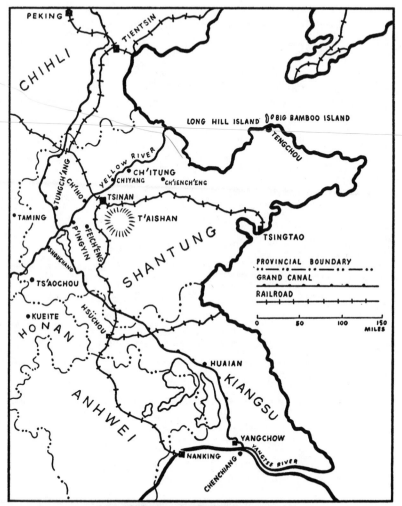

Map of Shantung and adjacent provinces.

Translator's Introduction to the Morningside Edition

MY NEW EDITOR is kindly allowing me to say a few words to the readers. I begin with some thoughts on what *The Travels of Lao Ts'an* (henceforth *The Travels*) has meant to me. I began teaching Western history and literature at Yenching University in Peking in 1925, just fourteen years after the abdication of the Manchu dynasty. A great empire was in ruins, but evidence of its past strength and beauty was everywhere to be found. I explored the City of Peking and the temples and villas in the Western Hills, all still permeated with the *mana* of the dynasty. The ashes from the last sacrifice at the Altar of Heaven had not been removed. At the Summer Palace the private rooms were as when they were last occupied. The last emperor had just been ousted from his inner courtyards in the Forbidden City. The bandit gangs, big and small, that had battened on the crumbling state were now succeeded by something worse. Warlord officers were flaunting their power in the streets of Peking and being glamorized in the windows of photographers' shops. I saw their ragtag and bobtail troops confiscating precious carts and draft animals and conscripting their peasant owners, all within a mile of the university. For teachers and students the university was a refuge from this chaotic world, but whenever a group gathered socially the inevitable topic of conversation was how China could be brought back to health and independence.

Most of my first year was spent in the beginners class at the Language School. When in 1929 I chanced on the novel *The Travels of Lao Ts'an*, it was, for me, a rare discovery: a book almost within my reading range that also seemed to have something interesting to say. I therefore made it my priority reading.

The early fascination of *The Travels* for me was that it confirmed or modified the way I was interpreting the endless novelties I encountered in this, to me, strange society. For instance, it struck me as quaint to hear a plumber say to his mate, "turn the handle to the west," rather than "to the left (or right)." The meticulousness with which the orientation of buildings and furniture is recorded in *The Travels*, together with my own observation that all buildings in China face south, made the plumber's words less quaint. And when I found this sentence: "The tables, chairs, stands, and desks were all *correctly* [*t'o hsieh*] placed" (p. 92, 1. 16), it became clear that in China such things are not a matter of choice or chance but of prescription. The fact that prescription is enforced by custom rather than law is clarified in the dictionary *Kuo Yü Tz'u Tien*, where the example cited of this meaning of *t'o hsieh* is the complete sentence quoted above, but the *locus classicus* is the eighteenth-century novel *Julin Waishih* (The Scholars). Buildings and furniture, of course, are only the stage setting for the human drama in which etiquette reigns. We see this in *The Travels* when the Governor places his guests on the heated *k'ang* while he sits below on a stool (p. 38, 11. 9–11).

If the plumber's words seemed quaint, the way two acquaintances of any social level meeting on the street bowed to each other with the stately elegance of an eighteenth-century European nobleman seemed touchingly beautiful as well as astonishing. The pervasiveness of such politeness is brought home in *The Travels* in, for instance, the convivial scene at the Ming Lake House (p. 25, par. 3), and in the many encounters of various officials. Thus, the novel, in faithfully describing life in the late Ch'ing period, concretizes the great Confucian principles of *Jen* (respect and consideration for others) and *Li* (the ceremonial rules by which the universe, including human society, functions harmoniously).

Similarly, the strength of the Buddhist belief in reincarnation and of the Confucian belief in the power of ancestors becomes plausible with the words of Yü Hsüeh-li—"I will go down first to prepare a dwelling for you!"—as she kills herself beside her husband, who is being slowly murdered in a garotte (p. 52, par. 5), and later with Tsui-huan's passionate concern for her little brother lest "the burning of incense to their ancestors would come to an end" (p. 190, par. 1).

It was not until 1934 that I seriously thought of translating the book. I happened to sit next to Dr. Hu Shih on a train from Peking to Tientsin, he bound for Nanking, I for Peitaiho. This was good fortune. He, the discoverer and "patron" of *The Travels* and its author, and editor of the edition I was using, filled me with information about the novel and encouraged me in the translation project. Some twenty years later when I had joined the faculty of Cornell University and the Cornell Press had published my translation, I saw Dr. Hu (a Cornell alumnus) frequently. He approved of the work.

On the Illustrations

I will also take this opportunity to make a few remarks about some of the photographs that appear on pp. 15–22. The caption to figure 2 does not identify everyone in the picture. Second from left is Wu Shih-ch'ang, best known as an authority on the *Hung Lou Meng*. He introduced me to the Liu family. Third from the left is Liu Hou-tzu (Hui-sun), son of Liu Ta-shen. He and Wu Shih-ch'ang were colleagues in Ku Chieh-kang's History Research Institute. Next is Helen Shadick and next to her, Mrs. Liu; between them, one of the many Liu grandchildren.

The rest of the photographs, figures 3–12, were taken on a pilgrimage to Shantung in late August 1936, when I visited all the places in Tsinan mentioned in *The Travels*. Figure 6 shows an enclosed area of lotus plants; at close hand one can see that the leaves grow up to thirty inches in diameter. It was too late in the season for the magnificent blossoms, which grow eight inches across on stems that rise five feet above the water.

The Wenshanghsien identified in the caption to figure 12 is about 125 kilometers southwest of Tsinan. It is a rather poor *hsien* on the river Wen that feeds the Grand Canal. At the time the *hsien chang* (magistrate) was my colleague, Professor Chang Hung-chün of the Department of Sociology at Yenching University. Several of his administrative staff were his students. This appointment of a scholar to the magistracy of a district was part of a larger local government reform and research project with headquarters at Chining on the Grand Canal, some 60 kilometers to the south of Wenshang. The helmeted man is

James Bertram, a New Zealander who was spending a year at Yenching University after finishing at Oxford, and who accompanied me on this trip. After seeing everything of interest in and about Tsinan, we went by train to Chining and thence by car to Wenshang. We stayed in the *yamen* for four days and became acquainted with the Hall of Justice, the prisons, the offices, and the treatment center for opium addicts.

It was not an entirely idyllic place. At night one heard the screams of the tax farmers being beaten to force them to disgorge more of what they had collected. The treatment of the opium addicts was rough, although in their own interest; at the time, government policy was to eliminate incorrigibles. Bertram and I went by bicycle with two armed *yamen* guards to visit the hill district of Liang Shan, the stronghold of the bandits in the novel *All Men Are Brothers* (*Water Margin*). The area was still infested by robbers, so our visit was made the occasion of maneuvers by the local militia. We then went south about 30 kilometers by boat on the Grand Canal to Nanwang, a strategic point where the river Wen divides as it enters the canal, sending half of its water north and half south. The officials at the Water Control Station treated us handsomely. I remember that breakfast in the orchard began with peaches and a fine big fish. Bertram, a budding journalist, was good company, full of curiosity. Two years later, he managed to be the first journalist to reach Sian when Chiang Kai-shek was kidnapped and wrote an account of the whole episode, *First Act in China: The Story of the Sian Mutiny* (1938).

Vocal Arts

Among the elements of Chinese life that *The Travels* celebrates is popular public entertainment, and specifically the art of the drum singer, described in chapter 2. This very demanding art is one of many that are usually presented in a mixed program comparable to that of a Western music hall. When I first read *The Travels,* I was already keen on Peking opera, which is closely related to drum singing. After undertaking the translation, I began visiting the teahouse in the East Market where the drum singers performed. In Tsinan, Bertram and I found a teahouse, more grand than any in Peking, where we heard an elaborate program climaxed by a performance by Liu Pao-ch'uan, the legendary King of Drum Singers. Too bad that it was not called the Ming Lake House! Since I had developed this interest it was natural for me to be one of a group of scholars who in 1969 organized the Conference on Chinese Oral Performing Literature (CHINOPERL), which meets annually and periodically publishes volumes of *CHINOPERL Papers*, which include studies of all types of spoken or sung performance: storytelling, comic dialogues, operas of many kinds, ballad singing. Volume 13 (1984–1985) includes a translation of the autobiography of Chang Tsui-feng, a drum singer who lived from 1913 to 1975.

Before 1949 the performers of all these entertainments were underprivileged and exploited. Under the People's Republic they have prospered. During a visit to Tientsin in 1986, I was taken on a tour of a new North China School for the Traditional Vocal Arts. This is a large, well-equipped institution, where the standard of instruction is very high. The students, well-fed, well-dressed, happy, devoted to their art, and assured of an honorable career, brought to my mind a contrasting image of the miserable life of their predecessors I had known in the twenties and thirties.

Studies in English

There is an extensive literature in Chinese on *The Travels*. In the years since I completed my translation, two substantial studies in English have appeared. While admitting the looseness of plot structure, both studies attempt to find a more definable unity than the rather vague "unity of feeling" with which I credited the book in my 1952 introduction.

C. T. Hsia, in "The Travels of Lao Ts'an: An Exploration of Its Art and Meaning," *Tsing Hua Journal of Chinese Studies* (August 1969), new series 7.2, shows great appreciation of the author's technical achievement. Hsia analyzes in some detail the night party of Lao Ts'an, his friend Huang Jen-jui, and two singing girls in a warm inn room insulated from the frozen world outside (chapters 12–16); "undoubtedly," Hsia concludes, "the longest night in traditional Chinese literature and, in terms of fictional art, the most triumphant." The "meaning" of the novel he finds in a political message, emphasizing what he sees as the author's preoccupation with the disaster of the Boxer Rebellion. He notes that the persons the author uses to typify the most dangerous officials, Yü Hsien (Yü Tso-ch'en in ch. 3, p. 34) and Kang I (Kang Pi in ch. 15, p. 171), were active promoters of the Boxers. So in the "Riddle of the Silver Rat" (ch. 10, p. 111), Hsia identifies the "swine"

as Kang I, who at the time of the Boxer attack on the foreign legations
had risen to the office of Associate Grand Secretary and was one of the
highest officials inciting them. In Hsia's words, "The prophetic section
of the book therefore places the hero's concern with injustice and
suffering in a larger historical and political perspective: the persecution
of the innocent by Yü Hsien and Kang I confirms their later crime of
precipitating a national calamity." Persuaded by Hsia, I have revised
the fourth line of the Second Clue on p. 111 from "Leaves a swine to
rule at ease" to "Where a swine rules at ease."

    The second study that must be noted is Donald Holoch's *"The Trav-
els of Laocan:* Allegorical Narrative," in Milena Dolezelova-Velinge-
rova, ed., *The Chinese Novel at the Turn of the Century* (University of
Toronto Press, 1980). Holoch begins with a close reading of chapter 1
of *The Travels,* which consists of two narratives that every reader will
recognize to be allegorical: the treatment of Mr. Huang's annual illness,
representing control of the annual flooding of the Yellow (Huang) River;
and an unsuccessful attempt to bring order to the ship's company of a
sinking vessel, representing the rejection of foreign technology and the
failure of all efforts at saving the Chinese empire from utter catastrophe.
But Holoch insists that when Lao Ts'an awakens from his dream the
allegory doesn't end. As he puts it on page 145, "A pervasive symbolism
integrates the varied handling of setting, character, and plot and gives
them a coherent texture, and also points toward the underlying ideolog-
ical unity: the gradual elaboration of a concept of human action through
a series of dramatic oppositions." With promptings from Vladimir Propp's
Morphology of the Folktale, he sees in *The Travels* a search for a
solution to China's problems in the guise of a series of quests by a hero.
Holoch sees Lao Ts'an as a reactionary whose reliance on reviving
traditional culture is doomed to failure and will neutralize the techno-
logical advances he supports.

On Sources in the Notes

    The notes frequently refer the reader to English translations of Chinese
works mentioned in the novel. Many of the translations referred to have
been supplanted by fuller and better ones—striking evidence of the
advances made in the study of Chinese literature in the past forty years.
A few examples:

Author's Preface, n.4: for *Li Sao,* see David Hawkes, *Ch'u Tz'u: Songs of the South* (1959).

Author's Preface, n.11: for *Hung Lou Meng,* see David Hawkes and John Minford, *The Story of the Stone* (1973–1982).

Chapter 2, n.25: for *Po Hsiang-shan,* see Arthur Waley, *Life and Times of Po Chü-i* (1949).

Chapter 3, n.21: for *T'ao Ch'ien,* see J. K. Hightower, *The Poetry of Tao Ch'ien* (1970).

Chapter 6, n.2 and chapter 11, n.29: for *Monkey,* see A. C. Yu, *The Journey to the West* (1977–1983)—though Waley's *Monkey* should still be read.

Chapter 8, n.8: for *Shih Shuo Hsin Yü,* see R. B. Mather, *A New Account of Tales of the World* (1976).

Chapter 10, n.7: for *Chuang Tzu,* see Burton Watson, *Complete Works of Chuang Tzu* (1968); also A. C. Graham, *Chuang Tzu: The Inner Chapters* (1981).

William H. Nienhauser, Jr., *The Indiana Companion to Traditional Chinese Literature* (1986), can be recommended as a comprehensive guide. It contains an entry on Liu E. (T'ieh-yün).

October 1989 HAROLD SHADICK

Note on Transliteration

Since 1970 the Wade-Giles transliteration system, used in *The Travels* for Chinese terms and names, has been largely replaced in popular use by the Pinyin system. About half of the initials and finals are identical in the two systems. The following table shows those that differ.

For production of the sounds, see Key to Chinese Pronunciation, pp. 275–277.

INITIALS

Wade-Giles Symbol	Pinyin Symbol	Wade-Giles Symbol	Pinyin Symbol
ch before i, ü	j	k'	k
ch before a, e, u, o	zh	p	b
ch' before i, ü	q	p'	p
ch' before a, e, u, o	ch	t	d
hs	x	t'	t
j	r	ts	z
k	g	ts'	c

FINALS

Wade-Giles Symbol	Pinyin Symbol	Wade-Giles Symbol	Pinyin Symbol
o after k, k', h	e	uei	ui
eh	e	ung	ong
erh	er	üeh	ue
ieh	ie	iung	iong
ien	ian		

SYLLABLES FORMED BY VOICING AN INITIAL

Wade-Giles Symbol	*Pinyin Symbol*	*Wade-Giles Symbol*	*Pinyin Symbol*
chih	zhi	tzu	zi
ch'ih	chi	tz'u	ci
shih	shi	szu	si
jih	ri		

Translator's Introduction

IN HIS ESSAY "Chinese Literature of the Last Fifty Years," [1] Hu Shih says, "During these fifty years [1872–1922] the literature which had the greatest force and the widest circulation, strange to say, was not the essays of Liang Ch'i-ch'ao, nor the novels of Lin Shu,[2] but was a number of vernacular novels. . . . They were the highest achievements, the works with the greatest literary value."

Hu Shih is here speaking of two schools of novel writing, the northern and the southern. The northern writers came first, with tales of adventure full of feats of superhuman strength, hairbreadth escapes from death and worse than death, gallant heroes, noble amazons, and wicked monks. They were and are popular among the common people, and many incidents from these books have already become part of the traditional stock of storytellers and theater managers. The most important novels of this type were the *Erh Nü Ying Hsiung Chuan* ("Tale of a Heroic Maiden"),[3] written about 1875 and attributed to a Manchu, Wen Kang; the anonymous *San Hsia Wu I* ("The Three Heroes and Five Champions"), of which the first part appeared in 1879; [4] and the *Hsiao Wu I* ("The Lesser Five Champions"), which is really a continuation of the latter, written in 1890. These all belong to what is known as the *p'ing hua* tradition. *P'ing hua* means "to amplify or comment orally" and refers to the contribution of the storyteller who adds his personal comment as he tells a traditional tale. Such stories began to be written down in the Sung period, 960–1278, and rose to epic heights with the *Shui Hu Chuan* [5] in the early Ming period, 1368–1644. Modeled after this last work and other great novels, the *p'ing hua* stories of the late nineteenth century reached a fair standard of lively narrative. Though they show very little reflective thinking, they are good stories, spiced with comedy and containing well-developed characters. The language is racily colloquial, the *Erh Nü Ying Hsiung Chuan* being perhaps the finest written record of pure Peking colloquial speech.

The southern school, which includes Kiangsu and Kwangtung men, made its appearance after the Boxer Rebellion. Whereas the northern writers had only unconsciously reflected the instinctive desire of the common people for champions who would right their wrongs and save the country, these southern men were acutely conscious of the perilous condition of China. All their lives they had heard accounts of the T'aip'ing and other rebellions and the foreign wars of 1840 and 1860. And they had themselves witnessed the abortive reform movement of 1898 and the disastrous Boxer Rebellion of 1900. Looking for the source of all these troubles, they found it not so much in foreign attacks as in the irresponsibility and corruption of the official class and the dead hand of the old examination system. They therefore set out to give expression in works of fiction to the critical attitude so fiercely expressed by Liang Ch'i-ch'ao:

What then is the path by which we may be saved from danger and seek progress? We must take the pernicious and filthy government system that has lasted several thousand years and smash it to pieces and grind it to powder; we must prevent those tens of thousands of tigerish, wolfish, locustlike, toadlike officials from battening like rats on the villages and foxes on the towns. Only so can we clean out our bowels and stomachs and set out on the forward path! We must take the obsolete and effeminate system of studies and sweep it away and expose it and say good-by to it; we must make it impossible for those tens of thousands of bookwormish, parrotlike, jellyfishlike, doglike scholars to shake their pens, wag their tongues, elaborate their style, work over their compositions, in support of the robbers of the people. Only then can we have new ears and eyes and really go forward.[6]

Just as the tales of heroes looked back to the *Shui Hu Chuan* as their great exemplar, so the southern novels of social and political satire took inspiration from the *Ju Lin Wai Shih* ("Unofficial Histories of the Literati") [7] written by an Anhwei man, Wu Ching-tzu, who lived from 1701 to 1754. This is a delightful book, consisting of a large number of separate incidents from the lives of the author's contemporaries. The narrative is fluent, and all sorts of human weaknesses are satirized, though the main attack is on the literati and the officials.

The social novels of the early twentieth century are for the most part more narrowly political in their interest than the *Ju Lin Wai Shih* and show a certain bitterness and intolerance. The most important authors were three in number: Li Pao-chia (1867–1906), Wu Wu-yao (1867–1910), and Liu T'ieh-yün (1857–1909). Li Pao-chia, a Kiangsu man, took his *Hsiu-Ts'ai* degree and then devoted himself to a literary life in Shanghai, editing several tabloid newspapers largely concerned with the city's amusements, writing poetry, and, most important, producing six novels. The longest and best known of his novels is the *Kuan Ch'ang Hsien Hsing Chi* ("Revelations of Official Life"). [8] It was begun in 1901, and the first thirty-six chapters were published in 1903, a further twenty-four chapters being written in 1904–1905. Even if half of the things described are discounted, it remains a formidable indictment of ignorance, bribery, peculation, philandering, and concubinage. From the literary point of view the book is uneven in quality, but as a social document it is of great importance. Wu Wu-yao, a Kwangtung man who came to Shanghai and worked for newspapers, wrote several novels, the best known being the *Erh Shih Nien Mu Tu Chih Kuai Hsien Chuang* ("Strange Things Seen in Twenty Years"), the first part of which was published in 1904 in the *Hsin Hsiao Shuo* ("New Fiction Magazine") edited by Liang Ch'i-ch'ao in Japan. The novels of both these writers bitterly satirize the whole social system and especially the activities of officials and scholars. In the eyes of Hu Shih and Lu Hsün they are weakened by their unrelieved censure and suffer, therefore, in comparison with the urbane satire of the *Ju Lin Wai Shih*. Hu Shih complains that in the more than 1,500 pages of the *Kuan Ch'ang Hsien Hsing Chi* there is not a single good official.

The Life of Liu T'ieh-yün

The third of the southern writers of social satire was Liu T'ieh-yün, [9] author of *The Travels of Lao Ts'an* (hereinafter referred to as *The Travels*). He was a man of unconventional and versatile nature who, living in a period of transition, was equally sensitive to the values in traditional Chinese culture and to the urgent needs of the new age in which the powerful influences of Western industrial civilization were making themselves felt.

Liu T'ieh-yün was born in 1857 at Liuho in Kiangsu,[10] in a family which traces its history in that region back to a General Liu Kuang-shih who came with the Emperor Kao Tsung (reigned 1127–1163) of the Sung dynasty when he was driven south by the Chin invaders. Liu T'ieh-yün's father was a *Chin-Shih* of 1852. He became a provincial censor in Honan and later a *taot'ai*. Liu T'ieh-yün himself spent his early years in Huaian, Kiangsu. He was an independent boy of impulsive nature who chafed under restraint and made his friends among the wilder youths of the common people. Before reaching the age of twenty he showed himself energetic and studious but refused to undergo the discipline of writing the "eight-legged" essays required for the official examinations. He studied the Sung philosophers with his father and spent much time with a group of friends who formed a sort of club with the intention of preparing themselves to help the country in her hour of need. They discussed questions of military science, economics, and mathematics, and practiced boxing. Liu T'ieh-yün himself specialized in the study of flood control and also showed great interest in music, poetry, astronomy, and medicine. All these interests are clearly reflected in his novel. He was so precocious and original that people came to speak of him as "that mad fellow."

After the death of his father, his brother, as head of the family, insisted that he should do something for his living. He had the idea, strange in the family of an official, of opening a shop at Huaian for the sale of Manchurian tobacco. Unfortunately, the accountant who was engaged to help him mismanaged the funds of the business and when the New Year settlement came committed suicide. This was the end of the tobacco venture and the first of many commercial failures.

Liu T'ieh-yün then went to Yangchow, where he studied with Li Lung-ch'uan, the chief teacher at that time of the T'ai-ku sect,[11] an esoteric religious society with a syncretic creed, embodying elements from Confucianism, Buddhism, and Taoism. Under the influence of this teacher, the young man who had been so headstrong and undisciplined apparently experienced what might very well be called a religious conversion, for though he continued to be bold and outspoken, his manner was greatly softened, and his taste in studies is said to have become "pure and simple." He developed a sense of social responsibility and was filled with the spirit of sympathy and pity for men. The set of highly metaphorical poems in chapter ix of the novel commemorates his teacher, Li Lung-ch'uan, while the whimsical hermit philosopher, Huang Lung-tzu (Yellow Dragon), in chapters x and xi, is a portrait of his friend, Huang Hsi-p'eng, who was a fellow disciple. His other great friend, Chiang Wen-t'ien (*hao* Lung-hsi) was also a follower of Li Lung-ch'uan.

He set up as practitioner of traditional Chinese medicine, but no business came his way. He next began to prepare for an official examination, but he detested the drudgery and soon gave it up. He was now thirty years of age, and it was obviously time for him to find a settled career. His next attempt was to start a printing establishment in Shanghai, the Shih Ch'ang Shu Chü. This was one of the first presses in China to adopt the lithographic process. Just when the business seemed to be prospering, some relatives connected with the firm without his knowledge sold the copies of a book he had printed for a third party. He became involved in a law suit; and by the time it was settled the printing house had gone bankrupt and he was forced to return to Huaian.

The next year, 1888, the Yellow River burst its banks near Chengchow in Honan and Liu T'ieh-yün decided to offer his services to Wu Ta-ch'eng,[12] a friend of his father who had been appointed Director General of Yellow River Conservancy. When he presented his scheme, the fruit of many years' study, Wu was much impressed and gave him a responsible position in the work of closing the great breach in the dike. He carried out his plans successfully, partly due to the fact that he discarded his long gown and went about on foot among the workmen, directing and urging them in person—an unheard-of thing for an official to do! Wu Ta-ch'eng recommended him to the capital and also had him put in charge of a commission to chart the course of the river through the provinces, Honan, Chihli, and Shantung. Hearing of his success in Honan, Chang Yao,[13] Governor of Shantung, invited him to his yamen as an adviser on flood control, with the rank of subprefect, later raised to prefect. He remained in Shantung in this capacity from 1890 to 1893, and during that time wrote several books on river conservancy and mathematics. The majority of Governor Chang's advisers advocated the method taught by Chia Jang [14] of which the main principle was to broaden the bed of the river so that there should be room between the dikes for the flood water. Liu T'ieh-yün proposed instead the method of Wang Ching,[15] which was to narrow and deepen the river bed so that the current would be swift and prevent the silt from forming a deposit. He finally won Governor Chang over to his method and so incurred the hatred of Kang I and Yü Hsien,[16] two Manchu reactionaries. Yüan Shih-k'ai was also in the Shantung yamen at this time. He turned against Liu because the latter could not or would not persuade Governor Chang to give him a position of responsibility. The enmity Liu undeservedly aroused against himself at this period was to be a major cause of his suffering fifteen years later.

In 1893 Liu T'ieh-yün's mother died, and he returned to Huaian for the funeral and the mourning period which custom demanded of an official. At this time he became intimate with Lo Chen-yü, 1866–1940,[17] a great scholar who was later to become the leading paleographer of China. They had known each other as boys, but Mr. Lo, who was younger, had avoided the wild youth Liu. Recently they had corresponded and found themselves in agreement on problems of flood control, and now in discussions on the conduct of the Sino-Japanese war (1894–1895) the two of them interpreted the strategy of the Japanese in the same way and foretold the fall of Port Arthur and Dairen in the face of the skepticism of all their friends.

In 1894, when Liu T'ieh-yün had completed his period of mourning, Fu Jun, who had become Governor of Shantung in 1891, recommended him for his great ability, and he was summoned to the capital to take a special examination in order to enter the Tsungli Yamen (Foreign Office). He spent some two years in Peking, and at this time became convinced that China would become strong and prosperous only when her commerce and industry developed, and that these could develop only if railways were built, if necessary with the help of foreign capital. He went to Hankow as adviser to the Viceroy Chang Chih-tung in connection with his scheme for building a railway from Peking to Hankow. After a difference of opinion with certain officials in Hankow, he returned to Peking and then promoted a railway which was to run from Tientsin to a point on the Yangtze opposite his native place, Chinkiang. His fellow townsmen who were officials at the capital, not realizing the benefits this railway would bring them, protested against it and finally struck him off the register of their club. Later, when the railway was built, it ran to Pukow, opposite Nanking. Disgusted with the attitude of the officials, Liu T'ieh-yün now gave up all thought of a government career and for the rest of his life devoted himself to private commercial and industrial projects, all of which were unsuccessful. First he co-operated with an English company, the Pekin Syndicate (Fu Kung Ssu), in making plans for building a railway into Shansi and opening coal mines there. In the end he felt that the foreigners were making demands inimical to the best interests of China and broke with them. They succeeded in obtaining a concession from the Peking government, however, and later Liu's enemies, particularly Kang I, his old colleague of Shantung days, accused him of being a traitor and made their first attempt to have him punished.

When the Boxer Rebellion of 1900 ended in the occupation of Peking by foreign troops, one result was a great shortage of food. People were dying in the streets while merchants cornered grain and made big profits. Liu T'ieh-yün discovered that the Russian troops quartered in the Imperial Granary were burning stores of rice for which they had no use, and through friends in the Russian Legation, he managed to buy this rice and distribute it to the populace at a nominal price. Mr. Lo Chen-yü says, "This was certainly the greatest act of mercy he performed in all his life." It was also one of the things that led to his later sufferings, for his enemies, led by Yüan Shih-k'ai, charged him with the serious crime of misappropriating Imperial property.

Liu's friendship with foreign diplomats made him a useful man in negotiating the treaty that concluded the occupation, and in settling questions relating to the indemnity. From Peking he went to Shanghai and there engaged in a fantastic series of business enterprises. He started building a department store but was bankrupt before it was finished. With the help of various friends he attempted to build a steam cotton mill at Sikkawei, a handicraft-weaving shop in Shanghai, a mechanized silk-weaving mill at Hangchow, and a steel refinery at Chuchow in Hunan. All of them failed.

It was in 1904, during his stay in the Shanghai region [18] that he started writing *The Travels of Lao Ts'an*. The novel was originally written to help a friend named Lien Meng-ch'ing, who had fled from Peking, where his life was in danger because he had made some revelations about the Imperial Court to a Tientsin newspaper. Lien was too proud to take money, but since he was trying to make a living by writing, he allowed Liu to write something for him which he sold to his publishers. The first eight chapters of the novel were thus printed in the *Hsiu Hsiang Hsiao Shuo* ("Illustrated Fiction Magazine"), published by the Commercial Press. The publishers made some arbitrary changes in printing chapter eight,[19] which aroused Lien Meng-ch'ing's indignation, and he refused to allow them to go on with the publication. The subsequent chapters were then printed at different times between 1904 and 1907 in the form of small single-sheet supplements to the *Tientsin Jih Jih Hsin Wen* ("The Tientsin Daily News") when Liu went north.

For many years Liu had been an enthusiastic collector of works of art and objects of archeological interest. He was one of the first collectors to show interest in the inscribed oracle bones of the Shang period, which have since become so important in the study of the early period of Chinese history. In 1903, he published the *T'ieh-yün Ts'ang Kuei* ("Tortoise Shells in the Collection of T'ieh-yün"), the first book of reproductions of these inscriptions ever made. Mr. Lo Chen-yü, who became the leading authority on this subject, said that his attention was first drawn to these inscriptions by Liu T'ieh-yün. Liu subsequently published several illustrated catalogues of pottery and seals and other objects of his collection.

Returning to Peking Liu T'ieh-yün tried to start a water works and a streetcar line. Then in Tientsin he helped organize the Hai Pei Kung Ssu (North Sea Trading Company) for manufacturing fine salt and distributing it in Korea, and in connection with this he traveled about a great deal. Returning to Shanghai, he started a company for trade with Dairen and Japan. Finally he became interested in the development of Pukow as a port and, gathering a considerable sum of money among his friends and relations, bought a large tract of land in anticipation of a rise in value with the opening of the railway. The evidence seems to show that, while there was an element of self-interest in this purchase, it was a perfectly legitimate undertaking and partly intended to prevent foreign interests from getting a foothold. Apparently certain officials became jealous and indignant because he would not let them share in the benefits of his foresight, and this transaction became the immediate occasion of his downfall. As might be expected of a man so gifted and original but so tactless and impulsive, he had incurred the hostility of many people during his lifetime, the two most powerful being Yüan Shih-k'ai and a man called Shih, who had earlier been offended by Liu's father. In 1907 both of these men were in the

Chün Chi Ch'u (Grand Council of State) in Peking and they charged him with being a traitor to the country and buying land at Pukow for certain foreign interests. An order was issued for his arrest, but he was protected by his brother-in-law, Ting Pao-ch'uan, Governor of Shansi, who enlisted the help of Prince Ch'ing, the chief Grand Councilor, in his defense. The attack was then dropped, but the following year Yüan Shih-k'ai again charged him with betraying the interests of the country by purchasing land at Pukow for foreigners and also revived the charge that he had sequestrated Imperial grain in 1900. Yüan sent a telegram to Tuan-fang, the Viceroy of Kiangsu, Kiangsi, and Anhwei at Nanking, ordering him to arrest Liu T'ieh-yün and send him into banishment in Sinkiang (Chinese Turkistan). The family heard of this and attempted to warn him, but through bad luck and bad management they failed.

Tuan-fang, who is known as the greatest collector of antiques of his time, was an old acquaintance of Liu T'ieh-yün—they had had several friendly rivalries over the possession of rare seals and rubbings of inscriptions—and tried to warn him, but through the stupidity or carelessness of a servant he did not receive the warning and was taken in July, 1908. He was carried on a warship to Hankow and then went on by road, crossing Hupeh, Honan, Shensi, and Kansu to Tihua in Sinkiang, an arduous journey of more than 3,500 miles. It is not surprising that he died at Tihua on August 23, 1909, thirteen months and seven days after leaving Nanking. All this time his family worked hard to obtain the repeal of his banishment and had great hopes of achieving it on the sixtieth birthday of the Empress Dowager, which fell in that year, but it was too late. Mao Shih-chün, the Governor of Kansu, who was a schoolmate of Liu T'ieh-yün and related to him by the marriage of their children, arranged for the body to be brought from Tihua to Lanchow in Kansu, where it was met by one of Liu's sons. Two other sons met it at Loyang, Honan, and the oldest son at Hankow. The next year Liu was interred in the family burial ground.

The Man and His Book

Liu T'ieh-yün lived the life of a pioneer in a period when farsighted Chinese were striving to break through the inertia of centuries and adapt themselves to the new conditions produced by the impact of Western civilization. His many attempts to promote railways, industry, and commerce failed, but it should not be concluded that they produced no effect in inspiring others. The whole period from about 1860 to well into the present century was littered with stillborn factories and mines, and he failed in good company. The Lanchow steam woolen factory started in 1879 by the Viceroy Tso Tsung-t'ang [20] ceased operation in 1883, and the Viceroy Chang Chih-tung, who started the Hanyang iron works in 1890, experienced as many failures as successes and in 1893 was impeached for "wasting public money on mines, causing disturbances in Hunan by trying to introduce the telegraph, and generally engaging in wild schemes." [21]

From the point of view of worldly career Liu T'ieh-yün's life was a failure, and *The Travels of Lao Ts'an* is the expression of his disillusionment. In the author's preface he compares himself with the ancient author of the famous poem *Li Sao* ("Encountering Sorrow") and other writers of novels and dramas, saying that he wrote in tears to express his lifelong sorrows. It would be wrong, however, to infer that the book is a long complaining wail. The prevailing mood is rather one of genial interest in life in all its forms, with a realization of the suffering that human beings inflict—mainly through ignorance or thoughtlessness—on one another. Whatever he writes about, Liu T'ieh-yün shows keen observation of reality and brings to his description a mellow mind steeped in literature and refined by music and art. He is a happy fusion of the man of action and the meditative man. Mr. Liu Ta-shen tells that no matter how occupied his father might be with business or politics, he never failed in the evening to light his pot of incense, play on his *ku ch'in* (the long horizontal lute, instrument par excellence of the scholar), and read some poetry or classics. Though Lao Ts'an, who represents the author, is an educated man and well received in official circles, and, though he enjoys whiling away an hour reading poetry, is always interested in painting and calligraphy, and goes about covering inn walls with poems of his own composition, he is as far removed as possible from the conventional literary man of the official class, dressed in silks and furs, who sits over his books and is afraid to soil his hands. He wears cotton clothes and refuses to accept a gown lined with fox; he is equally at home talking with high officials and talking with innkeepers. He buys some bean curd, peanuts, and wine and is not ashamed to carry these to his inn himself. The plight of people ruled by a tyrannical official arouses his anger, and when his intervention has resulted in the release of a father and daughter wrongfully accused of murder, he feels as though he has "eaten of the fruit of immortality."

After the literary renaissance began, and especially after 1925, when the Ya Tung edition of *The Travels* was published with a long critical introduction by Hu Shih, the literary merits of the book, its masterly use of the vernacular, and its descriptive power became recognized; it has now achieved a secure place of honor among the novels of China. It is hardly possible to open one of the school an-thologies of Chinese literature published during the last twenty years without finding several excerpts included as models of style.

Most genuine editions of the novel include only the twenty chapters translated here, but thirty-four chapters in all were published by the *Tientsin Daily News*. The Liu family kept a set of the original printed sheets, but unfortunately the last six have been lost. In 1935, Lin Yutang obtained the text of chapters xxi to xxvi [22] from a member of the Liu family and published them with the title *Lao Ts'an Yu Chi, Erh Chi* ("Second Part of the Travels of Lao Ts'an"), and in 1936 the Commercial Press of Shanghai published his English translation of these under the title *A Nun of T'aishan*. He has included an improved version in *Widow, Nun and Courtesan* (New York, 1951). They continue the story of Lao Ts'an's wanderings. He and his concubine start out for the south but turn aside to burn incense on T'aishan, the Sacred Mountain. Here they become interested in a charming young nun who tells her life story and reveals a strangely complex character which Buddhism and Taoism have both helped to form. The sixth chapter ends surprisingly enough with Lao Ts'an's concubine, the former prostitute, being received into a nunnery while Lao Ts'an continues his journey south alone.

The Moral Philosophy of Liu T'ieh-yün

Liu T'ieh-yün makes his novel a vehicle for expressing his ideas on a variety of subjects. His moral philosophy is most fully revealed in the words of the maiden Yü Ku, and Yellow Dragon, the eccentric sage, in the four-chapter episode (chapters viii to xi) of Shen Tzu-p'ing's visit to the Peach Blossom Mountain. Some Chinese critics have dismissed this section of the book as foolish fantasy. The foreign reader will find it interesting as an example of the jejune pedantry that Chinese writers are often given to; he will also find some profound insights in it.

The author's philosophy—it is almost a religion with him—is a fusion of Confucianism, Buddhism, and Taoism. Most educated Chinese, of course, move freely among these three systems of thought, but Liu is unusually positive in asserting that morality is really a simple matter and that these systems are nonessential elaborations. The important thing for him is to do good and to be unselfish. This is stated in chapter ix, and reiterated most forcibly in chapter xi, where he says that in heaven and earth there are only two parties. "One party preaches the common good: they are the sages and Buddhist Holy Ones, subject to Shang Ti. The other party preaches private interest: they are evil spirits and devils, subject to Ah Hsiu Lo." Doing good is not a matter of following particular rules and observing petty restrictions. Nor is it a matter of repressing the natural desires and inclinations of man. In this he is strongly opposed to the teaching of Chu Hsi who sums up his theory of morals in these words: "The thousands and tens of thousands of words of the Sages all amount to teaching man to hold fast to *t'ien li* (heavenly reason, i.e. innate moral principles) and to subdue *jen yü* (human desires)." [23]

Liu is willing to trust spontaneous human desires and is apprehensive of the tyranny of the reason, which so easily becomes a projection of individual prejudice. He gathers together in a rather arbitrary way passages from the classics to support an ideal of naturalness and sincerity. He daringly applies this to the subject of sex, admitting a freedom of relationship that avoids crass sensuality, though it seems to allow proximity and even physical intimacy, and is raised by intellectual and spiritual companionship to something comparable to, though different from, Western romantic love. This theme is more fully developed in the second part of the novel, *A Nun of T'aishan.*

He is prepared to face the facts of human experience and sees that apparent evil may contribute to ultimate good. The references in chapter xii to the overabundance of life and the necessary destruction of the surplus, as also to the key position of Force Supreme, show the influence of Darwinian biology and Western physics. The naturalism or positivism of Western scientific philosophy can easily be accommodated to Liu's Taoistic thought, which views life from an unsentimental and almost amoral point of view. Safeguarded from all dogmatism and fanaticism, it gives its blessing to anybody who lives freely and fulfills his destiny without encroaching on the freedom of others.

The Political Philosophy of Liu T'ieh-yün

One reason for the early popularity of *The Travels* was that on the strength of the conversation in chapter xi it was accepted by many people as a prophetic book written between 1894–1900 that foretold accurately the Boxer Rebellion in 1900. Since that "prophecy" was fulfilled, it was natural to expect that the great events promised for 1910 and 1914 would materialize. The novel was actually written between 1904 and 1907, but the "prophecy" of a revolution in 1910 (though the author, of course, thought that the revolution would fail) was a very near guess, as the monarchy was actually overthrown in 1911. The author was not, however, really attempting to write prophecy, but was expressing his intense awareness of impending internal changes in China, and was even thinking in terms of a new world culture in which China would take her place.

Liu T'ieh-yün was opposed to doctrinaire extremes and to violent revolution. This is clear from his description of the duplicity of a revolutionary demagogue in the allegory in chapter i, and from the attack on the Boxers and revolutionaries in chapter xi. Satire on office-hunting, jealousy, and other corruptions among officials which forms the staple of the *Revelations of Official Life* [24] plays a much smaller part in *The Travels*, but a great deal is suggested by a few words. Thus, in the first part of chapter iv we have a picture of selfish office-seekers that could only have been drawn by one who had been in the hurly-burly of official life himself.

The main political criticism in the book is reserved for the type of official who is honest and conscientious but bigoted, narrow, and without the suppleness of mind that will enable him to evaluate actual situations and make allowances for human nature. Honest officials in China have for hundreds of years been described as *ch'ing kuan* (pure officials), and as Hu Shih points out in his Introduction to *The Travels*, where honesty has been joined with intelligence as in men like Pao Cheng [25] of the eleventh century, such men are admirable in every way. But where a man is pure and at the same time bigoted and stupid, his honesty makes him all the more dangerous since he is liable to be trusted and given high position. In an article entitled "Lao Ts'an and

'Purity and Incorruptibility,' " [26] Hsü Ling-hsia shows that Liu T'ieh-yün is reiterating a warning that was sounded by the great Emperor K'ang Hsi (reigned 1662–1722). K'ang Hsi warned his officials against the common failings of honest men: stubbornness and pride, harshness, inefficiency, and misplaced economy. Hu Shih quotes the scholar Tai Chen, 1723–1777, as blaming the spread of a puritanical egotism on the Sung philosophers' exaltation of "innate moral principles." Thinking that they themselves are an embodiment of rational principles, scholar-officials identify these fixed principles with their own subjective opinions, which often, in turn, reflect their personal interests. Many chapters of the novel are devoted to the maladministration of justice of Yü Hsien (chapters iv, v, vi), and Kang Pi (chapters xv–xviii). The limitations of such "honest" officials are summarized when the wise Prefect Pai, having proved by a little common sense and ingenuity that Kang Pi's snap judgment in a murder case was wrong, proceeds to diagnose his weakness: "The pure and incorruptible man naturally arouses our admiration, but he often has one bad characteristic: he thinks that all other people in the world are little and mean, and that he is the only superior man."

If Liu T'ieh-yün opposes revolution, his positive recommendations for the political reform of China would seem to be these:

(1) A high standard of intelligence as well as honesty should be required of officials;

(2) The freemasonry of officials should not prevent the cashiering of the incompetent. This idea appears in Lao Ts'an's conversation with Governor Chuang (chapter xix);

(3) Foreign advice should be sought and foreign techniques adopted. This theme appears clearly in the allegory in chapter i. The naive expression of admiration for the business methods of Westerners shown in his comments on Taiku lamps and Shouchou pipe bowls (chapter xii), is also typical, though rather pathetic in view of Liu's own unsuccessful business ventures;

(4) Over-energetic government should be avoided. All positive reforms should be gradual, moderate, and adapted to existing conditions. This appears in the curious compromise solution of the problem of banditry suggested in chapter vii and in the paradoxical argument in chapter vi that overefficient officials are a greater menace than men of no ability. We feel here the moderating spirit of Chinese Taoism with its doctrine of "inactivity."

Literary Qualities of The Travels of Lao Ts'an

Judged by the Western conception of a novel, the book lacks unity both of plot and subject matter. It is the author's one attempt at this type of writing and was written in installments when he was about fifty years of age. This probably accounts for occasional carelessness and inconsistency in the text.[27] In spite of its desultoriness, however, the book has a unity of feeling produced by the author's tireless interest in people and things, his moral integrity, and his pervading sense of humor. Seen through his keen and sympathetic eyes, nothing is too humble to hold interest.

As in most Chinese literature before the revolution, whether in the classical or the vernacular language, the influence of tradition is everywhere present. Precedents could be found for almost every incident and every theme. The dream in the first chapter has its counterpart in the supernatural setting of the prologues to most Chinese novels. The idyllic, otherworldly atmosphere of Shen Tzu-p'ing's night in the Peach Blossom Mountain is a typical Chinese fantasy apt to be introduced into otherwise realistic tales. Poisoned cakes, "planted" stolen goods, and accusations of theft based on the measurements of a piece of stolen cloth occur in earlier stories. The theme of inviting a mountain recluse to assist in the government goes back to Chu-ko Liang, 181–234, and earlier. The historical and literary allusions include much of the stock in trade of any Chinese author. They also show evidence of wide reading in the less trodden paths of literature and are usually introduced aptly and with that strong feeling for historical continuity which is one of the striking features of Chinese literature. The book preserves the form of the traditional novel which purports to be a series of installments of a storyteller's narrative. Thus each chapter begins with a formula like "It is further told" and ends in suspense, with the promise that the suspense will be relieved in the next chapter, that is, the next recitation.

In the opinion of Hu Shih, the unique achievement of the author is in the descriptions of scenery and of music. In place of the stereotyped descriptions to be found in the earlier novels which reflect the sedentary bookishness of the Chinese scholar and the too-great wealth of ready-made phrases available to him from centuries of nature poetry and artistic prose, Liu T'ieh-yün attempts to express with precision and in his own words what he has seen and heard. The result is a direct yet imaginative style that convinces the reader of the reality of the experiences described. Passages that have been particularly admired are the description of the Ming Lake and the Springs of Tsinan (chapters ii and iii), the singing of the Fair Maid, Little Jade Wang (chapter ii), and the icebound Yellow River (chapter xii).

Apart from such elaborate passages of description the book abounds with fine touches which produce an impression of reality. The account of the arrival of Shen Tzu-p'ing at the mountain villa and the description of everything he saw there (chapters ix and x) employ subtle art to create an atmosphere in which the natural and the supernatural are blended. This unearthliness is something which can be felt even by the Westerner if he responds with sympathetic imagination to the influence of Chinese scenery and architecture, reinforced by literary and mythological associations. Similarly anyone who has traveled through the towns and villages of the great North China plain will recognize the authenticity of Lao Ts'an's descriptions of life in the inns and yamens and on the roads of Shantung.

The Translation

The translation endeavors to keep as close to the Chinese text as is consonant with readable English. The paragraphing follows that of Mr. Wang Yüan-fang in the Ya Tung edition. Where different names are used for the same person in the Chinese text they are generally retained, since degrees of intimacy and shades of feeling are often conveyed in this way. The notes should clear up any ambiguity that may result. A limited number of terms that recur and are difficult to translate without a circumlocution have been transliterated where they occur and explained in the Glossary. For Chinese terms and names (except for a few place names that have an accepted Anglicized form like Tsinan and Soochow) the standard Wade-Giles system of transliteration has been used, omitting, however, as superfluous all diacritical marks other than that in "ü" and the breath mark after initial consonants. In all but a few cases a place name is printed as one word; the division of syllables will usually become clear by reference to the Key to Pronunciation. It is to be noted that terms like *hsien* (district) and *fu* (prefecture) are sometimes added to and become part of place names. Thus Ts'ao, Ts'aochou, and Ts'aochoufu are variants of the same name. Short forms of the names are used on the map (frontispiece).

The photographs reproduced on pages 15–22 were taken in or about 1936.

Portions of this introduction appeared in the *Yenching Journal of Social Studies*, II, no. 1 (July 1939).

The translation was completed in Peking in 1939, but unsettled conditions prevented its publication at that time. Two abridged English versions of the novel have appeared in China: *Tramp Doctor's Travelogue,* translated by Lin Yi-chin and Ko Te-shun (Shanghai, 1939), and *Mr. Decadent,* translated by H. Y. Yang and G. M. Taylor (Nanking, 1947). They are not easily available, and in no sense duplicate the present complete annotated translation.

Chinese colleagues and friends in Peking were helpful in clearing up difficulties. I am particularly grateful to Miss Chou Nien-tz'u, Mr. Wang Shih-hsiang, and Miss Wu Hsin-min for reading the translation, and to Mr. Wu Hsing-hua for checking the notes. I am much indebted to Mr. Liu Ta-shen, the fourth son of the author, who went to great pains in preparing material on the life of his father, and also helped in the preparation of the notes and showed a friendly interest in the progress of the work. The late Dr. Bernard Read very kindly went over all the passages relating to Chinese medicine and drugs and his suggestions have been incorporated. My wife has been unstinting in her help, typing the manuscript and suggesting improvements in style. Finally I wish to acknowledge the generosity of Mrs. Charles William Wason of Cleveland, Ohio, in contributing funds that made possible the publication of the work.

Cornell University   HAROLD SHADICK
May 1952

Author's Preface

WHEN a baby is born, he weeps, *wa-wa;* and when a man is old and dying, his family form a circle around him and wail, *hao-t'ao.* Thus weeping is most certainly that with which a man starts and finishes his life. In the interval, the quality of a man is measured by his much or little weeping, for weeping is the expression of a spiritual nature. Spiritual nature is in proportion to weeping: the weeping is not dependent on the external conditions of life being favorable or unfavorable.

Horse and ox toil and moil the year round. They eat only hay and corn and are acquainted with the whip from start to finish. They can be said to suffer, but they do not know how to weep; this is because spiritual nature is lacking to them. Apes and monkeys are creatures that jump about in the depths of the forest and fill themselves with pears and chestnuts. They live a life of ease and pleasure, yet they are given to screaming. This screaming is the monkey's way of weeping. The naturalists say that among all living things monkeys and apes are nearest to man, because they have a spiritual nature. The old poem says:

> Of the three gorges of Eastern Pa, the Sorcerer's Gorge is the longest;
> Three sounds of monkeys screaming there cut through a man's bowels.[1]

Just think what feelings they must have!

1

Spiritual nature gives birth to feeling; feeling gives birth to weeping. There are two kinds of weeping. One kind is strong; one kind is weak. When an addlepated boy loses a piece of fruit, he cries; when a silly girl loses a hairpin, she weeps. This is the weak kind of weeping. The sobbing of Ch'i's wife that caused the city wall to collapse,[2] the tears of the Imperial Concubines Hsiang that stained the bamboo[3]—these were the strong kind of weeping. Moreover the strong kind of weeping divides into two varieties. If weeping takes the form of tears, its strength is small. If weeping does not take the form of tears, its strength is great: it reaches farther.

The poem, *Encountering Sorrow*, was Lord Ch'ü's weeping.[4] The book called *Chuang Tzu* was the weeping of the Old Man of Meng.[5] The book called *Historical Records* was the weeping of the Grand Astrologer.[6] The *Poems of the Thatched Hut* were the weeping of the *Kung Pu*, Tu.[7] Prince Li wept in lyric verse.[8] The Man of the Eight Great Mountains[9] wept with paintings. Wang Shih-fu put his tears into the *Story of the Western Chamber*.[10] Ts'ao Hsüeh-chin put his tears into the *Dream of the Red Chamber*.[11] Wang's words are: "Hatred of separation and sadness at parting fill my inward parts— it is hard to give vent to them. Without paper and pen as substitutes for throat and tongue, to whom can I tell my thousand thoughts?" Ts'ao's words are: "Paper covered with wild words; a handful of bitter tears. All say the writer is mad. Who understands his meaning!" When he says of his tea, "a thousand fragrances in one hollow," and of his wine, "ten thousand beauties in one cup," he means "a thousand lovely ones weeping together" and "ten thousand beauties mourning together."[12]

We of this age have our feelings stirred about ourselves and the world, about family and nation, about society, about the various races and religions. The deeper the emotions, the more bitter the weeping. This is why the Scholar of a Hundred Temperings from Hungtu[13] has made this book, *The Travels of Lao Ts'an*.

The game of chess is finished. We are getting old. How can we not weep? I know that "a thousand lovely ones" and "ten thousand beauties" among mankind will weep with me and be sad with me.

CHAPTER 1

The land does not hold back the water; every year comes disaster;

The wind beats up the waves; everywhere is danger.

THE STORY tells that outside the East Gate of Tengchoufu, in Shantung, there is a big hill called P'englai Hill,[1] and on this hill a pavilion called the P'englai Pavilion. It is most imposing with its "painted roof-tree flying like a cloud" and its "bead screens rolled up like rain."[2] To the west it overlooks the houses in the town, with mist hanging over ten thousand homes;[3] to the east it overlooks the waves of the sea, undulating for a thousand li. It is a regular custom for the gentlemen of the town to take wine cups and wine with them to the pavilion and spend the night there, to be ready the next morning before it is light to watch the sun come up out of the sea.

However, no more of this for the present.

It is further told that there was once a traveler called Lao Ts'an. His family name was T'ieh, his *ming* was of one character, Ying, and his *hao*, Pu-ts'an. He chose Ts'an as his *hao* because he liked the story of the monk Lan Ts'an roasting taros.[4] Since he was a pleasant sort of person, people deferred to his wish and began to call him Lao Ts'an, which eventually became a regular nickname. He was a Chiangnan [5] man. By the time he was thirty he had studied quite a lot of prose and poetry, but because he was not good at writing eight-legged essays,[6] he had taken no degrees and therefore nobody wanted him as a tutor. He was too old to learn a business and therefore did not attempt it. His father had been an official of the third or fourth rank but was too stubbornly honest to make money for himself, and after twenty years of office-holding he could only afford to travel home by selling his official clothes! How do you suppose he could have anything to give his son?

Since Lao Ts'an had nothing from his family and no definite occupation, he began to see cold and hunger staring him in the face. Just when he was at his wits' end, Heaven took pity on him, for along came a Taoist priest, shaking a string of bells, who said that he had been taught by a wonderful healer and could treat a hundred diseases. He said that when people met him and asked him to heal their diseases he had a hundred cures to every hundred treatments. So Lao Ts'an made obeisance to him as his teacher, learned the patter, and from that time on went about shaking a string of bells and filling his bowl of gruel by curing diseases. Thus he wandered about by river and lake for twenty years.

When our story begins, he had just come to an old Shantung town called Ch'iench'eng,[7] where there was a great house belonging to a man whose family name was Huang (Yellow) and whose *ming* was Jui-ho. This man suffered from a strange disease which caused his whole body to fester in such a way that every year several open sores appeared, and if one year these were healed, the next year several more would appear elsewhere. Now for many years no one had been found who could cure this disease. It broke out every summer and subsided after the autumn equinox.

Lao Ts'an arrived at this place in the spring, and the major-domo of the Huang household asked him if he had a cure for the disease. He said, "I have many cures; the only thing is that you may not do as I tell you. This year I will apply a mild treatment to try my skill. But if you want to prevent the disease from ever breaking out again, this too is not difficult; all we need do is to follow the ancients whose methods hit the target every time. For other diseases we follow the directions handed down from Shen Nung and Huang Ti, but in the case of this disease we need the method of the great Yü.[8] Later, in the Han period, there was a certain Wang Ching [9] who inherited his knowledge, but after that nobody seems to have known his method. Fortunately I now have some understanding of it."

The Huang household therefore pressed him to stay in the house and to give his treatment. Strange to say, although this year there was a certain amount of festering, not one open sore appeared, and this made the household very happy.

After the autumn equinox the state of the disease was no longer serious, and everybody was delighted because for the first time in more than ten years Mr. Huang had had no open sores. The family therefore engaged a theatrical company to sing operas for three days in thanksgiving to the spirits. They also built up an artificial hill of chrysanthemums in the courtyard of the west reception hall.[10] One day there was a feast, the next a banquet, all very gay and noisy.

On the day when our story begins Lao Ts'an had finished his noon meal, and having drunk two cups of wine more than usual, felt tired and went to his room, where he lay down on the couch to rest. He had just closed his eyes when suddenly two men walked in, one called Wen Chang-po, the other Te Hui-sheng.[11] These two men were old friends of his. They said, "What are you doing at this time of day, hiding away in your room?" Lao Ts'an quickly got up and offered them seats saying, "I have been feasting so hard these two days that I needed a change." They said, "We are going to Tengchoufu to see the famous view from the P'englai Pavilion and have come especially to invite you. We have already hired a cart. Put your things together quickly and we will go right away."

Lao Ts'an's baggage did not amount to much—not more than a few old books and some instruments—so that packing was easy, and in a short time the three men were getting into the cart. After an uneventful journey [12] they soon reached Tengchou and there found lodging beside the P'englai Pavilion. Here they settled and prepared to enjoy the phantasmagoria of a "market in the sea" and the magic of "mirage towers." [13]

The next day Lao Ts'an said to his two friends Wen and Te, "Everyone says the sunrise is worth seeing. Why shouldn't we stay up to see it instead of sleeping? What do you say?" They answered, "If you are so inclined, we will certainly keep you company."

Although autumn is that time of year when day and night are about equal in length, the misty light that appears before sunrise and lingers after sunset makes the night seem shorter. The three friends opened two bottles of wine, took out the food they had brought with them, and, what with drinking and talking, before they were aware of it the east had gradually become bright. Actually it was still a long time before sunrise; the effect was due to the diffusion of the light through the air.

The three friends continued to talk for a while. Then Te Hui-sheng said, "It's nearly time now. Why don't we go and wait upstairs?" Wen Chang-po said, "The wind is whistling so, and there is such an expanse of windows upstairs that I'm afraid it will be much colder than this room. We'd better put on extra clothes."

They all followed this advice and taking telescopes and rugs went up the zigzag staircase at the back. When they entered the pavilion, they sat at a table by a window and looked out toward the east. All they could see were white waves like mountains stretching away without end. To the northeast were several flecks of blue mist. The nearest was Long Hill Island; farther off were Big Bamboo, Great Black, and other islands. Around the pavilion the wind rushed and roared until the whole building seemed to be shaking. The clouds in the sky were piled up, one layer upon another. In the north was one big bank of cloud that floated to the middle of the sky and pressed down upon the clouds that were already there, and then began to crowd more and more upon a layer of cloud in the east until the pressure seemed insufferable. The whole spectacle was most ominous. A little later the sky became a shining strip of red.

Hui-sheng said, "Brother Ts'an, judging from the look of things the actual rising of the sun will be invisible." Lao Ts'an said, "The winds of heaven and the waters of the sea are sufficient to move me; even if we do not see the sunrise the journey will not have been in vain."

Chang-po meanwhile had been looking through his telescope. Now he exclaimed, "Look! There is a black shadow in the east that keeps rising and falling with the waves; it must be a steamship passing." They all took their telescopes and looked in that direction. After a while they said, "Yes! Look! There is a fine black thread on the horizon. It must be a ship."

They all watched for a while until the ship had passed out of sight. Hui-sheng continued to hold up his telescope and looked intently to right and left. Suddenly he cried, "Ayah! Ayah! Look at that sailing boat among the great waves. It must be in danger." The others said, "Where?" Hui-sheng said, "Look toward the northeast. Isn't that line of snow-white foam Long Hill Island? The boat is on this side of the island and is gradually coming nearer." The other two looked through their telescopes and both exclaimed, "Ayah! Ayah! It certainly is in terrible danger. Luckily it's coming in this direction. It has only twenty or thirty li to go before it reaches the shore."

After about an hour the boat was so near that by looking closely through their telescopes the three men could see that it was a fairly large boat, about twenty-three or twenty-four chang long.[14] The captain was sitting on the poop, and below the poop were four men in charge of the helm. There were six masts with old sails and two new masts, one with a completely new sail and the other with a rather worn one, in all eight masts. The ship was very heavily loaded; the hold must have contained many kinds of cargo. Countless people, men and women, were sitting on the deck without any awning or other covering to protect them from the weather—just like the people in third-class cars on the railway from Tientsin to Peking.[15] The north wind blew in their faces; foam splashed over them; they were wet and cold, hungry and afraid. They all had the appearance of people with no means of livelihood. Beside each of the eight masts were two men to look after the rigging. At the prow and on the deck were a number of men dressed like sailors.

It was a great ship, twenty-three or twenty-four chang long, but there were many places in which it was damaged. On the east side was a gash about three chang long, into which the waves were pouring with nothing to stop them. Farther to the east was another bad place about a chang long through which the water was seeping more gradually.[16] No part of the ship was free from scars. The eight men looking after the sails were doing their duty faithfully, but each one looked after his own sail as though each of the eight was on a separate boat: they were not working together at all. The other seamen were running about aimlessly among the groups of men and women; it was impossible at first to tell what they were trying to do. Looking carefully through the telescope, you discovered that they were searching the men and women for any food they might be carrying and also stripping them of the clothes that they wore.

Chang-po looked intently and finally couldn't help crying out wildly,

"The damnable blackguards! Just look, the boat is going to capsize any moment, and they don't even make a show of trying to reach the shore, but spend their time maltreating decent people. It's outrageous!" Hui-sheng said, "Brother Chang, don't get excited; the ship is not more than seven or eight li away from us; when it reaches land, we will go on board and try to make them stop, that's all."

While he was speaking, they saw several people on the boat killed and thrown into the sea. The helm was put about, and the ship went off toward the east. Chang-po was so angry that he stamped his feet and shouted, "A shipload of perfectly good people! All those lives! For no reason at all being killed at the hands of this crowd of navigators! What injustice!" He thought for a while and then said, "Fortunately there are lots of fishing boats at the bottom of our hill. Why don't we sail out in one of them, kill some of that crew, and replace the others? That would mean the salvation of a whole shipload of people. What a meritorious act! What satisfaction!" Hui-sheng said, "Although it might be satisfying to do this, still it would be very rash, and I'm afraid not safe. What does Brother Ts'an think?"

Lao Ts'an smiled at Chang-po and said, "Brother Chang, your plan is excellent, only I wonder how many companies of soldiers you are going to take with you." Chang-po answered angrily, "How can Brother Ts'an be so blind! At this very moment the lives of these people are in the balance. In this emergency we three should go to rescue them without delay. Where are there any companies of soldiers to take with us?" Lao Ts'an said, "In that case, since the crew of that ship is not less than two hundred men, if we three try to kill them won't we only go to our own deaths and accomplish nothing? What does your wisdom think of that?"

Chang-po thought for a while and decided that Lao Ts'an's reasoning was sound; then he said, "According to you, what should we do? Helplessly watch them die?"

Lao Ts'an answered, "As I see it the crew have not done wrong intentionally; there are two reasons why they have brought the ship to this intolerable pass. What two reasons? The first is that they are accustomed to sailing on the 'Pacific' Ocean and can only live through 'pacific' days. When the wind is still and the waves are quiet, the conditions of navigation make it possible to take things easy. But they were not prepared for today's big wind and heavy sea and therefore are bungling and botching everything. The second reason is that they do not have a compass. When the sky is clear, they can follow traditional methods, and when they can see the sun, moon, and stars they don't make serious mistakes in their course. This might be called 'depending on heaven for your food.' [17] Who could have told that they would run into this overcast weather with the sun, moon, and stars covered up by clouds, leaving them nothing to steer by? It is not that in their hearts they do not want to do the right thing, but since they cannot distinguish north, south, east, and west, the farther they go, the more mistakes they make. As to our present plan, if we take Brother Chang's suggestion to follow them in a fishing boat, we can certainly catch them, because their boat is heavy and ours will be light. If when we have reached them we give them a compass, they will then have a direction to follow and will be able to keep their course. If we also instruct the captain in the difference between navigating in calm and stormy weather and they follow our words, why shouldn't they quickly reach the shore?" Hui-sheng said, "What Lao Ts'an has suggested is the very thing! Let us carry it out quickly; otherwise the shipload of people will certainly be doomed."

The three men descended from the pavilion and told the servants to watch their baggage. They took nothing with them except a reliable compass, a sextant, and several other nautical instruments. At the foot of the hill they found the mooring place of the fishing boats. They chose a light, quick boat, hoisted the sail, and set out in pursuit of the ship. Luckily the wind was blowing from the north so that whether the boat went east or west there was a thwart wind and the sail could be used to the full.

After a short time they were not far from the big boat. The three men continued to watch carefully through their telescopes. When they were a little more than ten chang away, they could hear what the people on the boat were saying. They were surprised to find that while the members of the crew were searching the passengers another man was making an impassioned speech in a loud voice.

They only heard him say, "You have all paid your fares to travel on this boat. In fact, the boat is your own inherited property which has now been brought to the verge of destruction by the crew. All in your families, young and old, are on this boat. Are you all going to wait to be killed? Are you not going to find a way of saving the situation? You deserve to be killed, you herd of slaves!"

The passengers at whom he was railing said nothing at first. Then a number of men got up and said, "What you have said is what we all in our hearts want to say but cannot. Today we have been awakened by you and are truly ashamed of ourselves and truly grateful to you. We only ask you, 'What are we to do?' "

The man then said, "You must know that nowadays nothing can be done without money. If you will all contribute some money, we will give our energy and lifeblood for you and will lay the foundations of a freedom which is eternal and secure. What do you say to this?" The passengers all clapped their hands and shouted with satisfaction.

Chang-po hearing this from the distance said to his two companions, "We didn't know there was a splendid hero like this on the boat. If we had known earlier, we needn't have come." Hui-sheng said, "Let us lower part of our sails for the time being. We don't need to catch up with the ship. We'll just watch what he does. If he really has a sound scheme, then we can very well go back." Lao Ts'an said, "Brother Hui is right. In my poor opinion this man is probably not the sort who will really do anything. He will merely use a few fine-sounding phrases to cheat people of their money—that's all!"

The three then lowered their sails and slowly trailed after the big boat. They saw the people on the boat collect quite a lot of money and hand it over to the speaker. Then they watched to see what he would do. Who could have known that when the speaker had taken the money he would seek out a place where the crowd could not touch him, stand there, and shout to them loudly, "You lot of spineless creatures! Cold-blooded animals! Are you still not going to attack those helmsmen?" And further, "Why don't you take those seamen and kill them one by one?"

Sure enough, some inexperienced young men, trusting his word, went to attack the helmsmen, while others went to upbraid the captain; they were all slaughtered by the sailors and thrown into the sea.

The speaker again began to shout down at them, "Why don't you organize yourselves? If all you passengers on the boat act together, won't you get the better of them?"

But an old and experienced man among the passengers cried out, "Good people! On no account act in this wild way! If you do this, the ship will sink while you are still struggling. I'm certain no good will come of it."

When Hui-sheng heard this he said to Chang-po, "After all, this hero was out to make money for himself while telling others to shed their blood." Lao Ts'an said, "Fortunately there are still a few respectable and responsible men; otherwise the ship would founder even sooner."

When he had spoken, the three men put on full sail and very soon were close to the big boat. Their poleman pulled them alongside with his hook, and the three then climbed up and approached the poop. Bowing very low, they took out their compass and sextant and presented them. The helmsmen looked at them and asked them politely, "How do you use these things? What are they for?"

They were about to reply when suddenly among the lower ranks of seamen arose a howl, "Captain! Captain! Whatever you do don't be tricked by these men. They've got a foreign compass. They must be traitors sent by the foreign devils! They must be Catholics! They have already sold our ship to the foreign devils, and that's why they have this compass. We beg you to bind these men and kill them to avoid further trouble. If you talk with them any more or use their compass, it will be like accepting a deposit from the foreign devils, and they will come to claim our ship."

This outburst aroused everybody on the ship. Even the great speech-making hero cried out, "These are traitors who want to sell the ship! Kill them! Kill them!"

When the captain and the helmsmen heard the clamor, they hesitated. A helmsman who was the captain's uncle [18] said, "Your intentions are very honest, but it is difficult to go against the anger of the mob. You had better go away quickly."

With tears in their eyes the three men hurriedly returned to their little boat. The anger of the crowd on the big ship did not abate, and when they saw the three men getting into their boat, they picked up broken timbers and planks damaged by the waves and hurled them at the small boat. Just think! How could a tiny fishing boat bear up against several hundred men using all their force to destroy it? In a short time the fishing boat was broken to bits and began to sink to the bottom of the sea.

If you don't know what happened to the three men, then hear the next chapter tell.

CHAPTER 2

At the foot of Mount Li the traces of an ancient
    emperor;

By the side of Lake Ming the song of
    a beautiful girl.

IT HAS been told how the fishing boat Lao Ts'an was in was damaged
by the mob and sank with him into the depths of the sea. He realized
that there was no hope for his life. All he could do was to close his eyes
and wait. He felt like a leaf falling from a tree, fluttering to and fro.
In a short time he had sunk to the bottom. He could hear a voice at his
side calling to him, "Wake up, Sir! It is already dark. The food has been
ready in the dining hall for quite a long time." Lao Ts'an opened his
eyes in great confusion, stared around him, and said, "Ay! After all it
was but a dream."

Some days later Lao Ts'an said to the major-domo, "The weather
is now getting colder; your honorable master is no longer ill and the
disease will not break out again. Next year if you need my advice I
will come again to serve him. Now your humble servant wishes to go
to Tsinanfu to enjoy the scenery of the Ta Ming Lake." [1] The major-
domo repeatedly urged him to stay, but without success, so that night

he prepared a farewell feast and presented Lao Ts'an with a packet containing a thousand ounces of silver as an honorarium.

Lao Ts'an said a few words of thanks and put it away in his baggage. Then he said good-by, got into his cart, and started off. The road was among autumn hills covered with red leaves and gardens full of chrysanthemums so that he did not feel at all lonely. When he reached Tsinanfu and entered the city gate, the houses with their springs and the courtyards with their weeping willows seemed to him even more attractive than the scenery of Chiangnan. He found an inn called Promotion Inn on Treasury Street, took his baggage off the cart, paid the carter his fare and wine money, had a hasty evening meal, and went to bed.

The next day he got up early, had a light breakfast, and then took a turn up and down the streets shaking his string of bells in pursuit of his calling. In the afternoon he walked over to the Magpie Bridge [2] and hired a small boat. After rowing north for a short distance, he reached the Lihsia Pavilion,[3] where he stopped the boat and went in. Entering the main gate, he found a pavilion from which most of the paint and lacquer had peeled. On the wall hung a pair of *tui-lien* [vertical plaques] with the inscription:

> In Lihsia this pavilion is the oldest;
> In Tsinan there are many famous scholars.

In the upper right corner was written: "Composed by the *Kung Pu, Tu.*" [4] In the lower left was, "Written by Ho Shao-chi of Taochou." [5] There were several buildings near the pavilion, none of any great interest. He returned to his boat and, rowing to the west, before very long reached the enclosure of the memorial temple to T'ieh Kung.[6]

Do you know who T'ieh Kung was? He was the T'ieh Hsüan who at the beginning of the Ming period caused a lot of trouble to the Prince of Yen. Later generations have honored him for his loyalty to the lawful emperor. For this reason even today at the spring and autumn festivals the inhabitants come to this place to burn incense.

When he reached the T'ieh Kung Temple Lao Ts'an looked toward the south and saw facing him on the Thousand Buddha Hill groups of monastic buildings among the gray-green pines and blue-green cypresses.[7] The trees were crowded together, some red with a fiery red, others white with the white of snow, some indigo blue, others jade green, a few patches of maple red showing among the rest. It was as though a great painting by the Sung artist Chao Ch'ien-li [8] had been made into a screen several tens of li long.

He sighed with sheer delight. Suddenly the sound of a fisherman's song reached him. He bent his head to see where the sound came from and found that the Ming Lake had become as smooth and clear as a mirror. The Thousand Buddha Hill was reflected in the lake and appeared with perfect clarity. The buildings, the terraces, and the trees down there were extraordinarily gay and varied and seemed even more beautiful and clear than the hill above. He knew that beyond the south shore of the lake was a busy street, but a bank of reeds completely concealed it. It was now their blossom time, and the stretch of white bloom reflecting the vapor-filled beams of the setting sun was like a rose-colored velvet carpet forming a cushion between the hill above and the hill below. It was indeed a fascinating sight.

Lao Ts'an thought to himself, "Such an enchanting scene! How is it there are no visitors to enjoy it?" He looked for a while longer and then turned round and read the *tui-lien* on the columns of the great gate. The inscriptions were:

> On four sides lotus blossoms, on three sides willows;
> A city of mountain scenery, half a city of lake.

He quietly bowed his head and said, "It's absolutely true!" He then entered the great gate, and immediately opposite him was the ceremonial hall of T'ieh Kung. To the east was a lotus pond, round which went a zigzag gallery, and at the east end of the lotus pond was a circular gate. Beyond this was an old three-*chien* [three-unit] building with a weatherworn *pien* [horizontal plaque] on which were four characters forming the name "Ancient Water Spirit Shrine." [9] In front of the shrine were a pair of weatherworn *tui-lien* on which was written:

> A cup of cold spring water is offered to the autumn chrysanthemums;
> At midnight the painted boat pushes its way through the lotuses.

Leaving the Water Spirit Shrine, he went down to his boat and rowed to the back of the Lihsia Pavilion. On both sides the lotus leaves and lotus flowers crowded around the boat. The lotus leaves, which were beginning to shrivel, brushed against the boat with a sound, *ch'ih-ch'ih*. Water birds, startled by the coming of people, flew cawing into

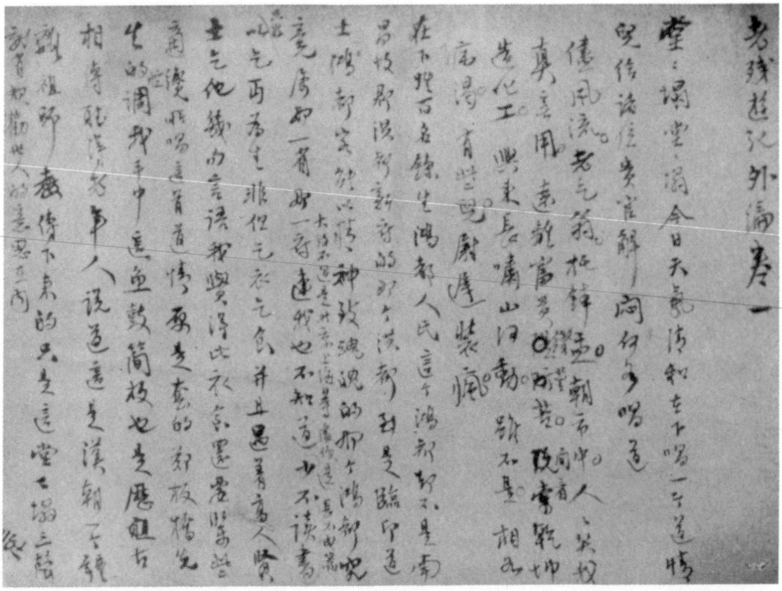

Fig. 1. Manuscript of the unpublished continuation of *The Travels of Lao Ts'an.*

Fig. 2. A visit to the home of Liu Ta-shen, son of the author of *The Travels.* Mr. Liu is at the extreme right, and the translator at the extreme left.

Fig. 3. Innkeeper at the door of what is claimed to be the three-*chien* room occupied by Lao Ts'an in the Promotion Inn at Tsinan.

Fig. 4. Entrance of the Lihsia Pavilion. The boy is holding a bundle of lotus pods. Note the *tui-lien* flanking the outer door and the *pien* above the inner door.

Fig. 5. A view of the Lihsia Pavilion.

17

Fig. 6. Looking toward Thousand Buddha Hill from the north of Ming Lake.

Fig. 7. The Temple of Patriarch Lü by the Leaping Spring.

19

Fig. 8. Women pounding clothes by the moat in Tsinan.

Fig. 9. Water jets of the Leaping Spring. One is being capped to serve the city water system.

Fig. 10. The Golden Spring Academy seen from the northwest. Note the plantain in the foreground.

Fig. 11. The harbor at Lok'ou, on the Yellow River north of Tsinan. Two wheel-barrows in the foreground.

Fig. 12. Residential quarters at the rear of a yamen (Wenshanghsien in Shantung).

the air, *k'e-k'e*. The ripe lotus pods kept catching on the side of the boat and scattering through the windows.

Lao Ts'an casually picked several pods, and while he was eating the seeds the boat reached the Magpie Bridge. Here he felt himself back in the press of human life. There were men carrying loads and men pushing small carts. There were a blue felt sedan chair carried by two bearers and behind the chair a yamen runner wearing a hat with a red tassel and carrying a folder full of letters under his arm. He was running with his head down as though his life depended on it and mopped his brow with a handkerchief as he went. Several five- or six-year-old children in the road did not know how to keep out of people's way. One of them was accidentally knocked over by a chair-bearer and got up crying, "Wa, wa!" His mother quickly ran up asking, "Who knocked you down? Who knocked you down?" The child could only cry, "Wa, wa!" She asked him again and again. At last through his tears he got out the words, "The chair bearer!" The mother raised her head and saw that the chair had already gone two or three li. She therefore took her child by the hand and muttering imprecations, *chi-chi, ku-ku,* went home.

As Lao Ts'an walked slowly south from the Magpie Bridge to Treasury Street, he happened to look up and saw pasted on a wall a strip of yellow paper about a foot long and seven or eight inches wide. In the middle of it were written three characters, "Recital of Drum Tales." [10] At the side was a line of small characters, "On the Twenty-Fourth at the Ming Lake House." The paper was not yet quite dry, so he guessed it had only just been put up. He did not know what it was about since he had never seen anywhere else an announcement of this kind. As he went along the road, he continued to puzzle over it. He heard two carriers talking, "Tomorrow the Fair Maid is telling stories. Let's leave our work and go to listen." And when he reached the main street he overheard a conversation behind a shop counter, "Last time you had a holiday to go and hear the Fair Maid sing; tomorrow it's my turn." Along his whole path the gossip was mostly on this subject. He wondered to himself: "What sort of person is this Fair Maid? What sort of tales are they? Why is the whole town so excited about this announcement?" He allowed his feet to lead him and very soon reached the door of Promotion Inn. He entered the inn and the servant asked him, "What will you have for supper, Sir?"

Lao Ts'an gave his order and then took the chance to ask, "What sort of local entertainment are these Drum Tales? Why is everyone so excited about them?" The servant replied, "You don't know, Sir! Drum Tales used to be a sort of popular country music in Shantung. Old stories were recited to the accompaniment of a drum and a pair of pear-blossom castanets, together called 'pear blossom and big drum.' There was nothing unusual about it. But recently Fair Maid and Dark Maid, two sisters from the Wang family have appeared. The Fair Maid's personal name is Little Jade Wang. She is the most amazing creature you ever heard of. When she was twelve or thirteen years old she learned this art of storytelling, but she soon began to despise the country tunes and said they were dull. She started going to the theater, and as soon as she heard a tune, she could sing it, whether it was a *hsi-p'i* or an *erh-huang* or a *pang-tzu-ch'iang*.[11] When she heard Yü San-sheng's, Ch'eng Chang-keng's, or Chang Erh-k'uei's [12] tunes, she could sing them right off. When she sings, she can go as high as you like. She can hold a note as long as you want. She got hold of those southern—what-do-you-call-'em—*k'un-ch'iang* [13] melodies as well. No matter what sort of style or melody, she puts them all into the singing of Drum Tales. In two or three years' time she created this kind of singing, and now, when people hear her sing, whether they are northerners or southerners, gentry or ordinary folk, there is nobody who is not stirred to the depths of his soul. The notices are up, so tomorrow she will sing. If you don't believe what I say, go and hear her and then you will see. Only if you want to hear her, you'd better go early. Although the performance starts at one o'clock, if you go at ten o'clock there won't be any seats."

Lao Ts'an heard what he said but did not take it very seriously. The next day he got up at six o'clock and first went to see the Shun Well [14] inside the South Gate. Then he went out of the South Gate to the foot of Lishan to see the place where, according to the tradition, the great Shun ploughed the fields in ancient times. When he returned to his inn, it was already about nine o'clock, so he made a hasty breakfast and then went to the Ming Lake House, where he arrived before ten o'clock. It turned out to be a large theater. In front of the stage were more than a hundred tables, and to his surprise when he entered the gate he found all the seats taken, except for seven or eight empty tables in the middle section. These tables had red paper slips pasted on them which said, "Reserved by the Governor," "Reserved by the Director of Education," and so on.

Lao Ts'an looked for a long time but could not find a place. Finally he slipped two hundred cash to an attendant, who arranged a short bench for him in a gap between the tables. On the stage he saw an oblong table on which was placed a flat drum. On the drum were two pieces of iron and he knew that these must be the so-called pear-blossom castanets. Beside them was a three-stringed banjo. Two chairs stood behind the table, but no one was on the stage. When you saw this huge stage, quite bare except for these few things, you couldn't help wanting to laugh. Ten or twenty men were walking up and down among the audience with baskets on their heads, selling sesame-seed cakes and *yu-t'iao* [fritters] to those who had come to the theater without having breakfast.

By eleven o'clock sedan chairs began to crowd at the door. Numerous officials in informal dress came in one after another, followed by their servants. Before twelve o'clock the empty tables in the front were all full. People still kept coming to see if there were seats, and short benches had to be wedged into the narrow spaces that were left. As this crowd of people arrived there were mutual greetings, many genuflections, and a few low bows.[15] Loud and animated conversation, free and easy talk, and laughter prevailed. Apart from those at the ten or so tables in front, the rest of the audience was made up of tradespeople, except for a few who looked like the scholars of the place. They all gossiped away, *ch'i-ch'i, ts'a-ts'a,* but since there were so many people, you couldn't hear clearly what they were saying. In any case, it was nobody's business.

At half-past twelve a man wearing a long blue cloth gown appeared through the curtained door at the back of the stage. He had a longish face, covered with lumps, like the skin of a Foochow orange dried by the wind. But ugly as he was, you felt that he was quiet and sober. He came out on the stage and said nothing but sat down on the chair to the left, behind the oblong table. Slowly he took up the three-stringed banjo, in a leisurely way tuned up the strings, and then played one or two little melodies, to which, however, the audience did not listen with much attention. After this he played a longer piece, but I don't know the name of the tune. I only remember that as it went on he began to pluck the strings in a circular motion, with all his fingers one after another, until the sounds now high, now low, now simple, now intricate, entered the ears and stirred the hearts of the listeners so with their variety that there might have been several tens of strings and several hundreds of fingers playing on them. And now continuous shouts of approval were heard, not interfering, however, with the sound of the banjo. When he had finished this piece, he rested, and a man from the wings brought him a cup of tea.

After a pause of several minutes a girl came out from behind the curtains. She was about sixteen or seventeen years old with a long duck's egg face, hair done into a knot, and silver earrings in her ears. She wore a blue cotton jacket and a pair of blue cotton trousers with black piping. Although her clothes were of coarse material, they were spotlessly clean. She came to the back of the table and sat down on the chair to the right. The banjo player then took up his instrument and began to pluck the strings, *chen-chen, ts'ung-ts'ung.* The girl stood up, took the pear-blossom castanets between the fingers of her left hand and began to clap them, *ting-ting, tang-tang,* in time with the banjo. With her right hand she took up the drumstick and then, after listening carefully to the rhythm of the banjo, struck the drum a sharp blow and began to sing. Every word was clear-cut and crisp; every note smooth-flowing like a young oriole flying out of a valley or a young swallow returning to the nest. Every phrase had seven words and every part several tens of phrases, now slow, now fast, sometimes high, sometimes low. There were endless changes of tune and style so that the listener felt that no song, tune, melody, or air ever invented could equal this one piece, that it was the peak of perfection in song.

There were two men sitting at Lao Ts'an's side, one of whom asked the other in a low voice, "I suppose this must be the Fair Maid?" The other man said, "No, this is the Dark Maid, the Fair Maid's younger sister. All her songs were taught her by the Fair Maid. If you compare her with the Fair Maid, it's impossible to estimate the distance that separates them! You can talk about her skill, but the Fair Maid's can't be put into words. The Dark Maid's skill can be learned by others, but the Fair Maid's can't possibly be learned. For several years now everybody has tried to sing like them. Even the singsong girls have tried! And the most anyone has done is to sing two or three phrases as well as the Dark Maid. As to the Fair Maid's merits, why, there's never been anybody who could do a tenth as well as she."

While they were talking, the Dark Maid had already finished singing and went out at the back. And now all the people in the theater began to talk and laugh. Sellers of melon seeds, peanuts, red fruit, and walnuts shouted their wares in a loud voice. The whole place was filled with the sound of human voices. Just when the uproar was at its height, another girl appeared at the back of the stage. She was about eighteen or nineteen years old, and her costume differed in no detail from that of the first. She had a melon-seed face and a clear white complexion. Her features were not particularly beautiful; she was attractive without being seductive, pure but not cold. She came out with her head slightly bent, stood behind the table, took up the pear-blossom castanets and clapped them together several times, *ting-tang*. It was most amazing! They were just two bits of iron, and yet in her hand they seemed to contain all the five notes and the twelve tones.[16] Then she took up the drumstick, lightly struck the drum twice, lifted her head, and cast one glance at the audience. When those two eyes, like autumn water, like winter stars, like pearls, like two beads of black in quicksilver, glanced left and right, even the men sitting in the most distant corners felt: Little Jade Wang is looking at me! As to those sitting nearer, nothing need be said. It was just one glance, but the whole theater was hushed,[17] quieter than when the Emperor comes forth. Even a needle dropped on the ground could have been heard.

Little Jade Wang then opened her vermilion lips, displaying her sparkling white teeth, and sang several phrases. At first the sound was not very loud, but you felt an inexpressible magic enter your ears, and it was as though the stomach and bowels [18] had been passed over by a smoothing iron, leaving no part unrelaxed. You seemed to absorb ambrosia [19] through the thirty-six thousand pores of the skin until every single pore tingled with delight. After the first few phrases her song rose higher and louder till suddenly she drew her voice up to a sharp high-pitched note like a thread of steel wire thrown into the vault of the sky. You could not help secretly applauding. Still more amazing, she continued to move her voice up and down and in and out at that great height. After several turns her voice again began to rise, making three or four successive folds in the melody, each one higher than the last. It was like climbing T'aishan [20] from the western face of the Aolai Peak. First you see the thousand-fathom cleft wall of Aolai Peak and think that it reaches the sky. But when you have wound your way up to the top, you see Fan Peak far above you. And when you have got to the top of Fan Peak, again you see the South

Gate of Heaven far above Fan Peak. The higher you climb, the more alarming it seems—the more alarming, the more wonderful.

After Little Jade Wang had sung her three or four highest flourishes, suddenly her voice dropped, and then at a powerful spirited gallop, in a short time, with a thousand twists and turns she described innumerable circles like a flying serpent writhing and turning among the thirty-six peaks of The Yellow Mountains.[21] After this the more she sang, the lower her voice became; the lower she sang, the more delicate it was, until at last the sound could be heard no more. Every person in the theater held his breath and sat intently, not daring to move. After two or three minutes it was as though a small sound came forth from under the ground. And then the voice again rose like a Japanese rocket which shoots into the sky, bursting and scattering with innumerable strands of multicolored fire. The voice soared aloft until endless sounds seemed to be coming and going. The banjo player too plucked his strings with a circular movement of all his fingers, now loud, now soft, in perfect accompaniment to her voice. It was like the wanton singing of sweet birds on a spring morning in the garden. The ears were kept so busy that you couldn't decide which note to listen to. Just as it was becoming most intricate, one clear note sounded, and then voice and instrument both fell silent. The applause from the audience was like the rumbling of thunder.

After a while the uproar abated slightly and from the front row one could hear a young man of about thirty say with a Hunan accent, "When I was a student and came across that passage where the ancient writer describes the merits of good singing in the words 'The sound circles the beams and stops not for three days,' [22] I could not understand what was meant. If you think of it in the abstract, how can sound go round and round the beams? And how can it go on for three days? It was not until I heard Little Jade Wang sing that I realized how appropriate the words of the ancient writer are. Every time I hear her sing, her song echoes in my ears for many days. No matter what I'm doing my attention wanders. Rather I feel that the 'three days' of 'stops not for three days' is too short. The 'three months' of the saying about Confucius, 'For three months he knew not the taste of meat' [23] would describe it much more adequately." Those around him all said, "Mr. Meng Hsiang [24] expresses it so aptly that he arouses my envy."

While they were talking, the Dark Maid again came on to sing.

After her the Fair Maid appeared again. Lao Ts'an heard a man near him say that this piece was called "The Black Donkey." It merely told the story of a scholar who saw a beautiful maiden riding by on a black donkey. Before describing the girl, it told all about the good parts of the black donkey, and when at last it came to tell about the maiden, in a few words it was finished. It was sung entirely in "rapid recitative"; the further it went, the faster it got. The poem by Po Hsiang-shan [25] expresses it perfectly,

> Big pearls and little pearls fall into the jade platter.

The marvelous thing about it was that though she recited so quickly that you would have thought the listeners could not follow, every word was clear; not one was lost to their ears. Only she could obtain this clarity. But even this piece, it must be owned, was inferior to the preceding one.

It was not yet five o'clock, and everybody assumed that Little Jade Wang would sing once again. It would be interesting to see what her next piece would be like.

To learn what happened, hear the next chapter tell.

CHAPTER 3

From Golden Thread eastward seeking Black Tiger;

A cloth sail goes west in search of Gray Falcon.

IT HAS been told that everybody expected Little Jade Wang to sing again. But instead her younger sister came out and sang off a few phrases which closed the performance. Then the audience noisily dispersed.

The next day Lao Ts'an remembered the thousand ounces of silver he was keeping in his inn and felt uneasy. He went to Government Street, found the banking house called Daily More Prosperous, and sent eight hundred ounces to his old home at Hsüchou in Chiangnan, leaving himself something more than a hundred ounces. The same day he bought a bolt of raw silk and a length of broadcloth for a short jacket, took them back to his inn, and called in a tailor to make him up a padded gown and a jacket. It was now the end of the ninth month, and although it was quite mild, he knew that if the northwest wind should blow up he would need padded clothing. His orders to the tailor finished, he had his midday meal, and walked out of the west gate. He first went to the Leaping Spring, where he had a cup of tea.

This Leaping Spring is the first in rank of the seventy-two springs in Tsinanfu. The big pool is about four or five *mou* in extent and is the source of two streams. The water flows through the pool with a continuous sound, *ku-ku.* In the middle three large springs gush up, rising two or three feet above the surface of the water. According to the natives, in former years the jets of water were five or six feet high, but after the pool had been repaired, for some unknown reason they became lower. The three jets are all thicker than a well bucket. On the north side of the pool is a Temple to the Patriarch Lü,[1] and in front of this a mat shed had been erected sheltering four or five tables and ten or more benches. Here the visitor could rest and buy tea.

After drinking some tea, Lao Ts'an went out by the back gate of the Leaping Spring enclosure and followed a winding path to the east till he found the Golden Spring Academy.[2] Here he entered the inner gate and came to the T'ou Hsia Well, reputed to be the place where Ch'en Tsun[3] entertained his guests. Going to the west through another gate, he came to a butterfly pavilion which had spring water flowing all around it. Behind the pavilion were many plantains, which in spite of several bunches of withered leaves, formed a continuous stretch of jade green. In the northwest corner surrounded by plantains was a pool about two chang square, the Golden Thread Spring. The Golden Thread ranks second among the four most famous springs.

Do you know which are the four most famous springs? The one we have just spoken of, the Leaping Spring; the one we are now visiting, the Golden Thread Spring; the Black Tiger Spring outside the south gate; and the Pearl Spring in the Governor's Yamen—these are known as the Four Famous Springs.

The Golden Thread Spring is reputed to have a thread of gold in its water. Lao Ts'an looked right and left for a long time, but there wasn't even an iron thread to be seen, to say nothing of golden threads. Happily, a scholar came along; Lao Ts'an bowed to him and asked to be enlightened whether there was anything in this name, Golden Thread. The scholar slowly led Lao Ts'an to the west side of the pool, leaned over, and with bent head gazed at the water, saying, "Look! On the surface of the water there is a line like a gossamer thread moving to and fro. Do you see it?"

Lao Ts'an followed his example. After looking for some time he said, "I see it! I see it! What is the cause of it?" He thought for a while and then said, "Can there be two springs underneath which match their strength against each other and so force up this thread in the middle?" The scholar said, "There are records of this spring for several hundred years. Is it possible that during this long period neither of the two springs has proved stronger than the other?" Lao Ts'an said, "Look! The thread keeps moving. This must mean that the two springs are not entirely of equal strength." The scholar on his side nodded his head in agreement. With that each went his way.

Lao Ts'an left the Golden Spring Academy and followed the west wall of the city south. When he had passed the corner of the city, he came to a street of shops and followed it straight east. Outside the south gate was a wide moat. The spring water in the moat was deep and pure, and the bottom was clearly visible; the water weeds in the moat had grown to more than a chang in length and were swept to and fro by the current—most beautiful to behold! As he went along looking about him, he saw several large oblong pools on the southern bank, where crowds of squatting women were pounding clothes on the stones at the side. Farther on was a big pond with a wattle building of several *chien* on its south bank. Finding it was a tea shop, he went in and sat down by the north window while a servingman steeped him a pot of tea. All the teapots looked like I-hsing [4] ware, though they were really of local make in that style.

When Lao Ts'an had settled down, he asked the servingman, "I hear you have a Black Tiger Spring here; can you tell me where it is?" The man smiled and said: "Lean on this window ledge and look out, Sir. There's the Black Tiger."

Lao Ts'an looked out, and there, indeed, just at his feet, was a carved-stone tiger's head, about two feet or so long and one foot and five or six inches across. A spring spurted out of the tiger's mouth with great force and dashed against the farther side of the pool, then divided and flowed out into the city moat. He sat for a while until he saw that the evening sun was beginning to go down behind the hills, paid for his tea, and with slow steps entered the south gate and returned to his inn.

The next day, feeling that he had done enough sightseeing, he took his string of bells and roamed up and down the crowded streets. Just past the Governor's Yamen he noticed at the entrance to a lane on the west a middle-class house with the main gate facing south. On a board by the gate were three characters, "Mr. Kao's Residence." At the gate stood a man with a long, thin face wearing a brownish-purple padded gown of fine *lo*. He was holding a foreign white brass "carriage-and-pair" [5] water pipe in his two hands. His face bore a melancholy look. Seeing Lao Ts'an he cried out, "Sir! Sir! Can you treat disorders of the throat?" Lao Ts'an answered, "I know something about them." The man then said, "Please come in." Entering the gate they made a turn to the west to a three-*chien* reception room, tolerably well furnished. On both sides there were scrolls, mostly from the brush of famous living men. In the middle hung a single scroll, a painting of a man who looked like Lieh Tzu riding the wind, his clothing, hat, and sash blowing in the gale, the brush strokes most powerful.[6] Above was the name of the painter, "Chang Feng, styled Great Wind," also excellently written.

They sat down and exchanged names. The man turned out to be from Kiangsu. His *hao* was Shao-yin, and he held the position of secretary in the provincial government. He said, "I have a concubine who has suffered from ulcerated throat for five days. Today she cannot even swallow a drop of water. Please, doctor, tell me whether there is any hope or not." Lao Ts'an answered, "I can't say anything until I have seen the patient."

Mr. Kao then ordered a servant, "Go to the women's quarters and warn them that a doctor has come for an examination." They then went together through the inner gate to a three-*chien* building. When they had entered the middle room, a maidservant lifted up the *lientzu* [curtain] on the door of the west room, saying, "Please come in." They went into the room where, in the northwest corner, was a big bed, hung with printed grass-linen curtains. There was an oblong table against the west wall by the head of the bed, and at the side of the bed were two stools.

Mr. Kao gave Lao Ts'an the stool to the west, and a hand was stretched out from behind the curtain. The maidservant brought several books and piled them up under the hand. He felt one hand, then the other. Lao Ts'an said, "The pulse in both hands is deep, quick, and taut,[7] showing that the fever is stopped up by the chill and can't get out. The longer this goes on, the more serious it is. Please let me see the throat."

Mr. Kao then lifted the curtain. The woman was about twenty years of age. Her face was flushed, yet she appeared to be quite exhausted. Mr. Kao gently raised her up toward the light of the window.

Lao Ts'an bent his head to look: the pale red swellings in the throat were about to meet. When he had looked, he said to Mr. Kao, "This attack was not so serious to begin with—only a little internal heat. But because a doctor has used bitter, cold medicine [8] to check it, the heat could not come out. Besides, the patient is inclined to be moody,[9] and the disorder was originally caused by the repression of her feelings. Even now two doses of pungent and cool diaphoretic [10] will set it right." He took a bottle of medicine and a tube out of his bag and blew some medicine into her throat. Returning to the reception room he drew up a prescription for a medicine called "Infusion of licorice and kikio root with additional flavors." [11] The ingredients were eight in number: licorice, kikio root, burdock, ground ivy, *fang-feng*, peppermint, magnolia, and talcum, while fresh lotus stems formed the adjuvant. When he had written the prescription he gave it to Mr. Kao.

Mr. Kao said, "That's splendid. But how many doses do we give her?" Lao Ts'an said, "Two doses today. Tomorrow I will come to examine her again." Mr. Kao further asked, "Please tell me what your fee is." Lao Ts'an answered, "As I go about practicing my mystery [12] I have no fixed charges. If I cure your concubine's sickness, then when I am hungry you may give me a bowl of rice or when I can't walk you may help with my travel expenses, and I shall be satisfied." Mr. Kao answered, "Since you say this, I will recompense you for everything when she is recovered. Where is your inn, so that if there should be a change I can send a man to fetch you?" Lao Ts'an said, "The Promotion Inn, on Treasury Street." Having said this he left.

From that time on they came every day to fetch him. In a few days the disease began to abate, and the patient returned to normal. Mr. Kao was overjoyed. He gave Lao Ts'an eight ounces of silver in token of thanks and honored him with a wine feast at the North Pillar Restaurant to which he invited his colleagues in the secretariat with the idea of making known Lao Ts'an's skill. One thing led to another until after a while not a day passed without a sedan chair coming for him from the officials and their aides.

One day a feast was given at the North Pillar Restaurant, this time by an expectant *taot'ai*.[13] The man sitting in an upper seat on the right side of the table said, "Yü Tso-ch'en [14] is going to fill the vacancy at Ts'aochoufu." The man at a lower seat on the left side, next to Lao Ts'an, said, "His place on the waiting list is very low. How can he fill the vacancy?"

The man on the right said, "He is so successful in dealing with bandits that in less than a year 'the thing dropped on the road is not picked up.' [15] The Governor considers him quite exceptional. The day before yesterday somebody said to him, 'I was traveling through a certain village near Ts'aochoufu when I saw with my own eyes a blue cloth bundle lying beside the road. No one had dared to pick it up, so I asked the inhabitants: "Whose bundle is this? Why does nobody pick it up?" A native of the place said, "Somebody we don't know put it here last night." I asked, "Why don't any of you take it away?" They all laughed and shook their heads saying, "We want all the members of our family to remain alive, thank you!" From this we see that "the thing dropped on the road is not picked up," and the ancient writer was not deceiving us, for what he wrote has actually been achieved today!' When the Governor heard this, he was delighted and is planning to send up a special memorial commending him."

The guest on the left said, "Tso-ch'en is certainly very efficient, but he is much too cruel. In less than a year he has choked to death more than two thousand people in his cages.[16] Do you suppose none of these were unjustly treated?"

Another guest said, "There certainly have been cases of injustice. That goes without saying. What nobody knows is the proportion of those not unjustly condemned."

A man on the right said, "Tyrannical government often looks well on the surface. You all remember that year when Flay-the-Skin Ch'ang was at Yenchoufu. Didn't the same thing happen there? It went on until everybody looked askance at the tyrant."

Another said, "Tso-ch'en's tyranny is indeed oppressive, but the people of Ts'aochou are certainly a bad lot! The year I was administering Ts'aochou scarcely a day passed without a case of banditry. I organized a band of two hundred gendarmes, but they were like a cat who couldn't catch mice—absolutely useless. Of all those who were arrested as bandits by the constables in the various *hsien*, those who were not honest country people were men compelled by the bandits to watch their horses and mules. Out of a hundred men arrested scarcely any were real bandits. But now thanks to the thunder and whirlwind methods of Yü Tso-ch'en, banditry has entirely ceased. All this makes me feel thoroughly ashamed!"

The man on the left said, "All the same, from my stupid point of view, it would be better not to kill so many people. This man may have a great name for a while, but I fear that what he will reap in the future will be too terrible for words." [17] When he had said this, every-body exclaimed, "We have had enough wine. May we have the rice!" After the rice they separated.

A day later Lao Ts'an was sitting idly in his inn in the afternoon when suddenly a blue felt sedan chair stopped at the door and a man came in calling out, "Is Mr. T'ieh at home?"

Lao Ts'an looked out; it was none other than Kao Shao-yin. He quickly went out to welcome him, saying, "At home! At home! Please come in; only the place is very poor; you demean yourself too much in coming." Shao-yin said, "You are much too polite," and came through the inner gate. They then entered Lao Ts'an's quarters. He had a two-*chien* room facing east. At the south end was a brick *k'ang* [bed] on which bedding was spread out. At the north end were a square table and two chairs. To the west were two small bamboo chests. On the table were several books, a small ink slab, some brushes, and a box of seal ink.

Lao Ts'an made Shao-yin sit in the place of honor. Shao-yin began to pick up the books and look at them carefully. Suddenly he said with great surprise, "This is a Sung period Chang Chün-fang [18] wood-block edition of *Chuang Tzu*. Where did it come from? No copy of this book has been seen for a long time. Neither Chi Ts'ang-wei [19] nor Huang P'i-lieh [20] ever came across one. It counts as a rare treasure!" Lao Ts'an said, "They're just a few old books left me by my father. They're not worth selling, so I carry them around with me in my traveling case to pass the time with when I am bored, instead of novels. Nothing worth mentioning." He turned over another. It was a volume of T'ao's poems [21] in the writing of Su Tung-p'o,[22] the original impression of Mao Tzu-chin's [23] wood-block edition.

Shao-yin sighed in admiration and then asked, "Since you come from such a scholarly family, why don't you find a position in the official world instead of following this thankless trade? 'Wealth and honor' may be 'floating clouds,' [24] but aren't you a bit too high-minded?"

Lao Ts'an sighed. "Your Honor's referring to me as 'high-minded' is truly too much of a compliment. It is not that I have no ambition for official life, but simply because my nature is too free and easy and doesn't fit the times, and because, as the saying is, 'the higher the climb, the greater the fall.' My intention in not climbing high is to make sure that I fall lightly."

Shao-yin said, "Last night I was at an informal dinner in the yamen, and the Governor was saying, 'In our provincial government we have a great deal of talent; all the gifted men we have heard of have been invited to join us.' Mr. Yao Yün, who was sitting with us, said, 'At this very moment there is a man in the city whom the Governor has not invited.' The Governor asked eagerly, 'Who is it?' Mr. Yao Yün reported on your scholarship, your character, your thorough understanding of men and affairs, until the Governor began to fiddle with his ears and stroke his cheeks, he was so pleased. He then told me to send you an official letter without delay. But I answered him, 'I'm afraid that won't do. This man is neither on the waiting list for an office, nor is he seeking office, and I don't even know whether he has any rank or degree. So it would be hard to write him an official letter.' The Governor said, 'In that case send an ordinary invitation.' I said, 'If you were to call him in to treat sickness, he would come instantly, but if you are inviting him into the administration I don't know whether he will want to come or not. It is better to sound him out first.' The Governor said, 'Very good. Go tomorrow to see what he says and bring him here to visit me.' This is why I have come today especially to find out whether or not you will come with me to the yamen to visit the Governor." Lao Ts'an said, "There is no reason why I shouldn't, except that to see the Governor I ought to wear an official cap and belt. I am not in the habit of wearing them, but if I may go in ordinary clothes then it's all right." Shao-yin answered, "Of course ordinary clothes will do. Let us wait a while and then go together. You can sit in my room, and when the Governor comes out of his living quarters in the afternoon, we can talk to him in his office." With this he ordered a chair.

Wearing his ordinary clothes, Lao Ts'an went with Kao Shao-yin to the Provincial Yamen. Now this Shantung Provincial Yamen was formerly the palace of Prince Ch'i [25] of the Ming dynasty, and many parts of it still keep the old names. They reached the third hall, called the Entrance to the Palace. To one side was Kao Shao-yin's office; opposite it was the room where the Governor signed official documents.

They went into Shao-yin's office and in less than half an hour saw the Governor come forth. His figure was majestic and his features kind and open. When Kao Shao-yin saw him, he immediately went forward to welcome him and said a few words in a low voice. All you could hear was Governor Chuang [26] saying again and again, "Please come over. Please come over." Then a minor official ran across and called out, "The Governor invites Mr. T'ieh to come."

Lao Ts'an hurriedly walked over and stood face to face with Governor Chuang. Chuang said, "Long have I admired you." Then he stretched out his hand and with a slight bow said, "Please come in." An attendant was already lifting up the soft *lientzu* over the door.

Lao Ts'an went into the room and made a low bow, his hands clasped together. The Governor gave him the seat of honor on the redwood *k'ang*. Shao-yin took the opposite seat, and a square stool was placed between the two. The Governor sat down there and began the conversation, "I have heard that Mr. Pu-ts'an's scholarship and knowledge of public administration are both far above the average. I am an unschooled person, but by Imperial Grace I have been appointed to take charge of this territory. In other provinces it is sufficient to put heart and soul into the work of administration, but in my province there is in addition the river work, which is certainly difficult to manage. The only thing I can do is to call in every man of unusual ability I hear of. It's a case of 'many minds, greater gain.' If anyone has a thorough grasp of certain problems and can give advice about them, it is of course greatly appreciated."

Lao Ts'an answered, "Every voice testifies to the fame of the Governor's rule: that goes without saying. However I have heard it rumored that in the matter of the river work, all the plans are based on Chia Jang's [27] 'Three Methods' and follow the principle that you must not struggle with the river for land." The Governor said, "You are quite right. Just consider: in Honan the river is very wide; but here it is very narrow." Lao Ts'an said, "The important thing is not that when the river is narrow there is no room for the water, for this only happens during the month or so when the river is in flood. The rest of the time, the current being weak, the silt is easily deposited. You must know that Chia Jang was only a good essayist. He had had no experience in river work. Less than a hundred years after Chia Jang a certain Wang Ching [28] appeared. His method of river control was derived in a direct line from that of the Great Yü. [29] He emphasized the 'curbing' which is referred to in the expression 'Yü curbed the flood waters.' [30] This directly opposed Chia Jang's views. After Wang Ching had directed flood control, there was no river disaster for over a thousand years. P'an Chi-hsün [31] of the Ming period and Chin Wen-hsiang [32] of the present dynasty both followed his doctrine to some extent and as a result enjoyed great fame. I take it the Governor knows this." The Governor asked, "What method did Wang Ching use?" Lao Ts'an answered, "He developed it from the two words 'united' and 'divided' in the passage which reads 'It divided and became nine rivers; these united again to form the "meeting" river.' [33] The *History of the Later Han Dynasty* [34] only tells how he 'built a water gate every ten li and regulated the flow of water from one to the other.' As to the details of the method, they cannot be dealt with completely in a short conversation. If you permit, I will later prepare a memorandum and offer it for your consideration. How would that be?"

Governor Chuang was so pleased that he said to Kao Shao-yin, "Tell them to prepare that three-*chien* south study as quickly as possible and we will invite Mr. T'ieh to move into the yamen to live so that he can give advice at any time." Lao Ts'an said, "The Governor's great kindness overwhelms me. But I have a relative living in Ts'aochoufu and I'm thinking of paying him a visit. Besides, having heard rumors about Prefect Yü's administration, I want to go and find out what sort of a man he really is. When I come back from Ts'aochou I will hope to profit further by the Governor's wisdom." The Governor's expression showed that he was very disappointed. The talk finished, Lao Ts'an excused himself, and he and Shao-yin left the yamen and went their several ways.

If you don't know whether or not Lao Ts'an went to Ts'aochou after all, then hear the next chapter tell.

CHAPTER 4

A Governor who loves ability and whose search for
  scholars is like thirst;

A Magistrate who suppresses bandits and hates
  wrongdoers as though they were foemen.

THE STORY tells that when Lao Ts'an came out of the Governor's
yamen he dismissed his chair and amused himself by strolling along
the street for a while. He spent some time in the curio shops, returning
toward evening to his inn. When the innkeeper rushed into his room
and shouted, "Congratulations!" Lao Ts'an could not make out what
it was all about.

The innkeeper said, "I have just heard that the Honorable Mr. Kao
of the Governor's yamen came in person to invite Your Honor saying
that the Governor wanted to see Your Honor and that you went with
him to the yamen. Your Honor is indeed fortunate. Mr. Li and Mr.
Chang, who occupy my main building, both came from the capital
with letters to the Governor. Half a dozen times they were unable
to see him, and when at last they did manage to see him once or twice,
they became overbearing, started to swear at everybody, and again
and again sent people with their cards to the yamen asking for them
to be beaten. And now take Your Honor! The Honorable Secretary

comes right from the Governor's yamen and invites you to go and have a chat! What a lot of face that gives you! There is no fear of your not getting an appointment very soon. Why shouldn't I congratulate Your Honor?" Lao Ts'an said, "No such thing. You've heard a lot of nonsense. I cured a case of sickness in Mr. Kao's family. I asked him if he could take me to see the Pearl Spring in the Governor's yamen, and so, since the Honorable Mr. Kao happened to be free today, he invited me to see the spring. What's all this about the Governor wanting to see me?"

The innkeeper answered, "I know all about it. Your Honor, don't deceive me. When the Honorable Mr. Kao was here, I heard his man say, 'When the Governor was going in to dinner and was passing the Honorable Mr. Kao's door, he called out: "As soon as you have had dinner, go and invite that Mr. T'ieh to come. If you go late, he may be out and we shall not be able to see him today."'" Lao Ts'an laughed, "Don't believe their foolish talk. There is nothing in it." The innkeeper replied, "Don't worry, Your Honor; I'm not asking you to lend me any money."

Then a voice was heard outside shouting, "Where is the proprietor?" and the innkeeper hurried out. He saw a man wearing an official hat with a bright blue button and a trailing peacock feather, a pair of "tiger boots,"[1] a lined gown of purple woolen cloth, and a sky-blue woolen jacket. In one hand he carried a lantern; in the other he held a folded red visiting card. He called out, "Innkeeper!" and the innkeeper said, "Here, Sir! Here, Sir! What do you want, Sir?" The man asked, "Do you have a Mr. T'ieh here?" The innkeeper answered: "Yes, Yes! He lives in the east building. I'll take you there."

The two men came in the courtyard and the innkeeper, pointing to Lao Ts'an, said, "This is Mr. T'ieh." The man took a step forward and made a genuflection. He presented the visiting card and said: "The Governor told me to convey his compliments to Mr. T'ieh. He had been invited to dinner by the Director of Education tonight, so he was unable to keep Mr. T'ieh at the yamen for dinner. He therefore ordered the kitchen to prepare a wine feast and send it over without delay. The Governor said, 'It is not really fit to eat, but ask Mr. T'ieh to be tolerant.'" The man then turned his head and gave the order: "Bring in the feast!"

Two attendants carried in a three-decked set of oblong boxes and lifted the lid. The top layer contained hors d'oeuvres and small bowls of food; the second layer, large bowls of such things as swallows' nests and shark fins; the third layer, a roasted suckling pig, a duck, and two plates of pastries. After it had been opened and seen, the man called out, "Innkeeper!"

All this time the innkeeper and his servingmen had been standing at the side, gaping with astonishment. Hearing the call he quickly answered, "What is it, Sir?" The man replied, "See that this is taken to the kitchen!" Lao Ts'an quickly said, "I am unworthy of all this attention from the Governor," and invited the man to come in and have some tea. He repeatedly refused. When Lao Ts'an became more insistent, he finally entered the room and sat in a humble place on a stool. He would rather die than sit on the *k'ang*.

Lao Ts'an took the teapot and poured him a cup of tea. The man quickly made a genuflection and expressed his thanks, adding, "I heard the Governor give orders to sweep the rooms in the south courtyard without delay and to invite Mr. T'ieh to move in tomorrow or the next day and live there. In the future if you have any errands to be run simply send to the headquarters of the *Wu Hsün Pu* [2] and I will come to attend you." Lao Ts'an said, "You are too kind." The man then got up again, made another genuflection, and said, "Good day, Sir, I must go back to the yamen to report. Please give me your card."

Lao Ts'an told a servingman to give the carriers four hundred cash, then wrote an acknowledgment, and started to see the man to the street. He firmly protested against this. Lao Ts'an, however, saw him out to the main gate and watched him get on his horse.

When Lao Ts'an came back from the gate, the innkeeper met him, all smiles, saying, "Does Your Honor still want to fool me? Wasn't this feast sent you by the Governor? I have heard that the man who just came in is the *Wu Hsün Pu*, the Honorable Mr. Ho. He is a lieutenant colonel. These two years the Governor has often sent wine feasts to guests staying at my inn, but they have all been ordinary feasts, and an ordinary messenger [3] was counted good enough to bring them. This is the first time anyone has received this kind of honorable treatment in my place."

Lao Ts'an answered, "It's all the same whether it's ordinary or extraordinary. The main thing is how I am to dispose of this food." The innkeeper said, "Either divide it up among some good friends or write an invitation tonight asking several honorable guests to come and eat it on the Ta Ming Lake tomorrow. What the Governor sends gives you much more credit than what money can buy."

Lao Ts'an smiled and said, "If it gives so much more face than what money can buy, is there anyone who will buy it? I'll be glad to sell it for two or three pieces of gold to pay you for my board and lodging." The innkeeper said, "Don't you worry. I'm not concerned about your board and lodging. There'll be plenty of people ready to pay Your Honor's bills. If you don't believe me, just wait and see whether I'm right or not." Lao Ts'an said, "Do what you like about that. As for this food now, as far as I can see the best thing is to hand it over to you and ask you to invite some guests. I certainly don't want to eat it. It's just a nuisance."

The two discussed the matter for some time. In the end it was Lao Ts'an who invited some guests. He asked all the people staying in the inn to go to the main building. In this building lived the man called Li and the one called Chang. They were both usually very arrogant, but today, seeing the Governor show so much respect for Lao Ts'an, they were wondering how they could make connections with him so as to ask him to put a word in for them with the Governor. Now that Lao Ts'an was borrowing their outer room in order to invite all the guests in the inn to dinner, it was natural for them to have the seats of honor, and they were happy as could be. In the course of the feast they made Lao Ts'an thoroughly uncomfortable by their flattery. There was no help for it. All he could do was to say a few words to pass it off. At long last the feast ended, and each went his way.

Who could have thought that Messrs. Chang and Li would come in person to the side building to express their thanks! They flattered Lao Ts'an without end; when one stopped, the other took it up. The one called Li said, "You can now buy the office of subprefect. Later this year you can buy a promotion. Next year at the general promotion in the spring you can again get a higher post and in the autumn be received by the Emperor. Then you can become the *Taot'ai* of the Chi, Tung, T'ai, Wu, and Liu circuit,[4] first being inscribed on the list and later appointed. This is all quite possible." The one called Chang then said, "Mr. Li is the wealthiest man in Tientsin; if you will help him get two promotions, Mr. Li will lend you the money for the purchase of an office. It will not be too late to return it when you have obtained a good post." Lao Ts'an answered, "I count myself fortunate to enjoy the good will of you two gentlemen, but just now I have no intention of 'leaving the mountains' and entering official life. In the future if I want to do so I will ask your help." The two urged him a while, then each went to his room to sleep.

Lao Ts'an thought to himself, "I was planning to stay here a couple of days more, but with things as they are I fear that these meaningless entanglements will get worse and worse. 'Of thirty-six plans, to get out is the best.'" That night he wrote a letter thanking Governor Chuang for the honor of his friendship and entrusted it to Kao Shao-yin. Before daylight he cleared his account at the inn, hired a wheelbarrow, and left the city. Once outside the west gate of Tsinanfu he traveled north for eighteen li, to a market town called Lok'ou. Formerly, before the Yellow River took the bed of the Tach'ing River,[5] the streams from the seventy-two springs in the city entered that river here and it was a very flourishing place. But ever since the Yellow River took the bed of the Tach'ing River, although there is still some coming and going of cargo boats, the traffic is not more than ten or twenty per cent of what it was formerly, a big difference.

Arrived at Lok'ou, Lao Ts'an hired a small boat with the understanding that he was to be taken upstream to Tungchiak'ou, the landing place for Ts'aochoufu. He advanced two strings of cash for the boatmen to buy some fuel and rice with. Luckily that day there was a southeast wind, the sail was hoisted, and they were blown along. They sailed until the sun was about to sink behind the hills, and when they had reached the town of Ch'ihohsien, they threw out the anchor and stopped for the night. The second day they stopped at P'ingyin, the third at Shouchang, and the fourth day they reached Tungchiak'ou where, as usual, they spent the night on the boat. At daybreak Lao Ts'an paid for the boat and had his luggage carried to an inn where he took a room.

Now this Tungchiak'ou is on the main road from Ts'aochoufu to Tamingfu, so there are a great many inns there. Lao Ts'an's inn was called The Old Inn of the Second Tung Brother. The innkeeper's name was Tung; he was more than sixty years old, and everybody called him Lao Tung. There was only one servingman, called Wang the Third.

Lao Ts'an settled in the inn. Originally he had planned to hire a cart and go directly to Ts'aochoufu, but since he wanted to find out about Yü Hsien's administration while on the road, he decided to stop here for a time in order to begin his investigations.

By the time the sun was up, even the latest risers among the guests in the inn had all left. The inn servant was sweeping out the rooms and the innkeeper had already made up his accounts and was sitting idly at the door. Lao Ts'an also sat down on a long bench at the door and said to Lao Tung, "I am told that the prefect in this *fu* [prefecture] is very good at handling cases of banditry; what is the true state of affairs?"

Lao Tung sighed and said, "Prefect Yü is no doubt an honest official and he certainly exerts himself in handling such cases; only his method is altogether too cruel. At first he arrested a number of bandits, but soon the bandits caught on to him, and then the tables were turned and he became the bandits' tool!" "What do you mean by that?" said Lao Ts'an. Lao Tung said, "In the southwest corner of this district there is a village called Yüchiat'un, containing about two hundred families. In this village there was a rich man called Yü Chao-tung who had two sons and a daughter. The two sons had both married, and there are two grandchildren. The daughter is also married.

"This family was living in peace and comfort when without warning calamity came to their door. Last year in the autumn they were robbed by bandits. Actually only a few clothes and pieces of jewelry were stolen, not worth more than a few hundred strings of cash. The family reported the robbery and Prefect Yü's energetic handling of the case ended in the capture of two fellows connected with the bandits. The stolen goods which were recovered were only a few pieces of cotton clothing but the bandit leaders had long before escaped where no one could find them.

"Who would have thought that because of this business the bandits would nurse a grudge? This year in the spring they robbed a house in the *fu* city. For several days Prefect Yü moved heaven and earth to find them but didn't catch a single man. After some days another house was robbed, and after the robbery they openly set fire to the place. Just think! How could Prefect Yü put up with that? Naturally he called out a troop of mounted men to go in pursuit.

"After the bandits had committed the robbery, they left the city carrying lighted torches and with rifles in their hands. No one dared to stop them. Outside the east gate they struck north some ten li or more and then the torches were put out. Prefect Yü called together his mounted men and went out on the street. The headman of the neighborhood and the watchman told him exactly what had happened.

The mounted troop then left the city in pursuit. In the far distance they could still see the torches of the bandits. They followed for twenty or thirty li and again saw the torches in front of them, and heard two or three rifle shots.

"When Prefect Yü heard the shots, how could he not be angry? He was very brave to begin with, and having twenty or thirty mounted men under him, all armed with rifles, what was there to be afraid of? So he started off in pursuit. When the torches could not be seen, there were still the rifle shots. When it was almost light, he saw that they were not far from their quarry. By that time they had come to this Yüchiat'un. They went past Yüchiat'un still in full pursuit, but there were neither shots nor torches.

"Prefect Yü thought for a bit and said, 'There is no sense in going any farther; the bandits must be in this village.' Immediately they reined in their horses and went back to the village. In the middle of the main street was a Temple of Kuan Ti,[6] and here they dismounted. He then gave orders to his troop, sending eight men east, south, west, and north, two to watch on each side and not let anybody go out. He also called out the headman and elders of the village.

"By this time it was already broad daylight and Prefect Yü himself led his troopers on foot from the south end of the village to the north in a house to house search. They searched for a long time but found no traces of the bandits. Then they searched from east to west, and when they came to the Yü Chao-tung house they discovered three shot guns, several knives, and ten or more staves.

"Prefect Yü was very angry and said, 'The bandits must be in this house.' He sat in the main hall, called the headman and asked, 'Whose house is this?' The headman answered, 'This family's name is Yü. The old man is called Yü Chao-tung; there are two sons, the elder called Yü Hsüeh-shih, the second Yü Hsüeh-li. They are all Collegians by purchase.'[7]

"Right away Prefect Yü ordered the father and two sons to be brought before him. Just think! How could any villager see a big official from the *fu* come in, and very angry at that, and not be afraid? Led into the hall, the three knelt down, already trembling, quite unable to speak.

"Prefect Yü said, 'What daring! Where have you hidden the bandits?' The old man was so frightened that he couldn't get a word out. The second son had studied in the *fu* city for two years and seen something of the world and so had a little more assurance. Still kneeling, he straightened his back, and looking up answered, 'My family have always been honest people and had no dealings with bandits; how could we dare to hide robbers?'

"Prefect Yü said, 'If you have no connection with the bandits, where do these arms come from?' Yü Hsüeh-li replied, 'Last year after we were robbed, bandits kept coming to our village. We therefore bought several staves and had some of our tenants and farm laborers take turns at guarding the house. Since the bandits all have rifles, while there is no place where we can buy rifles in the country—not that we'd dare buy them—we bought two or three guns from some bird hunters. We fire a couple of shots in the evening to frighten away the bandits.'

"Prefect Yü barked out, 'All lies! What honest people would dare to buy firearms; your family are certainly bandits!' Then he called out, 'Come forward!' The men under his command replied in unison like a clap of thunder: '*Tsa!*'

" 'Send men to watch the front and back gates and search the house thoroughly,' said Prefect Yü. The mounted soldiers then came to search the house, beginning with the main building. Clothes presses, wardrobes, chests of drawers—they ransacked everything. Pieces of jewelry that were light in weight and valuable were tucked away in the soldiers' belts. They searched for a long time but still discovered no unlawful articles. Who would have thought that later in the search in the northwest corner where there was a tumble-down two-*chien* building for farm implements they would discover a cloth bundle containing seven or eight pieces of clothing, including three or four of old silk? The soldiers took it to the main hall and reported: 'We found this bundle in an inside storeroom. It doesn't look like their own clothing. Please examine it, Your Excellency!'

"Prefect Yü looked, knit his brows, fixed his eyes on these things and said, 'These clothes look to me like those that were stolen from that house in the city the day before yesterday; we will take them to the yamen and compare them with the statement of that theft!' He then pointed to the clothes and said to old Yü and his sons, 'Tell me where these clothes came from.' They exchanged furtive glances. None could reply. Again it was Yü Hsüeh-li who at last said, 'Truly we don't know where these clothes come from!'

"Prefect Yü then got up and said, 'Twelve soldiers are to stay here and, with the headman, to bring Yü and his sons to the city to be tried.'

With this he went out. His followers brought his horse. He mounted and with the remainder of the troop set out for the city.

"And now the Yü father and sons, along with the members of their family, fell on each other's necks and wept bitterly. The twelve soldiers said, 'We have ridden all through the night and are very hungry. Hurry up and get us something to eat. Quick! Everybody knows the Prefect's temper. The longer we delay the worse it will be!' The headman too, all flustered, went to have a word with his family and get his things ready, telling the Yü family to order several carts to take them all into the city. They entered the city just after the second watch had struck.[8]

"Now Yü Hsüeh-li's wife was the daughter of the *Chü-Jen* [Provincial Graduate] Wu in the city. Seeing her husband with his father and elder brother taken under arrest to the city, she was filled with anxiety. She consulted her sister-in-law, saying, 'They have all three been arrested. They must have somebody in the city to help them. I think you had better look after the family, while I quickly follow them to town and ask my father to find some way of helping. What do you think?' Her sister-in-law answered, 'That's good; that's very good; I was just thinking that there ought to be someone in the city to help them. Our farm overseers are all country fellows. Even if we sent some of them to the city they'd be like simpletons, quite useless.'

"Saying this, Mrs. Yü got her things ready, chose a 'flying' cart with two animals, and hurried to the city. When she saw her father she began to sob aloud. It was just about the first watch, so she was some ten li ahead of the father and sons.

"Through her tears Mrs. Yü told her father of the sudden calamity. When Wu *Chü-Jen* heard it, he shook all over and still trembling said, 'To offend this "Baneful Star" is a most dangerous matter! I'll go right away and see what can be done!' He hastily put on his clothes and went to the *fu* yamen to ask for an interview. The gatekeeper went in but came out again saying, 'His Honor says he is about to try a case of banditry. He cannot see anybody, no matter who it is.'

"The *Chü-Jen* Wu was well acquainted with the secretary for criminal cases, and he quickly went in to see him and told him all about this case of injustice. The secretary said, 'If this case were in another's hands, certainly nothing would come of it. But up to now this superior of mine has not conducted cases according to legal precedent. If it comes down to my office I guarantee there will be no trouble. But I am afraid it will not come down. In that case nothing can be done.'

"The *Chü-Jen* Wu bowed several times in succession, commended his case again and again, and went out. Then he went to the east gate to wait for his son-in-law and the father and brother to arrive. After a short time the cart guarded by soldiers came. Wu *Chü-Jen* rushed forward and saw the three of them looking almost dead. Yü Chao-tung caught sight of him; he only said, 'Kinsman,[9] save us!' and a flood of tears streamed down his face.

"Wu *Chü-Jen* was just about to speak when one of the mounted guards shouted, 'His Excellency has been sitting in the court waiting for a long time. Already four or five detachments of soldiers have been sent to urge us on! Hurry up!' The cart could not stop any longer, so Wu *Chü-Jen* followed it saying, 'Kinsmen, set your hearts at rest! I'll go through fire and water to help you.'

"As he spoke they reached the yamen gate. He saw a great many runners come out to urge them saying, 'Take them into the court without delay!' Then came several attendants who made the Yü father and sons fast with iron chains, led them in, and made them kneel. Prefect Yü handed down the statement of the theft and asked, 'Have you got anything more to say?' The Yü father and sons had no sooner got out the words, 'Not guilty!' then the gavel struck the table and there was a roar: 'Caught redhanded with stolen goods and yet they cry "Not guilty!" Stand them in the cages! Go!' The attendants to left and right half-pulled, half-dragged them out."

If you don't know what happened afterwards, then hear the next chapter tell.

CHAPTER 5

A devoted wife determines to die faithful;

A village-dweller unexpectedly meets disaster.

WHEN Lao Tung reached this point in his story, Lao Ts'an asked, "Wouldn't that mean that the whole family, father and two sons, were choked to death in the cages?" Lao Tung said, "Of course! When Wu *Chü-Jen* went to the yamen to ask for an interview, his daughter, Yü Hsüeh-li's wife, went with him as far as the gate. She sat waiting in the Prolonging Life Medicine Shop to hear the news. She heard that since the Prefect had refused to see her father, he had gone into the yamen to ask the secretary's help. She then knew that things were not going well and immediately sent someone to ask the headman of the yamen runners [1] to come to her.

"The headman's name was Ch'en Jen-mei. He was well known in Ts'aochoufu as a capable officer. Mrs. Yü had him come, told him her wrongs, and entreated him to work on her behalf in the yamen. When Ch'en Jen-mei heard the story, he shook his head several times and said, 'This is a trick played by the bandits to get their revenge. Your family had both night watchmen and guards; how did you let the bandits bring stolen goods into a building in your house and know nothing about it? Why, it's the height of stupidity!'

"Mrs. Yü then pulled a pair of gold bracelets off her wrists and gave them to headman Ch'en saying, 'No matter what you have to do, I only ask you to do your best! If the lives of these three men can be saved, I am willing to spend any amount of money! I am not afraid to sell every bit of land and property we possess. Even if our whole family has to beg for food, we will do it!'

"Headman Ch'en said, 'I'll go and see what I can do for you, Mrs. Yü. Don't be too happy if I succeed; don't blame me if I fail. Whatever strength I have I'll use—that's all. The three of them will probably arrive sometime soon. His Excellency has already taken his seat in the hall of justice and is waiting. I'll go right away to do what I can for you!' With this he took his leave and went back to the guard room. He took the gold bracelets and put them on the table in the middle of the hall and said, 'My comrades! The charge brought against the Yü family today is clearly unjust. If any of you has a plan to propose, let us think it over together. If we can save these three lives, in the first place it will be a good deed; in the second place, we can each win several ounces of silver. If anyone of you can think up a good plan, this pair of bracelets is his!' They all answered, 'How can we plan in advance! We must wait and see what happens before we can decide what to do.' The first thing they did was to go and tell their comrades who were already on duty in the hall to keep their eyes open for a chance to do something.

"By this time the three men of the Yü family had already been taken to the hall, Prefect Yü had ordered them to be put in the cages, and the attendants had half-dragged, half-pulled the three of them away.

"At this point the chief guard for the day came to the front of the magistrate's table, went down on one knee, and said, 'I beg to report to Your Excellency that there are no cages vacant today. Will Your Excellency please give instructions.' When Prefect Yü heard this he said angrily, 'Nonsense! I do not remember having put anyone in these two days. How can there be none empty?' The guard answered, 'There are only twelve cages. They were filled in three days. Will Your Excellency please check in the register?'

"The Prefect checked the list, moving his finger down the register and saying, 'One, two, three; yesterday there were three. One, two, three, four, five; the day before yesterday there were five. One, two, three, four; the day before that there were four. There are none empty; yes, you are quite right.' The attendant again asked, 'For today shall we put these in the jail? Tomorrow there are bound to be several dead. When there are vacancies in the cages, we can put these into their places. Is that all right? Will Your Excellency please decide?'

"Prefect Yü frowned and said, 'How I hate these creatures! If we put them in the jail, won't that mean that they will live a day longer? That won't do at all! Go and take down those four who were put in three days ago. Bring them here for me to see.'

"The attendant went and had the four men taken down and brought into the hall. The Prefect himself came down from his table. He felt the noses of the four men with his fingers and said, 'There is still a little life!' He went back, sat down and said, 'Give each one two thousand blows; we'll see whether they'll die or not!' When they had received not more than twenty or thirty blows each, all four were dead.

"The attendants could do nothing but take the Yü father and sons, and put them in the cages. But they put three thick bricks under their feet, so that for three or four days they wouldn't die. They thought hard, but none of the suggestions that were made were of any use.

"This Mrs. Yü truly was a good and virtuous wife! Every day she came to the cages to make them drink some ginseng infusion. Having made them drink, she would go home and weep, then go to solicit help. I don't know how many thousand resounding kowtows she performed, but in spite of it all there was nobody who could move Prefect Yü's oxlike nature. Yü Chao-tung, who was after all a good many years older, died on the third day. By the fourth day Yü Hsüeh-shih was almost finished too. Mrs. Yü took away the body of Yü Chao-tung and with her own eyes saw it prepared for burial. She then changed into mourning clothes, and charged her father with the last rites of her brother-in-law and husband. Then she knelt at the yamen gate and cried her eyes out in front of Yü Hsüeh-li. Finally she said to her husband, 'You come slowly; I will go down first to prepare a dwelling for you!' With that she pulled a little sharp-edged knife out of her sleeve: one cut across her throat, and she breathed her last!

"Now the headman of the yamen runners, Ch'en Jen-mei, saw this and said, 'Men! This Mrs. Yü's courage and faithfulness are worthy of an Imperial Testimonial.[2] I think if Yü Hsüeh-li is taken out right away, he can still live. How would it be to make this an occasion to plead that mercy be shown him?' They all answered, 'Well said.'

"Headman Ch'en immediately went in to look for the clerk of the court [3] and told him about Mrs. Yü's courage and devotion. He further said, 'The people are full of sympathy for this faithful wife who has killed herself for the sake of her husband. Couldn't you beg His Excellency to have her husband set free and thus give rest to this brave wife's soul?' The clerk of the court replied, 'What you say is quite reasonable. I will go in immediately.' He picked up his official hat, put it on, and went in to see the Prefect, to whom he told how faithful and brave Mrs. Yü had been and how the people begged him to be merciful.

"Prefect Yü laughed and said, 'You're a fine lot! So you've suddenly become softhearted! You can be softhearted to Yü Hsüeh-li, but you can't be softhearted towards your own master! Whether this man is unjustly punished or not, if I release him he certainly won't rest content, and in the future even my position will be endangered. The proverb says right: "To cut down weeds you must get rid of the root." That applies here. Besides, this Yü woman is especially hateful. She is convinced that I have wronged her whole family! If she weren't a woman, although she's dead, I would give her a couple of thousand blows to give vent to my anger! Go and announce that if anyone comes again to ask mercy for the Yü family I shall take it as proof that he has accepted a bribe. No one needs to come in to appeal. I shall simply take the pleader and stand him in a cage too—and that will be the end of it!' The clerk of the court went out and repeated the words of the Prefect to Ch'en Jen-mei. They all sighed and then dispersed.

"Mr. Wu had already prepared coffins and brought them for the burial. By the evening Yü Hsüeh-shih and Yü Hsüeh-li had died one after the other. The four coffins of the one family were all placed in the Temple of the Goddess of Mercy [4] outside the west gate. When I went into the city this spring I saw them."

Lao Ts'an said, "What happened to the Yü family afterwards? Didn't they try to avenge the wrong?" Lao Tung said: "How could they do that! When an ordinary person is wronged by an official, what can he do but endure it? If an appeal is made, the rule is that the case is returned to the original court for trial so that it would be back in his hands again. Wouldn't that just give him another life to dispose of?

"Now Yü Chao-tung's son-in-law was a *Hsiu-Ts'ai* [Licentiate]. After the death of the four, Yü Hsüeh-shih's wife also went to the city to discuss whether they should make an appeal. But a certain old man who knew the world said, 'It's no good! It's no good! Who do you expect to send? If an outsider goes, they will say, "The matter is not his concern," and he will get a bad name as a busybody; if you say send the elder daughter-in-law, don't forget that the two grandchildren are still small and that the great property of the family is entirely her responsibility. If anything should happen to her, the family property will be divided among all the clan, and then who will protect and bring up the two little children? It might mean the end of incense-burning in the Yü family.' Others said, 'Certainly the elder Mrs. Yü cannot go, but surely there is no reason why the son-in-law shouldn't go!' The son-in-law said, 'It is certainly possible for me to go, only it won't help the main issue but rather will mean another corpse for the cages. Just think. The Governor will certainly send the case back to the original court for trial. Although he will delegate a deputy to be present at the trial, "official protects official." They will confront us again with somebody's statement of theft and some clothes. Even if we say, "Those were hidden by the bandits" they will say, "Did you see the bandits bring them in? What evidence have you got?" Then, of course, we shall have nothing to say. He is an official; we are ordinary people. He has the statement of the theft as evidence; we have nothing to rely on; we have no proofs. Tell me, can we win this case, or can we not?' All of them thought a while, but there was nothing they could do, so they dropped the matter.

"Afterwards I heard tell that when the bandits who had concealed the things learned what had happened, they were all filled with remorse and said, 'At the start we hated them for reporting their loss and causing the death of our two comrades. So we used the method of "killing with a borrowed knife," hoping their family would suffer several months at the hands of the law, and certainly lose one or two thousand strings of cash. Who could have known it would become as serious as the loss of four lives! We certainly didn't have that much hatred for their family!' "

Lao Tung finished the story, then added: "Just think, Your Honor! Wasn't I right in saying that Prefect Yü has become the bandits' tool?"

"Then who was it heard what the bandits said?" Lao Ts'an asked. Lao Tung replied, "Ch'en Jen-mei and his men having struck a snag when they tried to do something, and having seen the members of the Yü family die such a pitiful death, and also having received a pair of gold bracelets for doing nothing, were troubled in their hearts. They were all moved with righteous anger, and made a united effort to solve the mystery of the case. Besides, there were some bold fellows in the district who hated this band of robbers for acting too viciously, and so, before a month had passed, five or six of them were captured. Three or four, who had been involved in other cases, were choked to death; two or three, who were only concerned in the case of concealing stolen goods in the Yü house, were all released by Prefect Yü."

Lao Ts'an said, "This ruthless official Yü Hsien certainly arouses a man's hatred! Has he conducted other cases in the same way?" Lao Tung replied, "Lots of them. Be patient and I will tell Your Honor about them. Even in our own village here, there was a case, also a case of injustice. It was nothing much—it only involved one or two lives. I will tell you about it."

Just as he was going to tell the story, his servingman, Wang the Third, was heard calling out, "Master! What are you up to? We are all waiting for you to deal out the flour for the meal! Your windbag must have sprung a leak! Won't you ever finish talking?"

When Lao Tung heard this, he got up and went in to deal out the flour. Several wheelbarrows then arrived one after another, and guests began coming into the inn for a snack. Lao Tung was called hither and thither and had no more time for gossip.

When they had all eaten, Lao Tung was still bustling about, reckoning up the bills at each table and looking after his business. Lao Ts'an had nothing to do, so he went for a stroll down the street. Leaving the inn he walked twenty or thirty steps east to where there was a small shop selling oil, salt, and other provisions.

Lao Ts'an went in to buy two packets of Ch'ao tobacco [5] flavored with orchid seeds and took the chance to sit down. Looking at the man behind the counter, he judged that he was something over fifty years of age. He asked him, "Your honorable name?" "My name is Wang," said the man; "I'm a native of this place. Your honorable name, Sir?" Lao Ts'an said, "My name is T'ieh—I'm a Chiangnan man." "Chiangnan is certainly a fine place," said the man; " 'Above are the halls of heaven; below Su and Hang.' [6] Not like this hell of ours here!" Lao Ts'an said: "You have hills, you have water, you grow rice and you grow wheat. How is it different from Chiangnan?" The man sighed and answered, "It is difficult to tell in a word!" and said no more.

Lao Ts'an asked, "Your Prefect Yü here, is he all right?" The man answered, "He's an honest official! A good official! At the gate of his yamen are twelve cages which are usually full; it's a rare day when one or two are vacant!"

While they were talking, a middle-aged woman with a rough bowl in her hand came out from the back of the shop to look for something among the shelves. Noticing a man on the other side of the counter, she gave one glance at him and continued her search.

Lao Ts'an said, "How can there be so many bandits?" The man replied, "Who knows?" Lao Ts'an said, "Surely most of them must be unjustly condemned." The man answered, "Injustice! No, there's no injustice!" Lao Ts'an said, "I hear that if he happens to see a man who doesn't please his eye, he simply puts him in a cage and chokes him to death; or if somebody talks unwisely and falls into his hands, he's a dead man too. Is this true?" The man said, "No! Never!"

But Lao Ts'an noticed that as the man answered, his face began to turn gray, and his eyes reddened. When he heard the words, "if somebody talks unwisely," tears filled his eyes, though they did not fall. The woman who had come in to get things looked round and could no longer restrain the tears which rolled down her face. She stopped in her search, and carrying her bowl in one hand, and covering her eyes with her sleeve with the other, ran out through the back door. When she had reached the courtyard, she began to sob, *ju-ju.*

Lao Ts'an wanted to question the man further, but by his grief-stricken face he knew that he must be weighed down by some wrong or injustice of which he dared not speak, so he merely made a few meaningless remarks and went away.

He returned to his inn and went to sit for a while in his own room, where he read a few pages of a book. When Lao Tung was no longer busy, he wandered out to find him and have another chat. He told Lao Tung what he had seen in the little general store and asked him what it was all about.

Lao Tung said: "This man's name is Wang. There are only the two of them, man and wife, and they were not married until he was thirty. His wife is ten years younger than he. After marriage they had one son, who was twenty-one years old this year. They buy the rougher articles they sell in their shop at our village fair, but for the better-grade articles, this son of theirs always went to the city. This spring, when their son was in the *fu* city he must have had one or two cups of wine too many and let his tongue run away with him, for outside somebody's shop, he started to carry on about Prefect Yü, what a fool he was, how he took pleasure in treating people unjustly. This was overheard by some of Prefect Yü's spies, and he was dragged off to the yamen. The Prefect took his seat and railed at him, 'You thing, you! So you start rumors to disturb the people! What next?' He was then stood in a cage, and in less than two days choked to death. The middle-aged woman Your Honor saw just now is the wife of this man Wang. She is now more than forty. They had only this one son, not another soul in the world. Your mention of Prefect Yü couldn't help hurting her!"

Lao Ts'an said, "This Yü Hsien! Death wouldn't expiate all his crimes! How is it that his reputation in the provincial capital is so great? It truly is an astonishing thing! If I had power, this man would certainly be put to death!" Lao Tung said, "Your Honor had better watch what he says! While Your Honor is here, it doesn't matter if you talk freely. But in the city don't talk like this. It will cost you your life!"

Lao Ts'an said, "Thank you for your kind warning; I will be careful." That night, after supper, he had a good sleep. The next day he took his leave of Lao Tung, got on his cart, and set out. That night he stayed at Mats'unchi.

This market village was somewhat smaller than Tungchiak'ou and only forty or fifty li away from the city of Ts'aochoufu. Lao Ts'an looked up and down the street and found that there were only three inns. Two of them were already full. The third was deserted, and the gate was closed, so he pushed it open and went in. At first he could find nobody. After a long time a man came out who said, "We are not taking guests these few days." When asked the reason he wouldn't tell. Even had Lao Ts'an wanted to go elsewhere, there wasn't an empty corner to be found and this being his only hope, he pressed the man again and again. Finally the man listlessly opened up a room, still muttering, "There isn't any food, nor any hot water for tea, but if you have nowhere to sleep, this place is good enough for a makeshift. Our master has gone into the city to bring back a corpse, and there is nobody left in the inn. Just south of our gate is an eating house with a teashop attached where Your Honor can go to have your meals and drink tea." Lao Ts'an quickly said, "Thank you. Thank you. A traveler must make shift with anything." The man replied, "I sleep in the south room just inside the gate. If Your Honor needs anything, come and call me."

When Lao Ts'an heard the words, "to bring back a corpse," he wondered what was meant. In the evening when he had finished supper, he bought several pieces of bean curd flavored with tea, four or five packets of peanuts, and two bottles of wine and carried everything, including the earthenware bottles, back to the inn. The servingman had already brought in a lamp. Lao Ts'an said to him, "I've got some wine here. When you have barred the gate, come and have a cup." The servingman agreed with alacrity, ran out to bar the gate, returned immediately, and still standing said, "Please drink, Sir. It is too much of an honor for me." Lao Ts'an pulled him into a chair, poured a cup, and gave it to him. Baring his teeth in a grin, the man repeatedly said, "I wouldn't presume. . . ." But actually he had already carried the cup to his lips.

At first they talked idly, but after several cups Lao Ts'an asked, "Some time ago you said that your master had gone into the city 'to bring back a corpse.' What did you mean by that? Surely it isn't another person who has come to grief at the hands of Prefect Yü?" The servingman said, "Since we are quite alone here, I can speak freely. This Prefect Yü of ours is certainly terrible. Worse than a living King of Hell.[7] If you run up against him, you're a dead man!

"Our master has gone into the city on account of his sister's husband. This brother-in-law of his was a thoroughly honest man, and since my master and his younger sister were very fond of each other, they all lived together at the back of this inn. Whenever he could, the brother-in-law would buy bolts of cloth in the country and take them to the city to sell them and make a little money to add to the family income. The other day he went into the city with four bolts of white cloth on his back and spread them out for sale on the ground at the gate of a temple. In the morning he sold two bolts; later in the day he sold another five feet. Finally a man came along who wanted to have a piece of cloth eight-feet-five-inches-long torn off, but insisted that it be torn off the bolt that was whole. He said he was willing to give two big cash extra for each foot, but that he didn't want it from the bolt that had been started. When a country fellow sees a chance of making a little more money, is he not going to take it? Naturally he tore it off for the man.

"Who could have known that in less than the length of two meals Prefect Yü would pass the temple gate on horseback? From the side of the road a man came forward who said something or other to him.

Prefect Yü then looked in the direction of the clothseller and said, 'Take this man and his cloth to the yamen.' When he had arrived at the yamen, the Prefect took his seat, called for the cloth, rapped on the table with his gavel, and said, 'Where does this cloth of yours come from?' He answered, 'I bought it in my village.' The Prefect again asked, 'How much does each bolt measure?' He answered, 'I have sold five feet of one and eight feet five inches of the other.' The Prefect replied, 'If you sell it by the piece, and both are the same kind of cloth, why do you tear a bit off this and snip a bit off that? How much is left? Why don't you speak out?' He ordered his attendants: 'Measure this cloth for me!' They promptly measured it and reported, 'One is two chang, five feet; one is two chang, one foot, five inches!' [8]

"When the Prefect heard this, he was very angry, held out a slip of paper, and said, 'Can you read?' The man answered, 'I can't!' The Prefect said, 'Read it to him!' A clerk standing by took the slip and read: 'On the morning of the seventeenth, Chin Szu deposed, "Last night at sundown I was robbed at a place fifteen li outside the west gate. A man came out of the woods and cut me on the shoulder with a big sword. He stole from me a string of four hundred big cash and two pieces of white cloth; one two-chang-five-feet-long, one two-chang-one-foot-five-inches." '

"When he had read so far, Prefect Yü said, 'The material, length, and color of the two bolts all tally with the statement of the theft. You must have stolen them. Are you still going to stick to your story? Take him out and put him in a cage!' The bolts of cloth were handed to Chin Szu, and that was the end of it."

If you don't know what happened afterwards, then hear the next chapter tell.

CHAPTER 6

Blood of ten thousand families stains an official
button scarlet;

A conversational dinner; dispute over a white
fox gown.

THE INN servant was telling how his master's brother-in-law had been taken and stood in the cage and the case settled by giving the bolts of cloth to Chin Szu. Then Lao Ts'an said, "Now I understand it all. Of course it was a trap laid by the Prefect's men. And this being the case, of course your master had to go to bring back the corpse for his sister. But why should anybody want to harm an honest man like him? Didn't your master inquire about it?"

The servingman said, "As soon as he had been taken, we learned why it was. Someone told me the whole story. It was all because his tongue ran too fast and provoked trouble. In a little lane to the west of the main street, inside the south gate of the *fu* city, was a family of two, father and child. The father was forty-odd years old. The daughter was seventeen or eighteen and had grown up into a perfect beauty, but was not yet married. Her father was a small tradesman and they lived in a three-*chien* wattle house with a courtyard surrounded by a mud wall. One day this girl was standing at the gate when Wang the Third of the Tattooed Arm, captain of a troop of ten in the local cavalry, came by. Wang the Third saw she was a fine-looking girl and some-how or other managed to turn her head and have his will of her. After a while, of course, it came out; her father returned home and caught them. He nearly died of anger, gave his daughter a thorough beating, locked his front gate, and would not let her go out. In less than half a month Wang the Third of the Tattooed Arm had woven a plot and had her father convicted as a robber and choked to death in the cage. After this not only did the daughter become Wang the Third's wife, but even the little bit of a house became Wang the Third's property.

"My master's brother-in-law had sold cloth at their house once or twice, was acquainted with the household, and knew about this affair. One day he was in an eating house and drinking two cups too many, he must have gone quite mad; for drinking and talking with Bald-Head Chang the Second, of our North Street, he started telling what had happened and discussing this man's lack of all decency. That Bald-Head Chang the Second is another foolhardy fellow. He thoroughly enjoyed hearing it all and kept asking more questions: 'What, and he a brother in the Righteous Harmony Society!'[1] If good spirits like Erh Lang[2] and Kuan Yeh[3] often visit him, how is it that they don't restrain him?' My master's brother-in-law said, 'Yes, why don't they? I heard that some time ago he called upon the Great Monkey Sage. The Monkey Sage did not come, but the Pig of Eight Vows[4] did. If it was not because Wang stifles his conscience, why did the Monkey Sage send the Pig of Eight Vows instead of coming himself? It's my opinion that having such an evil nature, the day must come when he will run against the Great Sage in a bad mood, and the Great Sage will lift up his Gold-bound Staff[5] and give him a blow that he won't survive!'

"The two of them went on talking in high spirits, not knowing that a member of the society was listening to it all and would tell Wang the Third and give an accurate description of their faces. Before many months had passed my master's brother-in-law was destroyed, while Bald-Head Chang the Second, finding things unhealthy and taking advantage of the fact that he had no family—

> Break of Day
> Ssu-shih-wu
> Flew to Honan
> Kueitefu[6]

went away to see some friends.

"The wine is finished, Your Honor, you'd better go to sleep. If you go into the city tomorrow, whatever you do, be careful what you say! All of us here are in constant fear of danger. At the slightest slip the cage may fly to your neck!"

Then he stood up, fumbled on the table for a broken incense stick, stirred the lamp with it, and said, "I'll go and get a pot of oil to replenish the lamp." Lao Ts'an said, "Don't bother. Let's both go to bed." The two then separated.

The next morning Lao Ts'an put his things together and called his wheelbarrow man to carry them out to the wheelbarrow. The serving-man saw him off, saying again and again, "When you get into the city, don't talk too much. Take care! Take care!"

Lao Ts'an laughed and replied, "Many thanks for your interest in my safety." Meanwhile the wheelbarrow man had begun to push him along. They made for the south road and long before noon had reached Ts'aochoufu City. Entering by the north gate he found an inn on the road in front of the yamen and took up his quarters in a side room. A servingman came to ask what he would have to eat and brought what he ordered. After he had eaten, he went to the gate of the yamen to see what he could see and he found that the main gate was hung with red silk. There were indeed twelve wooden cages by the gate, but all were empty; there was not a single person in them. Greatly surprised he said to himself, "Surely all the accounts I heard on the road were not false!" He walked for a while, then returned to his inn. He saw a great many men wearing official hats going in and out of the main building while in the courtyard there was a blue-felt sedan chair, and a number of chair bearers, wearing padded jackets and trousers and official hats, were eating griddlecakes; there were also several men in livery with badges inscribed "Ch'engwuhsien Militia." He gathered that the magistrate of Ch'engwuhsien must be staying in the main building. After some time a servant called out, "Get ready!" The chair attendants then carried the chair to the foot of the steps, the bearer of the red umbrella of state lifted it up, two horses were led out of the stables, and immediately the red felt *lientzu* of the main building was lifted and a man about fifty years old came out wearing a hat with a crystal button, a jacket with embroidered medallion, and a court neck-lace. He came down the steps of the terrace and entered the sedan chair. The chair was lifted and carried out of the gate with a swishing sound.

When Lao Ts'an saw the official enter his chair, he thought to himself, "How is it his face is so familiar? I have never been to this Ts'ao region before. Where have I seen this man?" He thought for some time but couldn't remember, so gave it up. Since it was still early, he returned to the street to gather information about the administration of the *fu*. All with one voice said it was good, but all wore a look of gray misery; unconsciously he nodded his head as he realized that the ancient writer's saying, "Harsh government is fiercer than a tiger," [7] is absolutely true. He returned to his inn and had been sitting at the gate for a while when the magistrate of Ch'engwuhsien chanced to come back. Entering the gate, he looked out through the glass window of his chair, and as he passed Lao Ts'an their four eyes met.

In a few seconds the sedan chair reached the steps of the upper building. The magistrate of Ch'engwuhsien got out, and his servants lowered the *lientzu* of the chair and escorted him up to the terrace. In the distance he could be seen saying a few words to one of his men, who then ran down to the gate. The magistrate stood waiting on the terrace.

The servant came up to Lao Ts'an and said, "Is this the Honorable Mr. T'ieh?" "Yes, it is," said Lao Ts'an. "How did you know, and what is the name of your Honorable Master?" The servant replied, "My master's name is Shen; he has just come from the provincial capital. The Governor has appointed him to Ch'engwuhsien. He would like Mr. T'ieh to come to the main building."

It suddenly flashed on Lao Ts'an; he remembered that this man was Shen Tung-tsao of the secretariat. Although he had met him two or three times, he hadn't talked to him much and so had not recognized him.

Lao Ts'an then went up to see Tung-tsao and they bowed low to each other. Tung-tsao invited him into his private room saying, "I'll take the liberty of changing my clothes." He took off his official robes, changed into ordinary clothes, made his guest sit in the chief seat, and asked, "When did you arrive, Mr. Pu? How long have you been here? And are you staying at this inn too?" Lao Ts'an said: "I arrived today. I left the provincial capital not more than six or seven days ago and made my way here. When did you leave the capital, Mr. Tung? Have you been to your new district on the way?" Tung-tsao said, "I also arrived today. I left the capital two days ago; these servants and people went there to fetch me. The day before I left I heard Mr. Yao Yün say,

'When the Governor found that Mr. Pu had gone, he was very sad and said, "My whole life I have honored scholars of repute, and thought that none would refuse my invitation. Today I have met a certain Mr. T'ieh who really considers 'wealth and honor floating clouds'; looking into myself, I feel intolerably soiled by the world." ' "

Lao Ts'an said, "I deeply respect the Governor's appreciation of men of ability. As to my reason for leaving, it is not that I seek to live in 'lofty seclusion,' claiming to be 'high-minded.' [8] It is rather that I consider myself a man of insufficient ability and shallow knowledge —not worthy of praise; then too the reputation of this Prefect Yü is so great that I want to find out what sort of a man he really is. As to being 'high-minded,' not only am I not worthy of such a title, but I do not really consider it worthwhile in itself. The world produces a limited number of gifted men; stupid and mean people may use 'high-mindedness' to hide their stupidity, but if those who really have some ability to help society go into retirement, isn't that ungrateful to heaven for its will to produce men of ability?"

Tung-tsao answered, "I have often heard your wise words and have always admired you. What you have said today makes me want even more to prostrate myself before you. I can see now why such men as Ch'ang-chü and Chieh-ni [9] were not approved of by Confucius. But now from Mr. Pu's point of view what sort of man is this Prefect Yü of ours?" Lao Ts'an said, "He is a ruthless and base official, even worse than Chih Tu [10] and Ning Ch'eng!" [11]

Tung-tsao nodded his head again and again, then said, "The ears and eyes of men of my kind are fenced off from the world. But you, traveling about as you do in cotton clothes, must get to know the true state of the world. It seems to me that if this prefect is so fierce, much injustice must be done. How is it then that no appeals have been made against his decisions?"

Lao Ts'an began to give a detailed account of all he had heard on the road. When he was half way through, a servant came to announce dinner. Tung-tsao asked Lao Ts'an to stay and eat with him, which the latter agreed to do. After they had eaten, he continued his tale, and when he had finished said, "I have misgivings on only one point. Looking at the outside of the yamen gate today I saw that the twelve cages are all empty. I'm afraid that the tales the country people tell are not entirely to be relied on."

Tung-tsao said, "That is not so. I have just heard in the yamen of

Hotsehsien [12] that yesterday His Excellency received an official notification from the provincial government that his present position is to be made a substantive appointment. In addition he is to be specially recommended at the general promotion as an expectant *taot'ai* while holding his present office, and when he comes to take up his position as *taot'ai* he will be nominated to receive the button of an official of the second class. It is because of this that all punishments are discontinued for three days so that everyone may congratulate him. Didn't you see the red silk hung from the yamen gate? I heard that the first day punishments were discontinued, that is, yesterday, there were still several half-dead, half-alive men in the cages who are now being kept in the jail."

They both sighed, then Lao Ts'an said, "You've had a hard day on the road, and it is getting late. You'd better go to bed." Tung-tsao said, "Please favor me with your company again tomorrow evening. I have some extremely difficult tasks to perform and should like to receive your valuable instruction. I hope you will not refuse me." With this each went to his bed.

The next day when Lao Ts'an got up the sky was heavily overcast. Although the northwest wind was not blowing very hard, his padded gown floated about him like the garments of an immortal. Having washed his face he bought several *yu-t'iao* for his breakfast, and then feeling rather dispirited strolled aimlessly up and down the street for some time. He was just thinking of going up on the city wall to enjoy the distant view when snowflakes began to flutter down one after another. Before long the snow was coming down in wild flurries, whirling and crisscrossing, ever thicker and thicker. He returned in haste to his inn and told the servant to bring in a brazier. A sheet of the window paper, bigger than the rest, hung loose, and the wind, drumming on the paper wet from the snow, made a noise, *huo-to, huo-to*. The smaller strips of paper at the sides, though they made no noise, flapped to and fro without end. The chilling wind seemed to reach every corner of the room, making it desolate and eerie. Lao Ts'an sat with nothing to do. Even his books were in the trunk and not easy to get at. So he just sat, becoming more and more melancholy. He couldn't hold back his feelings, and finally, taking a brush and an ink slab from the box that formed his pillow, he wrote a poem on the wall, devoted to Yü Hsien's actions. The poem said:

Ambition pervades his flesh and marrow,
He zealously strives to make a name.
Injustice smothers the city in gloom,
Blood stains his hat-button red.[13]
Everywhere a rain of ill-omen,
In all the hills a tigerish wind;
He kills good people as though killing bandits:
This prefect who acts like a captain of troops.

Below he put the words: "Written by T'ieh Ying [14] of Hsüchou in Chiangnan." When he had finished writing, he had his noon meal. By this time the snow was coming down still more heavily. He stood in the doorway and looked out. The branches of the trees, big and little, appeared to be wrapped in fresh cotton wool. The rooks in the trees kept drawing in their necks to escape the cold and were flapping their wings for fear the snow would pile up on their backs; he saw, too, many sparrows hiding under the eaves of the house who also drew in their necks for fear of the cold. Their frozen and hungry appearance seemed to him most pitiful. He therefore thought to himself, "These poor birds! They have to depend on seeds collected from trees and plants and on little insects to satisfy their hunger and keep them alive. Now of course all the insects have gone into their winter sleep and are not to be found, and even the seeds of trees and plants are scarcely to be found under this covering of snow. Even if the sun shines tomorrow and the snow melts a little, as soon as the northwest wind blows the snow will become ice and again the birds will not be able to find them. Won't they go on starving until next spring?" When his thoughts reached this point, he felt so sorry for the suffering of the birds that he could hardly bear it. And then again he thought, "These birds may be cold and hungry, but even so they do not have men to shoot at them and hurt them; no snares are put out to catch them. They are only cold and hungry for the time being, but when it comes around to next year's springtime they will be as happy as can be. And now think of these people of Ts'aochoufu who have suffered calamities for several years —they are the unfortunate ones. For they have this tyrannical, 'paternal' official who, on every possible occasion, captures them and treats them as bandits, killing them in his cages. They are so frightened that not a word can they say. To cold and hunger is added fear. Are they not worse off than these birds?" At this point his tears began to fall. Again he heard a strident outburst of cawing from the rooks, as if they were not crying out from cold and hunger but rather showing off to the people of Ts'aochoufu because they enjoyed freedom of speech. And now he became so angry that "his angry hair pushed up his hat," [15] angry that he could not immediately kill Yü Hsien and so give vent to his anger.

He was just thinking these wild thoughts when a blue-felt sedan chair came to the gate followed by some attendants. He knew it was Shen Tung-tsao returning to the inn after paying some calls. He thought, "Why shouldn't I write a letter telling the Governor all these things I have seen and heard?" So he took out some letter paper and envelopes from his pillow box, lifted his brush, and began to write. The ink on the slab which he had used for writing on the wall was already frozen into solid ice. He had to breathe on it and write a few characters, and then breathe on it again. When he had written not more than two sheets, it was already quite late, for while he was breathing on the ink slab, his brush would freeze; and when he was breathing on his brush, the ink slab would freeze. After each attempt to melt the ink he could not write more than four or five characters, so he wasted a lot of time.

While he was kept busy in this way, it became so dark that he could not see. Being a dull day, it got dark even earlier than usual, so he called to the servant to bring him a lamp. After he had called for a long time, the man came in carrying a lamp, his hands and feet shaking with the cold, and as he put the lamp down he exclaimed, "It's cold all right!" He had a paper spill stuck between his fingers, and had to blow on it many times before it flared up. The lamp had been freshly filled with solid oil which was piled up like a big spiral snail shell so that when first lit it gave very little light. The servant said, "Wait a bit: when the oil has melted, it will be bright." He shook the lamp, then drew his hands into his sleeves again and stood and watched to see whether the lamp would go out. At first the flame was only the size of a big yellow pea. Gradually it took up oil and then became as big as a kidney bean. Suddenly the servant raised his head and looked at the characters written on the wall. Greatly alarmed he said, "Did Your Honor write this? What does it say? Don't stir up trouble! It's no laughing matter!" He then quickly turned his head and looked outside. There was no one there, so he said, "If you don't watch out, your life will be in danger; and we shall get into trouble too." Lao Ts'an laughed and said, "My name is written at the bottom, so don't worry."

While he was speaking, a man wearing a hat with a red tassel came in and called out, "Mr. T'ieh!" The inn servant shuffled out, and the newcomer said, "My master invites Mr. T'ieh to go and eat with him." It was Shen Tung-tsao's servant. Lao Ts'an said, "Ask your master to have his meal alone. I've already told them to bring me something here. It will come in a minute. Please thank him all the same." The man replied, "My master said, 'The inn food is not fit to eat!' We have a brace of pheasants someone has sent which have already been sliced, and there is also some sliced mutton. He said I am to tell Mr. T'ieh he simply must come and share the chafing dish. My master says that if Mr. T'ieh really won't come he will have the food carried over and eat it in this room. It seems to me much better for Your Honor to go over there. In that room there is a brazier four or five times as big as the one in this room, and it is very much warmer. Also it will be easier for us servants. Please oblige us."

Lao Ts'an had no excuse, so there was nothing to do but go. When Shen Tung-tsao saw him, he said, "Mr. Pu, what have you been doing in your room? Since it's such a snowy day, let's drink a cup or two of wine. Someone has sent me some very good pheasants. They are excellent eaten scalded in the chafing dish, so I will 'offer borrowed flowers to Buddha!' "

While he was speaking, they took their seats. The servants brought on the slices of pheasant, red and white, very good to look at. Eaten scalded they had a most savory taste. Tung-tsao said, "Do you notice a rather unusual flavor?" Lao Ts'an answered, "Indeed there is a sort of fresh fragrance. Why is it?" Tung-tsao said, "These pheasants come from the Peach Blossom Mountain in Feich'enghsien,[16] where there are many pine trees. The birds have this freshness and fragrance because they are so fond of eating pine flowers and pine kernels. The popular name for them is 'Pine-Flower Pheasant.' Even here they are very difficult to get."

Lao Ts'an murmured a few words of appreciation, and then the rice and other dishes were brought from the kitchen and placed on the table. When the two men had finished their rice, Tung-tsao suggested that they go into the inner room for their tea and to warm themselves at the fire. Suddenly he noticed that Lao Ts'an was wearing a cotton padded gown and said, "How is it you are still wearing a cotton gown in such cold weather as this?"

Lao Ts'an replied, "I don't feel at all cold. For us who have never worn fur-lined gowns from our childhood I think the amount of warmth given by our cotton gowns is greater than that given by your fox furs." Tung-tsao said, "This won't do" and then shouted, "Hello, there! In my flat leather trunk there is an extra gown lined with white fox. Take it out and put it in Mr. T'ieh's room."

Lao Ts'an said, "On no account do that! I am not just being polite. Think! Has there ever been an itinerant bell ringer who wore a gown lined with fox fur?" Tung-tsao said, "You didn't have to shake that string of bells of yours in the first place. Why must you go to such extremes in feigning vulgarity? Since you have favored me to the extent of treating me as Somebody, I have a few outspoken words I want to say, whether you get offended at me or not, Sir! Last night I heard you say that you despised those who 'live in lofty seclusion claiming to be high-minded!' You said, 'The world produces a limited number of gifted men; it is not good to belittle oneself unreasonably!' I prostrate myself in admiration of those sentiments! But your actions rather contradict your words. The Governor really wants you to come out of seclusion and be an official, but you run off in the middle of the night, determined to get away and shake your string of bells. Consider! How are you different from the one who 'knocked a hole in the wall and escaped'; [17] or the one who 'washed his ears and would not listen'? [18] What I say can't help being rather rash and is probably offensive to you, but please think about it. Am I right or wrong?"

Lao Ts'an said, "I admit that shaking a string of bells contributes little to the world, but then does it contribute anything to be an official? I should like to ask, now that you are magistrate of Ch'engwu-hsien and are 'father and mother' to a hundred li and to ten thousand people, where will be the benefit to the people? But perhaps you are like the painter of bamboo who 'had the complete bamboo in his mind.' [19] Why not favor me with a little enlightenment? I know that you have already held two or three official posts in the past. Please tell me what evidence you have had of achieving anything unusual by your good government?"

Tung-tsao replied, "This is not the way to look at it. All that mediocre talents like me can do is to muddle through. But if a man of vast ability and resourcefulness like you doesn't come out and do something, it really is a great pity! Men without ability are dying for official positions, while men of ability would die to avoid official positions; this truly is the most regrettable thing in the world!"

Lao Ts'an said, "On the contrary; what I say is that if those without ability get into office it does not matter at all; the really bad thing is when men of ability want to be officials. After all, isn't this Excellency Yü a man of ability? But just because he is overanxious to be an official, or rather hankers after being a great official, he acts as he does, wounding heaven and damaging all principles of justice. And with so great a reputation as an administrator I fear that within a few years he will become provincial governor. The greater the official position such a man holds, the greater the harm he will do. If he controls a prefecture, then a prefecture suffers; if he governs a province, then a province is maimed; if he rules the Empire, then the Empire dies! Looked at in this way, please tell me, is greater harm done when a man of ability is an official, or is the harm greater when a man without ability is the official? If he were to go about like me, shaking a string of bells and curing disease, people would not want him to treat serious disorders; and in treating minor troubles he couldn't kill anybody. And if in the course of a year he happened to cause the death of one man, in ten thousand years he would not harm as many people as he does as Prefect of Ts'aochoufu!"

If you don't know what else Shen Tung-tsao said, then hear the next chapter tell.

CHAPTER 7

"Borrowed chopsticks" for planning the control of a hsien;

In search of the Na Ying in a treasure house of books.

IT HAS been told that Lao Ts'an and Shen Tung-tsao were discussing Yü Hsien as an example of a man of ability so anxious to be an official that he wounded heaven and destroyed all principles of justice. Then they both sighed together for a while.

Tung-tsao said, "You are quite right! Last night I said that I had important matters to discuss with you in confidence. It was just this. Consider how cruel and oppressive this man is. And here am I, alas, doomed to be his subordinate. I simply can't bear to carry out his policy, but I see no way of avoiding it. You have had wide experience. As it is said, 'He has experienced perils, difficulties, and hardships; he is thoroughly acquainted with the truth and the falsehood of men.' [1] You must have some good suggestion to offer. What advice can you give me?"

Lao Ts'an answered, "Once you realize a thing is difficult, it is easy to do it. Since you have condescended to consult me, I must first ask you to tell me what your real aim is. If you want to get a good name with your superiors, you must be brilliant, and make a lot of noise and show. For this, the only thing is to follow Mr. Yü's policy, which is as the saying goes 'to compel honest people to become robbers.' If, on the other hand, you want to keep before you the ideal of a true 'father and mother official,' [2] and seek to remove those who harm the people, then there is the policy of turning robbers into honest people. If your official position is fairly high and the area under your control fairly large, it is quite easy to do this. But if you are limited to one *hsien* and your district is poor, you can't avoid pricking your hands somewhat; however, it is not impossible."

Tung-tsao said, "Naturally my chief aim is to remove those who harm the people. If only I can bring peace and quiet to my district, I shall be satisfied. Even though I get no special promotion, I shall not die of cold and hunger. Why should I want to found a great family and eat 'the offerings of my sons and grandsons'? But my district is really very poor. My predecessor kept a small troop of fifty soldiers, and, even so, cases of banditry kept occurring. Added to this, there was a deficit in the funds, and so he got into difficulties and was dismissed from office. I feel that even if there is a deficit, but the district becomes peaceful, I can find some way to make it up. But if I cannot do either, what is the good of trying?"

Lao Ts'an said, "The cost of keeping a troop of fifty men is obviously too great. Now how much money can you raise in your office without creating a deficit?" Tung-tsao replied, "I can raise up to a thousand taels without much effort."

"Well then," said Lao Ts'an, "there is a way of dealing with the matter. If you will provide twelve hundred taels a year and at the same time give me a free hand, I can outline a plan which will guarantee that not a single case of banditry will occur within your boundaries. And even if you do have some bandits, I can guarantee to catch them at once. What do you think of this?"

Tung-tsao said, "If I can get you to come and help me, I shall be eternally grateful!" "I shan't have to come myself," Lao Ts'an replied. "I will simply outline for you an absolutely flawless scheme." Tung-tsao said, "If you don't come, then who can put your scheme into effect?" Lao Ts'an answered, "I am going to recommend you a man who can carry out this scheme. But whatever you do, you must treat him with great respect, for he is the sort of man who will leave right away if you don't treat him well; and after he has gone, things will be even worse than before.

"This man's name is Liu Jen-fu, and he belongs to P'ingyinhsien in this region. His present home is in the Peach Blossom Mountain, in the south west of P'ingyinhsien. As a boy of fourteen or fifteen he learned boxing and quarterstaff at the Shaolin Temple [3] on Sungshan. After he had studied there for some time, he felt that the place had an empty reputation and was in no way outstanding, so he left it and wandered by river and lake. After some ten years he met a monk on Omei Mountain in Szechuan, who excelled in the art of self-defense. He forthwith made obeisance to him as his teacher and learned the *T'aitsu* and the *Shaotsu* styles of boxing. He asked the monk to tell him the origin of his method. When the monk said it came from the Shaolin Temple, he was greatly surprised and said, 'Your disciple was at the Shaolin Temple for four or five years and never saw any good boxing. From whom did you learn, Master?'

"The monk said, 'It is the Shaolin Temple style of boxing, but I did not learn it at the Shaolin Temple. Boxing is now a lost art there. The *T'aitsu* style that you have learned from me was handed down from the Dharma.[4] The *Shaotsu* style was taught by Shen Kuang.[5] They were originally developed for the use of the monks, who practiced the art in order to develop toughness and endurance. When they entered the mountains seeking the Way and went about alone, they were likely to meet tigers and panthers and fierce men. Monks are not allowed to carry weapons, so they practiced this art as a means of self-defense. Strong of bone and firm of muscle, they could endure cold and hunger. Just think! Wandering on foot in search of the antique virtue of noble men in barren hills and wild ravines, it is not easy for a monk to find good food and shelter! This was the original high purpose of *T'aitsu* and *Shaotsu* boxing. Who could have known that afterwards the Shaolin Temple art would become famous? Outsiders came in increasing numbers to learn it, and one would often hear that among those who went out masters of the art, there were bandits and seducers of men's wives and daughters. It was for this reason that the old monk who lived four or five generations before the present monk kept the genuine art of boxing hidden and would not pass it on, merely making a show of teaching some superficial and meaningless tricks. My style of boxing comes from a venerable monk of Hanchungfu.[6] If a man practices it faithfully he can attain the skill of Kan Feng-ch'ih.' [7]

"During the three years that Liu Jen-fu lived in Szechuan he completely mastered the art. That was the time of the disturbances caused by the Yüeh robbers,[8] and when he left Szechuan, he knocked about in the camps of the Hsiang and Huai armies [9] for some time. They were two distinct armies, and in the Hsiang army you needed to be a Hunan man, while in the Huai army you needed to be from Anhwei. Only such men received good treatment. A man from another province was merely tolerated; he could only get one or two minor promotions and had not the slightest chance of being given a responsible post. This man had been promoted to the position of captain, but when hostilities ceased, he did not wish to hold onto the post and returned to his home in the country and cultivated a few *mou* of land—just enough to live on. When he has nothing else to do, he wanders about at will in the two provinces of Shantung and Honan, and among the men who practice military exercises in these two provinces there are none who don't know of his prowess. However, he refuses to accept disciples. If he is quite sure that a man is a law-abiding person, then he will teach him a few movements of fist and quarterstaff, but he is very particular who it is. Thus, among the men of military skill in these two provinces none can beat him and all are afraid of him. Now suppose you invite him as your honored guest and hand over your monthly hundred ounces of silver to him, and let him do what he likes with it. Probably he will want to enlist a small troop of ten men as runners, each man's monthly pay six ounces, and the remaining forty ounces he will use as wine money for his bold friends—so it will be enough.

"The three provinces Honan, Shantung, and Chihli and the northern half of the two provinces of Kiangsu and Anhwei together may be considered as making one area. The bandits in this area can be divided into two types, greater and lesser. The greater bandits have chieftains, obey orders, and have regulations; and most of them are skillful in boxing. The lesser bandits are simply rogues and vagabonds who go about looting whenever and wherever they have a chance; they have no confederates and no guns or other weapons. After they have robbed somebody, they either get drunk or else gamble and are very easily caught and convicted. Thus for instance among the people that Prefect Yü deals with, probably nine-and-a-half-tenths are honest people, while half-a-tenth are these lesser bandits. As to the greater bandits, Prefect Yü has not been able to capture even one of their rank and file, to say nothing of their leaders, and yet it is easy to come to terms with them. Take the system of armed guards at the capital for example; no matter whether you are transporting a hundred thousand or two hundred thousand taels, only one or two men are needed to guard it on a journey and avoid all mishaps. Consider a huge sum of money like this! Even if one or two hundred robbers gathered and stole it, it would be ample for all of them. Do you think one or two guards could hold them off? But it is an accepted rule among the greater bandits not to harm the guards belonging to the insurance offices. So all the carts with escorts carry a mark. When they travel, they have a password, and when this password is called, even if the bandits meet them face to face, they merely exchange a greeting and will never make an attack. The bandits all know the marks of the various insurance houses, and they have several lairs which the guards know about. If a member of a band reaches a place where there is an insurance office and goes in and gives a secret sign, he is recognized as a comrade belonging to such and such a 'route' and he is at once made welcome and given wine and food, and on leaving must also be given two or three hundred cash for travel expenses. If he is an important leader, then they must make every effort to entertain him. This then is known as the law of river and lake.

"Just now I said that this Li Jen-fu is very well known by river and lake. The insurance offices in the capital have several times invited him to join them but he would never go, because he would rather hide himself and be a farmer. When he comes, treat him with all ceremony as an honored guest, and it will be as good as if you had opened an insurance office for the protection of your honorable *hsien*. When he has nothing else to do, he will sit around in the teashops and eating houses on the road, and will know at a glance which of the passersby are his bandit friends. He will then pay the teashop keepers to give them food and drink. Before ten days or half a month are gone, all the big bandit chiefs will know about it and will immediately issue an order that no man may make a disturbance in such and such a person's territory. The extra forty taels a month you simply give him for this purpose. As for the lesser bandits, they really have no system but act in a hit-or-miss fashion. When a robbery occurs near the city, someone will make a secret report, and long before the person robbed has come to the *hsien* to make a deposition, Liu Jen-fu's men will have captured the thieves. If a robbery happens at a place a little farther from the city, his friends in the byways will secretly arrest the culprits for him. No matter where they run to, they will all be caught. So this is why the troop of ten is needed. In fact four or five good men would be quite enough for the purpose. The function of the additional five or six is to spread awe in the path of the magistrate's sedan chair, to receive messages, go on errands, run with letters, and so on."

"What you have described is certainly an excellent scheme," said Tung-tsao. "But if this man was unwilling to accept the invitation of the insurance offices, I fear that he will not accept one from my yamen. What do you think?"

Lao Ts'an said, "If you invite him on your own account, of course he won't come. But if I write a letter describing the situation in detail and appeal to him by showing that he can help a whole *hsien* of innocent and honest people, then he will certainly agree to come. For he and I are very close friends, and if I urge him, he is sure to come. When I was about twenty, I saw that there would be disturbances in the empire and always kept my eyes open for future leaders. Many of my friends were interested in military affairs. When Liu Jen-fu was in Honan, he was my intimate friend. We swore to each other that if a time came when the country could use men like us we would all come forward and work together. At that time our group included experts on geography, military surveying, arsenals, and military exercises, and this man Liu was our chief expert on military exercises. Later we all realized that the government of the empire needed another kind of ability and that the subjects we had been discussing and studying were quite useless. For this reason we all turned to practical professions by which to make some sort of a living and threw our ambitions overboard into the eastern sea. But in spite of this, the friendship and idealism of that time can never be destroyed; so that if I write him a letter, he will certainly be willing to come."

When Tung-tsao heard this he bowed again and again and expressed his thanks, saying, "Ever since I was appointed to my new office, I haven't enjoyed a night of peaceful sleep. To hear you talk about these things is like waking from a dream, or recovering from sickness; it really is ten-thousand-fold good luck! But what sort of person is best to send with this letter?" Lao Ts'an replied, "It is better for a close and reliable friend to undertake this onerous task. If you just send a yamen runner with it, it may seem to show a lack of respect. Then he certainly won't come out of retirement, and even I shall be blamed."

Tung-tsao said repeatedly, "Very good. Very good. I have a younger cousin on my father's side who is coming here tomorrow. We can have him go. When will you write your letter? May I trouble you to write it now?" Lao Ts'an said, "I'm not going out all day tomorrow. I am just now writing a long letter to Governor Chuang, which I am asking Mr. Yao Yün to present to him, in which I describe in detail all I have seen of Prefect Yü's administration. I expect to finish writing it tomorrow, and I will write this letter at the same time. The day after I plan to leave."

Tung-tsao asked, "Where are you going the day after tomorrow?" Lao Ts'an said, "First I am going to Tungch'angfu, to visit the library of Liu Hsiao-hui.[10] I want to see his Sung and Yüan block-printed books. After that I am going back to Tsinanfu for the New Year. Where my footsteps will lead me after that even I myself do not know. It is already late. Let us go to bed." With this he got up.

Tung-tsao called to a servant, "Bring a light and take Mr. T'ieh back to his room." When the *lientzu* was lifted, sky and ground appeared of one color; the snow had swept into every corner until everything was white, and you felt your eyes bulging in the glare. The snow at the bottom of the steps was already seven or eight inches deep, so you could not walk through it. Only the path from the main building to the outer gate had been continually swept since there people had been going to and fro all the time. But not a vestige could be seen of the path to the side building; the snow was as thick there as everywhere else.

Tung-tsao ordered some men to shovel out a path quickly so that Lao Ts'an could go to his room. When Lao Ts'an opened his door, he found that his lamp had gone out. A candlestick and two red candles were sent down from the main building and lighted. Then he thought of writing his letters. But the brush and ink were extremely recalcitrant and would not obey his wishes, so the only thing was to go to bed. The next day, although it had stopped snowing, the cold was much greater than before. He got up and called the inn servant to measure out five chin of charcoal and start up a big brazier; he also told him to buy several sheets of "mulberry-bark" paper and to paste up the broken window. In a short time the air in the room became warm again, very different from what it had been the day before. He then melted the dry cake on his ink slab, carefully completed the letter he had left unfinished the previous day and sealed it, wrote the letter to Liu Jen-fu, and took them both to Tung-tsao in the main building.

Tung-tsao put the letter for Mr. Yao Yün in an official envelope and sent it to the post station and placed the letter for Liu Jen-fu in the case under his pillow. Then the midday meal was served.

The two men ate and had been chatting for a while when a servant came to announce: "Young Mr. Shen and the secretaries have all arrived. They are staying at an inn to the west of us. When they have washed, they will come over."

After a while a man arrived at the door who appeared to be something less than forty and was still without a beard. He was wearing a fur-lined gown of old Nanking silk in two shades of blue, and a long-sleeved, fur-lined black jacket. He had on a pair of velvet boots, the sides of which were covered with snow and mud. He walked hurriedly into the main room and bowed to his cousin. Tung-tsao said, "This is my cousin; his *hao* is Tzu-p'ing." Then turning toward Lao Ts'an he said, "This is Mr. T'ieh Pu-ts'an."

Shen Tzu-p'ing moved a step forward, made a bow, and said, "Long have I admired you." Tung-tsao then asked, "Have you had anything to eat?" "I have just arrived," said Tzu-p'ing. "I came over as soon as I had washed, but I'm in no hurry to eat." Tung-tsao said, "Order the kitchen to prepare a meal for young Mr. Shen," but Tzu-p'ing said, "It's not necessary. I'll wait awhile and eat with the other gentlemen." The servant came in and said, "The order has already been given in the kitchen. I told them to send a meal for young Mr. Shen and the secretaries!" Then another servant lifted the *lientzu* and brought in several big red *ch'üan-t'ieh.*[11] Lao Ts'an knew it was the secretaries come to see their superior, so he took the opportunity to leave.

After the evening meal Shen Tung-tsao again invited Lao Ts'an to the main building and asked him to explain in detail to Tzu-p'ing how he should go to Peach Blossom Mountain in search of Liu Jen-fu. Tzu-p'ing asked, "Which is the nearest way?" "I really don't know which is the best way from here," Lao Ts'an answered. "In the old days I used to go from the provincial capital following the Yellow River to P'ingyinhsien. From P'ingyinhsien I went thirty li to the southwest and thus reached the mountains. In the mountains you can't go by cart. The best thing is to take a donkey. In the level places mount your donkey, but where it is at all dangerous get off and walk a few steps. There are two roads into the mountains. When you have followed the one in the West Ravine for about ten or more li there is a Temple of Kuan Ti. The Taoist priest in that temple and Liu Jen-fu often see each other, so if you inquire at the temple you will find out exactly where he is. There are two Temples of Kuan Ti there, one to the east of the village and one to the west; this is the one to the west." When Shen Tzu-p'ing had found out all he wanted to know, the men went to their rooms to sleep.

Early next morning Lao Ts'an went out and hired a mule cart. He packed his things, and when Shen Tung-tsao had gone to the yamen to announce his departure for his district, Lao Ts'an took the fur-lined gown that had been given him two nights before, and gave it with a letter to the innkeeper, saying, "When Magistrate Shen comes back to the inn, give him this. Don't send it now or there might be a mistake."

The innkeeper quickly opened a wooden chest in his office and put the parcel in. After this he saw Lao Ts'an to his cart as he set out for Tungch'angfu. After an uneventful journey of two or three days, Lao Ts'an reached the city of Tungch'angfu and found a clean inn to stay at. That night he settled down there. The next day after breakfast he went out on the street to look for a bookshop. He looked for a long time and at last found a small bookshop with a frontage of three *chien*. In one half they sold paper, brushes, and ink; in the other they sold books. He went to the part that sold books, sat down by the counter, and asked what sort of books they had.

The proprietor said, "Our town of Tungch'angfu is famous for its scholarly atmosphere. The ten *hsien* we control are commonly known as the Ten Model Towns; not one of them but has lots of wealthy families and homes full of music and song. All the books used in these ten districts are bought at my little place here. This is my little shop; at the back is a warehouse, and besides that I have a workshop. We carve the blocks for many books here in our own shop—don't need to go to other places to buy them. But what is your honorable name, Sir? What is your honorable business in coming here?"

"My name is T'ieh. I've come to look for a friend," answered Lao Ts'an. "Do you have any old books here?" The shopkeeper said, "Yes. Yes. Yes. What books does Your Honor want? We have any number." So saying he turned round and pointed at the white paper labels on the book shelves, enumerating them, "Look, Sir! Here is *Writings Selected by the Master of the Hall of Discrimination* and the first, second and third series of the *Studio Where You Plough With Your Eyes*. I have still older ones, such as that *Schoolroom Textbook of Eight Inscriptions.*[12] All these are books of orthodox scholarship. If you just want miscellaneous writings, I have the *Pre-T'ang and T'ang Poetry with Collected Annotations,* and the *Three Hundred T'ang Period Poems.*[13] If you want something still earlier, I have the *Classical Prose with Explanations.*[14] I also have a very valuable book called *Essentials of Mental Philosophy.*[15] The man who can understand that is certainly a wonder!"

Lao Ts'an laughed, "I don't want any of these." The shopkeeper said, "I have others. I have others. Over there are the *Three Essentials of Geomancy,* the *Ghosts Pinching Feet,* and the *Cyclopedia of Astrology.*[16] My little place has complete sets of all the philosophers. Now Tsinanfu is a big city; that goes without saying. But north of the Yellow River our little place is the leading bookstore. No other cities have shops specializing in books. In most of them only the general store carries a few books. All the *Threes, Hundreds, Thousands,* and *Thousands* used in the schools for two or three hundred li around are bought at my little shop. I sell about ten thousand copies a year!"

Lao Ts'an said, "What sort of book is this *Threes, Hundreds, Thousands,* and *Thousands* that your honorable shop sells? I have never seen it. How is it you sell so many copies?" The shopkeeper exclaimed, "Ah! Don't try to fool me! I can see that you are a very well-educated man, Sir; you can't be ignorant of this. It's not one book. The Three is the Three of *The Three-Character Classic;*[17] the Hundred is the *The Hundred Surnames;*[18] the Thousand is *The Thousand-Character Essay.*[19] The other Thousand is *Poems of a Thousand Writers.*[20] This *Poems of a Thousand Writers* is mostly cold stock; I don't sell more than a hundred copies a year. The others —the *Threes, Hundreds* and *Thousands*—have a much wider sale."

Lao Ts'an asked, "Is it possible that nobody buys the *Four Books* and *Five Classics?*"[21]

He replied, "How could nobody buy them! Of course my little place has the *Four Books.* I've got the *Book of Odes, Book of History,* and *Book of Changes* too. If you want the *Book of Rites* and the *Commentary of Tso,* we can write a letter to the provincial capital to fetch them. Well, Sir, if you have come to look for a friend, what family is it you want?"

Lao Ts'an said, "It's the family of Liu Hsiao-hui.[22] Years ago when his father was our Commissioner for Water Transport, I heard that he had a very large number of books in his library. He had a series of reprints made, called *Na Shu Ying*, all taken from Sung and Yüan wood-block books. I want to widen my knowledge by seeing them, but I don't know if they are accessible." The shopkeeper said, "The Liu family is the leading family here in our town! Everybody knows that! But his Excellency Liu Hsiao-hui passed away long ago. The young gentleman is called Liu Feng-i. He is a *Liang-Pang*,[23] and has a position in one of the Boards. I've heard that there are lots of books in his house, all of them packed in big wooden cases. I guess there are many hundreds of boxes piled up in a special two-story building, but no one ever asks about them. A close relative of his, the Third Mr. Liu, who is a *Hsiu-Ts'ai*, often comes to our place for a chat. I once asked him, 'What sort of treasures are all those books in your house; won't you tell us about them?' He said, 'I haven't seen what they are like either!' I said, 'If they are kept in that way, aren't you afraid of bookworms eating them?' "

When the shopkeeper reached this point a man came in, pulled Lao Ts'an by the sleeve and said, "Go back quickly! There's a yamen runner from Ts'aochoufu waiting impatiently to talk to Your Honor! Hurry up!"

When Lao Ts'an heard this he said, "Tell him to wait. I'm staying here for a bit longer and then I'll come." The man said, "I have been looking for you on the street for a long time. My master is terribly worried. Do please go back quickly, Sir." But Lao Ts'an said, "Don't be excited. Since you have found me, you can't be blamed. You go along."

When the inn boy had gone, the bookseller watched him get well away and then in great excitement said to Lao Ts'an in a low voice, "How much is your baggage in the inn worth, Sir? Have you got any friends you can trust in this place?" Lao Ts'an said, "My baggage at the inn isn't worth much, and I haven't any reliable friends here. Why do you ask these questions?" The shopkeeper said, "The present Prefect of Ts'aochoufu is an official called Yü. It's most dangerous to arouse him. No matter whether you are innocent or not, if only he makes up his mind about you, you are stood in the cage. And now a yamen runner has come from Ts'aochoufu. I'm afraid somebody or other has made an accusation against Your Honor. Certainly it's more likely to mean evil than good! You'd better take this chance and make your escape. Since your baggage is not worth much, it's best to part with it. After all, your life is more important." Lao Ts'an said, "I'm not afraid. Surely you don't think he will take me for an armed robber? I'm not going to worry about it." So saying, he nodded his head and went out of the shop door.

On the road he met a wheelbarrow coming toward him, baggage piled up on one side, a man sitting on the other. Lao Ts'an's eyes were quick, and when he saw it he shouted, "Isn't it Second Brother Chin on that wheelbarrow?" and hurriedly went forward. The man on the wheelbarrow, too, jumped down, and then, recovering himself, said, "Aiyah! Isn't this Second Brother T'ieh? How did you get to this place? What are you doing here?" Lao Ts'an told him what he had come for, then said, "You must stop for a rest and come to my inn to talk. Where have you come from? Where are you going?" The man said, "What is the time? I've already had my rest. I simply must cover some more ground today. I'm going back to the south from Chihli.[24] I'm in a hurry to get back home because I have some business to look after; I can't afford to delay any longer." Lao Ts'an said, "In that case I won't keep you. But if you will wait for a few minutes I should like to give you a letter to take to Elder Brother Liu." With that he went back into the shop to the counter where they sold paper, brushes, and ink, bought a brush, several sheets of paper, and an envelope, borrowed the ink slab belonging to the shop, dashed off a letter, and gave it to Chin Erh. They both bowed to each other and he said, "Forgive me for not seeing you on your way. When you meet my friends in the hills, please ask after them all for me." Chin Erh took the letter and got on his wheelbarrow, while Lao Ts'an returned to his inn.

If you don't know whether the yamen runner from Ts'aochoufu will arrest Lao Ts'an or not, then hear the next chapter tell.

CHAPTER 8

Encounter with a tiger by moonlight in Peach Blossom Mountain;

Search for a sage through snow in Cypress Tree Valley.

IT HAS been said that Lao Ts'an was told by the inn boy that a yamen runner from Ts'aochoufu was looking for him. He was much surprised and thought to himself, "Surely Yü Hsien is not going to treat me as though I were a robber!" When he arrived at his inn, the yamen runner came forward and greeted him, holding a parcel in his hands. He put the parcel down on a nearby chair, and taking out a letter from his bosom presented it with both hands, saying, "Mr. Shen sends his compliments to Mr. T'ieh."

Lao Ts'an took the letter and read it. He found that when Shen Tung-tsao had returned to his inn and the landlord had sent the fur-lined gown in to him, he had been extremely put out, and had decided that the fox fur had not been accepted because it was not suitable for traveling. He therefore had picked out a sheepskin gown and jacket at an outfitter's shop and sent a special messenger with them. He said plainly that not to accept this time would be an affront.

When Lao Ts'an had read this, he smiled, then said to the messenger, "Are you a runner from the *fu?*" The messenger replied, "No, I'm a member of the guard of Ch'engwuhsien in Ts'aochoufu."

Lao Ts'an then realized that the inn boy had simply left out the three syllables, Ch'engwuhsien. He immediately wrote a letter of thanks, and gave the messenger two ounces of silver for traveling expenses. After he had sent him away, he stayed there two days more. By that time he had become convinced that the Liu family's books really were locked up in big boxes and that not only could no outsiders see them, but that even members of the clan could not see them. He felt so frustrated that he took up his pen and wrote a *chüeh-chü* [1] poem on the wall which said:

> *Ts'ang-wei, Tsun-wang, Shih Li Chü*
> *I Yün Ching She*, all four "shu" [2]
> Once arrived in Tungch'angfu
> Locked in library feed mildew. [3]

The poem finished, he sighed and went to bed. There we will leave him a while.

It is further said that on the day when Tung-tsao went to the *fu* yamen to take his leave, Prefect Yü admonished him, "Use severe punishments to put down disturbers of the peace." Tung-tsao contented himself with a few noncommittal words—that was all. Mr. Yü then raised his teacup and he was escorted out. [4] When Tung-tsao returned to his inn, the innkeeper took the fur gown and Lao Ts'an's letter in both hands and presented them to him very respectfully. Tung-tsao took them, glanced at them, and felt extremely mortified. Shen Tzu-p'ing was at his side at the time, and he asked, "What makes you unhappy, cousin?"

Tung-tsao then described how, noticing that Lao Ts'an only had cotton clothing, he had presented him with a fox-fur gown and how they had argued about it. He said, "And after all, when he was going, he left the gown behind. He really is overplaying the part." Tzu-p'ing said, "You have overlooked something in this business. It seems to me there is a twofold reason for his not accepting: firstly, he objected to the great value of this fur—and therefore couldn't accept it without demur; secondly, even if he had taken it, he really would have had no use for it—you can't possibly wear a fox-fur gown with a cotton jacket. If you really want to show good feeling, you ought to send a man to find a cotton or raw silk gown with a sheepskin lining and a jacket to match. If you send a messenger with these, he will certainly accept them. I don't believe he is a pretender and a fraud. What do you think?" "Excellent! Excellent!" Tung-tsao replied. "Tell someone to do as you have said."

Tzu-p'ing proceeded to carry out the plan, sent a messenger with the things, and saw his cousin off for his post. He then went into the city to get a cart and, with light baggage and a few attendants, set out for P'ingyin. When he reached P'ingyin he changed to two wheelbarrows for the baggage and, in the town, got a horse for himself. In less than a morning he arrived at the foot of the Peach Blossom Mountains, beyond which a horse couldn't well be used. Fortunately there was a village at the mouth of the mountain valley. The single inn provided only a place where one could stretch out on the floor, but he decided to stop there a while, hire a donkey at a villager's house, and send the horse back. Having rested and eaten, he set out into the mountains. As soon as they had left the village they saw a dry river bed in front of them rather more than a li wide, and all sand. Only in the middle was there a narrow stream over which the local people had thrown a bridge of planks, not more than a few chang in length. Although the stream under the bridge had become a sheet of ice, there was a gurgling sound of flowing water like hanging ornaments tinkling as they swing together. Tzu-p'ing decided it came from small pieces of ice striking against the large sheet of ice as they were carried forward by the current. Having crossed the dry river bed they passed the mouth of the East Ravine. Now these mountains stretched north and south in a continuous line, rising and falling with the pulse of the dragon.[5] You couldn't see the whole at one time, but the ridges, or better ranges that towered aloft to left and right joined in this place. There was a mountain water course called the East Ravine to the left of the central mass and a water course called the West Ravine to the right. The waters of the two ravines joined in front of the mountains, forming one stream which twisted and turned to right and left, making three bends, and then debouched from the valley. After leaving the mouth of the ravine, it became that dry river bed that they had crossed.

When Tzu-p'ing entered the West Ravine and lifted his head to look about, he saw a stretch of mountains rising before him like a great screen. Among the rocks were clumps of various trees; after a recent heavy snowfall the rocks were black against the white snow; the twigs on the trees were brown; and the many pines and cypresses were green in tufts like the moss that painters represent by dots. He rode along on his donkey, enjoying the scenery and feeling very happy indeed. He thought of composing some lines of poetry to describe the landscape.

As he went on, absorbed in his thoughts, he heard a sound, *k'o-to,* and suddenly felt a weakness in his legs. His whole body began to sway and he rolled down into the gully. Fortunately the path followed the bank of the water course, so that although he rolled down, there was not far to go. The snow on both sides of the gully was very deep, but there was a thin layer of ice over the surface which made a sort of crust, and as Tzu-p'ing rolled he broke a path through this thin sheet of ice. It was like rolling down a spring mattress. He rolled several paces until a boulder stopped his fall and prevented him from being hurt. With the boulder to support him he raised himself up. He found he had made two holes in the snow more than a foot deep. Up above, the donkey had already got his forelegs up, but his hindlegs were still buried in the snow at the side of the path and he couldn't move them. Tzu-p'ing called out in haste to his attendants; he looked in both directions, but of the men pushing the wheelbarrows which contained the baggage not a vestige was to be seen.

Do you know why? Well, the travelers on this path were very few, and, although there was less snow collected in the path than at the side, it was still some five or six inches deep. It was easy enough for the donkey to move along step by step, and Tzu-p'ing, absorbed in looking at the mountain snowscape, had not bothered about the wheelbarrows. He did not realize that as the barrows were pushed along, the wheels digging into the ground were clogged by the accumulated snow. Even with one man pushing and one man pulling they went very slowly and had fallen more than half a li behind the donkey.

Tzu-p'ing could not lift his feet out of the snow where he had fallen. He had to endure it until the wheelbarrows arrived. After about half the length of a mealtime, the wheelbarrows arrived, and they all stopped to see what could be done. The man down below certainly could not get up. The men above couldn't get down. They thought for a long while, then agreed, "The only way is to unloose two or three of the ropes from the baggage, tie them together, and let one end down into the gully."

Shen Tzu-p'ing himself tied one end around his waist and the four or five men above put their strength together to pull on the rope hand over hand and only thus could they haul him up. His attendants then beat off the snow and led the donkey forward. He mounted again, and slowly went on. Although it was no winding "sheep gut path," still it had sudden ups and downs, and the rock surface, frozen with ice and snow, was extremely slippery. Thus, although they had started at one o'clock, immediately after lunch, and kept going until four, they had not covered ten li. Tzu-p'ing thought to himself, "The people on the plain said it was not more than fifteen li to the mountain village, but we have traveled for three hours and only just gone half way." Since it was winter, the sun was likely to go down early; and, in the mountains, with high ridges shutting them in on both sides, it was still more likely to get dark early. So he thought to himself as he went on. Before he knew what was happening, night began to fall. He drew in his donkey's bridle and said to the wheelbarrow men, "It's already dark and we probably have another six or seven li to go. The path is rough. The wheelbarrows are slow. What's the best thing to do?" The men said, "There's nothing we can do about it. One good thing—it's the thirteenth of the month. The moon will come out early. In spite of everything the best thing is to push on to the village. There aren't likely to be any bandits along this deserted mountain trail. Even though we are traveling late, there's nothing to be afraid of." Tzu-p'ing said, "There may be no bandits, but even if there were, not having much baggage, I wouldn't be afraid of them. If they want to take it, let them, who cares? What I'm really afraid of is jackals, wolves, tigers, and leopards. At this time of night, if one or two come along, we're done!" The men said, "There aren't many tigers in these mountains, and in any case the king of the tigers keeps them under control, and they never do harm to men. It's only the wolves that are numerous. If we hear any coming, we will all take sticks in our hands, and then we don't need to be afraid of them."

As they talked, they reached a place where a gully cut across their path. It was the bed of a torrent which here fell into the main stream. Since it was winter, there was no water, but the channel that had been scooped out by the water yawned before them more than two chang deep and something more than two chang wide. Thus on one side there was a steep cliff, on the other a deep gulf. There was absolutely no other way for them to go round.

When Tzu-p'ing saw how things were he became very flurried. He quickly drew in his donkey's head, waited for the wheelbarrows to come up, and said, "Here's a fine thing! We've taken the wrong path! We've come to a dead end!" One of the men pushing a wheelbarrow put it down, panting, and said, "No! It's not possible! We've followed this path all the way and there is no other. We can't have made a mistake. Wait here while I go on and see which way we ought to go." He went forward several dozen steps, came back and said, "There is a path, but it's bad going. You must get off your donkey, Sir."

Tzu-p'ing got off, and leading his donkey, followed the man forward. When he had gone round a big boulder, he saw a man-made stone bridge. The bridge consisted only of two slabs of stone, each one not more than a foot and one or two inches wide. They did not fit closely together, and between them was a crack some inches wide; there was a layer of ice on the stone, making it very slippery. Tzu-p'ing said, "It frightens me to death. How can I ever get across this bridge? If my foot slips, I'll be a dead man! I certainly haven't the courage to cross it." The men looked at it and said, "Don't worry. We can manage it. One good thing is that we are all wearing straw shoes,[6] so that the soles of our feet can grip the slippery surface. There's nothing to be afraid of." One of the men said, "Let me go and try it," and scurried across with a skip and a jump. He shouted, "It's all right! Quite easy to cross," and immediately came back and said, "but you can't push the wheelbarrows. The four of us must make two trips and carry them over."

Shen Tzu-p'ing said, "You may be able to carry the barrows over, but I can't cross it. And what about the donkey?" The men said, "Don't worry. Let us help you over, Sir, and you don't need to concern yourself about the rest." Tzu-p'ing said, "Even if I have people holding me up, I don't dare to cross. I tell you frankly, my two legs are quite weak already. How do you think I can walk!" The men said, "We can get you over. You just lie down, Sir. Two of us will carry your head and two of us your feet. We'll get you across that way, Sir. What about that?" Tzu-p'ing said, "It's not safe! It won't do!" Another one of the men said, "How about trying this: undo a rope; you fasten it around your waist, Sir, and we fellows will hold the ends, one in front, one behind. If we go across like that, you will have more courage, Sir, and your legs will not be weak." Tzu-p'ing said, "Yes, that's the only way!"

So they first helped Tzu-p'ing over in that manner and then carried the two wheelbarrows across. But as for the donkey, the donkey would rather die than cross. They wasted a lot of time and in the end had to cover his eyes, and one man pulling, another beating, they at last bundled him across somehow. By the time it was all done, the ground was covered with shadows of the trees, and the moon was already bright.

Having at long last crossed the treacherous bridge, they rested a while, smoked a pipe of tobacco, and then went forward. When they had gone thirty or forty steps they heard in the distance two cries, "*Wu, wu.*" The men said, "A tiger!" They went on but strained their ears listening. When they had gone several dozen steps more, the men put their wheelbarrows down, and one of them said, "You'd better not ride, Sir; get off your donkey. The sound of the tiger comes from the west. Every time he calls, it sounds nearer. I'm afraid he will come to this path. We'd better hide for a bit. If we wait till he is on us, there will be no chance to hide."

When the man had said this, Tzu-p'ing got off his donkey. The head man said, "We'd better sacrifice the donkey to feed the tiger." There was a little pine tree beside the path. They tied the reins of the donkey to the pine tree, put the wheelbarrows beside him, and then went several paces away and hid Tzu-p'ing in a crevice in the rock wall. Some of the men hid at the foot of the boulders and covered themselves with snow; two of them climbed onto the branches of a tree on the slope of the mountain and all looked toward the west.

Slow in the telling, it was quick in the doing. They saw something bounding along in the moonlight on the western ridge. When it reached the top, there was another roar. No sooner had they seen it crouch to spring than it had already reached the bank of the west stream, where it gave another cry. The men hiding there, cold and frightened, were unable to control their trembling, and kept their eyes fixed on the tiger.

When the tiger reached the stream he stood still, his eyes reflecting the moonlight and glowing brightly. Instead of looking at the donkey, he roared in the direction of the men, then crouched again, and bounded past them.

All this time the air in the valley was absolutely still, but there was a rustling sound in the branches of the trees, *hu, hu.* Withered leaves fell to the ground with a sound, *sou, sou,* while the cold air bit into the men's faces, *lang, lang.* Their souls had long ago fled from their bodies! [7]

They waited quite a long while but saw no further signs of the tiger. One of the men up in the tree was the boldest of them all. He came down and cried to the rest, "Come out! The tiger is miles away."

The men came out one after another and pulled Tzu-p'ing, dumb with fright, out of his crevice in the rock wall. After some time he managed to open his mouth and asked, "Are we dead, or are we alive?" The men said, "The tiger has gone." Tzu-p'ing said, "How did he go? Is no one hurt?" One of the men who had been up in the tree said, "I watched how he came down the west slope of the gully; he darted through the air like a bird and here he was. The place where he landed was seven or eight chang higher than the top of our tree. After he'd reached that point, another leap and he was on the eastern ridge. He gave one roar and went off to the east."

Hearing this Shen Tzu-p'ing felt reassured and said, "My two legs are still like jellies; I can't get up. What shall I do?" The men said, "But aren't you standing up now, Sir?" Tzu-p'ing looked down, and sure enough he wasn't sitting any longer. He smiled and said, "This body of mine simply will not listen to what I tell it." Then the men supported him and made him take a few steps. He walked a few tens of paces and then recovered the use of his legs and was able to look after himself. He heaved a sigh and said, "Although I have escaped the jaws of the tiger, if I come to another bridge like that last one tonight, I shall certainly not be able to cross it. Stomach empty, body cold, I shall freeze to death!"

So saying he went up to the little tree to see the donkey. He found him still lying flat on the ground, frightened into this state by the tiger. His men pulled the donkey up, lifted Tzu-p'ing on its back, and they went forward slowly. They turned through a cleft in the rock and suddenly saw a cluster of lights which must have come from a group of houses. Everybody shouted, "Good! Good! Here we are at the village."

With this cry all of their spirits revived. Not only did the men feel that their feet were much lighter, but even the donkey was no longer timid and hesitant.

In a very short time they had come to the lights, which turned out to belong not to a market town, but to the houses of several families who lived on the mountain side. Because of the slope they looked like high buildings with several stories. When they arrived here, they talked things over and decided that nothing would make them go any further, that the only thing was to be brazen and knock on a door and ask for lodging.

By this time they had reached a gate in a "tiger-skin" stone wall. It belonged to a house that seemed to consist of quite a number of buildings, probably about ten or so *chien*. One of the men went forward and knocked on the door. After several knocks an old man with gray hair and beard came out, holding in his hand a candlestick with a lighted candle of white wax. He said, "What do you want?"

Shen Tzu-p'ing hurried forward and told him in his most pleasant manner about their troubles, saying, "I fully realize that this is not an inn, but unfortunately my attendants are absolutely unable to go on. I should like to ask you, Sir, to do a good deed." The old man inclined his head and said, "Please wait a while. I will go and ask our young lady." So saying, and without closing the gate, he went in.

Tzu-p'ing watched him and greatly surprised, asked himself, "Surely this family can't be without a master? Why does he go to ask a young lady? Surely the head of the family can't be a girl!" Then he thought, "I must be wrong! The family must be governed by an old lady. This old fellow must be her nephew; *ku niang* (young lady), must mean *ku mu* (paternal aunt). This is the only sensible explanation; I'm sure it can't be wrong."

Almost immediately the old man, still holding a candlestick in his hand, came out accompanied by a middle-aged fellow and said, "Will the guest please come in." On entering the gate of this house, a building of five *chien* in a row appeared, with a flight of about ten steps leading to a door in the middle. The middle-aged fellow held a candlestick in his hand and lighted the way for Shen Tzu-p'ing. Shen Tzu-p'ing ordered his men, "Wait in the courtyard for a bit while I go in to see how things are, and then I will call you."

Tzu-p'ing went up the steps; the old man was standing inside the door of the middle *chien* and said, "There is a slope on the north side. Tell them to push the wheelbarrows and lead the donkey up there and come into this building that way."

Now the main gate they had come through faced west. They all went into the building. The three *chien* in the middle formed one room which was separated by a partition from a one-*chien* room at each end. At the north end of the three *chien* there was a *k'ang;* the south end was empty. They put the barrows and the donkey at the south end, and the five men settled on the *k'ang.* Then the old man asked Tzu-p'ing his name and said, "Will the guest please go inside."

He passed through the middle *chien* and there was another flight of steps. It led to a level plot of ground planted with flowers and trees, which gleamed in the moonlight, strangely secluded and beautiful. Little gusts of elusive fragrance soaked the lungs and bowels with their freshness. To the north was a fine three-*chien* apartment that faced south, completely surrounded by a gallery with posts and railings of untrimmed fir. Upon entering the building Tzu-p'ing saw, hanging from the roof, four paper lanterns with cleverly made, mottled bamboo frames. Two *chien* were thrown together; one *chien* was separated off into another room. The tables, chairs, stands, and desks were all correctly placed. Between the two rooms was hung a *lientzu* of dull brown cloth.

When the old man reached the door of the inner room he called out, "Young lady, the guest, Mr. Shen, has come." Then the *lientzu* was lifted, and a maiden of eighteen or nineteen came out. She was dressed in cotton, a jacket of light blue, and a dark blue skirt. Her appearance was dignified and calm, attractive and graceful. Seeing the guest she bowed. Tzu-p'ing hastened to make a deep bow to return the greeting. The maiden said, "Please sit down." Then she said to the old man, "Hurry up and prepare the food; the guest is hungry." The old man went out.

The maiden said, "What is your honorable name? What brings you here?" Tzu-p'ing then told how his cousin had sent him specially to find Liu Jen-fu. The maiden said, "Mr. Liu used to live just to the east of this village. Now he has moved to Cypress Tree Valley." Tzu-p'ing asked, "Where is Cypress Tree Valley?" The maiden replied, "About thirty or more li west of the village. The path that leads there is much more out of the way than this and much rougher going too. The day before yesterday when my father came off duty he told us that today there would be a guest from afar who would have had a scare on the road, and told us to stay up late and prepare some food and wine for his entertainment. He further told us to ask you not to blame us if we do less than one should do for an honored guest."

When Tzu-p'ing heard this he was extremely surprised. "What sort of 'on duty' and 'off duty' can there be in a wild mountain where there is no yamen? How could anyone know about my coming the day before yesterday? How does this maiden have such dignity and grace? Surely this is exactly what the ancients meant by 'a silvan air.' [8] I must find out more about her."

If you don't know whether or not Shen Tzu-p'ing will be able to solve the mystery of who the maiden is, then hear the next chapter tell.

CHAPTER 9

A guest chants poems, hands behind back, facing a wall;

Three people sip tea, knee to knee, in intimate talk.

IT HAS been told that Shen Tzu-p'ing was just wondering at this maiden's dignity and grace of manner, so unlike that of a country girl, and at where her father could hold office. He was about to question her when he saw the outside *lientzu* move, and a middle-aged man come in carrying a tray of food. The maiden said, "Just put it down on the *k'ang* table in the west room."

In the west room under the south window, there was a heated brick *k'ang*. Against the window was a long *k'ang* shelf and at each end a short one. In the middle was a square *k'ang* table with places for people to sit on three sides. In the west wall was a big, round moon-window with a pane of glass let into the middle, and in front of the window was a desk. Although the room was not partitioned off from the central room, there was a carved wooden arch separating them. The man arranged the food on the *k'ang* table. It was only a plate of steamed bread, a pot of wine, a crock of millet gruel, and four dishes; no doubt some kind of rough mountain-vegetable food—no meat or fish. The maiden said, "Please have something to eat; I will come back in a little while," and went into the east room.

Tzu-p'ing really felt very cold and hungry, so he sat on the *k'ang*, drank some cups of wine, and then proceeded to eat some steamed bread. Although it was vegetable food, the fresh flavor which filled his mouth was much pleasanter than that of meat. When he had eaten the bread and finished the gruel, the man filled a basin of water and he washed his face. He then got up, and walked up and down the room to stretch his limbs. Lifting his head he saw a set of four large scrolls hanging on the north wall. They were covered with "grass" characters, very free, like flying dragons and dancing phoenixes, so unusual as to startle one. On the scroll at the extreme left were two names. At the top was written: "Presented for correction [1] to the Pillar Official of the Western Peak." At the bottom was written: "Yellow Dragon offers this writing." Although he could not decipher all of the characters, he could get eight or nine out of ten. On close examination it turned out to be six *chüeh-chü* poems of seven characters to each line. They were neither purely Buddhist nor Taoist writings, but when digested they had a good deal of flavor: they were not all "extinction of desire and emptying of the mind," [2] nor were they only about "lead and mercury" and "dragons and tigers." [3] On the desk below the moon-window he saw paper and pen ready for use so he copied down the poems to take back to the yamen to read as you would a newspaper. Do you know what sort of verses they were? Please look. The poems said:

(1)

I have worshipped the nine lotus-enthroned of the Jasper Pool,
Hsi-i has taught me the *Chih Yüan P'ien;*
Five centuries passed unnoticed like the grass:
The ocean now rolls where mulberries grew.

(2)

Tzu-yang bade me emulate the *Ts'ui Hsü Yin,*
It resounded like the Thunderclap Lute in empty hills;
I still could not remove the "Thee" and "Me":
Heaven-sent flowers clung to my encircling cloud.

(3)

The sky of lust and sea of sense are full of wind and wave:
Vast and uncrossable is the river of desire;

Led into the garden as River of Righteousness,
It is everywhere planted with Man T'o Lo flowers.

(4)

With cracking of rock and trembling of heaven a single crane flies aloft,
Blackness filled the night, at the fifth watch crows the cock;
The precept "Never three nights under one mulberry tree" once learned,
One sees not in the world of men distinctions of right and wrong.

(5)

"Wild horses" gallop night and day with clouds of dust;
Life teams, plants throng.
Steal into the joy of Condor Peak Nirvana;
Seize from Hu Kung his life-suspending power.

(6)

The peepul leaf is old; the *Lotus Sutra* is new.
North and south transmit the same true light;
Five hundred Heavenly Babes all received milk,
Incense flowers are offered to Hsiao Fu Jen.[4]

Tzu-p'ing finished copying the poems and turned his head to look out
of the moon-window. The moonlight, clear and bright, lighted up the
mountains which rose, layer on layer, tier on tier, ever higher and
higher. It was indeed a fairy land, far removed from the everyday
world. And now he felt not at all tired. Why not go out and wander
on the mountains a little? Wouldn't that be still better? He was about
to start when he thought, "But aren't these mountains the mountains
we have just come through? Isn't this moon the very moon under which
we trudged? Why did it seem so gloomy and fearsome when we came,
making us nervous and afraid? The mountain and the moon are still
the same. How is it they now bring me a feeling of liberation and delight?" And then he thought of what General Wang [5] says, "Alas, our
feelings change according to our surroundings; and melancholy follows." How completely true! For a moment he was undecided about
what to do next and thought of writing one or two poems, but he heard
behind him a musical voice saying, "Have you finished eating? How
neglectful I am!" He hurriedly turned his head and found that the
maiden had changed into a pale-green padded gown of printed cloth
and loose black trousers, and now her eyebrows were even more like
spring mountains, and her eyes like autumn water; her two cheeks

were plump and as though the vermilion were sheathed in silk. From under the white the color barely showed through—not like the present-day kind of make-up you see everywhere, where they plaster themselves with that rouge stuff until they look like a monkey's rump! A smile played about her mouth and cheeks, and her eyes and eyebrows had a look of grave dignity, arousing mingled feelings of love and respect. The maiden said, "Won't you please sit on the *k'ang?* It's much warmer there."

Then they both sat down. The old grayhead [6] came in and asked the maiden, "Where shall Mr. Shen's things be put?" The maiden replied, "When the master went away the day before yesterday, he ordered that the guest was to sleep in his bed in this building. You don't need to unpack his bedding. Have his men all had something to eat? Tell them to go to bed early. Has the donkey been fed?" The grayhead replied to all the questions, "Everything has been arranged properly." The maiden further said, "Bring us some tea." The grayhead said "Yes" several times.

Tzu-p'ing protested, "I wouldn't dare to rest my dusty and profane body here. On the way in I saw a big *k'ang;* let me sleep in that room with the others." The maiden replied, "You don't need to be so polite. These are my father's orders; otherwise a simple mountain girl like me wouldn't presume to entertain a guest alone." "You have shown me far too much kindness," Tzu-p'ing said, "I am deeply grateful. Only I have not yet asked your honorable name. What is your esteemed father's office? Where does he perform his duty?" "My name is T'u," said the girl. "My father does duty at the Palace of Colored Clouds.[7] He serves for five days at a time; this means half the month at home, half the month at the Palace."

Tzu-p'ing asked, "Who composed the poems on this set of scrolls? To look at them one would suppose it was an immortal." The maiden answered, "It was my father's friend. He often comes here for a talk, and he wrote them when he was here once last year. He is a man who goes about 'without gown or shoes.'[8] He is very intimate with my father." Tzu-p'ing said, "Well, then, is he a Buddhist monk or a Taoist priest? Why does he put into his poems a sort of Taoistic language? And isn't there also a lot of Buddhist lore?" The maiden said, "He is neither a Taoist priest nor a Buddhist monk; in fact he wears the clothes of a layman. He always says, 'The three schools—Confucianism, Buddhism, Taoism—are like the signboards hung outside three shops. In reality they are all sellers of mixed provisions; they all sell fuel, rice, oil, salt. But the shop belonging to the Confucian family is bigger; the Buddhist and Taoist shops are smaller. There is nothing they don't stock in all the shops.' He further says, 'All teachings have two layers: one can be called the surface teaching, one the inner teaching. The inner teachings are all the same; the surface teachings are all different. So Buddhist monks shave their heads; Taoist priests do their hair up into a coil; you can tell at a glance which is Buddhist and which is Taoist. If you ask the Buddhist monk to keep his hair and do it up in a coil and wear a feather-trimmed coat, and the Taoist priest to shave his hair and put on a gown of camlet, then people will call them by the opposite names. That is how people use their eyes, ears, nose and tongue, isn't it?' Again he says, 'Surface teachings differ; inner teachings are really the same.' For this reason Mr. Yellow Dragon doesn't hold to any one teaching, but freely chants them all."

"Listening to these wonderful arguments," Tzu-p'ing said, "I am filled with admiration. But I am extremely stupid, and since you say the inner teaching of the three schools is the same, I want to ask you where the similarities are and where the differences. Also why is one greater than the other? If the Confucian school is the greatest, wherein lies its greatness? I venture to ask you to explain."

The maiden said, "Their similarity consists in encouraging man to be good, leading man to be disinterested.[9] If all men were disinterested, the Empire would have peace. If all men scheme for private advantage, then the Empire is in chaos. Only Confucianism is thoroughly disinterested. Consider! In his life Confucius met many dissenters such as Ch'ang-chü, Chieh-ni,[10] and the 'old man with a basket of weeds,'[11] none of whom respected him very much, but he on the contrary praised them without end. This is his disinterestedness; this is his greatness. And so he said, 'To attack heterodoxy, this is truly injurious.'[12] Now the Buddhists and Taoists indeed were narrow-minded. They feared lest later generations should not honor their teachings, so they talked a lot about heaven and hell in order to frighten people. This was partly intended to spur people to well-doing, and to this extent they were disinterested. But when they teach that even to say that you believe their teachings is to have all your sins blotted out, while not to believe their teachings is to be possessed by devils and when dead to go down to hell—in this they are narrow and self-interested. As to all the foreign sects, they go even further and on account of doctrinal differences raise troops and war continuously, killing men as though cutting hemp. I ask you, does this agree with their original intention? This is where they are still more narrow than others. Islam, for instance, when it says that blood shed in a religious war shines like a rosy-red precious stone, cheats man to the extreme! Now Confucianism, unfortunately, has for a long time ceased to be taught. The Han-period scholars paid attention to chapter and verse, but they lost sight of the main thought; by the T'ang dynasty there was simply nobody who propounded it. Han Ch'ang-li [13] was a charlatan who understood the letter but did not understand the spirit and talked a lot of nonsense. He even wrote an essay called *In Search of the Original Tao*,[14] but his search led him to the opposite of the original teaching! He said, 'If the King does not give commands, he loses his kingship; if the people do not supply grain, rice, silk, and hemp and offer them to their superiors, they should be executed!' If this is true, shouldn't we say that since Chieh and Chou [15] were good at giving orders and good at executing people, therefore Chieh and Chou were good kings and the subjects of Chieh and Chou were bad? Isn't this to upset the whole idea of right and wrong? He also wanted to oppose Buddhism and Taoism and yet became the friend of a monk.[16] Therefore later students of Confucianism felt that it was too much trouble to follow the principles of Confucius and Mencius—not as easy as to throw together a few sentences of jargon attacking the Buddhists and Taoists, and so to count as disciples of the Sage. How much simpler that was! Even Chu Fu-tzu [17] couldn't escape this limitation. Merely on the authority of Han Ch'ang-li's *In Search of the Original Tao*, he changed the meaning of the *Analects* of Confucius, taking the 'attack' in 'to attack heterodoxy' and twisting it about in a hundred ways and in the end making no sense of it at all. Finally the Sung scholars made the Confucianism of Confucius and Mencius more and more narrow until it was quite destroyed."

As Tzu-p'ing listened, he was filled with respect and admiration, and he said, "An evening's talk with you is better than ten years' reading! Truly I am hearing what I have never heard before! But I still don't understand how Ch'ang-chü and Chieh-ni can be heterodox (*i tuan*), and Buddhism and Taoism not heterodox. How do you explain that?" The maiden answered, "They are all *i tuan*. You must know that the character *i* ought to be read to mean 'not alike,' and the character *tuan* must be read 'an extremity.' Thus 'To hold the two *tuan'* [18] expresses the idea 'hold the two extremities.' If *i tuan* is explained as 'heterodox,' then won't the 'two *tuan*' have to be explained as 'a forked teaching.' And in that case won't 'Hold the two *tuan*' then mean 'grasp a forked teaching'? What sort of sense does that make? The meaning of the Sage is that different roads may lead to the same goal; different melodies may achieve the same effect. If a doctrine sets out to persuade men to be good and lead men to take an unselfish view of life, there is nothing wrong with it. This is what is meant by: 'The greater virtue allows no overstepping of its limits; the lesser virtues permit some liberty.' [19] But if it sets out to make attacks on people, it may begin by attacking Buddhism and Taoism, but later when such differences as those between Chu and Lu [20] appear, members of the same family will take arms against each other. All being children of Confucius and Mencius, why did Chu's followers want to attack Lu, and Lu's followers want to attack Chu? This is what is called, 'losing one's proper nature,' [21] and is firmly condemned by the above-quoted words of Confucius, 'This is truly injurious.' "

When Tzu-p'ing had heard all this he sighed again and again in admiration and said, "I am indeed fortunate to meet you today; it is like meeting a distinguished teacher! But even though there are places where the Sung scholars may have misunderstood the Sage's intention, still, their development of the orthodox doctrine was an achievement beyond the reach of others. Thus, although the two terms *li* (reason) and *yü* (desire) and phrases like *chu ching* (stress seriousness) and *ts'un ch'eng* (maintain sincerity), come from the ancient sages, later men really received a great deal of gain from the Sung scholars' development of these conceptions. Men's sentiments were set right by them; customary morality was mellowed by them."

The girl smiled in a captivating manner and sent a glance in the direction of Tzu-p'ing like the seductive movement of autumn ripples. Tzu-p'ing felt the charm of her winged eyebrows and the grace of her parted red lips, and it seemed as though a subtle fragrance soaked into his flesh and bones. He couldn't prevent his spirit from fluttering about in the air. The girl put forth a hand, white as jade, soft as cotton wool, reached across the *k'ang* table, and took hold of Tzu-p'ing's hand. After she had taken it, she said, "I should like to ask you, how does this compare with the time when you were a boy in the study, and your esteemed tutor took your hand and 'beating was the school punishment'?" [22]

Tzu-p'ing was silent and could make no reply. The girl again said, "Tell me honestly, how do you like me compared with your esteemed tutor? The Sage says, 'What is meant by "making the thoughts sincere" is the allowing no self-deception, as when we hate a bad smell, and when we love a beautiful woman.' [23] Confucius speaks of 'Loving virtue as you love a woman.' [24] Mencius says 'It is the nature of man to eat and love.' [25] Tzu Hsia speaks of 'transferring your esteem from women to virtue.' [26] So this love of woman is fundamental to man's nature. The Sung scholars try to say that we should love virtue and not love women. Surely this is self-deception? To deceive yourself and to deceive others is the extreme of insincerity! But they perversely want to call it 'maintaining sincerity'—isn't that hateful? The Sage made a distinction between *ch'ing* (feeling) and *li* (good manners)—he did not consider *li* (reason) and *yü* (desire) opposed to each other; and he rearranged the *Book of Odes* so as to put the 'Kuan Chü' [27] at the head. Consider:

> Lovely is this noble lady,
> Fit bride for our lord!

and

> Sought her and could not get her

and

> Now on his back, now tossing onto his side.

Can we really say this only illustrates heavenly reason (*t'ien li*) and not a mere human desire (*jen yü*)? [28] From this we can see that the Sage did not deceive people. The *Preface* says on the 'Kuan Chü,' 'It arises from feeling; but stops within the limits of decorum and righteousness.' [29] 'Arising from feeling' is in the realm of the spontaneous. Thus tonight an honorable guest is bestowed upon us: I cannot help being happy: this arises from spontaneous feeling. When you came, you were tired and exhausted. A good deal of time has passed, and you ought to be still more tired. But instead, your spirit is bright and sparkling, and you seem very happy; this also arises from spontaneous feeling. When a young girl and a grown man sit together deep into the night, and they indulge in no improper talk, they have remained 'within the limits of decorum.' This indeed is in harmony with the Sage's teaching. As to the Sung scholars' various deceptions, they are too many to be recounted. Yet although the Sung scholars made many mistakes they were right in some places. As to the present-day disciples of the Sung school, they are really nothing but hypocrites; Confucius and Mencius would hate them deeply and would disown them."

They had barely finished talking when the grayhead brought in the tea—two old porcelain cups and pale green tea. As soon as they were put on the table a fragrance assailed the nostrils. The girl took her tea, rinsed her mouth, rinsed it again, and spat it all out into the pit under the *k'ang*, saying with a laugh, "What made us discuss these ethical questions tonight? You have made me pollute my mouth with these perverted doctrines. After this let us 'only talk about wind and moon.' " [30]

Tzu-p'ing readily agreed. He raised his cup and took a sip of tea. It was unusually refreshing. He swallowed it and felt purified to the very pit of his stomach. Around the root of his tongue the juices came in waves, fragrant and sweet. He swallowed two mouthfuls one after another, and it was as though the fragrant vapor stole up from his mouth to his nose, unspeakably pleasant to experience. He asked, "What tea leaves are these? Why is it so good?" The maiden replied, "The tea leaves are nothing wonderful; it is wild tea that grows on the mountain, and therefore has quite a full flavor. Luckily, too, our water is drawn from a spring on the east summit of the mountain. The higher the spring, the more delicious is the flavor of the water. Also we use pine cones as fuel and boil the water in an earthenware container. These three advantages combine to make the result good. Where you live, all the tea is brought from outside—you have no good varieties— and the flavor is bound to be thin. Add to this that your water and fuel are not right, and the taste naturally is inferior."

At this point somebody was heard outside the window, calling, "Yü Ku (Miss Jade), why didn't you tell me that you have a distinguished guest today?" When the girl heard this, she quickly got up and said, "Uncle Dragon, how is it you have come at this time of night?"

While she was still talking, the man had already come in. He was wearing a dark blue, cotton padded gown "of a hundred patches," [31] was bareheaded and beltless, and had no jacket. He was something more than fifty years old; he had a ruddy complexion,[32] and his whiskers and beard were pitch black. When he saw Tzu-p'ing, he saluted him with his hands together and said, "Mr. Shen, how long have you been here?" Tzu-p'ing replied, "About two or three hours. May I ask your honorable name?" The man said, "I keep my name hidden and use Yellow Dragon as a *hao*." Tzu-p'ing said, "What good fortune to meet you! I was reading and admiring your poems sometime ago." The maiden said, "Won't you come and sit on the *k'ang*?"

Yellow Dragon then sat on the *k'ang*, taking the inside place at the table, and said, "Yü Ku, you said you would invite me to eat bamboo shoots. Where are the bamboo shoots? Bring them in and I will eat." Yü Ku answered, "Some time ago I was planning to dig some up, but I forgot, and they were taken by Mr. T'eng Liu.[33] If Uncle Dragon wants to eat some, he had better find Mr. T'eng Liu himself and argue it out with him." Yellow Dragon raised his head to heaven and laughed aloud.

Tzu-p'ing said to the maiden, "I don't want to be rude, but I take it that the two words Yü Ku must be your honorable personal name?" The maiden replied, "My humble name is Yü, the Second Daughter. My older sister is called Fan, the First Daughter, and people of my father's generation are all accustomed to call me Yü Ku (Miss Jade)."

Yellow Dragon said to Tzu-p'ing, "Are you sleepy, Mr. Shen? If you are not, we are such a good company that we had better stay up tonight, and get up late tomorrow. In the Cypress Tree Valley region the paths are extremely steep and dangerous and very bad for traveling. Besides, this heavy fall of snow has made the roads hard to follow. If you slip, your life is in danger. Liu Jen-fu has been packing his bags tonight and will be at the fair at the Temple of Kuan Ti by noon tomorrow. If you start after breakfast tomorrow, you will be just in time to meet him."

Hearing this Tzu-p'ing was very happy. "To have chanced to meet you two immortals today is fortune enough for three incarnations," he said. "Please, Honorable Immortal, tell me the time of your birth; was it in T'ang or Sung?" Yellow Dragon again laughed very loud. "How do you know so much about me?" The answer was: "In your poem you say clearly:

> Five centuries passed unnoticed like the grass;
> The ocean now rolls where mulberries grew.

From this we can tell that you are certainly more than five or six hundred years old." Yellow Dragon said, " 'To believe everything in the *Book of History* would be worse than to have no *Book of History* at all.' [34] I was only playing with my pen and ink. You should read my poems as you read the *Story of the Peach Blossom Fountain*,[35] Sir!" With this, he lifted his teacup to taste the freshly made tea.

Yü Ku saw that the tea in Tzu-p'ing's cup was almost finished, so she took the little teapot to fill it for him. Tzu-p'ing half-rose several times and saying, "Please don't disturb yourself!" lifted his cup and tasted it like a connoisseur. Just then he heard a sound, *"Wu,"* outside in the distance, and noticed that the paper in the windows was moving with a slight rustling sound and the dust on the beams was coming down in a shower. He recalled what had happened on the road and unconsciously his hair stood up on end, his bones became stiff with fright, and his color suddenly changed. Yellow Dragon said, "This is a tiger's roar; nothing to worry about. Mountain folk look on this sort of animal as you city-dwellers look on donkeys and horses. Although you know they can kick a man, you are not afraid of them, for having been used to them for a long time you know that it is very unusual for them to harm people. Mountain folk and tigers are used to each other; the men usually avoid the tigers, and the tigers also avoid the men, so it is not often that a man is attacked. You don't need to be afraid of them."

Tzu-p'ing said, "You can tell from the sound that it is still far away; how is it that it makes the paper of the windows vibrate and the dust from the beams shower down?" "This is simply what is called 'the majesty of the tiger,'" [36] Yellow Dragon replied. "Since there are mountains on all four sides, the air is enclosed—one roar of a tiger and the four mountains all reply. It is like this for twenty to forty li around the tiger. If a tiger goes down to the plain, he no longer has this majestic power. For this reason the ancients said, 'If dragon leaves water or tiger leaves mountain, he suffers contempt of man!' It is just the same as when an official in the Imperial Court has experienced some difficulty, or been censured for something and goes home to vent his feelings on his wife and children. Outside his home he is afraid to utter a single determined word, nor has he the courage to give up his office. It is for the same reason that the tiger doesn't dare leave the mountains and the dragon doesn't dare leave the water."

Tzu-p'ing nodded his head several times, "That's true enough. But I still don't quite understand. When the tiger is in the mountains, how does he have such majestic power? What is the reason for it?" Yellow Dragon answered, "Haven't you read the *Thousand-Character Essay?* [37] It is for the same reason that 'Hollow ravine transmits sound;

in empty hall hearing is easy.' An empty hall is just a small hollow ravine. A hollow ravine is just a big empty hall. If you let off a cannon
cracker outside this door, it will reverberate for half a day. For the
same reason thunder in a mountain town sounds many times as loud
as on the plain." He then turned his head and said to the maiden, "Yü
Ku, I haven't heard you play the lute for a long time. Today we have
the unwonted pleasure of a distinguished guest here; bring your lute
and play him a tune! It will give me a chance to hear you, too." "Uncle
Dragon, why suggest it?" Yü Ku said. "You know how I play my lute.
It will make a laughingstock of me! When Mr. Shen is in the city, he
hears lots of good lute players! Why should he have to listen to our
rustic 'welcoming drum'? [38] However I will go and fetch a zither. If
Uncle Dragon plays a melody on the zither, that will be something
more rare." Yellow Dragon said, "All right. All right. Then I'll play the
zither, and you play the lute.[39] But to carry them back and forth is a lot
of trouble. It's better for us to go and play in your cave. Fortunately a
mountain maid is not like a young miss in a yamen, whose room may
not be visited by other people." With this he got down from the *k'ang*,
put on his shoes, took a candle, and beckoned to Tzu-p'ing, "Please
come along; Yü Ku will lead the way."

Yü Ku then got down from the *k'ang*, took the candle, and went first.
Tzu-p'ing was second, Yellow Dragon third. They went through the
middle *chien*, lifted the *lientzu*, and entered the inner *chien*. It had
two couches, one at each end; the one to the left had quilts and pillows
in place; the one to the right was piled with books and pictures. There
was a window looking out to the east, and under the window a square
table. In front of the couch on the left was a small door. Yü Ku said to
Tzu-p'ing, "This is my father's bedroom." They went through the little
door beside the couch. It was a sort of zigzag gallery, but had windows
and a roof. You walked on wooden planks over a hollow space. A turn
to the north, then a turn to the east. On the north and east it was all
glass windows. If you looked out of the north windows, the mountain
was very close—a sheer cliff that shot up into space; if you looked
down, it seemed to be very deep. Just as they were going forward they
suddenly heard the sound of falling rocks, *p'ing-p'eng, huo-lo;* as
though the mountain were toppling over. Underfoot was a shaking
and quaking. Tzu-p'ing was so frightened that his souls fled from his
body.

*If you don't know what happened afterwards, then hear the next
chapter tell.*

CHAPTER 10

A pair of black dragon's pearls shine on lute
and zither;

A single rhinoceros horn blends with an
ancient harp.

IT HAS been told that Tzu-p'ing heard the sound of heaven falling
and earth crumbling, and felt a shaking and quaking underfoot. He
was so frightened that his souls fled from his body fearing the mountain would topple over. Yellow Dragon was just behind him and said,
"Don't be afraid; it is because the frozen snow on the mountains has
been scoured hollow by the spring water. A large mass of packed ice
and snow has rolled down, and that's what makes the noise."

With this they made another turn to the north, and there was the
door of a cave. The cave was no bigger than a two-*chien* room. The
side facing away from the mountain was walled up halfway, and the
upper part was windows; the other three sides were smooth cut and
snow white. The roof was round like the barrel vault of a city gate.
The furnishings were extremely simple. There were several seats made
of the stumps of trees,[1] all different, some big, some little, but all polished to shine like silk. The tables and stands, too, were all of untrimmed vine stems, neither square nor round, but fashioned accord-

ing to the nature of the material. A narrow wooden couch, shaped like a boat and made of old logs, stood against the east wall, with covers and cushions all in place. Beside the couch were stacked up two or three yellow bamboo chests, no doubt containing clothes and such things. There were no lamps or candles in the cave, but in the north wall were fitted two "night shining pearls," [2] perfectly round like two drops of water, and the size of a bushel measure. They gave out a dull red light. On the ground was spread a soft, thick mat, which made a slight sound as you walked. North of the couch stood a bookcase in the form of a carpenter's rule,[3] on which were a great many books, all roughly bound, with the pages untrimmed. Between the two "night shining pearls" were hung several musical instruments. Tzu-p'ing recognized two zithers and two lutes; there were also a number he did not recognize.

When Yü Ku had entered the cave, she blew out the candle and put it on the window sill. As soon as they had sat down they heard the sound, *wu-wu-wu,* repeated seven or eight times outside, and then one after another several more sounds, but the window paper did not vibrate. Tzu-p'ing said, "How is it there are so many tigers in these mountains?" Yü Ku laughed and said, "When a country person goes to the city, there are all sorts of things he doesn't recognize, and people laugh at him. When a city man like you comes to the country, there are lots of things you don't recognize either. I'm afraid people will laugh at you!" Tzu-p'ing said, "Listen! That *wu-wu* sound out there! Isn't it tigers?" "That is the barking of wolves," Yü Ku said. "How could there be so many tigers? The sound of a tiger is long; that of the wolf is short. So the tiger's is called 'a roar'; the wolf's is called 'a bark.' The ancients always used careful thought in giving names to things."

Yellow Dragon pulled out two little oblong tables and took down a lute and a zither. Yü Ku also moved out three stools and made Tzup'ing sit on one. She and Yellow Dragon tuned their strings together, and each sat down on a stool. The strings tuned, they exchanged a few words and then began to play. At first they only plucked lightly and picked slowly, and the sound was sustained and gentle; after the opening section they separated and went against each other, the sound clear and crisp; after two more sections they began to slide their left hands up and down the strings, the tones of the zither alternating with the notes of the lute and answering them. Listening carelessly you would only have heard the twanging of lute and striking of zither, each making its own tune; listening more carefully you heard a pair of pearl birds singing in harmony, calling and answering each other. Four or five sections later they began to move their left hands less, but swept the strings promiscuously, *ts'ang-ts'ang, liang-liang, lei-lei, lo-lo*, bringing down their fingers with such force that the sounds rose in rich profusion. Six or seven or eight sections later the music became more sustained, with more and more turns and ever clearer, the melody more and more otherworldly.

Now Tzu-p'ing could play ten or more tunes on the lute, so he listened to it with absorption; he had never heard the zither played, and he listened to it with special attention. He found that the control of the zither also lay in the left hand. After the right hand had struck the strings, the left hand moved to and fro quivering and shaking as the continuing sound rose and fell in response, *i-i, mi-mi*. Indeed, he was hearing something he had never heard before. At first he was occupied in appraising the fingering and the changes of the notes. But soon there was only sound in his ears, and his eyes saw no fingers. Later still ears and eyes were both blank, and he felt his body fluttering to and fro as though carried by a strong wind, floating and again sinking in regions of glowing cloud. Still later, mind and body were all forgotten as though he was drunk or in a dream. Into the mysterious depths of his reverie several sounds at length forced their way, and lute and zither both became still. He began to see and hear again and suddenly was startled out of his dream. He half got up and said, "That tune is truly sublime! I have studied the lute for some years and heard many master hands. I have heard Mr. Sun Ch'in-ch'iu play a piece called *Autumn Comes to the Han Palace* [4] on the lute, and thought that it was quite out of the ordinary. I never imagined that one day I would hear this piece which is many times better than Mr. Sun's *Autumn Comes to the Han Palace.* Please tell me the name of it. Is there a written score?"

Yü Ku said, "The piece is called *Melody of Sea Water and Heavenly Wind.* It has never been written down. Not only is the tune unlike anything else in the world, but our way of playing is in the traditional mountain style not known to outsiders. The playing you people are used to is all unison music. If two of you were to play this piece together you would play the *kungs* and *shangs* [5] on both instruments together as one. If one played *kung,* then the other would play *kung;* if one played *shang,* then the other would play *shang.* On no account could they be *yü* and *chih*. Even if three or four people played together, it would still be the same. This is certainly *t'ung ts'o* (playing together), but it is not *ho ts'o* (playing in harmony). In the pieces we play, one person playing is quite different from two people playing; when one person plays it is called 'one-part music'; when two people play it is 'harmonious playing.' So that when this is *kung*, that may be *shang;* when this is *chüeh*, that may be *yü:* they harmonize, but the notes are not identical. The words of the Sage, 'Gentlemen are *ho* (harmonious), but not *t'ung* (identical),' [6] illustrate this principle. Later men have for a long time misunderstood this word *ho* (harmonious)."

At this point Yü Ku got up, went to a little door in the west wall, opened it, and shouted several words. You couldn't tell what she said —couldn't hear clearly. Yellow Dragon got up and hung the lute and zither on the wall.

Then Tzu-p'ing also got up, went to the wall, and looked closely at the "night-shining pearls" to see better what they really were like, that he might the better boast about what he had seen on his return. When he got close to them, he stretched out his hand to feel one of them. The "night-shining pearl" was quite hot, and he burned his hand. Greatly surprised he said to himself, "What's the meaning of this?" Seeing that Yellow Dragon had finished hanging up the lute and the zither, he asked, "What are these things, Sir?" Yellow Dragon replied with a smile, "They are a black dragon's pearls.[7] Don't you recognize them?" The question followed: "How can a black dragon's pearls be hot?" The reply: "They are pearls vomited by a fiery dragon, so of course they are hot!"

Tzu-p'ing said, "How can a fiery dragon have a pair of pearls so well matched as this? Even if you say they are from a fiery dragon, you can't tell me that they are perpetually as hot as this!" The laughing answer was: "So you are inclined to doubt what I say. If you don't believe me, I'll just open the source of the heat and show you." So saying he went to the side of a "night-shining pearl" where there was a little brass knob: one pull and the "night-shining pearl" opened like the wing of a door. It turned out to be a pearly shell. Inside was a deep oil reservoir; in the middle a wick of twisted cotton thread; around it a cylinder made of paper of many layers; above was a little chimney which went out through the wall, with lots of soot on it. It was made on the principle of a foreign lamp, but not as well made, so that you couldn't prevent its smoking. Having seen it, Tzu-p'ing laughed too. He looked at the pearly shell again, and found it was scraped out of a big oyster shell and therefore not as bright as a foreign lamp.

Tzu-p'ing said, "Wouldn't it be much simpler to buy a foreign lamp?" Yellow Dragon said, "Where do you expect to find a foreign-goods store in these mountains? This oil comes from the mountain in front of us; it's the same as the foreign oil you burn; only we are unable to refine it, so it is wretchedly crude, and the light it gives is feeble. This is why we have a place for it in the wall." Having said this, he shut the pearly shell; there was a pair of "night-shining pearls" as before.

Tzu-p'ing further asked, "What is this mat made of?" The reply: "It is usually called 'thatch rushes,' because it can be used for making thatch capes. You take the thatch rushes when they are still green, gather and dry them in the sun, split them very fine, and weave them with hemp. This, in fact, is Yü Ku's handiwork. In the mountains the ground is very damp, so we first spread mica on the floor, then put down this rush mat and in this way we don't get ill. This wall is also plastered with a mixture of mica and red clay, to keep out the wet and also to avoid the cold; actually it is far better than the lime which you use."

Tzu-p'ing then saw something hanging on the wall, like a bow for beating cotton wool, but provided with a great many strings. He knew it must be a musical instrument, so he asked, "What is this called?" Yellow Dragon said, "It is called a 'harp.'" [8] He brushed it with his hand, but it made very little noise. Tzu-p'ing said, "When we were young, we studied poems in which the title, *Harp Melody*,[9] appeared, but we did not know it referred to this kind of thing. Won't you play a little to show me what it is like? Please!" Yellow Dragon said, "There is no point in one person playing. Let's see what the time is. Perhaps we can ask someone else to come. Then it will be worth while." He went to the window and looked at the moon. "It's not more than the middle of *hai* [ten P.M.].[10] I don't suppose the Sang sisters have gone to bed yet. Let's send and ask them over." Then he turned to Yü Ku. "Mr. Shen wants to hear the harp. I wonder whether Sang A-hu can come?" Yü Ku said, "When grayhead brings the tea, I'll tell him to go and ask."

Then they all sat down again. The grayhead carried in a little red-clay stove, a jug of water, a little teapot, and several little teacups and arranged them on the short-legged stand. Yü Ku said, "Go to the Sang house and ask whether or not Hu Ku and Sheng Ku can come." The grayhead muttered a reply and went.

And now three sat around the "plum blossom" [11] table by the window, Tzu-p'ing being next to the window sill. Yü Ku gave tea to the two men. They all sat quietly sipping their tea. Tzu-p'ing saw several books on the window sill and picked them up. There was a title on them, four characters which read "Sayings of an Insider." When he opened a volume, he found that there were verse and prose, but the larger part was folk songs with long and short lines, all handwritten, the writing very beautiful. He looked at several pieces but didn't understand any of them very well. Then he happened to turn to a volume which contained a loose sheet of patterned writing paper on which were written four poems in lines of four characters. He thought of copying them down, so he said to Yü Ku, "I should like to copy this sheet. May I?" Yü Ku took it, looked at it and said, "If you like it, you may have it."

Tzu-p'ing took it back and looked more closely. The writing said:

The Riddle of the Silver Rat

First Clue:

> Eastern mountain, suckling tiger,
> Lies in wait at *men* and *hu;*
> A year from now devours the roebuck,
> Sorrow comes to Ch'i and Lu.

Second Clue:

> Dry bones in wolfish disorder,
> Suckling tiger unappeased;
> Flies aloft to visit heaven,
> Where a swine rules at ease.

Third Clue:

> Suckling tiger brindled over,
> Tyrannizes Western Hill;
> Father Adam's sons and grandsons,
> Persecutes and wastes at will.

Fourth Clue:

> Neighbors four are stirred to anger,
> Heavenly house takes flight to west;
> Violent death for swine and tiger,
> Black-haired people live at rest. [12]

Tzu-p'ing read it again and again, then said, "These verses are like an ancient folk song; they must contain references to current events. Please explain." Yellow Dragon replied, "Since it is called 'Sayings of an Insider,' it is obviously not intended for outsiders. If you will wait patiently for a number of years, you will be able to understand perfectly." Yü Ku said, "The suckling tiger of course is that Prefect Yü of yours. If you will think it out carefully you will be able to understand the rest."

Tzu-p'ing took the hint and did not ask any more questions. And now they heard the sound of laughter and talking in the distance. After a while there was the sound of many footsteps on the zigzag gallery, *ke-teng, ke-teng*. A few seconds later the footsteps reached the door. The graybeard first came in and said, "The Sang sisters have come." Yellow Dragon and Yü Ku both went out to meet them. Tzu-p'ing also got up and straightened himself. He saw that the one in front was about twenty years old, wearing a patterned jacket, purple with yellow flowers, and a skirt of swallow-tail blue, her hair swept up into a big coil but hanging down in a falling-from-horse style.[13] The one behind was about thirteen or fourteen and wore a kingfisher-blue jacket and red trousers with a white design. Her hair was tied in a knot on the top of her head and adorned with an ornament made of kingfisher feathers in the shape of a spearhead leaf,[14] which trembled and swayed at every step. They came in and were invited to sit down.

Yü Ku introducing them first said, "This is the younger brother of the Honorable Mr. Shen, magistrate of Ch'engwuhsien. He could not reach the inn at the market town today and accepted lodging here. Uncle Dragon happened to come, and we have had a splendid evening talking together. Mr. Shen wants to hear the harp, so we have ventured to trouble you too. It is really criminal to have disturbed your sweet slumbers."

The two answered in chorus, "You are too polite. But rustic music is an imposition on the ears of a gentleman!" Yellow Dragon said, "Now don't be overmodest!"

Yü Ku pointed to the older one, wearing purple clothes, and said to Tzu-p'ing, "This is my older 'sister,' Hu Ku." Then she pointed to the younger one, wearing kingfisher blue, and said, "This is my younger 'sister,' Sheng Ku. They are our nearest neighbors. We are very close friends."

Tzu-p'ing made one or two polite remarks, then looked at Hu Ku, and saw she had full, round cheeks, long eyebrows, eyes like the fruit of the ginko, a mouth set off by two dimples, red lips, white teeth, and with all of her beauty an air of nobility. Sheng Ku was quietly graceful, refined and attractive, with fresh, lively eyes and brows. The grayhead came forward, took up the bottle of water and filled the teapot, put fresh water in the bottle, and went out. Yü Ku picked up two cups and offered tea to both of them. Yellow Dragon said, "It's not very early, let's begin, please."

Yü Ku then took up the harp and handed it to Hu Ku. Hu Ku would not take it and said, "I can't play the harp as well as 'sister' Yü. I've brought a horn and my sister Sheng has brought her bells. It's much better for 'sister' Yü to play the harp. I'll blow my horn and my sister Sheng will ring her bells. That will be wonderful, won't it?" Yellow Dragon said, "Splendid! Splendid! That will be fine." Hu Ku again said, "But then what is Uncle Dragon going to do?" Dragon said, "I'm going to listen." Hu Ku said, "Aren't you ashamed of yourself! Why should we want you to listen? 'Dragon groans; tiger roars,' so you must groan!"

Yellow Dragon replied, "Water dragons may be able to groan, but I am a field dragon. I can only hide myself and do nothing." [15] "I have it!" Yü Ku said. She put down the harp, ran to the table against the wall, picked up a peculiar set of musical stones and put them down in front of Yellow Dragon, saying, "Then you can both roar and strike the musical stones and help us to keep the rhythm."

Hu Ku took from inside her jacket a horn that shone like a piece of polished black jade, and began to blow it slowly. There was a mouth-piece on it, and at the side were six or seven small holes. You could stop and open these with your fingers and make the various notes, *kung, shang, chih, yü*, unlike the conch horns that the military patrols use, which can only make one sound, *wu-wu*. This horn produced a deep rhythmic sound, very sad and strong.

By this time Yü Ku had lifted the harp to her knee and tuned the strings and was listening to the rhythm of the horn. Sheng Ku took out her little bells, and holding four in her left hand and three in her right, watched Hu Ku very closely. As soon as she saw Hu Ku about to finish the introduction on her horn, Sheng Ku lifted her two hands with the seven bells and shook them with abandon, *shang-shang*.

When the bells had started, Yü Ku lifted up the harp and began to play, *ts'ang-ts'ang, liang-liang*, quickly plucking the strings and slowly pulling at them, now tapping them lightly, now merely brushing them. The bells then stopped but the harp went on intermittently, *ting-tung*, in harmony with the horn which was like a fierce wind driving the sand before it, enough to shake the very tiles of the house. The seven bells then sounded again, not together, but at irregular intervals, though always ringing at the right time.

And now Yellow Dragon leaned on the table and looking up to heaven pursed his lips, and began to roar in concord. With that the sounds of voice, horn, strings, and bells, became indistinguishable, but the ear heard the sounds of wind and water, of men tramping and horses stamping, of banners flapping, of halberds clashing, and gongs and drums sounding the charge.

After about half an hour Yellow Dragon took up his mallet and struck the musical stones wildly, *k'eng-k'eng*, *ch'iang-ch'iang*, but all the sounds in tune and in harmony with the other instruments, filling the empty spaces and stepping in the gaps. Then the harp gradually sounded less frequently, the sound of the horn grew lower, and only the clear tinkling of the musical stones, *cheng-tsung*, had not yet died down.

A brief pause and Sheng Ku got up, stretched out her two hands, rang her bells wildly, and all the instruments ceased playing. Tzup'ing rose, raised his clasped hands and said, "You must be tired out, all of you. I am too grateful for words!" They all said, "Please don't laugh at us." Tzu-p'ing said, "Won't you tell me the name of this piece? Why are there so many sounds of fighting and killing in it?" Yellow Dragon answered, "The piece is called *The Melody of the Withered Mulberry Tree;* another name is *The Song of Tartar Horses Neighing in the Wind.* It is a battle song. None of the tunes played on the harp have a peaceful sound; most of them arouse feelings that are melancholy and desolate, but heroic. The more stirring ones have the power to make men weep."

While they were talking, each put his instrument back in its original place and sat down again. Hu Ku said to Yü Ku, "How is it that your sister Fan hasn't come home for such a long time?" Yü Ku answered, "My elder sister hasn't been able to come because for more than two months my nephew has not been well." Sheng Ku asked, "What illness does your little nephew have? Didn't they treat it right away?" "Of course they did!" Yü Ku said. "But children are so mischievous. When they get well, they immediately eat anything and everything, and then the illness breaks out again. He has had two attacks. Of course they looked after him!" They went on gossiping and then the guests rose to say good night. Tzu-p'ing got up also and said to Yellow Dragon, "Let us go back into the house too. It must be about the middle of *tzu* [midnight]. Surely Yü Ku wants to sleep."

With this they all left the cave and went along the zigzag gallery. Now the moon was no longer on the windows. Outside, the upper half of the cliff shone bright like pure snow, but the lower half was already raven black. It was a moon of the thirteenth day of the month, and it was already well down in the west. Arrived at the east room, Yü Ku said, "Won't you two wait here while I see Hu and Sheng out?" When they reached the main hall, Hu and Sheng said, "You don't need to see us any farther; we brought a grayhead along with us. He is out in front." You could hear them murmuring, *yü-yü nung-nung*, for a long time, and then Yü Ku returned. Yellow Dragon said, "You go back to your chamber. I'll sit here a little longer." Yü Ku then took her leave and went back to her cave, saying, "Mr. Shen, you will sleep on this couch. I will leave you now."

When Yü Ku had gone, Yellow Dragon said, "Liu Jen-fu is certainly a fine man, but his weakness lies in his being too sincere. In this mountain district he can get along all right; in the city I'm afraid he can't last long. You can expect to have him there for about one year. After this one year there will be changes in the political situation." Tzu-p'ing asked, "What is going to happen a year from now?" The reply was, "There will be a minor disturbance. Five years later a wave of political activity will gradually rise. Ten years later the situation will be completely changed." Tzu-p'ing asked, "Will it be for good or bad?" and the reply was, "Of course for the bad, but bad is good, good is bad, isn't it? Without bad nothing is good, without good nothing is bad."

"I simply don't understand this kind of talk," said Tzu-p'ing. "Surely good is good and bad is bad. Do you really mean that there is no difference between good and bad? I must ask you to explain what you mean in simple language. When a stupid person like me finds people reading in the Buddhist classics such illogical jargon as 'Form is emptiness; emptiness is form,' [16] it makes me dizzy in the head. Talking with you this evening, I felt as though all clouds had been driven away and I could see the blue sky. I didn't expect you would come out with this sort of unintelligible talk. It is enough to drive a man to distraction."

Yellow Dragon said, "I should like to ask you something. On the fifteenth of the month the moon is bright; on the thirtieth it is dark. At the first and third quarters, it is half bright, half dark. About the third and the fourth day of the month it is only a crescent. Please tell me how it manages gradually to become full, and after the fifteenth how it gradually rots away." Tzu-p'ing said, "This is easy to understand. The moon itself has no light, but receives light from the sun. So the half facing the sun is bright; the half away from the sun is in shadow. About the third and fourth the body of the moon slants toward the sun, so that the human eye sees only three parts bright, seven parts dark—and it looks like a crescent. In fact the moon itself doesn't change at all. The half-bright, half-dark phases, the waxing and the waning—all are due to illusions of the eye and have no connection whatsoever with the moon itself."

Yellow Dragon said, "Since you understand this principle, you ought to know that the principle of good being bad and bad being good is the same as that of the moon's brightness and darkness." Tzu-p'ing replied, "These things are certainly not identical. Although the moon doesn't become any less round, there is a real difference between brightness and darkness. There is always a bright half and a dark half, and so when the bright half is facing a man, the man naturally says the moon is round; when the dark half is facing a man, he says that the moon has become black. On the eighth and the twenty-third we look at it sideways and take it to be half bright and half dark; this is what we call the first and third quarters of the moon. Because what is seen by the eye varies, it is interpreted as the waxing and the waning. If a man could fly to the moon on the twenty-eighth or twenty-ninth, when it is all black, of course he would find it to be bright. This then is the principle of brightness and darkness. Everybody understands it. So that half-bright, half-dark is an unalterable principle. There is always a bright half; there is always a dark half. There is no way of proving by reason that darkness is brightness and brightness is darkness."

He was just feeling very satisfied with what he was saying when he heard somebody behind him say, "Mr. Shen, you are wrong."

To know who this was, hear the next chapter tell.

CHAPTER 11

A plague rat carrying calamity becomes a panic-making horse;

A mad dog spreading disaster develops into a poisonous dragon.

IT HAS been told that Shen Tzu-p'ing was disputing with Yellow Dragon when suddenly he heard someone behind his back say, "Mr. Shen, you are wrong." When he turned his head, he found it was none other than Yü Ku, who had changed her dress and was wearing a patterned cloth jacket and tight-fitting trousers which revealed her six-inch "gold lotuses" in a pair of slippers with *ling-chih* toecaps.[1] She looked more intelligent and beautiful than ever; her two eyes, black against white in strong contrast, were crystal clear.

Shen Tzu-p'ing got up quickly and said, "Yü Ku, you haven't gone to bed?" Yü Ku said, "At first I was going to bed, but I heard you two talking cheerfully, so I have come back to hear your discussion and learn something." Tzu-p'ing said, "How could I dare to dispute! I'm a stupid and rough fellow—can't understand anything easily—so I am bothering Mr. Yellow Dragon to instruct me. Just now you said I was wrong. Please enlighten me a little."

Yü Ku said, "It is not that you lack understanding, but that you have not thought much. Most people listen to what others say and then believe it. They don't use their own intelligence. Just now you said that the bright half of the moon is always bright. Now just consider the moon in the sky. Does it move or doesn't it? Everybody knows that the moon goes around the earth. If you know it goes around the earth, it is clearly evident that it cannot help moving or turning. And if the moon turns, how can the side which faces the sun at one time always be bright? Since the whole body of the moon is of the same substance, you can see that no matter how far round it turns, every part that faces the sun must be bright. From this you can see that no matter whether it is bright or dark, the actual substance of the moon neither increases nor decreases in the slightest; nor does it grow or decay. These principles are really very easy to understand; but the post-Sung disciples of the Three Teachings have stuffed into their commentaries a whole lot of ideas which deceive them and others. They have taken the essential ideas of the sages of the Three Teachings and glossed them crooked! For this reason heaven will send down strange disasters. The Boxers in the north and revolution in the south will strike out as at one stroke of the pen the sages of all the dynasties. This is perfectly natural too; there is nothing to be surprised at in it. No life, no death; no death, no life; where life, there death; where death, there life; how can there be a shred of doubt about this?"

"Just now I had two parts understood the principle of the brightness and darkness of the moon," Shen Tzu-p'ing said, "and now with your talking like this I am 'back in the paste pot' again! But I no longer expect to understand about the moon, so will you two please explain a little about the gradual rise of 'wind and wave' five years from now, and the great changes that will occur in ten years' time?"

Yellow Dragon said, "I suppose you know, Sir, about the doctrine of the three cycles of sixty years? [2] *Chia-Tzu* [1864], the third year of T'ung Chih,[3] was the first year of the first of three cycles. You must be aware of this, Sir?" Tzu-p'ing answered with a "Yes."

Yellow Dragon further said, "This cycle [the first of a new series of three] is different from the previous three cycles. This one is called a 'Pivotal Cycle.' Within sixty years this cycle will cause all former things to be completely changed. The thirteenth year of T'ung Chih, *Chia-Hsü* [1874], was the first change; the tenth year of Kuang Hsü, *Chia-Shen* [1884], was the second change; *Chia-Wu* [1894] was the third change; *Chia-Ch'en* [1904] will be the fourth; *Chia-Yin* [1914] the fifth. After these five changes everything will have been settled. If a man born in the *Chia-Yin* year of Hsien Feng [1854] lives to be eighty, he will have seen with his own eyes all changes of the six decades—a most interesting thing."

Tzu-p'ing said, "I suppose I have seen all the changes under the earlier three *Chia*. I suppose the death of the Emperor Mu Tsung I in *Chia-Hsü* [1874] was one important change. The French war in Fukien and Annam in *Chia-Shen* [1884] was another change.[4] The Japanese invading our Three Eastern Provinces in *Chia-Wu* [1894], and the Russians and Germans coming forward to mediate, taking 'the fisherman's profit,'[5] this was still another great change. I already know all this. Won't you tell me what the changes in the next three decades are going to be?"

Yellow Dragon said, "They will be just as I have said: Boxers in the north, revolution in the south. Preparations for the Boxer outbreak in the north began in *Wu-Tzu* [1888] and were already mature by *Chia-Wu* [1894]. In *Keng-Tzu* [1900] *Tzu* [Rat] and *Wu* [Horse] will clash with a great explosion.[6] Their rise will be sudden, their fall equally abrupt. They are 'the political force in the north.'[7] Those who believe in them will range from dwellers in the palace[8] to generals and ministers.[9] Their policy will be to suppress the Chinese. Preparations for the southern revolution, begun in *Wu-Hsü* [1898], will mature by *Chia-Ch'en* [1904]. In *Keng-Hsü* [1910], *Ch'en* [Dragon] and *Hsü* [Dog] will clash with a great explosion. Their rise will be gradual, their decline equally unnoticed. They are 'the political force in the south.'[10] Those who believe in them will range from the literati up to generals and ministers. Their policy will be to expel the Manchus. These two rebellious parties will both brew disaster, but together they will open up a new era. The Boxers in the north will gradually make inevitable the political changes of *Chia-Yin* [1914]. After *Chia-Yin* there will be great cultural developments. Chinese and foreign suspicions, Manchu and Han distrust will all be dissipated. The words of Wei the Taoist in his *Ts'an T'ung Ch'i*, 'In the beginning of the year the shoots sprout forth,'[11] refer to *Chia-Ch'en* [1904].[12] *Ch'en* is subject to earth. All vegetation grows on earth. Therefore, after *Chia-Ch'en* there will be a sprouting of cultural shoots, like 'a tree seedling bursting through the husk of a seed,'[13] like a bamboo shoot splitting a way through its sheath. All that the eye can see is tree seed and bamboo sheath, but the real living buds are concealed within. During the next ten years sheath and husk will gradually break, and by *Chia-Yin* [1914] the new life will be fully developed. *Yin* is subject to vegetable life and is a symbol of blossom. After *Chia-Yin* will be a time of cultural florescence, but although brilliant to look upon, still it will not equal the development of other countries. *Chia-Tzu* [1924] will be a time of a real independent cultural harvest. After that the introduction of new culture from Europe will revivify our ancient culture of the Three Rulers and Five Emperors,[14] and very rapidly we shall achieve a universal culture. But these things are still far off, not less than thirty or fifty years."

Tzu-p'ing listened with great delight and became most excited. Then again he asked, "What after all is the reason for the existence of such people as these northern Boxers and southern revolutionaries? Why does Heaven give birth to such people? You, Sir, are a man who understands the reasons of things. Won't you enlighten me, for I have never been able to understand this. Heaven's nature is to prosper life. If Heaven favors life and is also the ruler of the world, why then does Heaven give birth to such wicked men? Isn't there a common saying about 'blindly causing mischief'?"

Yellow Dragon inclined his head, and sighed. He was silent and spoke not a word. A short pause and he asked Tzu-p'ing, "You surely do not think that Shang Ti [Heaven or God] is a deity without equal?" Tzu-p'ing answered, "Of course he is." Yellow Dragon shook his head and said, "There is another August One more powerful than Shang Ti!"

Tzu-p'ing, greatly surprised, said, "This is most astonishing! Never since the time when there were books have we in China heard of anyone higher than Shang Ti, and in no country of the whole world has anyone ever said that there is any such deity above Shang Ti. This is indeed something that I have never heard before!"

Yellow Dragon said, "Have you never read in the Buddhist classics about the war between the Prince Ah Hsiu Lo [Prince of the Devils] [15] and Shang Ti?" "Of course I know about that," Tzu-p'ing said, "but I certainly don't believe it."

Yellow Dragon continued, "Not only do the Buddhist classics talk about this, but even the theologians of the Western countries know that there is a Prince of the Devils. There isn't the slightest doubt about it. You must know that every so many years Ah Hsiu Lo fights with Shang Ti, but always Ah Hsui Lo is defeated. After another period of years they fight again. I should like to ask why, when Ah Hsiu Lo is defeated, Shang Ti doesn't destroy him completely instead of letting him come again after a period of years to do harm to mankind? Not to have known he would harm mankind would be ignorance; to have known he would harm man and not to destroy him would be malevolence. How can Shang Ti be malevolent and ignorant? It is evident that Shang Ti's power is unable to destroy him: a moment's thought and you realize this. If two states fight together and one is victor and the other vanquished, yet the victor state can neither destroy the other, nor acquire it as a colony, isn't it clear that the two states are still equals even though a victory is won? So it is with Ah Hsiu Lo and Shang Ti. Since he can neither destroy him nor conquer him and make him obey his orders alone, Ah Hsiu Lo and Shang Ti are like equal states. Moreover neither Shang Ti nor Ah Hsiu Lo can escape from the sphere of the August One. So we must recognize that the rank of this August One is indeed above Shang Ti."

Tzu-p'ing quickly said, "I have never heard of this! Please tell me what the real name of this August One is." "His real name is 'Force Supreme,' " Yellow Dragon answered. "Even Shang Ti cannot disobey the authority of Force. I will give you an illustration. It is the virtue of Heaven above to prosper life. In the passage from winter to spring, from spring to summer, from summer to autumn, the power of High Heaven to prosper life is used to the full. Just imagine. If at that time of summer when trees, plants, and insects are all most abundant, life should go on multiplying according to the good nature of that old gentleman, in less than a year this earth would be unable to hold it all. Where would you go to find a patch of empty ground in which to put the surplus? For this reason frost and snow, cold and wind are allowed to appear and use all their strength to kill off the surplus life. Then High Heaven is allowed to come and show his love for life again. Now frost and snow, cold and wind, are the subordinates of Ah Hsiu Lo. The whole process of creating and killing is the activity of 'Force Supreme.' This is only a rough and superficial illustration and not very accurate. To get at the essence of the idea a day and a night would be insufficient."

Yü Ku listened and then said, "Uncle Dragon, how is it that you have launched into this extraordinary discussion today? Not only has Mr. Shen never heard all this, but even I have never heard it. After all is there really a 'Force Supreme'? Or is it a fable invented by Uncle Dragon?" Yellow Dragon said, "Well, now, do you agree that Shang Ti exists? If Shang Ti exists, then there certainly must be a 'Force Supreme.' You must know that Shang Ti and Ah Hsiu Lo are personifications of 'Force Supreme.' " Yü Ku clapped her hands and laughed aloud, saying, "I have it! 'Force Supreme' is simply the Confucian *Wu-Chi* [The Boundless].[16] Shang Ti and Ah Hsiu Lo put together are simply the *T'ai-Chi* [The Great Ultimate]. Am I right?" Yellow Dragon said, "Quite right. Quite right." Shen Tzu-p'ing also got up, very happy, saying, "Put in this way by Yü Ku, even I understand."

"Not so fast!" Yellow Dragon cautioned. "You may be right, but when you put it like this, don't you make Shang Ti and Ah Hsiu Lo into fables of the theologians? If they are fables, then they are not as satisfactory terms as *Wu-Chi* and *T'ai-Chi*. But you must know that these persons, Shang Ti and Ah Hsiu Lo, really exist; these things really are. So let me tell you about it in more detail. If you don't understand these principles, you can't possibly understand the ultimate source of the northern Boxers and the southern revolutionaries. And if you do understand, perhaps in the future Mr. Shen will not be ensnared by these two evils! Even Yü Ku's knowledge of the doctrine is shallow, and she must listen carefully.

"I will first explain how this 'Force Supreme' holds sway in the sun. The planets which travel around the sun all depend upon the sun as their controlling power. From this we know that all things in the sun's field of force are affected alike, quite impartially. Further, since there is contact between this power of attraction wherever it reaches and the responsive power of these places reached, many kinds of changes are produced—more than can be told. Therefore none of the books by the theologians are as good as the Confucian *Book of Changes* which is most profound. The *Book of Changes* is specially devoted to the *yao hsiang* [emblems].[17] Why are they called *yao hsiang?* Now just look at this *yao* character." Here he used his finger to draw on the table saying, "A downward stroke to the left, a cross stroke; this makes one intersection. Again a stroke and a cross stroke—another intersection. All things and the principles of all things above and below Heaven are fully present in these two intersections. The upper intersection is *cheng* [normal, even, rational], the second is *pien* [abnormal, odd, irrational]. An even and an odd multiplied and divided together have no end to them. This doctrine is infinitely subtle. The mathematicians show a rudimentary understanding of it when they say that similar terms multiplied together make a *cheng* [even, positive quantity], while dissimilar terms multiplied together make a *fu* [surd, negative quantity]. Whether you add, subtract, multiply or divide, whatever process you follow, you can never escape the sphere of *cheng* [positive] and *fu* [negative]. Thus it was said of Chi Wen-tzu, 'He used to think thrice and then acted.' Confucius said, 'Twice is enough'—only a twice not a thrice.[18]

"But enough of this talk. I will now proceed to discourse on the northern Boxers and southern revolutionaries. These Boxers are like a man's fist. He strikes, and if he succeeds, he succeeds; if he doesn't succeed, he stops, and nothing serious happens. Of course, a blow well delivered can end an opponent's life, but if he escapes, then nothing more happens. That blow of the northern Boxers will go near to smashing the country and will be very terrifying. Yet, since it will be only a single blow the country will get over it easily. Then there is the revolution (*ke*). The character *ke* means a hide, like a horse's hide or ox's hide. It covers the body from head to foot. However don't think that what we are talking about is merely a mild disease of the skin, for you must know that if eruptions appear all over the body, they can be fatal. The one good thing about it is that such a disease proceeds slowly and if you take pains to cure it, it doesn't cause serious harm. Now this character *ke* can be traced back to one of the hexagrams of the *Book of Changes*,[19] and therefore must not be neglected. Fear and avoid revolution, both of you! If you get drawn into that party, later you will rot away with them and lose your life!

"I will now say something about the *tse huo ke* hexagram [the water and fire hexagram of change and revolution, *ke*]. First take the character *tse* (water). Mountains and water communicate with each other. Water (*tse*) therefore means a mountain stream. There is water in a mountain stream, isn't there? Now the *Kuan Tzu* says, 'If rain water (*tse*) sinks in a foot, plants will rise up a foot.'[20] Also a common saying is 'The stream (*tse*) of mercy descends to the people.' Isn't it quite clear from all this that the character *tse* is a character with good implications? Why then should the *tse huo* hexagram be an inauspicious hexagram? Mustn't there be an auspicious water and fire hexagram of completion hidden there? Isn't it exasperating?

"If you want to know the difference between these two hexagrams you must find it in the distinction of *Yin* and *Yang* [the male and female principles]. The *k'an* water [trigram] is male water, and therefore produces a *shui huo chi-chi* hexagram [water and fire of completion, *chi-chi*]—an auspicious hexagram. The *tui* [trigram] is female water, and therefore makes a *tse huo ke* [water and fire of change and revolution, *ke*]—an inauspicious hexagram. The male virtue of *k'an* water arises from a compassionate heaven pitying the people, and therefore produces an emblem of completion. The female virtue of *tui* water arises from frustration and jealousy and therefore produces an emblem of change.

"Just look! In the *Treatise on the Definitions* [21] it says, 'The *tse huo ke* [water and fire of change] is like "two women living together, whose wills do not harmonize." ' Now if a man's family contains a wife and a concubine who are jealous of each other, how can that family prosper? It all comes from their both wanting to monopolize one husband. When they can't do this, the spirit of destruction is loosed. Because they love the husband, they fight. When they have once begun to fight, they don't mind if they harm the husband. Continuing to fight, they don't care if they destroy the husband's household. Again continuing to fight, they don't mind if they end their own lives. This is the nature of a jealous woman. The Sage simply uses these two phrases, 'two women living together, whose wills do not harmonize' to show forth the wretched character of the leaders of the southern revolution. He shows them much clearer than a photograph could.

"The southern revolutionary leaders will all be official and commercial people; they will all be clever men who have risen above their fellows. But being in the grip of a female-water nature like that of a jealous woman, they will only consider themselves and not consider others; for this reason they will not make their way very successfully in the world. Frustration gives birth to jealousy; jealousy gives birth to general destruction. Can this destruction be brought about by one man alone? No! but men of the same kind always seek each other out. Water goes where it is wet, fire goes where it is dry. Gradually they will flock together more and more, drag in the dissolute youth and finally burst into action like a 'military display.' [22] Those who have already attained the rank of *Chü-Jen, Chin-Shih*, Member of the Hanlin Academy,[23] or President of a Board will begin to talk about a dynastic revolution. Those who are unable to read and have no occupation will learn a little A, B, C, D, E or ah, ee, oo, e, oh [24] and then talk about a revolution in the family. If you claim to believe in revolution you don't need to submit to the control of justice, national law, or social custom. What a great satisfaction that is! You must know that to be too satisfied is not a good thing. To eat to satisfaction is to be surfeited. To drink to satisfaction is to be cloyed. The men of today do not follow justice, do not fear national law, do not keep to social custom, but act without restraint. This sort of indulgence is bound to result either in disaster caused by men or calamity caused by devils. How long will it last?"

Yü Ku said, "I have often heard my father say the Jade Emperor [25] has lost his power and Ah Hsiu Lo occupies the throne. If so, are northern Boxers and southern revolutionaries all due to evil agents and devils under the command of Ah Hsiu Lo?" Yellow Dragon said, "Of course they are! What sages or Buddhist Holy Ones would do these things?"

"But how can Shang Ti lose his authority?" Tzu-p'ing asked, and Yellow Dragon answered, "The expression 'lose authority' is used, but actually it is only 'yield authority.' Even the expression 'yield authority' is misleading. To speak truly you can only call it 'conceal authority.' Take for example the slaughter that occurs in fall and winter. Surely it is not real slaughter? It is merely a holding back of the breath of life, saving up a little strength to make the next year's growth. The Taoist writer says: 'Heaven and Earth are ruthless; to them the Ten Thousand Things are but as straw dogs. The sage too is ruthless; to him the people are but as straw dogs.' [26] And again: 'If a man sleeps under used straw dogs, he will certainly have a nightmare.' [27] All the things that grow up in spring and summer, by fall and winter become 'used straw dogs' and are only worth being discarded. I therefore said this was the activity of 'Force Supreme.' From the Thirty-three Heavens above to the Seventy-two Earths below,[28] among mortals and immortals there are only two parties. One party preaches the common good: they are the sages and Buddhist Holy Ones, subject to Shang Ti. The other party preaches private interest: they are evil spirits and devils, subject to Ah Hsiu Lo."

Shen Tzu-p'ing was puzzled. "Since the southern revolution destroys heavenly justice, national law, and social custom, how is it there are still people who believe in it?" Yellow Dragon replied, "Do you consider that heavenly justice, national law, and social custom will only be destroyed at the time of the southern revolution? They were overthrown long ago! The *Journey to the West* is really a sort of sermon, every page an allegory. It says that the king who was on the throne in the Black Chicken Country [29] was a false king. The true king was imprisoned in the Octagonal Glazed Well. Thus the truth, law, and custom of today are the false king on the throne in the Golden Imperial Hall of the Black Chicken Country, so that the strength of the southern revolution must be used to kill the false king. Then the true king can be rescued from the Octagonal Glazed Well. When true justice, law, and custom appear, the whole empire will enjoy peace."

Tzu-p'ing further asked, "What sort of a distinction is this between true and false?" Yellow Dragon said, "In the *Journey to the West* it says, 'Tell the Crown Prince to ask the Queen Mother—then you will know!' The Queen Mother said, 'Three years ago it was mild and warm. Three years from now it will be cold as ice.' 'Cold' and 'warm' here simply represent true and false. Those who consider the common good are of one heart in loving other men and therefore breathe out warmth. Those who teach private interest are of one mind in hating other men, and they breathe out coldness.

"There is another secret I want to tell you about in some detail. Please remember it well so that when the time comes you won't be drawn into the Boxer and revolutionary conflagration. The Boxers will use belief in spirits.[30] The revolutionaries use disbelief in spirits. If you say there are spirits, you can pretend to be spirits yourselves, practice magic, and mislead simple rustic fools. This is the value of teaching people to believe in spirits. If you say there are no spirits, the uses of it are even greater. First, if there are no spirits, then you don't need to respect your ancestors: this is the prime source of revolution in the family. If you say there are no spirits, then there is no retribution from Hell, no punishment from Heaven, and you can act in any way, defying Heaven's laws, and so arouse the unholy joy of dissolute youths. They will live in concessions or foreign countries in order to practice their illegal acts; they will abuse those who say there are spirits in order to practice their blasphemous tricks. They will say that rebels and traitors are noble heroes and that loyal and good officials have a slavelike nature. In these several ways they will practice their tricks against morality. Most of them are eloquent and embroider everything they say. Like those jealous women who destroy the whole house, they preach what seems like a reasonable sounding doctrine, but anyone can see that the house will be destroyed by them. In short, the arguments of the southern revolutionaries have such surprisingly brilliant and attractive features that it is clear all morality will be twisted and destroyed by them.

"In conclusion, when these trouble-making factions are in Shanghai or in Japan they are easy to distinguish; but when they are in Peking, the provincial capitals, and other large cities, it is difficult to distinguish them. But remember carefully: those who ascribe things to spirits are northern Boxers; those who explain things without spirits are southern revolutionaries. If you meet these people, 'respect them but keep away from them' [31] and so avoid the danger of being killed. That is the important thing!"

When Tzu-p'ing had heard this, he was filled with the deepest admiration. Just as he was about to ask some more, he heard the morning cock already begin to crow outside the window. "It is very late," Yü Ku said. "We really must go to bed." Then she bade them good night, opened the door in the corner, and went out. Yellow Dragon gathered some books to make a pillow on the opposite couch. No sooner had he lain down than a snoring like thunder began. Shen Tzu-p'ing carefully went over the night's conversation in his mind a couple of times and then fell asleep.

If you want to know what happened afterwards, hear the next chapter tell.

CHAPTER 12

Winter wind freezes over Yellow River water;

Warm air inspires "White Snow Song."

THE STORY tells that when Shen Tzu-p'ing woke, the red sunlight was already filling the window, so he hurriedly got up. Yellow Dragon had already gone, he didn't know how long before. The old grayhead brought in hot water for him to wash with, and after a while brought some plates and bowls of food for his breakfast. Tzu-p'ing said, "Don't worry about me, but go and express my thanks to your young lady. I must get on the road."

As he was saying this, Yü Ku came out and said, "Didn't Uncle Dragon tell you last night? There's no use your going early. Liu Jen-fu will only get to the Temple of Kuan Ti by noon. If you don't go till you've had breakfast, you still won't be late."

Hearing this Tzu-p'ing had his breakfast and sat a while longer. He then took his leave of Yü Ku and hurried off to the market place. The market was thick with people. There were not many shops, but on both sides the ground was covered with things for sale—farm implements and things of every possible kind for everyday use in the country. Having inquired of some country people he soon found the Temple of Kuan Ti, where Liu Jen-fu had already arrived. They met, talked

128

a little about the weather, and then Tzu-p'ing took out Lao Ts'an's letter.

Jen-fu read it and then said, "I'm a rough fellow and don't understand the formalities of yamen life. Besides I have little ability, and I'm afraid I should only cause your honorable cousin to lose his reputation as a judge of men. All in all it is best for me not to go. I received a letter from brother T'ieh brought by second brother Chin, asking me to be sure to go, and expressing the fear that it would be difficult for you to go to Cypress Tree Valley where I live, and not easy to find the place; I have therefore come to meet you here to decline in person. I must ask you please to pass on my firm refusal. It's not that I am lazy or that I want to seem proud, but I'm really afraid I cannot undertake the responsibility and might mismanage your business for you. I sincerely beg your pardon." Tzu-p'ing said, "You don't need to be so modest. My cousin was afraid that nobody else would be able to persuade you and therefore sent me, his cousin, to give you a most sincere and respectful invitation."

Liu Jen-fu, seeing it was impossible to refuse, could but settle his private affairs and go back to Ch'engwu with Tzu-p'ing. Shen Tung-tsao did indeed treat him as a most honorable guest and in all other ways acted as Lao Ts'an had told him. At first there were still one or two cases of robbery, but after a month or so conditions were such that "at night no dog barked."

However, we won't say any more about that.

It is further told that Lao Ts'an started out from Tungch'angfu, planning to return to the provincial city. One day he came to the south gate of Ch'ihohsien and looked for an inn. Finding that every inn on the main street was full, he was greatly surprised and said to himself, "Surely there has never been as much commotion in this place before; what's the cause of it all?"

He was just standing there, wondering what to do, when a man came through the gate shouting, "All's well! All's well! It will soon be broken through. We'll probably be able to cross tomorrow morning."

Lao Ts'an had no time to ask what it meant, but found an innkeeper of whom he asked, "Do you have a room?" The innkeeper said, "We're full up. You'll have to go somewhere else." Lao Ts'an said, "I've already been to two places and neither of them have rooms. Can't you give me a makeshift? Never mind whether it's good or bad." The innkeeper said, "It's quite impossible for us to manage it. But a group of guests left the inn to the east of us this afternoon. If Your Honor will go there quickly, they may not be filled up."

Lao Ts'an then went to the inn to the east and asked the landlord. By good luck there was still a two-*chien* room empty, so he moved his baggage in. The inn boy ran in with some water for washing and brought a lighted stick of incense which he put on the table saying, "Will you smoke, Sir?"

Lao Ts'an asked, "Why is there so much stir in the town? All the inns are full." The inn boy answered, "A strong north wind has been blowing for several days, and for three days blocks of ice as big as a house have been floating down the river. The ferryboat didn't dare to cross, afraid of striking a piece of ice and getting damaged. Yesterday the upper bend of the river became packed tight, and while below the bend boats could have gone across, the ferryboats were all frozen solid in the ice at the edge of the river. Last night His Excellency, Prefect Li of Tungch'angfu arrived on his way to report to the Governor. When he reached this place and couldn't cross, he was very impatient. He stayed at the *hsien* yamen and had the river workers and local headmen break the ice. They have been breaking it all day today, and it looks as though they will get through. But they can't rest their hands during the night, for if they once stop it will freeze again. So you see, Sir, the inns are all full of people who can't get across the river. Our inn was full up this morning. But among one group of guests there was an old man who watched on the river bank for half a day and then said, 'They can't break through that ice. There's no sense in waiting here forever. Let's go on to Lok'ou and see what we can do there. We can make up our minds when we get there.' So at noon they started off in carts. You are really very fortunate, Sir! Otherwise there would be absolutely no rooms free!" Having said all this, the inn boy went out.

When Lao Ts'an had washed his face and arranged his baggage, he locked his room and walked out to the river dike to see what was happening. The Yellow River came from the southwest and, making a bend here, went due east. The bed of the river was not very wide, the two banks being not more than two li apart. Lao Ts'an saw piled up before him layers of packed ice which rose seven or eight inches above the surface. He wandered up the river a couple of hundred paces. The ice from above kept coming down block after block, until at this point it was caught by the ice in front, couldn't move, and came to a standstill. More ice came and pressed it with a rustling sound, *ch'ih-ch'ih,* until the ice behind, pressed harder by the flowing water, simply jumped on top of the ice in front. Pressed down in this way the ice in front gradually went under. The surface of the water was not more than a hundred chang wide. In the middle the main stream was not more than about twenty or thirty chang, and on both sides was smooth water. This smooth water had long before been frozen over completely and the surface of the ice was smooth but had been covered with dust by the wind so that it looked like a sandy desert. The main stream in the middle, however, continued to roar on with noise and power, pushing the packed ice so that it jumped away on both sides, until the ice on the smooth water was crushed by the pieces from the main stream and driven five or six feet up on the shore. Many broken pieces of ice were stood on end by the pressure, forming a low screen. Lao Ts'an watched it for about an hour, until the packed ice was wedged solid.

He wandered back down the river past the first place he had come to, and went on down to where there were two boats. On the boats ten or more men were breaking the ice with wooden clubs. They would break their way forward for a while, and then backward. On the opposite bank of the river were two boats breaking the ice in the same way. Seeing that night was falling, Lao Ts'an prepared to return to his inn. He then noticed that each willow tree on the dike cast a shadow of moving threads on the ground, for the moon was already shining brightly. Back at the inn, he opened his door, called the boy to come and light a lamp, and had his supper. Then he wandered out to the dike again.

By now the north wind had abated, but surprisingly enough the cold air was even more severe than the north wind had been. Luckily Lao Ts'an had long before this changed into the sheepskin gown presented to him by Shen Tung-tsao, so he was able to endure the cold. He found that the boats were still there breaking the ice. On each boat a small lantern had been lit, and in the distance he thought he could make out on one side "Magistrate's Boat" and on the other, "Ch'ihohsien"; this satisfied his curiosity. He raised his head and looked up at the hills to the south. The snow-white line reflected the light of the moon; it was extraordinarily beautiful. The mountain ranges rose tier on tier, but they could not be clearly distinguished. A few white clouds lay in the folds of the hills so that you could hardly tell cloud from hill unless you looked intently. The clouds were white, and the hills were white; the clouds were luminous, and the hills were luminous too. Yet because the moon was above the clouds and the clouds beneath the moon, the clouds were luminous with a light which had penetrated from behind. This was not true, however, of the hills; the light there flowed directly from the moon and was then reflected by the snow, so that the light was of two kinds. But only the nearer parts were like this. The hills stretched away to the east farther and farther until gradually the sky was white, the hills were white, and the clouds were white, and nothing could be distinguished from anything else.

Faced with this landscape where the brightness of snow and moon met, Lao Ts'an recalled the two lines of Hsieh Ling-yün's [1] poem:

> Clear moon lights up snow drifts;
> North wind strong and doleful.

If you haven't experienced the bitter cold of the north, you cannot know how well chosen the word "doleful" is, in the line: "North wind strong and doleful." By this time the moonlight was making the whole earth bright. Lao Ts'an looked up. Not one star appeared in the sky except for the seven stars of the Dipper which could be seen clearly, gleaming and twinkling like several pale points. The Dipper was resting slantwise on the west side of the "Imperial Enclosure," [2] the handle on top, the bowl below. He thought to himself, "Months and years pass like a stream; the eye sees the handle of the Dipper pointing to the east again; another year is added to man's life.[3] So year after year rolls along blindly. Where is an end to be found?" Then, remembering the words of the *Book of Odes,*

> In the North there is a Dipper
> But it cannot scoop wine or sauce,[4]

he mused, "Now indeed is a time when many things are happening to our country; the nobles and officials are only afraid of bringing punishment on themselves; they think it is better to do nothing than to risk doing something, and therefore everything is allowed to go to ruin. What will the final result be? If this is the state of the country how can an honest man devote himself to his family?" When he reached this point in his thinking, unconsciously the tears began to trickle down his face, and he had no heart left for the enjoyment of the scenery. He went slowly back to his inn. As he walked along, he felt that there was something sticking to his face. He touched it with his hand and felt on each cheek a strip of smooth ice. At first he couldn't understand it. Then he understood and smiled to himself. The tears he had just shed had immediately frozen solid in the cold air. There must have been many other "frozen pearls" on the ground. He returned to his inn feeling very melancholy and immediately went to bed.

The next morning he went to the dike again to see what was happening. He found that the two ice-breaking boats had been frozen solid near the bank of the river. He questioned some men on the dike and learned that they had worked half the night, that when they broke the ice in front it froze behind them, and when they broke the ice behind it froze in front of them, so that they were now resting their hands and would not do any more. No doubt they were waiting for the ice to freeze firm and strong so that people could walk over it. This being the case Lao Ts'an would have to wait too. Having nothing to do, he strolled into the city. There were only a few shops on the main street and the back streets had very few brick buildings. The whole town had a barren and deserted appearance, but since most places in the north are like this he was not greatly surprised. Back in his room he opened his case of books and pulled one out at random. He happened to take out a copy of the *Poetic Anthology of Eight Dynasties*. He remembered that it was given him by a Hunan man in the provincial capital as a token of thanks for curing a sickness. Busy in the city he had been unable to examine it closely and had slipped it into his box. Being free today, why shouldn't he look it over more carefully? It turned out to be in twenty volumes. The first two were poems in four-word lines; volumes three to eleven were five-word lines; twelve to fifteen were in "new style" verse; fifteen to seventeen were in lines of different lengths; volume eighteen was verses for music; nineteen was folk songs; volume twenty was miscellaneous compositions. As he looked over the detailed table of contents he saw that among the new-style verse selections were twenty-eight pieces by Hsieh T'iao and fourteen by Shen Yüeh, while among the old-style pieces were fifty-four by Hsieh T'iao and thirty-seven by Shen Yüeh.[5] He couldn't understand this at all, so he took out volumes ten and twelve together in order to compare them. He was unable to distinguish any difference between the new and old styles. He further thought, "These poems were selected by Wang K'ai-yün.[6] He had a great name at one time and his *History of the Hunan Army* was really well done. All who have eyes for a good book praised it. Why should he have made an anthology which is so unsatisfactory?" Then he remembered how Shen Kuei-yü's anthology, *The Spring of Ancient Poetry*,[7] throws together in a chaotic way folk songs and regular poems—a serious fault—and that Wang Yü-yang's *Anthology of Early Poems* [8] too is quite unsatisfactory. After all, Chang Han-feng's *Early Poems Reprinted* [9] is the most nearly satisfactory. However it was no use worrying about these questions—he merely used the chantings of these old poets to drive away his cares and boredom. After reading for quite a long time he returned to the inn door and stood there idly. He had been there some time and was about to go back when a servant wearing a hat with a red tassel came up to him and made a genuflection saying, "Mr. T'ieh, when did you come here?" Lao Ts'an answered, "I arrived yesterday." He said this with his mouth, but he couldn't bring to mind whose servant this was.

The servant saw Lao Ts'an's bewilderment and knew that he hadn't recognized him, so he laughed and said, "I am Huang Sheng. My master is the Honorable Mr. Huang Ying-t'u." Lao Ts'an said, "Oh! Of course! Of course! My memory is certainly bad. I have often been to your master's residence. How was it I didn't recognize you?" Huang Sheng said, "Your Honor is merely a case of 'the important man often forgets practical matters' that's all." Lao Ts'an laughed. "I am not an important person, but I do indeed often forget practical matters. When did your honorable master come here? Where is he staying? I was just feeling at a loose end. I'll go and have a chat with him." Huang Sheng said, "My master has been deputed by His Excellency Mr. Chang, the Comptroller, to buy eight million units of material [10] in this Ch'iho district. He has now bought all he needs. The inspector has also examined it and he was just planning to return to the provincial capital to report on his commission when the river got blocked up so that we have to wait a couple of days before we can go. Is Your Honor also staying in this inn? In which room?"

Lao Ts'an pointed to the west and said, "In that west room there." Huang Sheng said, "My master is staying in the main building on the north. He arrived the day before yesterday in the evening. Until then he was busy with his work, but now that the inspector has been and gone he has come to stay here. At this moment he is having lunch at the *hsien* yamen. After lunch, Mr. Li has asked him to go and have a chat. I still don't know whether he is coming back to dinner or not." Lao Ts'an nodded, and Huang Sheng went out.

Now this man's personal name was Huang Ying-t'u, his *hao* Jen-jui; he was more than thirty years of age, a Kiangsi man. His elder brother, a member of the Hanlin Academy,[11] had become an Imperial Censor and was very intimate with Ta-la-mi of the Grand Council of State. Huang Jen-jui was therefore able to buy the rank of subprefect and had come to Shantung to offer his services for the river conservancy. Receiving a letter from the Grand Council, the Governor treated him with special consideration. Shortly he was to be recommended to the Emperor at the general promotion for the office of prefect. However, he was not at all a bad person in himself. Lao Ts'an and he had had dealings together a great many times in the provincial capital, and so they knew each other.

Lao Ts'an again stood for a while at the door of the inn and then went to his room. It was almost dusk. When he reached his room, he read a volume of poems until he could no longer see and then lit a candle. Soon he heard someone come in and call out, "Mr. Pu! Mr. Pu! I haven't seen you for such a long time!"

Lao Ts'an hurriedly got up to see who it was; it proved to be Huang Jen-jui. They bowed to each other, sat down, and told each other what had been happening to them since they had parted. Huang Jen-jui said, "I hope Mr. Pu hasn't had dinner yet. Somebody sent me a chafing dish and several small dishes of food, but I was afraid it wouldn't be enough, so this morning I told the cook to stew a fat chicken with mushrooms. It should be enough to help the rice down. Please come to my room for dinner. The ancient writer says, 'Rare is it to meet an old friend in stormy weather.' The misery of this frozen river is harder to bear than a storm. But meeting with a good friend it is no longer lonely." Lao Ts'an said, "All right! All right! If the victuals are good, even if you hadn't invited me, I'd have come."

Jen-jui noticed the book on the table and idly picked it up to look at it. It was the *Poetic Anthology of Eight Dynasties*. He said, "On the whole this isn't a bad selection of poems." He glanced over a few pieces, then dropped it saying, "Let's go and sit in my room."

Then they both went out, Lao Ts'an first tidying his books a bit and locking the door, before following Jen-jui to the main building. It was a three-*chien* building, one inner *chien* and two *chien* without a partition between them. On the outer door of the middle section was hung a *lientzu* of woolen cloth stiffened with wooden strips. In the middle was placed a square table covered with oil cloth. Jen-jui asked, "Is the food ready?" The servant replied, "You must still wait a little while; the chicken is not quite tender yet," and so Jen-jui said, "Bring the cold dishes first and we'll drink some wine."

The servant obeyed. In a short time he returned to set the table, putting out four pairs of chopsticks and four wine cups. Lao Ts'an asked, "Who else is coming?" Jen-jui replied, "Wait a bit and you'll see."

When the wine cups and the chopsticks had been properly arranged, the servant found that there were only two chairs so he went out again to find more. Jen-jui said, "Let's sit on the *k'ang*." Now at the west end of the outer room there was an earthen *k'ang* covered with reed mats. Jen-jui had spread a tiger-pattern velvet rug in the middle of the *k'ang*, and placed a smoking tray on the rug and a wolfskin rug on each side of the tray. In the middle a T'aiku lamp was burning very brightly.

You ask what a T'aiku lamp is like? Since there are lots of wealthy men in Shansi and they all smoke opium, the smoking appliances there are much finer than in other provinces. T'aiku is the name of a district. The lamps made in this *hsien* are of a good shape and produce ample heat and plenty of light, so that they can be counted as the best in the five continents. It is unfortunate that they are produced in China. If they were produced in any European or American country, all the newspapers there would help the first maker of such lamps to become known, and the government would grant him a patent! Alas! This is not the rule in China; the first maker of T'aiku lamps and the first maker of Shouchou [12] pipe bowls produced things which have come to be used and known through the whole country, but the names of the men themselves are lost. You may not approve of how they employed their talents, but clearly it was the fault of the times that they achieved no fame by it.

However, let us leave this idle talk. In the smoking tray there were several blue cloisonné boxes and two Kwangtung bamboo opium pipes. It was flanked by cushions at each side. Jen-jui made Lao Ts'an take the upper seat, stretched himself out, took the opium *ch'ientzu*,[13] picked up some opium, and roasted it. "Mr. Pu, you still don't smoke?" he said. "Of course if you smoke this kind of stuff to the extent of wasting your time and neglecting your business for it, it is bad; but if you don't become an addict and simply pass the time with it, then it's an excellent thing. Why do you have to abstain so completely?" Lao Ts'an replied, "I have many friends who are smokers. Not one of them set out to become an addict. They all smoked to pass the time. But they passed the time so well that finally they passed into the clutches of the habit. And when it had become a habit, not only were they not contented merely to pass the time with it, but it became a serious handicap to them. From my point of view, my friend, you would do much better not to pass the time with it." Jen-jui replied, "I have a limit which I keep. I shall never be led astray."

As he spoke there was a rustling of the *lientzu* and two prostitutes came in. The first one was seventeen or eighteen years old with a duck-egg face; the second was fifteen or sixteen with a melon-seed face. Having entered the door they bowed toward the *k'ang*. Jen-jui said, "So you've come!" Pointing to the inner seat, he said, "This Mr. T'ieh is a friend of mine from the provincial capital. Ts'ui-huan, you shall wait on Mr. T'ieh, so go and sit over there." The seventeen- or eighteen-year-old one then sat next to Jen-jui on the edge of the *k'ang*, but the fifteen- or sixteen-year-old one remained standing, too embarrassed to sit down. Lao Ts'an therefore took off his shoes, moved to the inside of the *k'ang*, and sat cross-legged so that she would have room. She then sat down timidly on the very edge of the *k'ang*.

Lao Ts'an said to Jen-jui, "I was told there weren't any of these creatures here. How is it there are now?" Jen-jui said, "You're wrong. There still aren't any here. Until recently these two 'sisters' plied their trade at Twentymile Village near P'ingyüan. Their master and mistress belong to this town, but their mistress and the two of them have been living at Twentymile Village. Two months ago, however, their master died and their 'mother' came back here. She was afraid they might run away, so she brought them back, but they don't usually visit the inns here. Being in low spirits and with nothing to do, I had them called in. This one is Ts'ui-hua. That one of yours is Ts'ui-huan.[14] They both have snow-white skin—most desirable. Look at their hands. I guarantee you will be satisfied." Lao Ts'an laughed, "I don't need to look. How could anything you say be false?"

Ts'ui-hua, leaning against Jen-jui, said to Ts'ui-huan, "Roast some opium and give it to Mr. T'ieh." "Mr. T'ieh doesn't smoke," Jen-jui replied. "Tell her to light it and give it to me." Then he handed the opium *ch'ientzu* to Ts'ui-huan. Ts'ui-huan bent down, roasted a portion, put it in the bowl and handed it across. Jen-jui finished it in a few breaths. As Ts'ui-huan was roasting some more, the servingman brought in the cold dishes and the chafing dish and said, "Please take your wine, Gentlemen."

Jen-jui got up and said, "Let's drink. It's very cold today." Then he made Lao Ts'an take the upper seat, himself sat opposite, told Ts'ui-huan to sit at Lao Ts'an's left, Ts'ui-hua at his left. Ts'ui-hua took the winepot and filled the cups, put it down, and then lifted her chopsticks to put food in Lao Ts'an's plate. Lao Ts'an said, "Please don't bother. You don't need to serve me. We are not newly married brides; we can feed ourselves." Then Ts'ui-hua proceeded to serve Jen-jui while Jen-jui helped Ts'ui-huan to something with his chopsticks. Ts'ui-huan hastily got up and said, "Please don't." Again he prepared to put something on Ts'ui-hua's plate, but saying, "I can help myself," she received it in a spoon, carried it to her mouth, ate a little, and put it down.

Jen-jui repeatedly urged Ts'ui-huan to eat. Each time she said "Yes" but never actually took anything. Suddenly Jen-jui thought of something, rapped on the table and said, "I know what! I know what!" Then he shouted at the top of his voice, "Hey, there!" A servingman came from behind the *lientzu* and stood about six or seven feet from the table. Jen-jui nodded and told him to come a step nearer, then whispered a few words in his ear. The servant said repeatedly, "Very good, Sir," turned round, and went out.

After a while a man came in wearing a blue padded gown and holding two three-stringed banjos in his hand. He handed one to Ts'ui-hua and one to Ts'ui-huan, and muttered to Ts'ui-huan, "When they tell you to eat, wait on the gentlemen in everything."

Ts'ui-huan seemed not to have heard clearly and glanced up at the man. The fellow said, "You're to eat. Do you still not understand?" Ts'ui-huan nodded and said, "I understand." Immediately she gave Huang Jen-jui a piece of ham with her chopsticks, then picked up a piece and gave it to Lao Ts'an. Lao Ts'an said, "Please don't help me." Jen-jui raised his cup and said, "Let's empty a cup. The girls can sing a couple of songs while we drink."

As he spoke, they finished tuning up their strings and sang through a song. Jen-jui fished about with his chopsticks in the chafing dish for some time and decided there was nothing good in it. He said, "The things in this chafing dish all have distinguished names. Do you know them?" Lao Ts'an said, "No, I don't." Jen-jui then pointed with his chopstick, "This is called 'hair-so-angry-that-it-pushes-up-your-hat' [15] shark fins. This is 'unyielding' sea slug. This is 'virtuous-from-age' chicken. This is 'emaciated-by-dissipation' duck. This, 'refuse-arrest-by-force' pork. This 'official-with-a-heart-as-pure-as-water' soup."

When he had finished, they laughed loudly together. The two sisters then again sang two or three songs. The servingman carried in the chicken that he himself had stewed. "We've had quite enough wine," Lao Ts'an said. "Why not serve the rice while the food is hot?"

The servant immediately brought in four bowls of rice. Ts'ui-hua stood up, took the rice bowls, placed one in front of each person, and poured some chicken soup over them. Each ate his fill. After the meal they wiped their faces and Jen-jui said, "Let's sit on the *k'ang* again."

The servant came to remove the leftovers, and all four went to sit on the *k'ang*. Lao Ts'an leaned back in the upper place, Jen-jui in the lower. Ts'ui-hua leaned against Jen-jui to light his pipe. Ts'ui-huan sat on the edge of the *k'ang*. Having nothing to do she took a banjo and began to strum idly, *peng-erh, peng-erh*.

Jen-jui said, "Lao Ts'an, I haven't seen any of your poems for a long time. After all, today is a case of 'strange place, chance on old friend,' so you must write a poem, and we will read it." Lao Ts'an replied, "Looking at the frozen river these two days, I have wanted very much to write a poem. I was just getting my ideas in order when your invasion mixed my poem up with that 'emaciated-by-dissipation' duck of yours." Jen-jui said, "Now don't you 'refuse-arrest-by-force' or I shall be 'hair-and-hat-raising-angry.'" At this both laughed aloud, *ha-ha*.

Lao Ts'an said, "All right. All right. I'll write it tomorrow and show you." Jen-jui said, "That won't do. Look. Here on this wall is a piece of fresh plaster as big as a bushel measure, specially prepared for you to write poetry on." Lao Ts'an shook his head and said, "I leave it to you to write on." Jen-jui put down his pipe in the tray and said, "If you take things so easy, all your ideas will be gone from you. We can't await your pleasure." Then he got up, ran into his room, brought some brushes, an ink slab, and a block of ink, put them on the table and said, "Ts'ui-huan, you grind the ink." Ts'ui-huan poured out a little cold tea and ground the ink.

After a short time she said, "The ink is ready. Please write, Sir!" Jen-jui took a cloth duster and said, "Ts'ui-hua, take the candle. Ts'ui-huan, hold the ink slab. I'll dust the plaster." He put a brush into Lao Ts'an's hand. Ts'ui-hua lifted the candlestick. Jen-jui first jumped onto the *k'ang*, stood below the newly plastered portion and dusted it off. Ts'ui-hua and Ts'ui-huan both climbed onto the *k'ang* and stood to left and right. Jen-jui beckoned with his hand and said, "Come on! Come on!" Lao Ts'an laughed. "You certainly know how to make a nuisance of yourself!" He stood on the *k'ang*, dipped the brush into the ink on the slab, breathed on it, and began to write in sprawling characters on the wall. Ts'ui-huan, afraid that the ink on the slab would freeze, blew without stopping, but the brush still picked up bits of ice and the more Lao Ts'an wrote the thicker the tip became. He soon finished writing. The poem read:

> The earth cracks; the north wind howls;
> An ice sheet covers the river below.
> Ice behind pursues the ice before,
> Piling up and pressing down.
>
> The river bend jams solid;
> It forms a jagged silver bridge.
> The homeward-bound sigh long sighs,
> The traveler vainly groans and plains.
>
> Only a narrow strip of water,
> But a canopied carriage cannot cross;
> An elegant feast with girls and music
> Makes a riot of the bitter night.

When Jen-jui saw it he said, "A splendid poem! A splendid poem! Why don't you leave a signature?" Lao Ts'an said, "All right, I'll write Huang Jen-jui from south of the Yangtze." Jen-jui said, "That would be no laughing matter! It's hardly worth the risk of being degraded from office for cuddling courtesans and tippling wine merely to get the name of a poet."

Lao Ts'an then wrote "Pu-ts'an" and jumped down from the *k'ang*. The two sisters put down the ink slab and candlestick, and they all went to the brazier to toast their hands. Finding the ashes almost burned out, they added some fresh charcoal. Lao Ts'an stood beside the *k'ang*, bowed with clasped hands to Huang Jen-jui and said, "I have troubled you too much. Now I am going to my room to sleep." Jen-jui pulled him back, saying, "Don't be in such a hurry! Today I heard of a most amazing law case involving a great many lives. The circumstances are puzzling and very unusual, and I was just going to discuss it with you. I have to make a report on it tomorrow at dawn. Wait while I take two puffs of opium to raise my spirits, and I will tell you." Lao Ts'an could only sit down again.

If you don't know what sort of a law case it was, then hear the next chapter tell.

CHAPTER 13

Bright lamplight and a girl's sad story;

Vicious Yellow River water and a taot'ai's
*   ingenious plan.*

IT HAS been told that Lao Ts'an returned to his seat and stretched himself out, waiting while Huang Jen-jui took a few puffs of opium the better to tell his story of an amazing law case.

Ts'ui-huan by this time was much more at home, so she sat against Lao Ts'an's leg and asked, "Mr. T'ieh, where is your honorable home? What does this poem of yours say?"

Lao Ts'an told her in simple words. She thought it over gravely for a while and then said, "What it says is certainly very true! But is it proper to say this sort of thing in poetry?" Lao Ts'an replied, "If poetry is not good for saying this sort of thing, what should it say?"

Ts'ui-huan replied, "When I was at Twentymile Village I saw a great many passing guests, and many of them wrote poems on the wall. I used to enjoy very much asking them to explain their poems to me. Among the many I have heard explained, this is what they amounted to: the better-class men could never talk about anything but how great their own ability was and how the world didn't recognize them; as for the men of poorer class, they could never talk about anything but how attractive such and such a girl was and how much she loved them.

"How great the ability of those gentlemen really was we couldn't know; why is it that all these who come and go are men of ability and we never see a man without ability?

"I'll say something foolish. Since there are so few incompetent people, if the saying is right, 'rarity makes things valuable,' surely then incompetent people are very precious?

"Well, I won't say any more about them. The girls they praised were all girls we knew ourselves. Many of them didn't even have properly shaped noses and eyes, and yet if these men didn't compare them with Hsi Shih,[1] then they compared them with Wang Ch'iang;[2] if their beauty did not 'make fish sink and birds fall,'[3] it 'obscured the moon' and 'shamed the flowers.'[4] We girls don't know who Wang Ch'iang was. Some say she was Lady Chao Chün. It seems to me that Lady Chao Chün and Lady Hsi Shih could hardly have been as ugly as the girls we know.

"As to what they said about their relations with the girls being so good, and how deep their love was, I was once foolish enough to ask one of the girls. The girl said, 'A night with him was a night of misery! In the morning I asked him to give me a couple of taels for myself. He immediately pulled a long face, and began shouting, "I paid the full price last night. What other private payment do you expect?"' The girl further begged him saying, 'Out of what you paid, the inn servant takes one tenth, the landlord takes a tenth, and all the rest is taken by the house mistress. She doesn't give me a single copper. Our rouge and powder and all our underclothes—all are bought with our own money. We cannot ask anything of the gentlemen who merely listen to our singing. It is only to gentlemen who stay the night that we can open our mouths and ask a little payment for our services.' After she had begged many times, he gave her a small string of two hundred cash, throwing it on the ground and saying roughly, 'You thievish harlots! You're less than dirt! Addled turtle's eggs!' Now what sort of love do you call that? And so I thought this business of writing poems was all a fake, nothing but the telling of a lot of lies. How is it that Your Honor's verses are not like this?"

Lao Ts'an smiled. "'Every teacher has his teaching; every magic has its art.' When our teacher taught us it wasn't that sort of instruction—hence the difference."

Huang Jen-jui had just finished smoking. He put down his pipe and said, "It is certainly true: 'A man cannot be judged by his looks: the water in the sea cannot be measured by the bushel.' Making verses is nothing but the telling of a lot of lies. The child is right in saying this! From now on I'll make no more verses and so avoid telling lies and being laughed at by these girls!"

Ts'ui-huan said, "Who would dare to laugh at Your Honor? We are simple country girls who haven't seen the world. We talk a lot of nonsense. Please don't blame me, Sir. Let me kowtow to you, Sir!" She turned towards Huang Jen-jui and bowed her head several times.

Huang Jen-jui said, "Who has blamed you? What you say is the absolute truth! Only no one has ever said it! It is like the saying, 'The player is blind: the onlooker sees clear.'"

"Enough of this," Lao Ts'an said. "Why don't you quickly tell me about that strange and wonderful case of yours. If you have to make a report at dawn tomorrow, why all these delays and preliminaries?" Jen-jui said, "Don't be in a hurry. First of all I'll explain why there is no hurry, and then I'll tell you that story. I should like to ask you, 'Will the river be free of ice by tomorrow?' Reply: 'No, it can't be!' Question: 'If the river is not clear will you venture to cross on the ice? That is, will you be able to start tomorrow?' Reply: 'No, I won't.' Question: 'If you can't start, have you any important business to get you up early tomorrow?' Reply: 'No, I haven't.'"

Huang Jen-jui said, "Well then, since that is the case, why are you in such a hurry to get back to your room? Surely to talk with a friend on such a lonely and desolate night should count as 'joy in the midst of sorrow.' And besides, even if these two sisters cannot be compared with peonies and *shao yao* [5] surely you won't say they are not as good as morning glory or bamboo blossom.[6] And it is very pleasant to have them pour the tea and trim the candles. Now this is what I want to say: when we were in the provincial capital, you were busy and I was busy. We were always wanting to have a good talk, but we never had a free moment. Surely our meeting today is an excellent opportunity. As I often say, the most miserable thing in life is to have no chance to talk. But now, if we talk from morning to night we shall not be in that unhappy situation! With most men the words that come forth have two centers of origin: one kind comes from the bottom of the heart: [7] this is the real language of the individual; the other comes from the throat and is the language of social intercourse. Among the people at the capital, those who are not above me are below me. Those who are above me look down on me so that I can't talk with them, while the man who is not my equal is envious of me and I can't talk with him. You ask if there aren't any who are about equal with me. In their circumstances they may be like me, but in their hearts they don't think they are so. If they think themselves greater than I, then they look down on me; if they think themselves less than I, then they envy me: thus there is no common ground for conversation. But you, my old friend, after all you are beyond all that, and today I have the rare pleasure of meeting you. I have always had great respect for you; you ought to take pity on me and talk to me, but you keep wanting to go. Isn't that rather harsh?"

"All right, all right," Lao Ts'an said, "I'll stay with you and talk. I don't mind telling you that if I went to my room I would sit up anyway, so why should I be unreasonable? Since you had already called in two girls I thought you would want to fool and laugh with them, and that I would be in the way here. As a matter of fact I'm no Confucian moralist and I have no ambition to be an 'eater of cold pork,' [8] so why should I pretend to be one!"

Jen-jui said, "It's precisely about their affairs that I wanted to consult you." He stood up, pulled back Ts'ui-huan's sleeve, and pointed to her arm, saying, "Look! don't all these scars arouse a man's pity?" When Lao Ts'an looked he saw line upon line of black, blotch after blotch of purple. Jen-jui further said, "If the arm is like this, the rest of the body must be still more pitiable! Ts'ui-huan, open your clothes for us to see."

All this time Ts'ui-huan's eyes were brimming with tears, but she restrained them from falling; but when her arm was taken in this way the tears began to pour down. She said, "What do you want to see? It's not modest!" "Just look!" Jen-jui exclaimed. "What a foolish child it is! What is there to be afraid of if we do look? Surely there's no room for modesty in your trade!" Ts'ui-huan answered, "Why shouldn't I be modest?"

And now Ts'ui-hua's eyes filled with tears and she said, "Please don't ask her to take her clothes off." Then she turned round, looked out of the window, and whispered something, I don't know what, into Jen-jui's ear. Jen-jui nodded and was silent.

And now as Lao Ts'an stretched out on the *k'ang*, he thought to himself, "These are both children from perfectly good homes. Their parents no doubt brought them up at great pains, and went to infinite trouble. If in their play the children hurt themselves a little, the parents would rub the place tenderly, and not only rub the wound, but feel it in their hearts; and if somebody else's children should hurt their children, they would resent it greatly. Such love and kindness is beyond words to express. Who could have foreseen that when they grew up, either because of famine or because the father was fond of gambling, or smoked opium, or became involved in a lawsuit, their parents would be driven to an extremity would sell their daughters into this sort of a house to be cruelly treated by a procuress and to live an indescribable life." These thoughts brought to his mind all he had seen and heard of the universal cruelty of brothelkeepers. It was just as if they had all learned from the same teacher; they all had the same tricks. It filled him with anger and grief, and, before he knew it a slight moistness made itself felt in the corners of his eyes.

They all sat quietly without saying a word. Then a man came in carrying a roll of bedding on his shoulder. He was led by Huang Jen-jui's servant into the inner room. The servant came out and said to Huang Jen-jui, "Please, Your Honor, hand over the key to Mr. T'ieh's room so that we can put Ts'ui-huan's things in there." Lao Ts'an said, "No, no! Put them in your master's room." Jen-jui said, "Come, come. Don't be a 'cold-pork eater.' Hand over your key to me." Lao Ts'an said, "That won't do. I've never done that sort of thing." But Jen-jui argued, "I arranged it all long ago. The money is already paid. What are you worrying about?" "Never mind if you've paid the money," Lao Ts'an said. "I'll pay you back whatever it is tomorrow, and that will settle it. Since you've already paid, her mistress will have nothing to say and can't treat her badly, so what is there to worry about?" Ts'ui-hua replied, "If you really send her back, she can't possibly escape a thrashing. They are certain to say she has offended a guest."

"I have it!" Lao Ts'an cried. "Send her back tonight, but say she is to come again tomorrow. Then it will be all right. Anyhow she was called in by Mr. Huang, so what has it got to do with me? I'm willing to pay the cost. Isn't that the simplest way out?" Huang Jen-jui said, "I called her in for you. Last night I kept Ts'ui-hua here. How can we send her back tonight? It's only a matter of cheering each other up. I am not set on your doing anything else. Last night Ts'ui-hua sat talking in my room until dawn. I only did this to pass the time, and, incidentally, to save her a couple of thrashings. Isn't this a way of piling up merit? I really kept her here because according to their custom, if no one keeps them for the night, they don't get anything to eat. If they come home before dark, they have to sit into the middle of the night with an empty stomach, and very likely can't escape a thrashing. For their mistress is bound to say, 'Since the customer kept you this long he must have been attracted by you, and why should he send you back again? You must have entertained him badly!' As likely as not, it will be a thrashing. For this reason I said that they would both stay. Didn't you notice that that servant of theirs told Ts'ui-huan to eat? That was a secret sign."

At this point Ts'ui-hua turned to Ts'ui-huan, "You plead with Mr. T'ieh to have pity on you." Lao Ts'an said, "I don't have anything against her. But the money is paid in full. Let her go back. She will be satisfied, and I shall be more than satisfied."

Ts'ui-hua sniffed and said, "It's true that you will be satisfied, but she certainly won't be." Ts'ui-huan turned around and raising her face to Lao Ts'an said, "Mr. T'ieh, I can see by your appearance that you are a very kind gentleman; why won't you be a little kind to us girls? The *k'ang* in your room is twelve feet long and your bed is not more than three feet wide, so that there is nine feet left. Surely you won't mind giving me a chance to avoid a night's suffering? If you will allow me to stay and let me wait on you, I can prepare your pipe and pour tea; if it is distasteful to you, I beg you to be lenient and give me a corner of your bed as a makeshift for the night; this will be a great kindness!"

Lao Ts'an put his hand into his pocket, pulled out a key and gave it to Ts'ui-hua saying, "All right, do what you like, but on no account are my things to be disturbed."

Ts'ui-hua stood up and gave the key to Jen-jui's servant saying, "Please see that the man takes the things in and then comes straight out. Then lock the door, if you please. Thank you very much." The servant took the key and went out.

Lao Ts'an stroked Ts'ui-huan's face with his hand and said, "Where do you come from? What is your mistress' name? How old were you when you were sold to her?" Ts'ui-huan answered, "My mistress' name is Chang." That said, she was silent. She took out a handkerchief from her sleeve and wiped her tears. She wiped them and wiped them but made no sound. Lao Ts'an said, "Don't cry. I only ask you about your old home in order to cheer you up. If you don't want to talk, just don't say anything. Why be so unhappy about it?" Ts'ui-huan said, "I've never had a family."

Ts'ui-hua said, "Don't be angry, Sir. The girl has an awkward temper and she often gets a beating for it. In fact it is not surprising that she finds life hard. Two years ago her family was still very wealthy. She was only sold to our mistress last year. Since she never suffered such hardships when she was little, she can't get used to it. Actually our mistress treats us quite kindly. But I'm afraid that by next year Ts'ui-huan won't have even as good a life as she is having now."

At this point Ts'ui-huan covered her face and began to sob. Ts'ui-hua shouted at her, "Hey! The girl doesn't know what's good for her. Just look! The gentlemen call you in for their amusement, and you amuse yourself by crying! It's an insult! Stop crying, quick!"

"No, no, let her cry by all means," Lao Ts'an said. "It's good for her. Just think. Where could she weep out all the misery which has been pent up in her belly and has suffocated her? Now that she has the rare chance of being with us two men who are good natured, let her have a good cry, and then she'll feel happier." He touched Ts'ui-huan with his hand. "Cry out loud—it doesn't matter. I can promise that Mr. Huang is not superstitious. Just cry. Don't worry." Huang Jen-jui then shouted out in a loud voice from the side, "Little Ts'ui-huan. Good girl! Cry away. Please weep out for Mr. Huang the bellyful of misery which is pent up in him and is suffocating him!"

When they heard these words, none of them could help laughing. Ts'ui-huan covered her face and burst out laughing. She knew perfectly well that she ought on no account to cry in front of a customer. It was only because Lao Ts'an had asked her about her family, and Ts'ui-hua had told how two years before they were still wealthy that her wounded heart had been hurt again, and unwilling tears had started from her eyes. Restrain them as she would, she could not hold them back. And when she heard Lao Ts'an say that she had been suffocated by her pent-up misery, and that she had had nowhere to weep it out, heard him encourage her to have a good cry, and heard him say that then she would feel better, she thought to herself, "Ever since my hardships began, nobody has shown me so much sympathy. This proves that not every man treats girls as refuse to be trampled on. Only I don't know whether there are many men in the world like this one. How many more shall I meet in my lifetime? I think since I have met one there must be more." Her heart was so full of these thoughts that she forgot to think about the pain she had just suffered and instead bent her ear to hear what the others were saying. Now that Huang Jen-jui suddenly shouted at her to weep for him, how could she not want to laugh? And so, with eyes still full of tears, she burst out laughing and lifted her head to look at Jen-jui. When the others saw her appearance, they were still less able to restrain their laughter.

A last Lao Ts'an said, "Well, we've cried and we've laughed. And now I want to ask you what you mean by saying she belonged to a wealthy family two years ago? Ts'ui-hua, tell me all about it." Ts'ui-hua began: "She belonged to our town, Ch'itunghsien. Her family was called T'ien. They owned more than two *ch'ing* of land outside the south gate of Ch'itunghsien and had a general store in the town. Her parents had only her and her little brother who is about five or six years old now. There was also an old grandmother. Most of the land on the banks of our Tach'ing River is cotton-growing land worth more than a hundred strings of cash a *mou*. If they had more than two *ch'ing*, doesn't that make more than twenty thousand strings of cash? If you add the shop, it's more than thirty thousand. The proverb says, 'Ten thousand strings—wealthy house.' If a family with ten thousand strings is wealthy, and they had thirty thousand, don't you call that a very wealthy family?"

Lao Ts'an said, "Then how did they become poor?" "It happened very quickly," Ts'ui-hua said. "Less than three days and the house was destroyed and the people dead. It was the year before last. Now our Yellow River overflows its banks twice in three years, doesn't it? Well, Governor Chuang was worried to death about this, and they say a certain official, a famous southerner of great literary ability, brought some sort of book and gave it to him to read. The book said that the trouble was that the river was too narrow, that unless it was widened there would be no room for the water, that the people's dikes [9] must be destroyed and they must again use the main dikes.

"When this idea had been brought forward, every one of the expectant officials said 'Yes.' Then the Governor said, 'What are we to do with all the people living within the big dikes? We shall have to give them money and tell them to move away.' Who would have thought that all those 'turtle's eggs' [10] of department heads and expectant officials would say, 'But we can't let the people know. Just think, the space within the big and the little dikes is five or six li wide and six hundred li long. Altogether there are more than a hundred thousand families.

If they know of it, these several hundred thousand people will protect the people's dikes, and then how will you destroy them?'

"Governor Chuang could do nothing. He nodded his head, heaved a sigh, and I have heard he shed a few tears. That year in the spring, they quickly built up the big dikes, and at Chiyanghsien they built a dam out from the south bank. These two things were the 'big sword' that killed these several hundred thousand people. Alas! How could the poor peasants know what was going to happen?

"In the first few days of the sixth moon people were saying, 'A great flood is coming. A great flood is coming.' The troops on the dike ran up and down. The water in the river rose more than a foot a day, and in less than ten days the water was not very far from the top of the people's dike and one to two chang above the land on the other side of that dike! By the thirteenth and fourteenth, the mounted messengers on the people's dike were rushing to and fro, one moment one, the next another. On the following day at noon the horns sounded in all the camps to gather the men together and the troops all moved over to the big dike.

"At that time people with more foresight said, 'It's bad. It looks as if there is going to be trouble. We must go quickly and prepare to move our families!' And that night at the third watch a great storm arose, and the Yellow River water could be heard swirling, *hsi-li-hua-la*, as it poured over like a falling mountain.

"Most of the village people were still asleep in their houses. With one roar the water rushed in. They woke in alarm, but no matter how they tried to run, the water had already reached the eaves of the houses. The sky was black, the wind strong, the rain sharp, the water fierce. Just think, Your Honor, under such circumstances, what could they do?"

If you don't know what happened, hear the next chapter tell.

CHAPTER 14

The inhabitants of a hsien float like frogs on the face of the water;

Small boats like ants distribute steamed bread.

THE STORY tells that Ts'ui-hua continued: "By the fourth watch the wind dropped, the rain stopped, the clouds went away, and a moon shone through clear as crystal. Nothing could be seen of the destruction in the villages. You could only see the people who, by holding on to doors, tables, chairs, and benches, had floated over to the people's dike and were climbing up it. You could also see those who lived on the dike pulling people out with bamboo poles; and they pulled out quite a number. When these people had been saved and had recovered their breath, they began to realize that none of their families were there, that only themselves were left. Not one of them but wept aloud. Crying out for fathers, calling for mothers, weeping for husbands, wailing for children—a continuous sound of lamentation more than five hundred li long! Isn't it a sad thought, Your Honor!"

Ts'ui-huan then took up the story. "On that day, the fifteenth of the sixth month, my mother and I were in our shop at the south gate. In the middle of the night we heard people shouting, 'The flood is coming!' Everybody heard it and we got up quickly.

"Now it had been very hot that day and most people were wearing short jackets and trousers and sleeping in the courtyard. When the rain came, we went indoors. We had barely fallen asleep when we heard the shouting outside. We ran out into the street to see what was the matter. The city gate was open, and a lot of men were running out. Now there was a little dike, something more than five feet high, outside the city wall, a protection against the annual high water. The men were going out to strengthen this small dike. By that time the rain had stopped, but the sky was still overcast.

"After a short while, we saw the men outside the wall running for their lives into the town; then we saw the *hsien* magistrate, who had left his sedan chair, run into the town and go up on the wall. Then we heard a voice shouting, 'The people outside mustn't take time to bring their things in. Tell them to come in quickly. We're going to shut the gates! We can't wait!'

"We all climbed up on the wall to look, too. A lot of men were filling rush bags with mud, ready to pile against the gate. The *hsien* magistrate shouted from the wall, 'Everybody is inside; shut the gates as quickly as you can!' Now bags of earth had already been prepared inside the walls of the city. When the gate was closed, these bags of earth were piled up against it.

"My second uncle Ch'i, who lived outside the city, had also come up on the wall. By this time the clouds had already gone back to the mountains, and the moon was very bright. My mother saw second uncle Ch'i and said, 'It's really terrible this year, isn't it?' Uncle Ch'i replied, 'It certainly is! In most years when the water broke through and the flood began, it didn't rise more than a foot, and when the main head of water came, it still didn't rise more than about two feet, never more than three feet; and in less than the length of a meal time the flood had passed. In any case it was never more than about two feet of water. This year the water is certainly fierce! Right at the start it was over a foot! In a short while, more than two feet. Our magistrate saw how bad things looked and was afraid the small dike wouldn't hold, so he told everyone to come inside the wall quickly. By that time the water was getting to be about four feet. I haven't seen elder brother these two days; surely he isn't out in the country? If he is, then it's bad!' Mother began to cry and said, 'It is indeed!'

"And then a noise of shouting was heard from the top of the wall, 'The small dike is covered! Small dike covered!' The men on the wall rushed down, *hu-hu*. Mother sat down on the ground weeping and said, 'Let me die here and not go back!' I could do nothing but weep with her. Then we heard men saying, 'The water is coming through the cracks of the gate.' Then crowds of men began running wildly about and without a by-your-leave entering people's houses, and warehouses, and shops. If they found bedding, they grabbed it; if they found clothing, they grabbed that. They took everything they could find to stop up the cracks of the gates. In a short time they had taken all the clothes in the secondhand-clothes shop and the cloth in the cloth shop in our street and stuffed them into the cracks. Gradually we began to hear, 'The water isn't coming through!' Then we heard a shout, 'The bags of earth are not strong enough; they won't hold!' And now we saw a number of men go to our warehouse and carry out bags of grain and take them to fill up the archway of the gate. A short time and they had emptied the warehouse. And paper from the paper shop and cotton from the cotton shop—all were emptied.

"By then it was daylight, and mother had cried herself into a daze. I could do nothing but sit and watch over her. My ears kept hearing, 'This flood is certainly awful. It's already above the eaves of the houses outside the wall. The water will be more than a chang deep soon! I've never heard of such a flood before!'

"Later on several men from our shop came to help my mother and me back home. Back at the shop—oh, how changed everything was! I heard our men say, 'The grain in sacks has all been stuffed into the archway of the city gate; every bit of the loose grain in the bins has been stolen by ruffians; we have left only what was spilled on the floor. We have swept it up, and it makes two or three piculs.' Now there were two servantwomen in the shop whose homes were in the country. When they heard how bad the flood was, they decided that all, young and old, must have lost their lives, and wept continuously as though they wanted to die.

"The disturbance went on until the sun began to go down in the west, and then the servants poured some ginger tea into my mother's mouth to bring her to. When we had all drunk a couple of mouthfuls of millet gruel, mother woke, opened her eyes wide, and said, 'Where is grandmother?' They said, 'In her room sleeping; we didn't like to wake the old lady.' My mother said, 'You must ask the old lady to get up and eat a little.'

"But when they went into her room, to everyone's surprise the old lady was not sleeping, but was dead—from fright. They felt her nostrils; she had stopped breathing. When my mother saw it, she gave forth a cry, vomited out the two mouthfuls of gruel she had eaten, along with a clot of blood, and again fell into a swoon. Our old maidservant Wang rubbed grandmother's body without stopping and suddenly gave a cry: 'It's all right. Her heart is still warm!' Then she quickly put her mouth to grandmother's mouth and breathed in and out. Again she called out, 'Quick! Bring some ginger tea.' By the late afternoon grandmother had come to, and my mother had come to, and the whole household was more or less peaceful.

"Two servants were talking in the courtyard: 'They say there is a chang and four or five feet of water outside the wall. I'm afraid that this old wall can't stand it. If it comes into the town, there won't be one person left alive!' Another servant said, 'The *hsien* magistrate is still in town, so I reckon it's all right!' "

Lao Ts'an said to Jen-jui, "I've heard vague reports about all this. Whose idea was it really? What book did he follow? Do you know, my friend?"

Jen-jui answered, "I arrived in the year *Keng-Yin* [1890]. This all happened in *I-Ch'ou* [1889]. I have heard it talked about, but I don't know for certain. According to the talk, it was a scheme proposed by the *taot'ai*, Shih Chün-fu, and he followed Chia Jang's *Methods of River Control*.[1] He quoted Chia Jang as saying that in early times 'the River was the frontier between Ch'i on the one side and Chao and Wei on the other. Chao and Wei sloped up to the hills, while the land of Ch'i was low. Ch'i made a dike twenty-five li from the river. The river water went east towards the Ch'i dike and then overflowed to the west in Chao and Wei. Chao and Wei then made a dike twenty-five li from the river.'

"One day when the provincial officials were all in the yamen Shih Chün-fu quoted this passage to them and said, 'You see, at the time of the Warring States[2] the two dikes were fifty li apart, and therefore there were no floods. Today the two people's dikes are not more than three or four li apart and the main dikes not more than twenty, not half the distance the ancients had. If you don't destroy the people's dikes, disasters will never cease.'

"The Governor said, 'Yes, I understand the argument; but this strip of land between the dikes is dotted with villages; it is all flat and fertile

land. Surely we don't want to destroy the livelihood of several tens of
thousands of people.'

"He then again directed the Governor's attention to the *Methods of
River Control,* saying, 'Please read this passage: "An objector may say,
'If this is done, walled cities and suburbs, fields and peasant huts, and
mounds and tombs will be destroyed by the ten thousands, and then
the people will be full of resentment.'" Chia Jang answered, "Of old
the Great Yü ruled the waters; when the mountains were in the way, he
destroyed them. Thus he chiseled out the Dragon Gate, opened up the
Gap of Yi, snapped the Whetstone Pillar, and split the Chieh Rock; [3]
he acted even when it meant interfering with heaven and earth; but
our obstacles are the works of man, so what need is there to say anything about destroying these works of men?"' Then he said further,
' "If the small does not suffer then the great scheme is thwarted." The
Governor thinks that the peasants who live between the dikes with
their huts, and graveyards, and their crops, are to be pitied. Does the
annual bursting of the dikes, then, do no harm to human life? It is a
question of "one great effort and then perpetual peace." Therefore
Chia Jang says, "The dominion of the Great House of Han is over ten
thousand li. Is it worth while to struggle with the water foot-by-foot?
This good work once done, the river bed will be fixed, the people's
life settled in peace, and for a thousand years there will be no disaster.
And so I call it the best of the three plans." The dominion of the Han
dynasty was not more than ten thousand li, and yet it seemed wise to
them not to struggle with the water for land; our national territory is
many ten thousands of li; if we on the contrary, struggle with the
water for land, don't you think this will cause the sages of former times
to laugh at their progeny?' And again he pointed to Ch'u T'ung-jen's [4]
commentary, reading, ' "*The Three Methods* then became an unalterable standard, but from Han till today the river-control officials have
always followed the last and the worst of the three methods. Alas! After
the Han through the Chin, T'ang, Sung, Yüan, Ming periods, although
the scholars all knew that Chia Jang's *Methods of River Control* was
as authoritative in its field as a Sacred Classic, the river-control officials, unfortunately, were not scholars, and no great success has been
achieved!" If the Governor can carry out the scheme that Chia Jang
considers best, won't that mean that after two thousand years Chia
Jang will have found an understanding disciple? Your merit handed

down on "bamboo and silk" will not decay through ten thousand generations!'

"The Governor wrinkled his eyebrows and said, 'But there is one important question..I can't get away from the thought of these ten to twenty tens of thousands of peasants and their property!' Two officials said, 'If by one great effort we can ensure perpetual security, why not set aside an additional sum on the budget and move the people out of the region?' The Governor said, 'That's the only thing to do; it's the best solution we can find.' Afterwards I heard that they raised three hundred thousand ounces of silver in preparation for moving the people. But why they didn't move them I simply don't understand."

Jen-jui said to Ts'ui-huan, "What happened to you afterwards? Tell us." Ts'ui-huan said, "Afterwards my mother made up her mind: 'What will happen will happen. If the flood comes, we can only be drowned.'"

Tsui-hua said, "That year I was in Ch'itunghsien too. I lived at the north gate and my third maternal aunt's house was outside the north gate near the people's dike. Now the shops along the street outside the north gate were large and prosperous so that the dikes at the back of the houses on both sides were quite high. I have been told they were thirteen feet to the top. Besides, the land there was high so that the north gate was not flooded. On the sixteenth I went onto the city wall and looked at the things floating on the river. I don't know how many there were. There were chests; there were tables, chairs, benches; there were windows and doors. Still less do I know how many dead bodies I saw. They were floating here and there all over the river, and there was nobody to bother to fish them out. There were rich people who wanted to leave the place, but there were no boats to be hired."

Lao Ts'an said, "No boats? Where had they gone?" Ts'ui-hua said, "They were all taken by the officials for carrying steamed bread." "Who were they sending steamed bread to?" Lao Ts'an asked. "Why did they need so many boats?"

Ts'ui-hua said, "This sending of steamed bread was certainly a meritorious act! More than half of the people in the villages were drowned. The rest were quicker-witted. When they saw the water coming, they climbed on the roofs so that in every village there were a hundred or more people on the roofs. Water on all sides; where could they go to get something to eat? Some grew so hungry that they jumped into the water again and drowned themselves. Fortunately the Governor sent commissioners who went by boat from place to place distributing steamed bread, three to each adult and two to each child. The next day some more officials came in empty boats to take the people to the north bank of the river. Wasn't that an excellent piece of work? Who would have thought that some of the 'addled eggs' would squat on the roofs and refuse to come down? Ask them why—they said that the Governor would send them steamed rolls while they were in the river, but that once on the north bank no one would bother about them, and they would die of starvation. Actually the Governor sent food for several days and then stopped, and then they starved to death. Weren't they a stupid lot?"

Lao Ts'an said to Jen-jui, "This business was certainly badly muddled. Although we don't know whether it was *Taot'ai* Shih or not, we do know that the one who suggested this policy had no bad intentions, and was not at all prompted by selfish interest, yet because he had only read books and was not experienced in practical affairs, every movement of his hand or foot was a mistake. This is why Mencius said, 'To believe everything in the *Book of History* would be worse than to have no *Book of History* at all.'⁵ And do you think that river conservancy is the only case where this is true? The cases where the welfare of the Empire is prejudiced by wicked officials are three or four in ten. But those due to ignorance of practical matters on the part of good men are six or seven in ten!" Again he asked Ts'ui-huan, "And afterwards, did you find your father again? Or was he carried away by the flood?" Ts'ui-huan answered, holding back the tears, "He must have gone down with the flood. If he was alive, wouldn't he have come home?"

They all sighed for a while. Then Lao Ts'an again asked Ts'ui-hua, "Just now you said you were afraid that next year her life won't be even as good as it is this year. Why did you say that?" Ts'ui-hua replied, "Well, you see our mistress' husband has just died! The funeral expenses were well over a hundred strings of cash.⁶ Two days ago our mistress was gambling with dice and again lost two or three hundred strings. Altogether her debts are more than four hundred strings of cash. She can't possibly balance her accounts at the end of the year, and so she has already made plans to sell sister Huan to Baldhead K'uai the Second. This Baldhead K'uai is famous for his cruelty. If you don't get a guest during the course of a day, he takes red-hot chopsticks and burns your flesh. Our mistress wants three hundred ounces from him. He has offered her six hundred strings of cash, so it is not settled yet. Just think, Sir. How many days is it to the end of the year? She's in a tight corner, and every day it gets worse for her. And when it comes to the end of the year, do you think she won't sell? And when Ts'ui-huan is sold, she will certainly have plenty to put up with!"

When Lao Ts'an had heard all this, he sat quietly and said not a word. Ts'ui-huan merely wiped her tears. Huang Jen-jui said, "Brother Ts'an, I was just saying that I wanted to discuss their affairs with you. Well, this is the reason. It seems to me that it is really a shame to see a child of a decent family sent into this 'Gate of Ghosts.' [7] It's a matter of not more than three hundred ounces. I am willing to produce half and find some friends who will make up the other half. You'll give a few ounces, won't you? Never mind how much. The only thing is that I definitely can't take her in my name. If you could take her along with you, then the whole thing would be easy to manage. What do you think about it?"

Lao Ts'an said, "It's not a difficult business. As to the money—if you are willing to produce half, I'll certainly make up the other half. It's not a good idea to 'beg alms' from anybody else. But I certainly don't want to ask for her. We'll have to think of some other way."

When Ts'ui-huan heard this, she hurriedly jumped off the *k'ang* and kowtowed twice to the two gentlemen, Huang and T'ieh, saying, "Oh, you two gentlemen Bodhisattvas, lifesaving benefactors, if you are willing to give up your silver to save me from the fiery furnace, I am most willing to be anything you like, no matter what it is, slave girl or amah! But there is one thing I must tell you about first. I don't blame our mistress for all the blows I have received. It must be because of my own wickedness. At the beginning my mother sold me to this mistress because our family was simply starving to death. She got twenty-four strings of cash, but items like the fees to the middleman took three or four strings so that there were only twenty left. Then last year my grandmother died, and the money was all used up. Mother then led my brother out to beg, and in less than six months she too died from hunger and hardship. This left one little brother who is six years old now. Fortunately we had an old neighbor, the Fifth Mr. Li, who now lives in Ch'ihohsien, where he has a small business. He took charge of him and gives him something to eat; but he doesn't really have enough for himself, so how can he give my brother enough to eat? Still less can he give him clothes. Therefore while I was at Twentymile Village, whenever I happened to have some good customers who gave me a thousand or eight hundred cash, I put it by, and in the course of one or two months collected two or three thousand cash and sent it to him. Now that you two gentlemen are rescuing me, if I go to a place only two or three hundred li away, that's all right, for surely I can save a little money to send him. But if I have to go a long way, won't you kind gentlemen please think of a way to let me take the little boy with me, or send him to a Taoist or Buddhist monastery, or else find some family that will look after him? The ancestors of the T'ien family for a hundred generations, who are now spirits, will be grateful to you two gentlemen for your kindness. 'Knotted grass' [8] and 'bracelets carried in the beak' [9] will certainly be the reward of you two gentlemen. Have pity on this last remaining offshoot of the house of T'ien." When she had reached this point, she again began to weep and wail.

Jen-jui said, "This is certainly another difficulty," but Lao Ts'an replied, "There's no difficulty here. I'll arrange it." Then he said in a louder voice, "Miss T'ien! You don't need to cry. I promise you that you two, brother and sister, shan't ever be separated—so that's all right. Stop crying so that we can make plans to help you. If you upset us with your crying, how can we make good plans! Hurry up and stop crying."

When Ts'ui-huan heard this, she immediately stopped crying and performed several resounding kowtows before each of them, *ku-tung, ku-tung.* Lao Ts'an quickly lifted her up. Just think! When she was kowtowing, she used such force that a big swelling appeared on her forehead. Then the swelling broke and the blood flowed.

Lao Ts'an helped her to a seat and said, "Why do you do that?" Then he gently wiped away the blood on her forehead and made her lie down on the *k'ang* and came over to Jen-jui to discuss what they should do. He said, "In carrying out this piece of business, we must proceed by definite stages. The first stage is to buy her freedom. The second is to find her a mate. There are two steps to the business of buying her freedom. The first is the private negotiation; the second is the legal confirmation. Somebody else has already offered six hundred strings. Tomorrow we must call her mistress here and first offer six hundred strings. Then afterwards we can add to it. It's not good to appear too ready to pay with this sort of person. If you are too ready to pay she will think that she has 'rare merchandise that should be held.' [10]

At present an ounce of silver exchanges for two strings and seven hundred cash. Three hundred ounces will bring eight hundred and ten strings, which is enough to cover everything, including all expenses. We will see what sort of attitude the mistress adopts. If she is not obstinate, of course it's better to do it privately. If she is suspicious and tricky, we will ask the magistrate of Ch'ihohsien to give a formal decision in the public court and then complete the transaction privately. What does Mr. Jen think of the plan?"

"Excellent! Excellent!" Jen-jui exclaimed. Lao Ts'an further said, "If you really under no circumstances can do it in your name, neither can I do it entirely in mine. I'll say I am arranging it for a relative of mine. That'll seem all right. When the whole thing is settled, only then will we reveal our intention of finding a mate for her. Otherwise the mistress will refuse to let her go."

Jen-jui said, "Good. The scheme is absolutely foolproof." Lao Ts'an said, "As to the money, we each supply half. No matter how much it costs, we divide it that way. The only trouble is that I haven't enough money with me in my chest. I'll have to ask you to advance it, and when I get to the provincial capital, I'll return you my share."

Jen-jui said, "Never mind that. I've got more than enough money here to buy two Ts'ui-huans. As long as we can carry the thing off successfully, I don't care whether you pay me or not." Lao Ts'an said, "I certainly will pay you. I have a deposit of more than four hundred ounces of silver at the Yu Jung T'ang.[11] You don't need to be afraid that I can't afford it or that it will make me starve. Set your mind at rest."

"Then we'll leave it at that," Jen-jui said. "Early tomorrow morning we'll send somebody to fetch her mistress." Ts'ui-hua said, "Don't send early in the morning. We two must go back early tomorrow morning. If you call them early, and they get to know what is afoot, they will certainly first take her away and hide her in the country and then begin to discuss their price. And then you'll be in their hands. Besides, these opium smokers never get up early. It's better to wait till the afternoon. First send somebody to tell us to come and then call our mistress. Then you don't need to be afraid of her. And another thing. Whatever you do, don't tell them that I suggested all this. Sister Huan is being rescued from hell, and doesn't need to be afraid of her, but I have still got to live some time in this fiery furnace."

Jen-jui replied, "Of course, of course. You don't need to tell us that.

Tomorrow when I go to the *hsien* yamen I will take the opportunity to bring a runner back with me. If your mistress gets ugly, I'll hand Ts'ui-huan over to the runner to look after, and that will be a way of managing her."

With this everybody felt very happy. Then Lao Ts'an said to Jen-jui, "Well, I suppose that settles their business. But what about that law case you mentioned? I can't help thinking about it. Were you serious or not? Tell me, and set my mind at rest."

If you don't know what happened afterwards, hear the next chapter tell.

CHAPTER 15

Fierce flame by its noise startles the two Ts'uis;

Severe punishment without measure oppresses a defenseless widow.

IT HAS been told that Lao Ts'an and Jen-jui had just brought to a satisfactory end their discussion of how to rescue Ts'ui-huan, and that Lao Ts'an then had said to Jen-jui, "A little while ago you were going to tell me about an amazing law case involving a great many lives and in which the circumstances are puzzling and very unusual. Well, is there really such a case, or is there not? I'm impatient to know." Jen-jui replied, "No hurry. No hurry. We've just spent half the night talking about the affairs of this little slave, and my proper work, my smoking, has been neglected. Let me take one or two puffs to refresh myself and then I'll tell you."

Ts'ui-huan was now so happy in her heart that she simply didn't know what to do with herself. Hearing that Jen-jui wanted to smoke she immediately took the *ch'ientzu* and helped him light his pipe.

Jen-jui then said, "To the northeast of this Ch'ihohsien, forty-five li from the city, there is a big market town, called Ch'itungchen. It happens to be the home of the 'uncultivated person of the east of Ch'i' in the Chou period.[1] There are three or four thousand families in this place; there's a main street, and ten or more side streets. In the third turning to the south of the main street is the home of the venerable Mr. Chia.

"This old gentleman would be not much more than fifty years old this year. He has had two sons and one daughter. If the elder son had lived, he would be over thirty years old. When he was twenty, he married the daughter of the Wei family in the same town. The Wei and Chia families both depend on farm lands for their living, each owning forty or fifty *ch'ing* of land. There are no sons in the Wei family, only this one daughter, and therefore they adopted a distant nephew into the family to be in charge of all their business. But this adopted son wasn't very fond of his studies, and so old Mr. Wei wasn't pleased with him, whereas he loved his son-in-law as something very precious. Quite unexpectedly in the seventh month of last year this son-in-law caught an infection, and by the middle of the eighth month, alas, he had died. After the hundred days of mourning old Mr. Wei, fearing his daughter was too unhappy, frequently took her home with him for ten days or half a month in order to relieve her sorrow.

"As to the Chia family, the second son was twenty-four this year, and had been studying at home. He had grown up into a handsome young man and was very gifted in literary composition. Since the elder son was dead, this second son was old Mr. Chia's treasure. Afraid that the young man was working too hard, he didn't allow him to study any more. His daughter is nineteen this year. She is as beautiful as a flower or a piece of jade. In addition she is very capable, and it is she who is in charge of all the business great or small in the household. For this reason the people of the town have given her a nickname, Chia T'an-ch'un.[2] The second son married the daughter of a scholarly family, also this town, a girl of so gentle a disposition that she rarely ventured to open her mouth. For this reason people considered him simple-minded and useless, and invented a nickname for him, 'Second Simpleton.'

"And if this Chia T'an-ch'un has grown up to nineteen years, why is she still not married? It is simply because her intelligence and her beauty are both perfect. Where in these country families was there a young man handsome enough to pair with her? There was only a certain Wastrel Wu the Second of a neighboring village. He is a rare fellow, quite a young blood, and very handsome. He is a clever talker, and his family is prosperous. He is fond of riding horseback and fond of archery. He was related to the Chia family, so that when their families met, the womenfolk did not retire. This Wastrel Wu the Second had entrusted someone with the task of coming to propose marriage.

"Old Mr. Chia thought to himself, 'This match may seem quite all right. But I have heard people say that this Wastrel Wu has already seduced several country girls, that he is fond of gambling, and that he frequently runs off to the provincial capital on a spree for one or two months at a time without coming back.' He decided that this sort of a man, though he was considered the wealthiest man in the district, in the end wouldn't be able to preserve his property. He therefore didn't accept his offer. After this, no matter how he tried to find a man of equal ability and wealth, he was unsuccessful, and the marriage question was shelved.

"The thirteenth day of the eighth month this year was the anniversary of the elder Chia son's death, and Buddhist priests were called in to say masses for three days: on the twelfth, the thirteenth, and the fourteenth. When the ceremonies were finished, old Mr. Wei took his daughter home with him for the festival.[3] Who would have dreamed that in the afternoon of that day they would suddenly hear that everybody in the Chia family was dead! Their confusion and terror were indescribable! Mr. Wei rushed back to see what had happened, and when he got there, the headman and the elders had already arrived. All the members of the household were dead except for Chia T'anch'un and her aunt, who came in crying as though they were made of tears. When, after a little while, the daughter of the Wei family—that is, the eldest daughter-in-law of the Chia family—arrived, entering the gate, she heard a continuous sound of weeping. Without really knowing what it was all about, she gave herself up to bitter weeping and wailing.

"By this time the headman had finished his examination. In the gate house there were three dead, the gatekeeper and two farm hands. In the anteroom of the reception hall the page was lying dead on the floor. In the inner room of the main reception hall old Mr. Chia was on the *k'ang*, dead. In the main hall of the second courtyard were the younger Chia son and his wife, near them a womanservant, and on the *k'ang* a child of three years; in the kitchen were a womanservant and a slavegirl; in the side building a womanservant; in the side room of the front courtyard where the reception hall was, an accountant. In all, big and little, male and female, there were thirteen dead. A statement was drawn up on the spot and without delay sent to the *hsien* magistrate.

"Early the next morning the magistrate came down to the town bringing the coroner with him to examine the corpses one by one. Not one of them showed signs of injuries. None of the joints were stiff, and the skin had not turned black or purple. It was not a case of assault; neither was it poisoning. This mysterious case obviously presented many difficulties. While the Chia family began making arrangements for the funeral, the district magistrate prepared a report to submit to the Governor. Suddenly, just as the magistrate was drafting his report, the Chia family sent in a petition saying that they had found evidence of an intention to murder on the part of some persons."

When the story had reached this point, Ts'ui-huan happened to look up and shouted, "Look! Why is the window all red like this?" The words were scarcely out of her mouth when a crackling sound, *pi-pi, po-po,* was heard, and a confused noise of men's voices shouting loudly and saying, "Fire! Fire!" while several people rushed out of the main building. When they had raised the *lientzu*, they saw that the fire was just behind the side building Lao Ts'an was living in.

Lao Ts'an quickly pulled out his key and went to open the lock of his door. Huang Jen-jui shouted, "Send a couple of men to help Mr. T'ieh get his things out."

When Lao Ts'an had unlocked and pushed open the door, a cloud of black smoke swept out, while tongues of flame darted out of the windows. Overcome by the smoke, Lao Ts'an hastily took a step back, stumbled over a brick, and fell, but luckily the men who were to move the things had just arrived and were able to pick him up and help him to the east side of the court.

And then it began to look as though the fire would be strong enough to catch the main building, so Huang Jen-jui's servant led the men in to rescue his things. Huang Jen-jui stood in the middle of the courtyard shouting, "Bring out the box of accounts first, and then look after the other things!"

While he was talking, Huang Sheng appeared with the box of accounts. The men scrambled out carrying Huang Jen-jui's various chests and baskets and put them down at the foot of the east wall. The innkeeper soon brought them some benches and asked them to sit down. Jen-jui counted his things. None were missing; in fact there was one piece extra. He hastily called the men to carry this to the inn office.

Reader! Can you guess whose the extra piece was? It was Ts'ui-hua's bedding. Jen-jui knew that the district magistrate was bound to come to look at the fire. If he should see the bundle, it would be rather embarrassing, so he told them to carry it away. Moreover he said to the two Ts'ui's, "You go and hide in the office too. The district magistrate will be coming soon." The two Ts'ui's heard this and went out along the outside wall.

It is further told that when the fire started all the neighbors and the river workers looked about for tubs and buckets to help put it out. Unfortunately both banks of the river were frozen solid; and although the water was flowing in the middle, they couldn't get at it. Behind the inn there was a pond full of water, but it was frozen solid like the ground. Only two of the wells outside the city wall had water in them. Just think! What good could it do to bring water slowly bucket by bucket? However, "when man is pressed, intelligence is born." The men broke up the ice in the pond and threw it chunk by chunk on the fire. Strange to say, the ice was more effective than water would have been. Wherever a lump of ice fell, the flames were put out. The pond was just behind the main building. There were seven or eight men standing on the ridge of the roof and several tens of men outside, who passed the ice up to the roof. As the men on the roof received it, they threw it into the fire; or rather they threw half of it into the fire and dropped the other half on the roof of the main building so that the fire would not come in that direction.

Lao Ts'an and Jen-jui were by the east wall watching the men put the fire out when they saw a stream of torches and lanterns; the district magistrate had arrived. He brought with him yamen servants armed with long hooked poles and other instruments to help put the fire out. When they got inside the gate, they found that the force of the fire had been weakened, and while some used their hooks to tear down the building, other men were ordered to get some thin ice from a shallow place in the Yellow River to throw on the fire in order to extinguish it. Thus gradually the fire died down.

When the *hsien* magistrate saw Huang Jen-jui standing beside the east wall, he stepped forward and saluted him, saying, "I'm afraid Your Excellency has been badly disturbed." Jen-jui said, "Nothing to speak of: but our venerable friend Pu has suffered from the fire." And then he said to the magistrate, "Mr. Tzu, I should like to introduce someone to you. His name is T'ieh, his *hao* Pu-ts'an, [4] and he should be of great interest to you. If you entrust that case of yours to him, it will be successfully handled." The *hsien* magistrate said, "Ai-yah-yah! Is Mr. T'ieh Pu here? Please bring him over and introduce us." Jen-jui then beckoned with his hand and shouted, "Lao Ts'an! Please come here."

Lao Ts'an had been sitting on a bench with Jen-jui; but when he saw the magistrate arrive, he stepped over into the crowd and looked at the fire as an excuse for avoiding a meeting. Now, hearing himself called, he went over and bowed to the *hsien* magistrate, and they exchanged a few polite greetings. The magistrate of Ch'ihohsien turned out to be a Mr. Wang. His *hao* was Tzu-chin. He was another Chiang-nan man of the same district as Lao Ts'an. Although he had entered official life as a *Chin-Shih,* still he wasn't exactly a fool.

Then Jen-jui said to Wang Tzu-chin, "In my opinion all you need do in the matter of your Ch'itungts'un case is to ask Mr. Pu to write a letter to the Governor. He will then send Pai Tzu-shou and justice will be done. That 'childless creature' [5] won't dare to be obstinate any more. All of us are officials and colleagues so that it's not very good for us to offend him, but Mr. Pu is an outsider and need not be so cautious. What is your honorable opinion?"

When Tzu-chin heard this he was extremely glad. "Mrs. Chia Wei's deliverer has come. Marvelous! Splendid!" When Lao Ts'an heard this, he couldn't make head or tail of it. To agree would be bad; not to agree would be just as bad. He could only mumble assent.

By this time the fire was quite out, and the *hsien* magistrate wanted to drag them both off to lodge at the yamen. Jen-jui said, "Since the main building has not been burned, I can move in there again; it's only Mr. T'ieh who has no home to return to." Lao Ts'an said, "It doesn't matter, it doesn't matter. It is already well into the night and before long it will be light. Then I will go out to buy some new things. It is quite all right."

The *hsien* magistrate then again pressed Lao Ts'an most urgently to come to the yamen. Lao Ts'an said, "If I impose myself on brother Huang, it won't matter. Please don't worry." The *hsien* magistrate then asked with much concern, "What have you had burned? You must have lost a great many things, but as far as the resources of my humble *hsien* go I will do the little I can to make up the loss." Lao Ts'an laughing said, "One cloth coverlet. One bamboo box. A cloth gown and a pair of cloth trousers. Several old books. A set of iron bells on a string. That's the lot." The magistrate laughed and said, "That can't be all!" and laughed again.

They were just going to separate when the headman came in with a yamen runner leading a man on an iron chain. The man kneeled on the ground, and kowtowed again and again, like a chicken picking grain, crying, "Mercy, Your Honor! Mercy, Your Honor!"

The headman went down on one knee and cried, "The fire started in this old fellow's room. Please, Your Honor, will you have him taken to the yamen for trial; or will you try the case here?" The *hsien* magistrate asked the man, "What's your family name? What are you called? Where's your home? How did the fire start?" The man on the ground continued to kowtow and said, "My humble family name is Chang. I'm called Chang the Second. I belong to this town. I work in the inn on the other side of the wall. Yesterday I got up at daylight and worked until the second watch of the night. When at last I was free, I went back to my room to sleep. But my shirt and trousers were wet through with sweat, and when I lay down I was very cold. The colder I got, the more I shivered, and in the end I couldn't get to sleep. When I saw that there were some bundles of corn stalks piled up in the room, I pulled out several stalks and burnt them to dry myself. Then I remembered that on the window ledge there was some leftover wine which a guest in the main building had given me to drink, so I took it and warmed it in the ashes and drank a few cups. Well, when a man who is tired out and wet after a day's work gets a bit of warmth and a couple of cups of wine in his belly, what happens? Before I knew it, while I was sitting there, I fell asleep. A few seconds after I'd fallen asleep, I felt a painful stinging in my nose from the smoke. I quickly opened my eyes. A big patch of my padded gown was already burned, and the wall that was built with corn stalks had already caught. I rushed out to look for water, but the fire was already through the roof, and there was nothing I could do. What I have said is the truth. Please, Your Honor, have mercy!"

The *hsien* magistrate shouted, "The addlepate!" and said, "Take him to the yamen for punishment!" Having spoken, he got up and took his leave of Huang and T'ieh, enjoining Jen-jui to find a way of settling that difficult case. Then he hurried out.

By now the fire had completely died down, and only white smoke rose from it. Jen-jui saw Huang Sheng lead in the gang of men. They carried his things in again and put them in their original places. Jen-jui said, "The smell of smoke is very strong in the room. Light a pot of 'long-life' incense to sweeten it." Then he laughed at Lao Ts'an and said, "Mr. T'ieh, I wonder if you are still in a hurry to go back to your room!" Lao Ts'an said, "It's all because I was kept here by your insistence. If I had been in the room, I shouldn't have been cleaned out by the fire so completely." "Eh! Aren't you ashamed of yourself!" Jen-jui replied, "If I'd allowed you to go back, the chances are that you would have been burned to death there along with your things. Instead of thanking me properly, you blame me. You don't know the difference between good and bad treatment." Lao Ts'an said, "What do you take me for? If you don't make good my losses, see whether I'll give you any peace."

While they were talking, the *lientzu* was raised and Huang Sheng led in a man wearing the "big hat" of a yamen runner. He made a genuflection and said, "My master sends his compliments to the Honorable Mr. T'ieh. He is sending you a set of bed coverings, some that he uses himself. May it please Your Honor not to refuse them because they are a little soiled. Tomorrow a tailor will be ordered to make some new ones without delay. For tonight this is the best we can do. And here is a fox-lined gown and jacket. May it please Your Honor to use them." Lao Ts'an stood up and said, "I am causing your honorable master too much trouble. If you will leave the bundle here for the time being, I will use it for one or two days until I have bought some things for myself, and then I'll return it. As to clothes, I was wearing all I possess, so that none were burned, and I don't need to trouble your master. Please go back and express my deepest thanks."

But the servant was afraid to take the clothing back. Then it was Huang Jen-jui who said, "Mr. T'ieh will really not accept the clothing. Say that I said so, and take it back." The man again made a genuflection and went away.

Lao Ts'an said, "My things being burned doesn't matter. But through your stupid meddling you have got Ts'ui-huan's bundle burned up for no reason at all. Is there any justice in that?" Huang Jen-jui said, "That's even less important. I don't suppose all her bedding together was worth ten ounces of silver. Tomorrow we'll give her fifteen ounces. Her mistress will be so pleased she won't be able to contain herself." Ts'ui-huan said, "You're quite right. But I'm afraid that because I am such an ill-fated person, my bundle of bedding has caused Mr. T'ieh's fine things to be destroyed."

"None of the things were valuable," Lao Ts'an said. "I'm only sorry about my two Sung wood-block books,—for money can't buy them. It's a pity about them. But it's fate, and we can only accept it."

Jen-jui said, "Sung wood-block books aren't anything wonderful. The only really regrettable thing is that that string of bells that you ring is destroyed too, for doesn't that mean the loss of your means of livelihood?"

Lao Ts'an said, "Without a doubt. And it's for you to replace it. What more is there to be said?" Jen-jui said, "Tut, tut, tut! Her bedding burned! Your bells destroyed! It's wonderful luck. Congratulations!" He made a bow to Ts'ui-huan and then bowed to Lao Ts'an and said, "From today on she won't need to be a harlot who sells her body, and you won't have to be a prating quack!"

Lao Ts'an cried out, "All right! All right! Go on with your insults! Ts'ui-huan, how is it you don't go and pinch his mouth?" Ts'ui-huan said, "Amitofo! [6] How kind you two gentlemen are!" Ts'ui-hua nodded her head and said, "Ts'ui-huan from now on is to be a virtuous girl. Mr. T'ieh from now on is to be an official. This fire certainly was a fire of good luck and of profit. I really must congratulate you both."

Lao Ts'an said, "According to what you say, she is to follow virtue and I to follow dishonor." Huang Jen-jui said, "No more of that nonsense. I want to ask you—are we going to talk some more; or are we going to sleep? If we're going to sleep, then let us get our bedding out. If we're going to talk, then I'll tell you about that strange case." Then he cried out in a loud voice, "Huang Sheng! Come here!"

Lao Ts'an said, "Go on. I want very much to hear." "Let's see," Jen-jui continued, "I had just got to where the Chia family sent a messenger with a petition, saying that they had discovered evidence of intended murder, hadn't I?

"Well, on old Mr. Chia's table there was a half-eaten moon cake. In most of the rooms there were traces of moon cakes' having been eaten, and these moon cakes had been sent two days before by the Wei family. Chia T'an-ch'un and Chia Kan, a son who had been newly adopted to continue the line of the Chia family, therefore accused their elder brother's wife, Mrs. Chia Wei, of committing adultery with somebody and planning to poison thirteen members of the family!

"The magistrate of Ch'ihohsien, Wang Tzu-chin, therefore called in this Chia Kan and asked with whom the adultery had been committed, but he couldn't point to anyone. Of the partly eaten moon cakes there was only half of one left, and that was already crumbling, but in the sweet filling there was some arsenic.

"Wang Tzu-chin had Mrs. Chia Wei called in and asked her to explain. She gave evidence: 'The moon cakes were sent on the twelfth, when I was still in the Chia house. Some of them were eaten then, but nobody died!' Then old Mr. Wei was called in. He gave evidence: 'The moon cakes were made at the Studio of the Four Virtues in the High Street. They can witness whether there was poison or not!' So the master of the Studio of the Four Virtues was called in, and he gave evidence that although the moon cakes were made in his shop, the sweet filling was supplied by the Wei family. Though this was the only evidence, there was nothing to do but take the Wei father and daughter into custody for the time being. Although they were imprisoned, they were not shackled but simply put into an empty room and allowed to furnish it as they wanted.

"Knowing that the coroner's investigation showed it was not a case of poisoning, Tzu-chin examined the matter carefully himself. He was convinced that it was not a case of poisoning, and even supposing the moon cakes did contain poison, they couldn't have all eaten them at the same time; and wouldn't there have been a difference in the degree of poisoning?

"The bereaved family were urgently demanding a trial without delay, so he reported the case to the Governor, asking him to send a deputy to be associated with him in a joint trial. It happens that some days ago Kang Sheng-mu was sent. This man's family name is Kang and his personal name Pi.[7] He is a disciple of Lü Chien-t'ang who imitates his master in everything and is utterly incorruptible! As soon as he arrived, he had old Mr. Wei put in the ankle-squeezers and Mrs. Chia Wei in the thumbscrews. Both fainted completely away, but neither confessed anything.

"But 'it is difficult to avoid one's enemy.' Mr. Wei's major-domo was an honest fellow, simple but loyal. Seeing his master unjustly accused, he raised some money for him and came into the town to see what he could do. He found his way to the house of a landed gentleman, the *Chü-Jen* Hu."

When the story had reached this point, Huang Sheng raised the *lientzu* and came in saying, "You called, Sir?" Jen-jui said, "Get the bedding ready." Huang Sheng said, "How do you want it arranged?" Jen-jui thought a bit and said, "The outer room is cold. We'll all sleep inside." Then he turned to Lao Ts'an, "The *k'ang* in the inner room is very big. You and I will sleep one at each end and the two girls can unroll their things and sleep in the middle. All right?" "Very good, very good," Lao Ts'an answered. "But won't it be a lonely perch for you?" Jen-jui said, "With both of them here—how can you call that lonely?" "Whether you're lonely or not," Lao Ts'an said, "hurry up and tell me—when he got into this *Chü-Jen* Hu's house, what happened?"

If you want to know the later events, hear the next chapter tell.

CHAPTER 16

Six thousand gold pieces buy the lingering death;

A letter drives away the star of mourning.

IT HAS been told that Lao Ts'an, greatly agitated, was asking what happened when the major-domo got into the *Chü-Jen* Hu's house. Jen-jui said, "The more impatient you become, the less impatient I am! I want to have a couple of pulls at my pipe!" Lao Ts'an was very anxious to hear him tell the story so he called, "Tsui-huan, quickly roast two pipefuls, and let him smoke so that he can talk." Ts'ui-huan took the *ch'ientzu* and began to prepare the opium. Huang Sheng came out of the inner room where he had unrolled the bedding and said, "I must tell their man to get their things ready." Jen-jui nodded. After a while the manservant who had appeared before came in with Huang Sheng.

Now it is the regular custom [1] that a singsong girl's bedding must be brought and arranged by her own man. An ordinary domestic will on no account help her with it. The same is true of the things she needs besides her bedding: her man knows where to put them so that the girl can get them easily. If somebody else arranged them, she wouldn't know where to find them.

When the servingman had made the bed, he came out, saying, "Ts'ui-huan's is burned. What's to be done?" Jen-jui said, "You don't need to worry about that." "I know," Lao Ts'an said, "come tomorrow, and I'll pay twenty ounces of silver to make a new set." The man said, "It's not a question of the money, don't worry, Sir; it's a question of what she is to sleep on tonight." "I tell you not to worry yourself about it," Jen-jui said. "You still don't understand?" Ts'ui-hua, too, said, "You're told not to worry. You can go home." The man then inclined his head and went out.

Jen-jui said to Huang Sheng, "It's very late. Put some more charcoal in the brazier, and put a pot of hot water beside it; take out my ink box and brushes; get out some sheets of eight-line white paper and an envelope; prepare two candles; put them all on the table, and then you can go to sleep." Huang Sheng replied, "Very good," and went to do as ordered.

By now Jen-jui had finished smoking. "What happened when he got into the *Chü-Jen* Hu's house?" Lao Ts'an asked, and Jen-jui continued, "When this stupid country fellow saw *Chü-Jen* Hu, he crouched on the ground and kowtowed saying, 'If only you will help my master, may your descendants for ten thousand generations be marquises!' The *Chü-Jen* Hu said, 'A marquisate won't help the matter. You've got to have money before you can do anything. Now I know His Excellency; I've been at feasts with him. If you'll first produce a thousand ounces, I'll do it for you. My reward, extra, of course.' The old fellow then pulled from under his gown a leather purse, took out two bills of five hundred and passed them to *Chü-Jen* Hu. He further said, 'If only you can settle this law case without harm to my master, no matter how much more has to be spent, I will get it!' *Chü-Jen* Hu nodded his head. After his midday meal he put on his formal gown and hat and went to pay his respects to Old Kang."

Lao Ts'an struck the edge of the *k'ang* and exclaimed, "That's bad!" Jen-jui said, "When this addled egg, *Chü-Jen* Hu, arrived, Lao Kang invited him in and they exchanged a few polite words. *Chü-Jen* Hu then took the notes for a thousand ounces in his two hands and offered them saying, 'I have come about the case of Mrs. Chia Wei. The Wei family wishes to show respect to Your Honor. They beg Your Honor to be especially kind to them.'"

Lao Ts'an said, "Of course he was very angry!" Jen-jui said, "It would have been all right if he'd got angry. But he didn't get angry." "What happened then?" Lao Ts'an asked. Jen-jui replied, "Lao Kang received it eagerly, looked at it with a chuckle, and said, 'What house are these bills on? Are they reliable?' *Chü-Jen* Hu said, 'They are on the House of Universal Abundance. It's the biggest money shop in our *hsien*. They're absolutely reliable!' Lao Kang said, 'Do you think a thousand pieces is enough for handling a case as serious as this?' *Chü-Jen* Hu answered, 'The man from the Wei family said that if only the case can be settled quickly without any trouble, he is willing to spend more!' Lao Kang said, 'Thirteen lives; let's say a thousand pieces each —that makes thirteen thousand. Very well, since you, elder brother, have come, I'll agree to reduce it by half—sixty-five hundred pieces of silver.' *Chü-Jen* Hu immediately accepted, saying, 'Yes, that's all right. That's all right.'

"Lao Kang further said, 'You, elder brother, are only a middleman; you can't take the full responsibility. Please go back and ask him to confirm the arrangement. He doesn't need to send the money. All that is necessary is for you to write saying that he is willing to make this half payment of sixty-five hundred some time later. I will trust to this and settle the case tomorrow.' The *Chü-Jen* Hu was delighted and as soon as he had left went to discuss the matter with the old country fellow. When the major-domo heard that the case could be settled without trouble, he decided to take the responsibility himself; he felt that since he had been his master's servant so many years, he would not be blamed, especially as the actual money was not wanted. Therefore in the highest spirits he wrote a promissory note for fifty-five hundred ounces and gave it to *Chü-Jen* Hu, also a note for five hundred ounces as a gift for *Chü-Jen* Hu himself.

"This addled egg, *Chü-Jen* Hu, then wrote a letter and sent it to the *hsien* yamen, together with the promissory note for fifty-five hundred ounces. Lao Kang took it and gave a receipt. The next day he went into the hall of justice to hear the case in conjunction with Wang Tzu-chin. Tzu-chin had no inkling of all that had happened. When the officials had taken their seats, the prisoners were called in. The yamen attendants brought in the father and daughter of the Wei family— both looking half dead. The two knelt in the front of the hall. Kang Pi pulled out the thousand-ounce bill and the promissory note for fifty-five hundred ounces together with the *Chü-Jen* Hu's letter and handed them to Tzu-chin to look at. Tzu-chin could say nothing, but in his heart secretly he felt very sorry for the Wei father and daughter.

"Kang Pi waited till Tzu-chin had looked the papers over. Then he called to old Wei, 'Can you read?' Old Wei replied, 'I have been brought up as a student. I can read.' Then he asked Mrs. Chia Wei, 'Can you read?' Reply: 'I studied for several years when I was little. I can recognize a few characters.'

"Old Kang then told an attendant to take the bill and the promissory note to the father and daughter for them to see. They both answered, 'I don't understand what this is about.' Kang Pi said, 'If it was something else you didn't understand it might be genuine ignorance. Whose writing is this note? And the signature at the bottom—you don't recognize that?' Then he ordered an attendant, 'Give the old fellow another look at it!' Old Wei looked and said, 'This promissory note is written by the major-domo of my house. But I don't know why he wrote it.'

"Kang Pi laughed out 'Ha! Ha!' and said, 'You don't know! Well, let me just tell you and then you'll know! Yesterday a certain *Chü-Jen* Hu came to visit me. First he gave me 1,000 ounces of silver asking me to find a way of acquitting you of this charge. Then he said that if you were acquitted, you were willing to give more. I decided that since you two wretched criminals stood out so much against torture the day before yesterday it was better to take the chance to get the truth out of him. So I said to *Chü-Jen* Hu, "Go and tell their major-domo that for killing thirteen people it is one thousand ounces each, so he must pay thirteen thousand ounces." *Chü-Jen* Hu said, "I'm afraid they can't pay as much as that in a short time." I said, "Let them know what they have to pay: it doesn't matter if they don't pay till some time later. If they can't pay one thousand each then I'll halve it and say five hundred each. That will make sixty-five hundred ounces. I can't take less." *Chü-Jen* Hu immediately agreed. But I was afraid *Chü-Jen* Hu was making a wild promise, so I insisted that he go with this offer of a half-rate to explain to your major-domo and to tell him that if he really was agreeable he should send me a promissory note and that a delay in the payment didn't matter. The next day this note was written.

" 'Let me tell you. I have neither hatred nor enmity for you. Why then do I want to ruin you? You had better realize that I am an official of the Imperial House and besides this the Governor has specially deputed me to assist His Honor Mr. Wang in hearing this case. If I were to take your silver and acquit you, not only should I betray the Governor's trust, but how would those thirteen wronged souls leave me in peace?

" 'Let me speak plainer. If you didn't maliciously cause the death of these thirteen people, why is your family willing to pay out several thousands of ounces? This is the first proof.

" 'Sixty-five hundred ounces is being paid to me. I don't know how much more has been paid to other people, but it's not necessary for me to look further into that. If you didn't cause the deaths, when I told him that we would count at the rate of five hundred ounces a person, that is sixty-five hundred ounces, that servant of yours should have said, "It really wasn't our family that did the murders, and if the Honorable Deputy will establish our innocence we will give as much as seven or eight thousand ounces, but we cannot agree to the sum of sixty-five hundred." Why did he have no hesitation but agree to calculate five hundred ounces per person? This is the second proof. I adjure you to confess everything without delay and so escape additional suffering on the instruments of torture.'

"The father and daughter then kowtowed without stopping and said, 'Most Just Sir, we really are wrongly accused!' Kang Pi struck the table and shouted in great anger, 'I have exhorted you in this way and you still don't confess! Put them in the ankle-squeezers and the thumbscrews again!' Down the hall the attendants replied like a thunder clap, 'Sha!' The ankle-squeezers and thumbscrews were brought to the front of the hall and dropped with a noise loud enough to startle and put to flight all a man's souls.

"Just as they were about to apply the torture, Kang Pi said, 'Wait a bit. You men who administer the torture, come forward. I've got something to say to you.' Several attendants advanced a few steps and knelt on one knee, calling out, 'We await Your Honor's orders.' Kang Pi said, 'I know all of your tricks. When you think a case is not very serious and you are given money, you make the torture light so that the criminal shall not suffer so much. When you think the case is very serious and there is no chance of a reversal of the judgment, if you are given money you make the torture so severe that the criminal dies right in the hall of justice and his corpse is preserved whole. Then the official is blamed for torturing people to death. I understand it all. Now you are to apply the thumbscrews to Mrs. Chia Wei, but don't turn them so that she swoons. Watch till she looks faint and then relax the pressure. When she has recovered a bit, then turn them again. If you are prepared to do this for ten days, then no matter how brave a fellow the victim is there is no danger of his not confessing!'

"Poor Mrs. Chia Wei! In less than two days she couldn't endure it. She wept aloud and could scarcely breathe. Besides she couldn't bear to have her father tortured, so she said, 'You don't need to torture me any more: I'll confess, and that will be the end of it. I poisoned them! My father knew absolutely nothing about it.' Kang Pi said, 'Why did you kill them—the whole family?' Mrs. Wei replied, 'I quarreled with my sister-in-law and intended to poison her.' 'If you quarreled with your sister-in-law,' Kang Pi said, 'it would have been quite enough to poison her. Why did you poison the whole family?' Mrs. Wei said, 'I only wanted to hurt her, but I didn't have an opportunity, so the only way was to put poison in the sweet paste for the moon cakes. She was very fond of moon cakes, so I thought she would be poisoned first, and the rest of them wouldn't be hurt.' Kang Pi asked, 'What poison did you put into the moon cakes?' Reply: 'It was arsenic.' 'Where did the arsenic come from?' Reply: 'I sent someone to buy it in a medicine shop.' 'Which medicine shop was it bought in?' 'I didn't go myself but sent someone to buy it, so I don't know what shop.' Question: 'Who did you send to buy it?' Reply: 'It was a workman from my mother-in-law's family, Wang the Second, who later died of the poison.' Question: 'If Wang the Second bought it for you, how is it that he ate a moon cake and was poisoned to death?' Reply: 'When I sent him to buy the arsenic, I said it was to poison rats with, so he didn't know.' Question: 'You say your father didn't know about it. Do you mean to tell me that you didn't consult him?' Reply: 'The arsenic was bought from my mother-in-law's house. I bought it a long time ago. I was hoping to find an opportunity to put it in my sister-in-law's rice bowl. For several days no chance offered itself, and then it happened that when I went home I found that they were making the filling for moon cakes. I asked why they were making it, and they said it was to send to my house as a present for the festival. I watched for a time when nobody was about and then stirred the arsenic into the paste.'

"Kang Pi nodded his head and said, 'Very good. Very good.' Then he further said, 'I perceive that you are a very straightforward person. What you have confessed is no doubt quite true. But I have heard it said that your father-in-law was accustomed to treat you very harshly. Is that true?' Mrs. Wei said, 'My father-in-law treated me as kindly as he treated his own daughters: he couldn't have been more kind.' Kang Pi said, 'Your father-in-law is dead, so why do you want to protect him?'

"When Mrs. Wei heard this she lifted up her head, her willow-leaf eyebrows slanted upwards, her almond eyes became round and in a loud voice she said, 'Mr. Kang! You wanted to convict me of a crime punishable by the lingering death. I have already satisfied your wish. Since I have killed my father-in-law, I am liable to the slow death! Why must you try to make it into an intentional murder? You have boys and girls in your own family! I implore you to withdraw your insinuation.' Kang Pi laughed and said, 'As an official it is my duty to trace things "to the source of the stream and the end of the mountains." [2] Now that we have got so far, first of all let her put her signature to this testimony.' "

Huang Jen-jui then went on, "All this happened two days ago. Now he wants to settle accounts with the old fellow. Yesterday I had a meal in the yamen. Wang Tzu-chin was nearly dead with anger, but he had to force himself not to speak, for if he were to open his mouth it would have seemed as though he had received a sum of money from the Wei family. Prefect Li is also here, and he too thinks that the case is not being properly conducted, but he can't do anything. We agreed that the only way to put things right would be to get Prefect Pai, Pai Tzu-shou, here. This Killer Kang prides himself on being honest and incorruptible, but I have no doubt that Prefect Pai's probity is more to be relied on than his. Pai Tzu-shou's character and learning are praised by everybody so that Kang Pi would not dare to treat him with contempt. Apart from him there is not a man who can overrule Kang Pi. The only trouble is that a final report on the case is going to be sent up within a day or two. The Governor is very hasty by nature, and when once the report is forwarded to the Emperor, it will be almost impossible to do anything. The main difficulty is in approaching the Governor. We officials [3] have to avoid arousing suspicion. Yesterday when I saw you, my friend, I was happy to the core of my heart, for surely you can find a way of doing something about it."

Lao Ts'an said, "I have no very satisfactory plan of action. But in a case of this kind where circumstances are already so pressing, you can't make a perfect plan, but have to meet the situation as it is. I'll write a detailed letter, reporting the case to the Governor, and asking him to send Prefect Pai to re-examine it. Whether it will come off or not, that I can't promise. There are many injustices in this world. When they come to my knowledge, I do what I can to help, and that's all."

Jen-jui said, "Splendid! Splendid! There's no time to waste. Brush, ink, and paper are all ready. Please start right away, my friend. Ts'ui-huan, you go and light the candles and make some tea."

With an air of absorption Lao Ts'an went into Jen-jui's room. Ts'ui-huan lit the candles. Lao Ts'an opened the ink box, pulled out a brush, spread out the paper, took up the brush, and began to write. To his surprise the ink in the box was frozen hard like a block of stone; the brush too was frozen like a date stone: he couldn't write even half a stroke. Ts'ui-huan carried the ink box to the brazier and warmed it, while Lao Ts'an took the brush in his hand and went to the brazier where he warmed it meditatively. In a very short time white vapor rose from the ink box, showing that the bottom had melted. Lao Ts'an dipped into the ink and wrote. After every two lines he had to warm it again, but in less than half a watch the letter was finished. He put it in an envelope and was ready to say to Jen-jui, "The letter is finished; who shall we send it by?" So he ordered Ts'ui-huan, "Ask Mr. Huang to come in."

Ts'ui-huan lifted up the *lientzu* and then began to giggle uncontrollably, *ke-ke*. She called in a low voice, "Mr. T'ieh, do come and look!" Lao Ts'an looked out. There was Huang Jen-jui at the south end of the *k'ang* nursing his pipe with both hands, his head sprawled across the pillow, three or four inches of saliva hanging from his mouth, his feet covered with a wolfskin rug. A look in the other direction showed Ts'ui-hua sleeping on a tigerskin rug, her two feet curled up in her clothes, her two hands tucked into her sleeves; her head wasn't on the pillow; one half of her face was buried in the overlap of her jacket, the other half was pressed against her sleeve. Both of them were fast, fast asleep.

Lao Ts'an looked and said, "But they mustn't do this. Let's wake them up! Quick!" He then went and tapped Jen-jui saying, "Wake up! You'll catch cold if you lie around like this." Jen-jui woke with a start and, half-dazed, opened his eyes and said, "Ah! Ah! Have you finished the letter?" "Finished!" Lao Ts'an said. Jen-jui pulled himself together and sat up. The thread of saliva slid down his sleeve and into the smoking tray and broke into several parts. What do you think? It had turned into an icicle!

While Lao Ts'an was tapping Jen-jui, Ts'ui-huan went over to Ts'ui-hua. She felt around under her clothes for her two feet and using all her strength tugged at them. Ts'ui-hua came to with a start, and cried,

"Who is it, who is it?" Then she rubbed her eyes and said, "I'm perishing with cold!"

Both of them got up and rushed over to the brazier to get warm. Since there had been nobody to put on more charcoal, all that was left was a layer of white ash and a few sparks but it was still warm. Ts'ui-huan said, "The fire in the other room is still blazing. Let's go in there right away to get warm."

All four then went into the inner room. Ts'ui-hua saw three lots of bedding laid out neatly and evenly, so she went to look at the one sent from the yamen. There was a quilt of blue Huchou silk crepe,⁴ a quilt of red Huchou silk crepe, two big woolen pads, and a pillow. She showed them to Lao Ts'an saying, "Look at this bedding! Isn't it beautiful!" Lao Ts'an said, "Much too good." Then he said to Jen-jui, "The letter is finished; won't you look at it?"

Continuing to toast himself by the fire, Jen-jui took the letter and read it from start to finish, then said, "Very well put. I should say it's bound to produce results." "How shall we send it?" Lao Ts'an said. Jen-jui pulled out his watch from his waist, looked at it, and said, "Four o'clock. If we wait a bit, it will be light, and I'll ask the yamen to send a man." Lao Ts'an said, "People in the yamen rise late. It'll be better to discuss it with our landlord when it gets light and hire a man to take it—much more reliable. The only difficulty is in crossing the river." "People got across the ice already last night," Jen-jui said. "One man alone can cross the river quite easily."

They all hugged the fire, chatting freely. Two or three hours passed very pleasantly and before they were aware of it, the east was bright. Jen-jui woke up Huang Sheng and told him to arrange with the innkeeper to hire a man to take a letter to the provincial capital. He said, "It's not more than forty li. If he delivers it before noon and brings back a receipt in the afternoon, I'll give him ten ounces of silver."

After a while the inn servant came in with a man and said, "This is my brother; if you want to send a letter, Sir, he can take it. He has often taken letters. He's quite good at doing errands, and when he reaches the yamen, he won't be afraid to go in, so please set your mind at rest." Jen-jui immediately gave him the petition to the Governor. He then got ready and went to deliver it.

Here Jen-jui said, "Now we really must go to sleep." Huang and T'ieh lay down at the two ends; the two Ts'uis slept in the middle. In no time at all they were all snoring away. When they woke up, it was already noon and the servant from Ts'ui-hua's house had been waiting in the outer court for a long time, ready to take the two "sisters" back. He rolled up the bedding, put it on his shoulder, and prepared to go.

Jen-jui said, "Bring them again tonight: we won't send anyone specially to call for them." The servant replied, "Very good, Sir," and started off with them. Ts'ui-huan turned round, her two eyes pools of tears. "Don't forget!" she said. Jen-jui and Lao Ts'an both laughed and nodded.

The two men washed, rested awhile, and then had their noon meal. When they had finished, it was past two o'clock. Jen-jui now had to go to the yamen, so he said, "If the reply comes, let me know." "All right," Lao Ts'an replied. "Don't you worry."

Not more than two hours after Jen-jui had gone, the landlord led in the messenger, his head covered with sweat. He came in and pulled from under his jacket a large official envelope with a big purple seal.[5] When opened, it was found to contain two replies: one in Governor Chuang's own writing, characters bigger than walnuts; one a letter from the secretary, Yüan Hsi-ming, saying that Prefect Pai was now at T'aian, but that someone was being sent to take his place and that he would probably arrive in six or seven days. It further said, "The Governor hopes very much that you will wait a few days until Prefect Pai has arrived to discuss the whole matter."

When Lao Ts'an had read it he said to the messenger, "Go and have a rest. Come tonight for your reward. Tell Huang Sheng to come." The landlord said, "He's gone into the yamen with the Honorable Mr. Huang." Lao Ts'an thought to himself, "Who shall I send these letters by? The best thing is to go myself." So he told the landlord where he was going, locked the door, and betook himself to the *hsien* yamen. Inside the main gate he saw a great many runners going in and out and knew there must be a case in process. When he had gone through the inner gate, he soon became aware of the awe-inspiring atmosphere of the hall of justice, with its rows of attendants lined up on the two sides. He thought for a while, then said to himself, "Why shouldn't I go on in and see what sort of a case it is?" He took up a position behind the attendants but could see nothing.

He heard only a loud voice in the hall saying, 'Mrs. Chia Wei, I want you to understand! Your death for murder is settled; that can't be changed. But you have done all you can to exculpate your father, saying that he knew nothing about the crime. This shows your filial piety, and we have no objection to his life's being saved. But if you do not confess who your paramour was, your father's life cannot be guaranteed. Just think of what your paramour has done! He has brought you into all this suffering while he hides far away and doesn't even send you a bowl of rice. This man's love must be pretty thin, and yet you will suffer death rather than be willing to confess who he is, and prefer to let your father suffer death in his place! The Sage has said, 'Any man may be husband to a woman, but she can have but one father.' [6] If even a proper husband is not to be considered before a father, what is to be said about a casual lover! I adjure you to make a full confession." All that could be heard was a sound from below the magistrates' table of sobbing and crying, *ying-ying*. Then a loud voice was heard from the presiding desk, "You still won't confess? If you won't, I shall torture you again!"

From below an almost inaudible voice said a few words, but you couldn't hear what they were. Then a loud voice from above: "What does she say?" A secretary went up and answered, "Mrs. Chia Wei says that in things that concern her alone, whatever Your Honor orders she will agree to; but if you want her to fabricate a paramour, she can not do so."

Again the judge struck the table with his gavel and with a menacing voice cried, "This adulterous woman is indeed cunning and deceitful! Put her in the thumbscrews!" Down in the body of the hall countless voices shouted, "Sha!" You could hear several men run forward and throw down the thumbscrews with a sudden noise, *huo-ch'o,* enough to startle the heart and put to flight the souls.

When Lao Ts'an had heard thus far, his anger rose within him, so that disregarding the sanctity of the hall of justice, he parted the attendants with his hands, shouting with a loud voice, "Stand aside! Let me pass!" The attendants moved out of the way.

Lao Ts'an walked to the middle of the hall. He saw that an attendant had grasped Mrs. Chia Wei's hair and was lifting up her head. Two others were just pushing her hands into the thumbscrews. Lao Ts'an went up, pulled the men away and said, "Hold!" Then he marched with great strides up to the *nuan ke.*[7] There were two men sitting at the presiding desk: in the lower seat [8] Wang Tzu-chin; in the upper seat he knew it must be Kang Pi. He first bowed to Kang Pi.

When Tzu-chin saw it was Lao Ts'an, he hurriedly rose. But Kang Pi didn't know him. He didn't get up but shouted, "Who are you that dares to come in and disturb the hall of justice! Drag him out!"

If you don't know how Lao Ts'an was dragged out and what happened afterwards, then hear the next chapter tell.

CHAPTER 17

At the sound of an "iron cannon" torture is relaxed;

Three airs on an inn lute—"jade bracelet reward."

IT HAS been told that when Lao Ts'an saw Mrs. Chia Wei about to be put to torture he quickly pushed his way forward and called to them to halt. Kang Pi, not knowing who Lao Ts'an was or where he came from, and seeing that he wore a blue gown and an ordinary cap, ordered the attendants to drag him out. But somehow when the attendants saw that their own *hsien* magistrate had stood up they realized this must be a man of some antecedents, and though they responded with a shout, *Sha!*, not a single man of them ventured to move forward.

When Lao Ts'an saw that Kang Pi's face was absolutely flushed with anger and when he heard him shout, he intentionally led him on and said to him gently, "Won't you first ask who I am and let me say a few words? If what I say is not satisfactory, you have lots of instruments of torture down there, and I shan't mind if you give me a few blows and squeeze me in your presses. But I want to ask you: here is an old gentleman with not long to live, and here a cloistered maid—I am not concerned with the nature of the case—and you put manacles on their hands and fetters on their feet; what is it all for? Surely you're not afraid they will break prison and run away? These are tools for handling fierce bandits. If you freely use them on honest subjects, where is divine justice? And where is your conscience?"

Wang Tzu-chin couldn't imagine that the Governor's reply had already come, and fearing that Lao Ts'an and Kang Pi would begin an altercation in the hall of justice, which would be intolerable, he quickly called out, "Venerable Mr. Pu, won't you come into the reception room? This is the hall of justice, not a convenient place for talking in." Kang Pi was so angry that his eyes started from his head and his lips refused to move. But hearing Tzu-chin address this man as "Venerable Mr. Pu," he realized he must have some sort of antecedents, and didn't dare to be too highhanded with him.

Lao Ts'an knew that Tzu-chin was in a dilemma, so he went over to the west end of the table and bowed to him. Tzu-chin immediately returned the greeting and said "Come and sit in the reception room at the back." Lao Ts'an said, "There's no hurry." Then he took the Governor's reply out of his sleeve and presented it to Tzu-chin with both hands.

When Tzu-chin saw the big purple seal, unconsciously joy lighted up his whole face. He took the letter with both hands, opened it, and read in a loud voice, "Your letter received. Prefect Pai Ch'i will arrive soon after this letter. Please inform the two magistrates, Wang and Kang, they are not to torture indiscriminately. Let Wei Ch'ien and his daughter offer bail and go home and wait for the arrival of Prefect Pai for further examination. Your younger brother Yao greets you." He handed it to Kang Pi to read, and at the same time gave the order in a loud voice, "The Governor's order has been received to release Wei Ch'ien and his daughter from their shackles. They are to offer bail and go home. When his Excellency Mr. Pai has arrived, the hearing will be resumed." From below came the sound in reply, *Sha!*, and a shout, "Release the prisoners! Release the prisoners!" Immediately many hands got to work and made a clean job of removing the manacles and fetters from the hands and feet of the father and daughter and the iron chains from their necks. Then the men told them to go forward and kowtow and said on their behalf, "They wish to thank the Governor for his mercy. They wish to thank their Excellencies, Kang and Wang, for their mercy."

When Kang Pi had read the letter he "dared to be angry, but dared not speak." [1] And when he heard them thanking their Excellencies,

Kang and Wang, for their mercy, it was like a dagger stabbing him in the heart. He couldn't keep his seat but went out to the rear hall.

Tzu-chin then raised his clasped hands towards Lao Ts'an and said, "Please come and sit in the reception room. I must go and settle a few things about this case, and then I will come and talk to you." Lao Ts'an raised his hands in thanks and said, "Please proceed with your work. I have some other business to do. Excuse me." Then he left the hall and swaggered out of the yamen.

Wang Tzu-chin now ordered a clerk to tell Wei Ch'ien and his daughter to produce their bail as soon as possible so that they could go away that night. The clerk went to obey. Then the drum was sounded, and the court was dismissed.

The story goes on that as Lao Ts'an went back, all along the way he was very elated, thinking to himself, "The other day I was hearing of Yü Hsien's various oppressions and was unable to do anything. To-day again I have with my own eyes seen a tyrannical official, but by means of a letter I have been able to save two lives. My heart is lighter than if I had eaten of the fruit of immortality!" Walking along in this way, without realizing it, he went out of the city gate and soon was at the Yellow River dike. He climbed up onto the dike. It was approaching dusk; the Yellow River was frozen and like a great highway; already wheelbarrows were going to and fro without ceasing. He began to think, "Baggage all burned; there's nothing at all to hold me back. Tomorrow I can travel light to the city. It's a good opportunity to go and buy some new things." But again he remembered, "Yüan Hsi-ming has written asking me to wait till Mr. Pai arrives in order to help in the consultation. I know that Mr. Pai will conduct this affair 'with ample room for the knife,' [2] but if there are points which he does not completely understand, won't my going perhaps be a loss? I had better contain myself and wait a few days and then see." While thinking these thoughts, he had reached the gate of his inn. As he strolled in, he saw a number of men busy clearing up the debris of the fire. They had heaped up a pile of fragments of silk and cloth. He didn't go to look at it but went to the main room and sat down alone.

After two hours or so Jen-jui came in saying, "Wonderful! Wonderful!" He explained, "After that Killer Kang had left the hall, he told his men to prepare his baggage in order to return to the capital. Tzu-chin, knowing that the Governor has a credulous ear, was afraid that

if Kang got back to the city there would be further complications, so
he did all he could to keep him here. He said, 'The Governor has only
deputized Prefect Pai to hold a new inquiry: there is no order calling
you back to the capital. So long as this case is not finished, you can't
go. If you go like this and resign your charge, won't it be venting your
anger on the Governor? And surely that is not in keeping with your
principles of reverence and sincerity.' Kang thought it over and finally
resigned himself to staying. Tzu-chin intended to invite you in to dine.
I said, 'That's not wise. It's better for you to send him a table of good
food and let me play host for you.' I have come entrusted with this task.
What do you think of that?"

"You've done very well for yourself," Lao Ts'an said. "You get a free
meal; I have the burden of receiving a favor. It's very fine for you!
And if I decline, then what will you eat?" Jen-jui said, "If you are
capable of refusing, then refuse, and I'll go hungry with you."

While they were talking, a man in a red-tasseled hat appeared at
the gate holding a *ch'üan t'ieh;* after him came a man bearing a set of
boxes containing food. They went directly to the main building, raised
the padded *lientzu,* and entered. The first said to Jen-jui, indicating
Lao Ts'an, "Is this the Honorable Mr. T'ieh?" Jen-jui said, "Quite
right." The servant then took a hurried pace forward, made a genuflection, and said, "My master says that his poor district produces no good
food; he is sending you a table of coarse dishes and hopes that Your
Honor will be tolerant." Lao Ts'an said, "The food in this inn is quite
good enough. I won't trespass on your master's good nature. Please
carry it back so that he can send it to somebody else." The servant said,
"My master has ordered it. Please, Sir, do him the honor of accepting.
I dare not on any account carry it back. I should get a severe scolding."

Jen-jui placed a sheet of letter paper on the table, took the cap off a
brush, and said to the servant, "Tell them to take it out to the kitchen."
The servant raised the lid and asked the gentlemen to have a look. It
was a sumptuous shark's fin feast. Lao Ts'an said, "I am not worthy of
even a simple meal; this wine feast is far too much of an honor: I don't
dare to accept."

Jen-jui had already finished working with his pen on the flowered
paper, and handed it to the servant saying, "This is Mr. T'ieh's reply:
go back and express his thanks. That's all." Then he told Huang Sheng
to give the servant a string of cash and the carrier two hundred cash.
The servant made two genuflections.

At this point Huang Sheng brought on the lamp, and before half an hour had elapsed, Ts'ui-hua and Ts'ui-huan both arrived. Their man didn't wait for the order, but carried their two bedding rolls into the inner room. Jen-jui said, "Your bedding certainly didn't take long to make! Half a day and all finished!" Ts'ui-hua said, "There is lots of bedding in our house. By sharing around we can make it enough."

Huang Sheng came in to ask whether he should serve the dinner. "Serve it," Jen-jui said. After a quarter of an hour the cold dishes were arranged on the table. Jen-jui said, "Although the north wind is not blowing today, still it's very cold. Let's have some wine heated and drink a few cups. Today is such a happy day we ought to drink a little extra." The two Ts'uis took up their banjos and sang a few airs to encourage the drinkers. Then Jen-jui said, "Don't sing. You come and drink too."

Ts'ui-hua, seeing the two of them in such good spirits, asked, "Why are you in such good spirits? I suppose the man who took your letter to the Governor must be back?" Jen-jui said, "Do you think it's only because the reply has come? Why, old man Wei and his girl are probably both already back in their home by now!" Then he told the whole story to the two Ts'uis. It goes without saying that the "sisters" were pleased beyond measure.

When Ts'ui-huan had heard this story, she kept laughing quietly to herself. Suddenly again she knit her willow-leaf brows and became quite silent. Do you know why? She laughed when she heard how much trust the Governor put in a letter from Lao Ts'an. Surely he could settle her affair as easily as blowing dust off the table. And then she began to wonder whether, though their power was sufficient, their talk of last night was serious or not. If they were only talking for the sake of talking, then this opportunity would be lost to her, and to the end of her life she would have no hope of escape. This is why she knit her brows. And then she remembered how her mistress was certain to sell her off by the end of the year and how brutal that Baldhead K'uai the Second was—sooner or later she would die at his hands—and unbeknown to herself, her face turned the color of dead ashes. And then she began to think of herself, the daughter of a respectable family, somehow or other sunk into this kind of degraded life—it would be better to die—and then a new expression of courage and determination came into her eyes. Again she thought: while death might be the best thing for her personally, who would look after her little six-year-old brother; wouldn't he starve to death? And if he starved to death, not only would her father and mother have no one to sacrifice to them, but also the burning of incense to their ancestors would come to an end. No, she couldn't afford to die. She turned it over and over in her mind: she could not live, and yet she must not die. Before she was aware of it, the tears began to stream down her cheeks; she hastened to wipe them with her handkerchief.

Ts'ui-hua saw it and said, "You miserable little fool! The gentlemen are in good spirits tonight. What's come over you this time?" Jen-jui looked at her and merely grinned. Lao Ts'an nodded to her and said, "You don't need to think a lot of stupid thoughts. We are certainly going to help you." "That's right. That's right," Jen-jui said, "Mr. T'ieh will rescue you by himself, and you won't need to count on what I said last night."

Ts'ui-huan was startled when she heard this and felt that her anxiety had not been misplaced. She was just going to question Jen-jui when Huang Sheng came in with a man who made a genuflection to Jen-jui and handed him a red envelope. Jen-jui took it, held open the end of the envelope, and peeped inside; then he put it under his gown, said that it was quite all right, and began to chuckle. Huang Sheng said, "Will you please come out for a few words, Sir?" Jen-jui then went out.

After about half a watch, he came back to find the three of them looking at each other and not saying a word. Jen-jui was in even better spirits than he had been before. Then the servant from the yamen came in, made a genuflection to Lao Ts'an, and said, "My master told me to fetch back the roll of old bedding that was borrowed yesterday." Lao Ts'an was taken aback and thought to himself, "What does this mean? If you take it away, what shall I sleep on tonight?" But, after all, it was somebody else's property, and he couldn't very well hold on to it, so he said, "You may take it," but in his heart he felt rather puzzled. He watched the servant go into the room and take it away. Then Jen-jui said, "We started by being very cheerful tonight, but this Ts'ui-huan's unhappiness has made me unhappy too. We won't drink any more. Let them take away all the dishes." Then Huang Sheng came in and actually did take away the dishes.

By this time not only were the two Ts'uis wondering what it all meant, but even Lao Ts'an felt that something queer was afoot. Next Huang Sheng led in Ts'ui-huan's man to take away her bedding roll.

Ts'ui-huan quickly asked, "What's the matter? What are you doing? Why can't I stay here?" The servant said, "I don't know. I was only told to take the bedding back."

And now Ts'ui-huan couldn't control herself, for she was convinced that her doom had come. Impulsively, holding back her tears, she threw herself at Jen-jui's feet and said, "Even if I am unworthy, since you are honorable gentlemen, won't you be patient with me? If you are displeased, then we are lost." Jen-jui said, "I am very pleased with you. Why shouldn't I be pleased? But I can't do anything to help you. You had better go and beg Mr. T'ieh to help."

Ts'ui-huan then knelt in front of Lao Ts'an and begged, "Won't you help me, Sir?" Lao Ts'an said, "What's that? You want me to help you?" Ts'ui-huan said, "Since they are taking back the bedding, they must have got wind of what was said last night. My mistress knows the plan and won't let me stay here tonight, but is forcing me to go back today so that tomorrow I can be taken far away. Do you think she could stand up to an official? Her only chance is to run." "There's something in what you say," Lao Ts'an replied. "Brother Jen-jui, you must think of a solution. We must keep her here. If she is once back in the hands of her mistress, it will be difficult to do anything." Jen-jui said, "There's no need to tell me that! Of course she must be kept here. And if you don't keep her, who can?"

Lao Ts'an then lifted Ts'ui-huan up, saying to Jen-jui, "I think I understand what you are saying. But surely you don't mean that what you said last night is not really to be counted on?" Jen-jui said, "I've thought the matter over thoroughly; the only thing for me is to withdraw. You must realize: to rescue one of the 'sisterhood' someone must be pledged to take her. If neither you nor I will take her openly, what pledge can we give? If we just get her out, where are we going to put her? If we keep her in the inn and neither of us acknowledges her, people will certainly blame me; there's no doubt about that. I have just got a good appointment. Well, there are lots of envious people about. Do you think nobody will tell the Governor? And, if they do, I shan't need to hang about in Shantung any more! And what sort of promotion can I hope for? No! It's out of the question for me!"

Lao Ts'an realized there was some truth in these remarks, but he couldn't bear to see Ts'ui-huan left to her fate on this account. Add to this that Ts'ui-huan wept without ceasing, and it was indeed a difficult situation. So he said to Jen-jui, "In spite of all this, we must find a satisfactory solution." Jen-jui said, "Well, you think it over; if you can think of something, I'll certainly help you."

Lao Ts'an thought a while but without success. Then he said, "There seems to be no way out, yet we must all try to think of a way." Jen-jui said, "I have a solution, but you won't want to act on it, so I might as well keep quiet." "Speak out," said Lao Ts'an, "I'll certainly do what I can." Jen-jui said, "The only thing is for you to agree to take her as your concubine. Then we can claim her." "All right then," Lao Ts'an replied, "I'll agree to take her." "Are empty words any use?" Jen-jui said. "If I make the arrangements and just tell people that you want her, who will believe me? I can't do anything unless you yourself will write me a letter. Then I can settle it." Lao Ts'an said, "That's rather hard to do." "I said you wouldn't do it, didn't I?" Jen-jui replied.

While Lao Ts'an sat irresolute, the two Ts'uis came forward to plead with him, "Don't take it too seriously; it's not a very big responsibility." Lao Ts'an said, "What do you want me to write? And to whom?" Jen-jui said, "Naturally you will write to Wang Tzu-chin. Just say, 'I have seen a certain prostitute, originally of a respectable family, very pitiful. I propose to rescue her from the life of "wind and dust" and take her to be my concubine. I entreat your powerful influence [3] to support me. I will pay according to the price set.' With such a letter I can manage it. And afterwards it will rest with you either to send her away or find her a mate. You will be quite free to do either. And then I won't be blamed. Is there any other solution besides this?"

While he was speaking, Huang Sheng came in and said, "Miss Ts'ui-huan, come out; a person from your house wants you." When Ts'ui-huan heard this her souls flew beyond the sky. She said she was coming, and at the same time she pleaded desperately with Lao Ts'an to write the letter. Ts'ui-hua then went into the inner room to get paper, ink, brush, and ink slab, dipped the brush, and put it into Lao Ts'an's hand.

Lao Ts'an took the brush, sighed, and said to Ts'ui-huan, "Is there any justice in this, that I should put my signature to such a statement on your account?" Ts'ui-huan said, "I will make you a thousand kow-tows! By this one small sacrifice you will gain more merit than if you built a pagoda of seven stories." When Lao Ts'an had finished writing as he was told, he gave the letter to Jen-jui, saying, "I've done my part. And now if the thing is not successfully carried out, the fault will be yours." Jen-jui took the letter, gave it to Huang Sheng, and said, "After a while send it to the yamen."

While Lao Ts'an was writing the letter, Huang Jen-jui had whispered several words into Ts'ui-hua's ear. When Huang Sheng took the letter, he said to Ts'ui-huan, "Your mistress is waiting to speak to you. Go to her right away." Ts'ui-huan still held out and wouldn't go. Then she looked at Jen-jui as though pleading for help. Jen-jui said, "Go on. It's all right. I'll look after everything."

Ts'ui-hua got up, took Ts'ui-huan's hand and said, "Sister Huan, I'll go with you. Don't worry; there's nothing at all to worry about." There was nothing for Ts'ui-huan to do but take her leave and go out.

And now Jen-jui lay down on the smoking *k'ang*, lit his pipe, and chatted with Lao Ts'an in a desultory way. After about an hour, when Jen-jui had smoked enough, Huang Sheng came in wearing a brand new official hat and said, "Will the gentlemen please come to the other room?" Jen-jui said, "Ah," got up, and pulled Lao Ts'an, saying, "Let's go over there." Lao Ts'an was greatly surprised, "Since when has this 'over there' existed?" Jen-jui said, "This 'over there' has made its appearance only today."

Now the main building of the inn was divided into two suites of three *chien*. Jen-jui was living in the three *chien* to the west. The other three *chien* to the east had been occupied by another person who had left that morning to cross the river, so the rooms were now empty.

The two of them, Huang and T'ieh, walked hand in hand till they were in front of the east suite; as they went up the steps somebody raised the padded *lientzu*. Inside they saw an "altar cloth" [4] attached to the square table in the center, a pair of red candles alight on the table, and a red carpet spread on the floor.[5] When they got inside the door they saw another square table arranged in the *chien* to the east, with an "altar cloth" attached to the side facing south, two chairs arranged in the places of honor, and one chair on each of the two sides, all with coverings. Moreover the table was almost completely hidden by the plates of fruit and delicacies of a feast much finer than the one they had just been eating. The *chien* to the west was walled off, with a red wool *lientzu* hung in the doorway.

Greatly surprised, Lao Ts'an said, "What's the meaning of this?" Jen-jui's only reply was to call out in a loud voice, "Lead out the new mistress to be presented to her lord." Then the *lientzu* was raised and a beautiful girl came out supported on the left by an old womanservant and on the right by Ts'ui-hua. The girl's head was covered with ornaments; she wore a plum-colored jacket, a sunflower-green gown, and a pale pink skirt. Hanging her head, she went over to the red carpet.

A close look showed Lao Ts'an that this was Ts'ui-huan, so he cried out, "What's the meaning of this? This is quite impossible." Jen-jui said, "You've signed the declaration with your own hand. What tricks are you up to now?" and, without giving him a chance to reply, dragged Lao Ts'an over and sat him on his chair. But Lao Ts'an refused to be sat there.

And now Ts'ui-huan went down to kowtow. Lao Ts'an couldn't help responding with a half-bow. Then the old womanservant said, "Mr. Huang, please take your seat," and then, "Thank the honorable matchmaker." Ts'ui-huan then kowtowed again. Jen-jui said, "I don't deserve any credit," and returned the salutation. Then the "new one" was led into the inner room. Ts'ui-hua soon came out, kowtowed, and felicitated the husband. The maidservant and all the others also expressed their congratulations. Then Jen-jui dragged Lao Ts'an into the inner room.

The inner room had been fitted up very comfortably with new bedding, to wit, a coverlet of red Huchou crepe and one of green; a pad of fine red wool cloth, and one of green; two pillows; in front of the *k'ang* was hung a reddish purple Lushan silk curtain; on the table was spread a red table cover with a pair of red candles; while on the wall were hung a pair of red *tui-lien* on which was written:

> May all lovers under the sky achieve the marriage state;
> These things are fixed in heaven: do not miss your mate.

Lao Ts'an recognized the work of Jen-jui's pen—the ink was barely dry—so he laughed at Jen-jui, "You certainly are a mischievous rascal! This is the *tui-lien* from the Shrine of the Man in the Moon at West Lake [6] that you've cribbed." Jen-jui replied, "Anything which fits the occasion is a piece of good writing. Do you dare to say it doesn't fit?"

Jen-jui proceeded to pull out from under his gown the red envelope that had been sent from the yamen some time before and handed it to Lao Ts'an saying, "Look, this is your honorable concubine's original deed of sale; and this is the new deed. Allow me to hand them to you together. What do you say; does this stupid little brother do things thoroughly or doesn't he?" Lao Ts'an said, "Since it's already done, I'm very grateful. But why did you have to trick me into it?" Jen-jui said, "Haven't I said to you, 'These things are fixed in heaven: do not miss your mate'? I was thinking of Ts'ui-huan's good. If you're going to help somebody, you must help them thoroughly. Without this, it couldn't be a hundred per cent safe. And on your side, you don't lose anything. In this world things have to be done in this way; there is no doubt about it." With this he guffawed and then continued, "Let's not waste our breath. Our bellies are crying out for food. Let's eat."

Jen-jui dragged Lao Ts'an along. Ts'ui-hua led Ts'ui-huan, and they tried to make them take the seats of honor. Lao Ts'an refused obstinately, and finally they took off the "altar cloth" and sat, one at each side of the table. It goes without saying that at this feast each person had his own particular cause for happiness. And no doubt they had enjoyed themselves fully when they separated. Then of course the newlyweds were escorted to their bedchamber, and we don't need to say anything further.

It is further told that having been forced into his felicity by Jen-jui, Lao Ts'an was rather disgruntled and wanted to be revenged. He had noticed the night before that, though Ts'ui-hua was cold herself, she had used the tigerskin rug to cover Jen-jui's legs; also that she had taken a lot of trouble to arrange things for Ts'ui-huan. Seen with a cool eye, she was truly a virtuous girl. She deserved to be rescued too. Some time in the future he would plan how to do it.

Next morning Jen-jui ran in and smiling said to Ts'ui-huan, "Did you sleep peacefully in the corner of the *k'ang* last night?" Ts'ui-huan answered, "Everything has been done through Mr. Huang's great kindness. I will always worship your immortal spirit-tablet." "Don't say that," Jen-jui replied, "I've done very little." Then turning to Lao Ts'an he said, "It was Tzu-chin who advanced the three hundred ounces yesterday; I'm going to the yamen today to pay it back for you. It was Tzu-chin who supplied the clothes, quilts, and pillows, but you don't need to be sensitive about accepting them. If you send money for them, he won't take it." Lao Ts'an said, "What do you mean? Let somebody else spend all that money! Please thank him for me, and I will find some way of repaying him."

When this had been said, Jen-jui went to the yamen. Since Ts'ui-huan's name was in rather poor taste, Lao Ts'an didn't want to use it

any more, so he turned it around and changed it into Huan-ts'ui.[7]
This then became her *pieh hao*, much better sounding. In the afternoon a man was sent and fetched her little brother. Seeing that the
boy's clothes were very shabby, Lao Ts'an gave him several ounces
of silver and told Li Wu to take him to buy some new clothes.

Time went very quickly, five days passed unperceived. Then one
day when Jen-jui had gone to the yamen and Lao Ts'an was in the
inn teaching Huan-ts'ui to recognize characters, suddenly the inn
servant announced, "His Honor the *hsien* magistrate, Mr. Wang, is
coming."

A few moments and Tzu-chin's sedan chair reached the foot of the
steps, and he got out. Lao Ts'an went to the main door to welcome
him. Tzu-chin came in, they sat down as guest and host, and then he
said, "Prefect Pai is arriving soon; I am on my way to meet him; I have
taken the opportunity to come and congratulate you and to chat for
a while." Lao Ts'an said, "I asked Jen-jui to convey to you my sincerest
thanks for all your kindnesses of the other day. Since Mr. Kang was
at the yamen, it wasn't convenient for me to come myself to thank you;
I hope you will forgive me." Tzu-chin said very modestly, "Don't mention it." Then the "new one" was called out to pay her respects. Tzu-
chin gave her several pieces of jewelry as presents on the occasion of
his congratulatory visit. Suddenly a yamen runner rushed in at a
great speed to announce, "His Excellency Mr. Pai has arrived. He has
left his chair on the other side of the river and is crossing on the ice."
Tzu-chin quickly got in his chair and went to meet him.

*If you don't know what happened afterwards, then hear the next
chapter tell.*

CHAPTER 18

*Prefect Pai talks and laughs and rights
a strange injustice;*

*Mr. T'ieh through wind and frost begins
an investigation.*

IT HAS been told that Wang Tzu-chin hurried to the river bank to welcome Prefect Pai, who had just crossed the ice. Tzu-chin presented his official card, stepped forward, and made a genuflection, saying, "Your Excellency must be fatigued." Mr. Pai returned the greeting and said, "Why did you trouble to come out to meet me? Naturally I was planning to come to your honorable yamen to pay my respects." Tzu-chin repeatedly said, "You honor me too much, Your Excellency."

A tea booth, hung with colored silks, had been put up on the riverbank, and the guest was led into it to rest a while. Mr. Pai asked, "Has Mr. T'ieh gone yet?" Tzu-chin replied, "Not yet; he is waiting for Your Excellency to arrive in case there is need to talk things over. I have just come from Mr. T'ieh's lodging." Mr. Pai nodded and said, "Good. But I had better not go to visit him just now. It might make Mr. Kang suspicious."

By the time they had drunk a cup of tea, the sedan chair and the lackeys bearing official insignia provided by the *hsien* were made ready. Mr. Pai then entered the chair and they went to the yamen. Nothing was omitted in the raising of flags, firing of cannon, playing of music, opening of gates. So they entered the yamen, and Mr. Pai was lodged in the west reception hall.

Kang Pi had already put on his official robes and hat, and as soon as Mr. Pai arrived he presented his card and requested an audience. Greetings over, Mr. Pai asked a lot of questions as to how the Wei and Chia case had been conducted. Kang Pi, with an appearance of great satisfaction told him what had happened, finally saying, "Judging by the Governor's letter, he must have given ear to the idle talk of some meddlesome person. In my humble opinion this is already a 'cast iron' case; there is not a shadow of doubt about it. But this old fellow Wei has lots of money. He offered me a thousand ounces, and since I wouldn't accept it, he bribed somebody to go to the Governor in order to make black appear white. I'm told there is some sort of drug-selling quack who accepted a lot of money from him and wrote a letter to the Governor. Having got the money, this doctor fellow immediately bought a singsong girl. He is still staying at an inn just outside the city walls. I'm also told that if the judgment in the case is really reversed, they plan to give him several thousand ounces more, to show their appreciation. This is why this doctor does not leave; he is waiting for his fee. It seems to me that we ought to bring him in and examine him. A confession from him that he has been bribed will be an additional proof in the case."

Mr. Pai said, "What you say is quite right I'm sure; but first I should like to go over all the records relating to the case this evening, and tomorrow call all the witnesses. Then I will make my decision. Perhaps I shall come to the same conclusion as you, but I don't yet know. At the moment I prefer not to commit myself to an opinion. A person as wise and as straightforward as yourself has 'the complete bamboo in his mind' before drawing it and never makes a mistake. But I am very dull by nature. I decide about things according to the things themselves, and make detailed investigations. I can't say I never make mistakes; but if I don't make very many, I'm quite satisfied." Then he went on to gossip about events in the capital.

After the evening meal Mr. Pai returned to his room, carefully examined all the documents in the case twice, and issued an order calling the witnesses to appear on the morrow. The next day at about nine in the morning an attendant came to his door and said, "The witnesses are all here ready. Will Your Excellency please give orders whether the session shall be held this afternoon or tomorrow morning?" Mr. Pai said, "If the witnesses are already here, the session can take place immediately. Prepare three seats at the presiding table."

Mr. Kang and Mr. Wang hurried forward, genuflected, and said, "May it please Your Excellency, we might make some false judgments; it is only right that we should withdraw." Mr. Pai said, "What do you mean! I am quite stupid. My strength is insufficient to handle the case alone. I want you two to help me." The two men did not dare to excuse themselves further.

After a while, when everything in the hall was ready, the clerk of the court came up to ask the magistrates to take their places. The three magistrates donned their official robes, went in, and took their seats. Mr. Pai took up the vermilion brush; the first name to be called was that of the original plaintiff, Chia Kan. An attendant led Chia Kan foward, and he kneeled in front of the judges.

Mr. Pai asked him, "Are you Chia Kan?" From below came the answer, "Yes." Mr. Pai asked, "How old are you this year?" Reply, "Seventeen." Question: "Are you the late Chia Chih's son by birth or by adoption?" Reply: "I was originally his nephew, but then I was adopted." Question: "When were you adopted?" Reply: "The day after my late father had been poisoned. When it was time for the funeral, there was nobody to wear mourning for him, so it was decided in the clan council that I should be adopted in order to wear the mourning."

Mr. Pai further asked, "When the *hsien* magistrate held his inquiry, had you already come into the family?" Reply: "Yes." Question: "At the time of the funeral did you personally witness the placing of the jewel in the mouth and the enshrouding?" Reply: "Yes, I saw it with my own eyes." Question: "What color were the faces of the corpses when they were being put in the coffin?" Reply: "Completely white, the color of dead men." Question: "Were there any black or purple marks?" Reply: "I didn't see any." Question: "Were the joints stiff?" Reply: "Not at all stiff." Question: "If they weren't stiff, did you feel their chests to see if they were warm?" Reply: "Someone felt them and said that they weren't warm." Question: "When was it discovered that the moon cakes had arsenic in them?" Reply: "The day after the funeral." Question: "Who discovered it?" Reply: "My elder sister discovered it." Question: "How did your sister know there was arsenic in them?" Reply: "At first she didn't know, but she suspected that there was something wrong with the moon cakes, so she opened one and looked more closely, and saw pink specks. She took it to show the other people, and somebody said it was arsenic, so she called in a man from the medicine shop to examine it. He also said it was arsenic, so then we knew they had been poisoned."

Mr. Pai said, "I see. You may go." Making a mark with the vermilion brush, he said, "Bring in the man from the Studio of the Four Virtues." An attendant led him forward. Mr. Pai asked, "What's your name? What's your position at the Studio of the Four Virtues?" Reply: "My name is Wang Fu-t'ing.[1] I'm the proprietor." Question: "How many chin [catties] of moon cakes did you make to the order of the Wei family?" Reply: "I made twenty chin." Question: "Was the sweet filling sent by the Wei family?" Reply: "Yes." Question: "You made twenty chin: that is to say exactly twenty chin—not more and not less?" Reply: "Twenty chin were ordered; I made exactly eighty-three cakes." Question: "The moon cakes they ordered, did they have one kind of filling or two kinds?" Reply: "One kind. They all had a filling of crystallized sugar, sesame seeds, and walnuts." Question: "How many kinds of filling do you make in your shop?" Reply: "A great many." Question: "Do you make the sugar, sesame, and walnut variety?" Reply: "Yes." Question: "Which is better, the filling made in your shop or the filling that was made in their house?" Reply: "Theirs was better." Question: "In what way was it better?" Reply: "I don't know, but I heard our man who makes moon cakes say that they used good materials and that their flavor was more spicy and more sweet than ours."

Mr. Pai said, "Well then, when your workman tasted it, didn't he notice any poison?" Reply: "No, he didn't." Mr. Pai said, "I see. You may go." Again he made a mark with the vermilion brush, saying, "Bring in Wei Ch'ien."

Wei Ch'ien came forward and kowtowed repeatedly, saying, "Your Excellency! Not guilty!" Mr. Pai said, "I didn't ask you whether you are guilty or not guilty. Just listen to what I ask you! It's not for you to speak when I haven't asked you anything!" The yamen attendants on both sides then made a loud noise, *Sha!*

Reader, do you know the reason for this? Whenever an official hears a case, the attendants give a variety of shouts. This is called "the roar of official majesty." The idea is to frighten the prisoner out of his wits so that he will confess to anything. I don't know what dynasty the custom dates from, but it is the practice in all of the eighteen provinces. Here was Wei Ch'ien accused of a serious crime, so they gave him a roar of official majesty to frighten him.

But enough of this idle talk. The story goes on that Mr. Pai asked Wei Ch'ien, "How many moon cakes did you order?" Reply: "Twenty chin." Question: "How many chin did you send to the Chia family?" Reply: "Eight chin." Question: "Did you send to any other houses?" Reply: "We sent four chin to my son's wife's family." Question: "And the remaining eight chin?" Reply: "They were eaten by the members of my own family." Question: "Are any of your people who ate the moon cakes here now?" Reply: "I divided the cakes among all the people in my household. Every one of the men who have come here with me ate some." Mr. Pai said to the attendant, "Find all those who have come with Wei Ch'ien and bring them forward."

Shortly afterward, an old man and two middle-aged fellows came forward. They all knelt down, and the attendant reported, "Here are the major-domo of the Wei family and two farm hands." Mr. Pai asked, "Did you all eat some of the moon cakes?" They answered with one voice, "We all ate some." Question: "How many did each of you eat? Tell me, all of you." The major-domo said, "My share was four. I ate two and kept two." The laborers said, "We were each given two and we ate them up the same day." Mr. Pai asked the major-domo, "The moon cakes that you didn't eat right away: when did you eat them?" Reply: "I still hadn't eaten them when this case started and it was said that the moon cakes had poison in them; so I didn't dare eat them, but kept them as evidence." Mr. Pai said, "Good! Have you brought them with you?" Reply: "Yes, they're down there." Mr. Pai said, "Very good!" and sent an attendant with him to get them. Then he said, "Wei Ch'ien and the laborers may go." Next he asked a clerk, "Was the half moon cake containing arsenic exhibited in the court the other day?" The clerk said, "It was exhibited and is in the repository." Mr. Pai said, "Have it brought out."

In a little while the attendants brought forward the major-domo with the two moon cakes; the half moon cake from the repository was also produced. Mr. Pai then ordered Wang Fu-t'ing of the Studio of the Four Virtues to be brought forward again. While waiting for him, he compared the two kinds of moon cakes with great care and showed them to Mr. Kang and to Mr. Wang, saying, "These moon cakes certainly look alike on the outside; don't you think so?" Both of them leaned forward and agreed that they did.

By this time Wang Fu-t'ing of the Studio of the Four Virtues had been brought forward; Mr. Pai broke open one of the cakes and handed it to him telling him to examine it. He said, "Was this ordered from you by the Wei family?" Wang Fu-t'ing looked at it closely and replied, "There's not a bit of doubt; it was made in my shop." Mr. Pai said, "Let Wang Fu-t'ing give bail and go home."

Mr. Pai next took the fragments of the half-eaten moon cake from his table and looked at them closely. Then he said to Kang Pi, "Brother Sheng-mu, look carefully at this. This filling is made of crystallized sugar, sesame seeds, and walnuts—all materials of an oily nature. If the arsenic had been put in during the making of the paste, surely it would have melted into the rest of the paste. You will see that this arsenic was evidently put in later, for it has not become mixed with the other ingredients at all. Besides, the Studio of the Four Virtues has given evidence that there was only one kind of filling used. And now that we have compared the two specimens of filling, there isn't a shadow of doubt that apart from the addition of the arsenic they are absolutely identical. Now since only one kind of filling was used and other people ate it without being poisoned, surely we can conclude that the deaths in the Chia family were not due to the moon cakes. In the case of soups or liquid foods it is possible to introduce poison after they are prepared, but a moon cake is a thing with a solid crust of pastry so that it is impossible to put anything into it afterwards. What do you gentlemen think?" They both leaned forward and said, "Quite right."

Mr. Pai continued, "Since there was no poison in the moon cakes, clearly the father and daughter of the Wei family are innocent people, and we can give orders to wind up the case against both of them." Wang Tzu-chin immediately agreed, saying, "Certainly." Kang Pi felt extremely ill at ease, but could say nothing, so all he did was to agree with a "Yes."

Mr. Pai then ordered Wei Ch'ien to be brought forward and said, "This court finds that the moon cakes were not poisoned and that you and your daughter are innocent. The case is closed; you may go home." Wei Ch'ien kowtowed several times and departed.

Mr. Pai then called for Chia Kan to be brought forward. This Chia

Kan was a useless stupid fellow, but his "sister" had sent him for appearances' sake. Now, seeing the case against the Wei father and daughter dismissed, and the prisoners released, he became somewhat frightened and when he heard that he was called for, not only was he incapable of saying the things he had been primed to say, but even those who had coached him didn't know now what words to put in his mouth.

Chia Kan went forward and Mr. Pai said, "Chia Kan, since you are the adopted son of your late father, it was your duty to do all you could to discover how these thirteen lives were lost. If you couldn't manage it, then you should have asked somebody else to do it for you. Why did you put arsenic into the moon cakes and so get innocent people into trouble? You must have been incited to it by some evil counselors. Confess the truth. Who was it told you to make this false accusation? Don't you know that there is a retributory clause in the law which provides for the accuser the penalty that would have been paid by the falsely accused?"

Chia Kan kowtowed nervously; he was so frightened that he trembled all over. Through his tears he said, "I don't know! My sister told me to do it all! And it was my sister who found the arsenic in the moon cakes and told me about it. I don't know anything else." Mr. Pai said, "Then according to you the truth about this question of the arsenic will never come out unless we call your sister to the court?"

Chia Kan only kowtowed. Mr. Pai laughed out loud and said, "It's lucky for you that you've got me for judge. If it had been one of your thorough and efficient deputies, the moon cake case being settled, this question of the arsenic would have become an affair of world-shaking consequences. But I do not like to bring people's womenfolk into the court if it can be avoided. You go home and tell your sister that this court asserts that the arsenic was put in the moon cakes after the event. For the time being I am not in a hurry to find out who put it in, because the death of thirteen people in your household is a very great mystery and must be probed to the very bottom till 'the water has gone down and the rocks emerge.' [2] For this reason we can proceed slowly with the question of the arsenic. What have you got to say?"

Chia Kan kowtowed and said, "I accept Your Excellency's most just decision." Mr. Pai then said, "In this case take Chia Kan's bond that he has left it at our discretion to investigate the case." As he was leaving, Mr. Pai again called out, "If you play any more tricks, I shall look further into your arsenic and false accusations!" Chia Kan quickly answered, "I wouldn't dare, Sir; I wouldn't dare!" And left the court.

At this point, Mr. Pai said to Wang Tzu-chin, "Have you a really smart yamen runner in your *hsien?*" Tzu-chin said, "Hsü Liang is quite good." Mr. Pai said, "Let him come forward." Then a yamen runner of forty-odd years, who had not yet let his beard grow, walked up to the magistrate's table and knelt, saying, "The runner Hsü Liang pays his respects." Mr. Pai said, "I am sending you to Ch'itungts'un to investigate and make secret inquiries as to whether these thirteen people died of poison and to find out whether anything else was involved. Report within a month. You are not to use your authority as an official employee. If you do, and attract attention to yourself and force people to give bribes, the penalty will be death!" Hsü Liang kowtowed and said, "I wouldn't dare to do such things."

By this time Wang Tzu-chin had issued a warrant which he handed to Hsü Liang. Mr. Pai then said, "The witnesses we have heard need not give bail but can go." In this way the original verdict was reversed. Then he pulled out Wei Ch'ien's promissory note and said, "Bring in Wei Ch'ien again."

Mr. Pai said, "Wei Ch'ien, do you want the money that your majordomo sent?" Wei Ch'ien said, "I have been deeply wronged. Your Excellency has established my innocence. As to the money, I leave it to Your Excellency to dispose of it as you see fit." Mr. Pai said, "I will return the promissory note for fifty-five hundred ounces, but this court would like to borrow the bills for a thousand ounces. Not for my use, of course, but to put in the treasury. The inquiry in the Chia family case is bound to involve some expense. When the case is settled, and this court has reported to the Governor, we will return it to you in full." Wei Ch'ien replied, "Willingly, willingly," took the promissory note, and left the court.

Mr. Pai gave the bills for a thousand ounces to the clerk to be cashed at the money shop where they were issued against an order for payment from the court. Then he turned to Kang Pi and, laughing, said, "Brother Sheng-mu, I suppose you will scorn me for accepting a bribe in the court!" Kang Pi muttered, "I wouldn't dare." Then the drum was beaten, and the court adjourned.

It is further told that all the inhabitants of Ch'ihohsien knew about this important case. Yesterday Prefect Pai arrived; today the witnesses were called. Both the Chia and the Wei families had been prepared to stay in the *hsien* town for at least ten days or half a month. Who could have expected that in less than an hour the case would have been settled? Everywhere up and down the streets "speaking tablets" [3] praised the magistrate, *tse-tse.*

It is told that when Mr. Pai went back to the west reception hall, just as he was stepping over the threshold, he heard a clock in the room striking eleven as though to welcome him. Wang Tzu-chin came in with him and said, "Will Your Excellency change and eat?" Mr. Pai said, "There's no hurry." He saw that Kang Pi had come in too, so he said, "Will you both please sit down. I have something to say."

They both sat down and Mr. Pai turned to Kang Pi, "Have I done rightly in my decision in this case or not?" Kang Pi said, "Your Excellency's just decision could not be wrong. The only thing I don't understand is why the Wei family paid out money if they had not done something wrong. In my whole life I have never offered anyone a single copper."

Mr. Pai laughed a loud *ha-ha* and said, "If you have never offered a copper to anybody, how then did the authorities come to have such a high opinion of you? Isn't it a clear proof that not everybody in this world sees only with an eye for money? The pure and incorruptible man naturally arouses our admiration, but he often has one bad characteristic: he thinks that all other people in the world are little and mean and that he is the only superior man. This obsession is very harmful. It has caused I don't know how many disasters! You, elder brother, have made this mistake. Please don't take offense at my plain speaking. As to the bribe offered by the Wei family, it was done by a country fellow—a servant—with no experience of the world, and is nothing to be surprised at." Then he said to Tzu-chin, "Now that the session is over let's send a man with our two cards and invite Mr. T'ieh to come and join us," and he smiled at Kang Pi saying, "Sheng-mu, you don't know who this is? Why it's the drug-selling quack you were talking about. His family name is T'ieh; his personal name Ying; and his *hao* Pu-ts'an. He is a man of strong character, and extremely wide and profound scholarship; his nature is urbane and amiable, and he despises nobody. But you took even him to be a little and mean person. That's why I say that you go too far."

Kang Pi said, "Then it can't be any other Lao Ts'an than that Lao

Ts'an everybody was talking about in the capital. Is it he?" "That's who it is," Mr. Pai replied. Kang Pi went on, "I've heard it said that the Governor wanted him to move into the yamen to live and offered to purchase him an office and recommend him for promotions, but that he refused, and ran away during the night. Is it really he?" Mr. Pai said, "It certainly is. And you wanted to summon him for trial."

Kang Pi's face flushed as he said, "I have been very clumsy. I have often heard of this man, but have never met him." Tzu-chin then got up saying, "Will Your Excellency change?" Mr. Pai answered, "Let us all change so that we can loosen up and drink well."

Wang and Kang went each to his room, changed, and returned to the reception hall. Just at that moment Lao Ts'an also arrived. He first bowed to Tzu-chin and then to Mr. Pai and Kang Pi, and was made to sit in the seat of honor on the *k'ang.* Mr. Pai sat beside him. Lao Ts'an said, "To settle an important case like that in half a watch, what miraculous speed, Mr. Tzu Shou!" "You are too flattering," Mr. Pai answered, "I have only done the first and easy part of the job. The second and more difficult part will have to be Mr. Pu-ts'an's responsibility." Lao Ts'an said, "What do you mean? I am neither a great official personage nor am I a minor yamen runner. What has it got to do with me?" Mr. Pai said, "Well then, who wrote the letter to the Governor?" "I did," Lao Ts'an replied, "how could I watch people die without helping them?" "You're right," Mr. Pai said, "but if it is one's duty to help someone who is not yet dead, shouldn't you seek justice for people already dead? Just think! Can an ordinary yamen runner handle this sort of extraordinary case? There is no alternative but to ask the help of a Sherlock Holmes [4] like you!" Lao Ts'an laughed, "I haven't enough perseverance to be that, but if you want me to go I'm willing. Ask His Excellency Mr. Wang to give me an appointment as head of the yamen runners and draw up a warrant, and I'll go!"

While they were talking, the food was all set out. Wang Tzu-chin said, "Please come to the table." "Isn't Huang Jen-jui here?" Mr. Pai said; "Why not ask him over?" "I've already sent to ask him," replied Tzu-chin.

Before he had got the words out, Jen-jui arrived and bowed all around. Tzu-chin raised the wine pot and then became embarrassed. Mr. Pai said, "Of course Mr. Pu will take the seat of honor." "On no account," replied Lao Ts'an. They wrangled a while, but in the end it was Lao Ts'an who had the seat of honor and Mr. Pai the second seat.

When they had drunk a few cups of wine and had a few rounds of the wine game,[5] Mr. Pai returned to his theme, explaining that his sending Hsü Liang to make inquiries was only a blind, and insisting that he must ask Lao Ts'an to suffer a few hardships and go to Ch'i-tungts'un too. Tzu-chin and Jen-jui added their entreaties. Lao Ts'an could only agree.

Mr. Pai further said, "To begin with there is the Wei family's thousand ounces; you can use that first. If that is not enough, brother Tzu-chin will find some more for you. Don't stint yourself. The important thing is to solve the mystery." Lao Ts'an said, "I don't need any money. I have already drawn out the four hundred ounces I had deposited in the capital. I was going to repay a debt to brother Tzu-chin. It's better for me to use that. If I clear up the case, we can ask Lao Chuang [6] to return it. If I don't clear it up, I will take myself off and not stay here to be a laughingstock." Mr. Pai said, "All right, but if you do need anything come and get it. The important thing is not to let small economies interfere with the main task." Lao Ts'an agreed. Soon they finished eating, and Mr. Pai started across the river to make his report to the Governor. The next day Huang Jen-jui and Kang Pi both returned to the capital.

If you don't know what happened afterwards, then hear the next chapter tell.

CHAPTER 19

Once again the string of bells is rung
   in Ch'itungts'un;

With great skill a golden snare is set in Tsinanfu.

THE TALE continues that in the afternoon, after receiving Mr. Pai's commission, Lao Ts'an went back to his inn and thought over how he was to carry it out. The landlord came in and announced, "Hsü Liang, a yamen runner from the *hsien*, wishes to see you." "Tell him to come in," Lao Ts'an said.

Hsü Liang came in, made a genuflection, and stepped forward. "Will Your Honor please give orders: shall I wait here for Your Honor's directions or do you want to send me ahead somewhere? A thousand ounces has been paid out by the *hsien* office. Is it to be sent here or is it to be deposited in the moneyshop till needed?"

Lao Ts'an said, "I don't need the money, so deposit it in the money-shop. This case is certainly not going to be easy to handle. There is no doubt it is a question of poisoning, but it's no ordinary poison. The joints were not stiff, the color of the faces hadn't changed. These two points are very significant. I'm afraid it's some sort of Western poison, probably some sort of 'Indian Grass.'[1] For a start I'm going to the provincial capital tomorrow. There is a Sino-European medicine shop there where I'll make inquiries. You can go ahead to Ch'itungts'un and inquire discreetly whether there are any people who have dealings with foreigners. If we can track down the origin of this poison, it will be a clue. The only problem is where am I to meet you?"

"I have a younger brother called Hsü Ming," Hsü Liang said. "I've brought him with me and he can wait upon Your Honor. He knows lots of people. If you have any errands, give your orders, and he will carry them out well." Lao Ts'an nodded, "Excellent."

Hsü Liang waved his hand to someone outside, and a thirty-year-old man came in, stepped forward, and made a genuflection. Hsü Liang said, "This is my younger brother, Hsü Ming." Then he turned to Hsü Ming, "You don't need to go back. Stay here and wait upon His Honor, Mr. T'ieh." Finally Hsü Liang said, "May we pay our respects to the new mistress?"

Lao Ts'an raised the *lientzu* and looked in. Huan-ts'ui was sitting near the window, so he called the two men to come in and pay their respects. They each made a genuflection, and Huan-ts'ui replied with two movements of her clasped hands on her side.[2] Hsü Liang then took Hsü Ming home with him to fetch his baggage.

When it was time to light the lamps, Jen-jui came back to the inn and said, "I wanted to start off two days ago, but I was concerned about this law case and Tzu-chin insisted on keeping me here. Now that the case is finished, I am going to the capital early tomorrow morning to make my report." Lao Ts'an said, "I'm going to the capital too. First, I want to make inquiries about poisons at the Sino-European medicine shop and such places. Second, I want to find a place for this encumbrance of mine. If I unload her, I can get things done." "There is lots of room in my house," Jen-jui said. "You had better make your home with me for the time being. If you are not comfortable there, then you can look for a house at your leisure. How is that?" Lao Ts'an answered, "That would be splendid."

When it appeared that Huan-ts'ui's maid didn't want to go to the city, Hsü Ming said, "My wife can accompany the mistress to the city, and when you have engaged a maid, she can come back."

So everything was well settled. As might have been expected, Huan-ts'ui called her little brother in and gave him some money and they wept together for a while. Hsü Ming looked after such details as getting the carts.

Early next morning they all started off together. When they reached the bank of the Yellow River, Lao Ts'an and Jen-jui were afraid to ride, so they got off their carts and prepared to walk across the river. To everyone's surprise there was already a cart waiting on the river-bank. When they were seen approaching, a woman jumped off the cart, embraced Huan-ts'ui, and wept loudly.

Do you know who it was? Well, since Jen-jui was starting off early this morning, he hadn't told Ts'ui-hua to come the night before, but had sent Huang Sheng to settle his account with her. Also since Ts'ui-hua was afraid there might be officials from the *hsien* seeing him off, she hadn't dared to come to say good-by in the evening. She hadn't slept all night, and in the early morning had hired a cart so that she could wait on the riverbank, with the idea of "accompanying the part-ing guest to the pavilion at the tenth li." [3]

After she had wept for some time, Lao Ts'an and Jen-jui said a few words to comfort her and then walked over the ice. Across the river and to the city was not more than forty li, and when the bell had struck one, they were at the door of Huang Jen-jui's residence in East Arrow Way. They got off the carts and went in. It isn't necessary to enlarge on the way in which Huang Jen-jui performed his duties as a host.

After they had eaten, Lao Ts'an sent Hsü Ming to buy some things to replace those lost in the fire, and himself went to the Sino-European medicine shop to begin his inquiries with one of the managers there. It turned out that this shop dealt only in bottles of prepared medicine sent up from Shanghai and had no unprepared drugs. He asked a few questions about the names of certain chemicals. But as they didn't even understand what he was talking about, he decided that the poison had certainly not come from here. Feeling rather baffled, he went to call on Yao Yün-sung. Fortunately Mr. Yao was at home and made him stay for the evening meal.

Mr. Yao said, "Pai Tzu-shou arrived last night. He has already seen the Governor and told him all about the Ch'ihohsien case and that he has entrusted you with continuing the inquiry. The Governor is ex-tremely pleased. He doesn't know yet that you have come to town. Are you going to see him tomorrow?" "I shan't go to see him," Lao Ts'an replied, "I have other business." Then he asked about his letter from Ts'aochou, "What did you say to the Governor?" Mr. Yao said, "I gave your original letter to the Governor to read. He read it and was very disturbed for many days. He said, 'From now on I will not recommend Prefect Yü any more.'" Lao Ts'an said, "Why didn't he recall him to the capital?" Yün-sung laughed and said, "After all you are an outsider! Whoever heard of one who has just been recommended to the Emperor being recalled to the capital? What Governor is there in the Empire who doesn't cover up the faults of his subordinates? It's not easy to find a Governor even as good as this one!"

Lao Ts'an inclined his head, and when they had talked a while longer, he went home. The next day he went to the Roman Catholic mission to find the father known as K'e-ch'e-ssu.[4] Now this father was proficient in Western medicine and also in chemistry, so Lao Ts'an was more than delighted to be able to tell him all about the case of poisoning. He asked him what poison it could have been. K'e-ch'e-ssu thought for a long time but couldn't decide. Then he consulted his books, but found nothing corresponding to the symptoms described and said, "My knowledge is insufficient; I will have to ask someone else about it."

When Lao Ts'an heard this, he was again greatly discouraged. There was now nothing for him to do in the city, so he packed his things and returned to Ch'ihohsien with Hsü Ming. He began to consider how he should go about his investigations in Ch'itungts'un. He quickly had a string of bells made to replace his old ones, bought an old medicine chest, and stocked it with various medicaments. He told Hsü Ming he was not to travel with him and that when they met in the village he was to appear not to recognize him. When Hsü Ming had gone, he hired a wheelbarrow in Ch'ihohsien and settled a price for the month at the rate of three mace of silver a day. Then, fearing that the wheelbarrow man might let his plan leak out, in order to put him off he said, "I practise doctoring, but there is no business in this *hsien* city. Are there any biggish market towns in the neighborhood?" The man said, "Forty-five li to the northeast there's a big market town called Ch'itungts'un which is quite a busy place. Every month on the 'threes' and 'eights'[5] there are market days when people from several tens of li around come to market. You'd better go there to look for business, Sir." Lao Ts'an said, "Good!" The next day he packed his things on the wheelbarrow and, riding part of the way and walking the rest, he soon got to Ch'itungts'un. It was quite true, the main street of the town running from east to west was a very busy place, and there were small streets going off to the north and the south.

Lao Ts'an took a turn up and down and found that there were inns at each end. At the east end was a hostelry called Threefold Prosperity. It seemed on inspection to be fairly clean, so he took a room on the west side and settled there. There was a big *k'ang* in the room. He told his wheelbarrow man to sleep at one end, and he slept at the other. He slept till the beginning of *ssu* [9–11 A.M.] the next day, got up, had breakfast, and went along the street ringing his bells. He went aimlessly along the main street and through the little alleys, and by *wei* [1–3 P.M.] found himself in a small turning to the north of High Street where there was a big entrance gate. He thought to himself, "This must be an important family." So he stopped there and gave his bells a good shake. Soon after an old fellow with a black beard came out and asked, "Can you treat injuries, Sir?" Lao Ts'an said, "I know something about them."

The old fellow went in and then came out again saying, "Please enter." Inside the great gate was a second gate and beyond that the reception hall. He went into the side building and saw an old man sitting on the edge of the *k'ang*. When he saw Lao Ts'an, he stood up and said, "Please be seated, Sir."

Lao Ts'an recognized him to be Wei Ch'ien but he purposely asked, "What is your honorable name, Sir?" Wei Ch'ien said, "My name is Wei. What is your honorable name, Sir?" "My name is Chin," was the reply. Wei Ch'ien said, "I have a daughter who has pains in the joints of her arms and legs. Have you any medicine to treat them with?" Lao Ts'an said, "How can I prescribe medicine until I have examined the case?" Wei Ch'ien said, "You are quite right." Then he sent a man in to warn of a doctor's arrival.

After a while word was brought from within, "Please come in." Wei Ch'ien then took Lao Ts'an to a side room in the east court, behind the reception hall. It had three *chien*, two light, the other dark.[6] Going into the inner *chien*, he saw a woman of thirty-odd years, her face haggard from suffering, sitting on the *k'ang* with her legs crossed, leaning against the *k'ang* table. She tried to get down from the *k'ang*, but you could see she didn't have the strength to do it. Lao Ts'an quickly cried out, "Don't move. It is better for taking your pulse if you don't move." Old Mr. Wei then made Lao Ts'an take the seat of honor and himself sat on a stool.

When Lao Ts'an had taken the pulse of both hands, he said, "The lady suffers because the blood has been stopped and is clotted. Please let me see the two hands." Mr. Wei's daughter stretched out her hands on the *k'ang* table and Lao Ts'an looked. The joints were all black and blue. He couldn't help sighing deeply and saying, "There is something I would like to say, Sir, but I am afraid it is too impertinent." Old Mr. Wei said, "Say it; there's no harm." "Please don't be angry at me," Lao Ts'an said, "but this looks like the result of torture in a hall of justice. If it is not treated in time, she will be maimed for life." Old Mr. Wei heaved a sigh and said, "Unhappily you are quite right. Please apply the necessary treatment. If it is successful you shall be well rewarded."

Lao Ts'an then drew up a prescription and said, "If my treatment works, you can send for me to the Inn of Threefold Prosperity, where I am staying." From now on he called every day. After a few days they became quite well acquainted, and old Mr. Wei made Lao Ts'an stay in the reception hall to drink wine.

Lao Ts'an took the opportunity to ask, "How does it happen that a member of such a distinguished family as yours should undergo torture in a law court?" Old Wei said, "Mr. Chin, you being a stranger don't know. My daughter was married to the elder son of the Chia family. Last year my son-in-law died. He had a sister, Chia T'an-ch'un who had made eyes at Wastrel Wu the Second of the East Village, and they had become eager for each other. Last year, when negotiations were going on, my foolish daughter caused them to be broken off. The Chia girl therefore hated my daughter to the marrow of her bones. This spring she was in her aunt's house and had improper relations with Wastrel Wu. I don't know what sort of drug they used, but they poisoned the whole Chia family and then accused my daughter before the *hsien* magistrate of having committed the crime. Then we came under a ruthless official—I'd like to cut a thousand slices off him and hack at him ten thousand times—called Kang, who got the bit between his teeth and insisted that some moon cakes we had sent contained arsenic. My poor girl went into a dead faint, I don't know how many times. They tell me that she had already been condemned to the lingering death. But the good Lord of Heaven has eyes. The Governor sent a relative to make a private inquiry; he stayed at an inn in the south suburb, discovered the injustice that was being done to my family, and reported it to the Governor. The Governor immediately sent an official letter ordering the magistrate to release us from our shackles. In less than ten days the Governor further sent a certain Excellency Pai—he is indeed a just official of great nobility. In one hour he washed us clean of all the false charges against us. They say he also sent someone here to continue the investigation of the case. While we were in prison, that bastard Wastrel Wu the Second was with the Chia girl every day. When he heard that the case against us was demolished, he ran away."

Lao Ts'an said, "Since you have suffered so much injustice, why don't you denounce him?" Old Wei said, "Do you think it's easy to go to law? If I accuse him, won't he demand proofs? 'To prove adultery you must catch them together.' If we can't 'catch them together,' then they will bite back at us, and we shall be unable to withstand the charge. But Heaven has eyes; there is certain to be a day of vindication!"

Lao Ts'an asked, "What was this drug they used? Have you heard anyone say?" Old Wei said, "Who knows? But we have an old woman-servant whose husband is called Wang the Second; he's a water carrier. That day, the day of the deaths in the Chia family, Wang the Second was taking water there when he saw Wastrel Wu go into their house to gossip. They were just then cooking noodles in the Chia house, and Wang the Second saw Wu pour something from a little bottle into the noodle-boiler and then run away. Wang was rather suspicious of this, so a little later, when the Chia cook offered him some noodles to eat, he wouldn't eat them. Less than four hours later the commotion began. Wang the Second never dared tell anybody. Only his wife knew, and she told my daughter. But when I called Wang in, he persisted in saying 'I don't know' and stuck to it. When we asked his wife again, she too was afraid to say anything more. They say that when his wife got home, Wang gave her a sound thrashing. Just think, Sir, how do we dare go to law about it?"

Lao Ts'an sighed for a while and soon after left the Wei house. He sought out Hsü Liang, told him all he had heard in the Wei family, and told him to call in Wang the Second.

The next day Hsü Liang came with Wang. Lao Ts'an gave him twenty ounces of silver to leave with his family and asked him to come with him as a witness, saying, "We will pay all your expenses, and when the case is finished we will give you a hundred ounces."

At first Wang would have nothing to do with it, but when he saw the twenty ounces lying on the table he began to realize that the offer was real. He said, "And if you don't give me the hundred ounces when the case is finished, what shall I be able to do?" Lao Ts'an said, "That's no difficulty. We'll give you the hundred ounces now. We'll deposit it in a reliable shop, and you shall give us a written contract saying, 'I agree to bear witness that I saw with my own eyes the man called Wu pour out some poison. When the case is closed, a reward of a hundred ounces deposited at such and such a shop is to be paid to me. Agreed to by both parties in perfect sincerity.' Will that do?"

Wang still hesitated, so Hsü Liang took a hundred ounces and handed them to him, saying, "I'm not afraid that you will run off. Take the money first. How about that? If you don't want it, then we'll give up the whole thing." Wang thought it over for a bit, but in the end he couldn't resist the money, and agreed.

Lao Ts'an took up his brush and wrote as above, told Wang to take the money, and then read the contract to him and told him to draw a cross and put his thumb print on it. When do you suppose this country water carrier had seen two ingots of fifty ounces each? Of course he was only too glad to put his thumb to the paper!

Then Hsü Liang said to Lao Ts'an, "I've found out for certain that Wastrel Wu is now in the provincial capital." Lao Ts'an said, "Then we'll go to the city. You go first and find a spy to seek him out." Hsü Liang said, "Yes, Sir," and then, "We'll meet in the city, Sir."

The next day Lao Ts'an went first of all to Ch'ihohsien to give Tzu-chin a general idea of the state of the investigation, then on to the city. He gave his wheelbarrow man a few ounces and sent him back. That evening he told everything to the venerable Yao Yün and asked him to make a report to the Governor and also to order the magistrate of Lich'enghsien [7] to appoint two yamen runners to work with Hsü Liang.

The next evening Hsü Liang came and reported: "I've found Wastrel Wu. He is very thick with a low-class harlot called Little Silver, in the Chang house, in the south lane off the Street of the Provincial Court. He spends his days gambling with a crowd of idle fellows. He spends his nights in Little Silver's house."

Lao Ts'an asked, "Is there just one girl or are there several girls in this Little Silver's house? How many *chien* are there? Have you found that out?" "There are the two 'sisters' who occupy three *chien*," Hsü Liang answered. "Their 'father' and 'mother' live in the two-*chien* side building on the west. Of the two *chien* on the east, one is the kitchen, the other the entrance gate."

When Lao Ts'an heard this, he nodded his head and said, "With a man like this it's not safe to act in a hurry. The case involved is too important. It will certainly not be easy to make him confess. With Wang the Second as the only witness we can't get the better of him." Then he whispered a detailed plan of action into Hsü Liang's ear, how to do this and that, to act thus and so.

After Hsü Liang had gone, a letter came from Yao Yün-sung which said, "The Governor is most anxious to see you. Please come to the Secretariat tomorrow at noon. Most important." Lao Ts'an wrote a reply and the next day went to the yamen. First he went to the office of the Secretary, Mr. Yao. Mr. Yao's servant announced his arrival to the Governor's servant, and after a while he was asked to go into the Governor's office for an interview. Governor Chuang came to the door to welcome him and led him in. Lao Ts'an bowed and sat down.

Lao Ts'an said, "When I seemed to turn my back on Your Excellency's kindness some time ago, it was truly because I had some private business. It was impossible for me not to go. I hope you have forgiven me." The Governor said, "Until I read your letter, I had no idea that Prefect Yü was so ruthless. I am indeed to blame. I shall certainly have to do something about it. But at the moment I dare not 'recommend a man and then cashier him'; it would appear disrespectful to the Emperor." Lao Ts'an said, " 'To save the people is to serve the King.' It seems to me that this principle is also sound." The Governor made no reply to this. They continued chatting for about half an hour, and then the Governor raised his teacup and Lao Ts'an took his leave.

The story continues that when Hsü Liang had received his orders from Lao Ts'an, he went to the third-rate brothel and made the acquaintance of Little Gold. Gambling and dissipating together, in a few days he and Wastrel Wu had mixed like milk and water. At the beginning Hsü Liang lost four or five hundred ounces to Wu, all in silver. Wastrel Wu then took Hsü Liang to be a foolish rustic, but afterwards Hsü gradually got it back and even won some seven or eight hundred ounces from Wu. Wu paid one or two hundred in silver. He had to give an I.O.U. for the rest.

One day Wastrel Wu was playing *p'ai-chiu* [8] and lost more than two hundred to Hsü Liang and more than three hundred ounces to the others. He had already used up all the money he had brought with him, but the others demanded their money at once. Wastrel Wu said, "Let's play another round and settle accounts all together." Nobody would agree to this. They all said, "You can't pay what you've already lost; if you lose again, you will be still less able to pay." Wu Erh got excited and said, "I've got lots of money at home. I've never gone back on a debt. When we've made up accounts, I'll send a man home to get it." But they all shook their heads.

Then Hsü Liang up and said, "Brother Wu Erh, how will this do? When can you return the money? I'll lend you some, but I shall need it back in three days for some important business. Whatever you do, don't let me down." Wastrel Wu was so eager to play that he said right away, "There is no danger of that!" Hsü Liang then counted out bills for five hundred ounces and gave them to him, deducting the two hundred or so already owing him, thus handing over some two hundred-odd.

Wastrel Wu saw that this was still not enough to cover his debts so he begged Hsü Liang saying, "Elder Brother, Elder Brother, lend me another five hundred. As soon as my luck changes I'll return it." Hsü Liang asked, "And supposing your luck doesn't change?" Wastrel Wu said, "I'll still give it back tomorrow for sure." "A spoken promise is no guarantee that you'll return it tomorrow," Hsü Liang said, "I must have a written I.O.U." Wu said, "All right! All right!" There and then he took out a brush, wrote an I.O.U. and handed it to Hsü Liang, who counted out five hundred ounces more. Wu then paid the three hundred-odd he already owed and had some four hundred-odd left. With money, his courage became great, and he said, "Let me be banker for a round." He won two throws in succession and became very pleased with himself. But when the wind began to blow in his direction, all the others began to lower their stakes. He became annoyed at this, and his luck got worse and worse; the more he played, the more he lost; the more he lost, the angrier he became. Before half a watch was over, he had lost every bit of the four hundred-odd ounces.

There was a man in the crowd called T'ao, generally known as Fat T'ao the Third. Fat T'ao said, "Let me be banker for a round." By now Wastrel Wu had no capital and had to sit idle and watch the others play.

T'ao the Third went to the banker's seat. The first throw he drew a one-spot, so that he lost to everybody. The second throw he drew eight. The Gate of Heaven had an eight, but including a two of Earth. The Upper and Lower Places each had nine, so again he lost to everybody. It looked as if his luck was even worse than Wu's. Wu Erh was now so excited that he couldn't keep his seat, and again he pleaded with Hsü Liang, "Elder Brother, my dear Elder Brother! Dear Father! Lend me two hundred more!" So Hsü Liang lent him two hundred more.

Wastrel Wu then put a hundred ounces as a special stake on the corner between the Gate of Heaven and the Upper Place, and a hundred as an ordinary stake. Hsü Liang said, "Stake a little less, brother." Wu said, "That's all right!" When they turned over the pieces, the banker had a dead ten, and Wu Erh won two hundred ounces. He was so delighted that he didn't take away his original stake. The fourth throw the banker lost to the Gate of Heaven and to the Lower Place, but ate up the Upper Place. Wu Erh's two hundred ounces were neither lost nor won. In the first throw after they had shuffled the dominoes the banker got a Heavenly Bridge and swallowed up everybody. Wu Erh still had two hundred left.

But now the banker began to burn up everything. Not only was Wastrel Wu exhausted, but even Hsü Liang was cleaned out. Hsü Liang got very angry, took Wu's I.O.U., and put it on the table, saying, "I'll play alone on the Gate of Heaven. Will you dare to be banker?" T'ao the Third said, "I'll play. Sure I'll play. But I don't want this sort of worthless bit of paper that can't be cashed." Hsü Liang said, "Mr. Wu might cheat you, but do you think that I, the Honorable Mr. Hsü, would cheat you, too?" This brought them almost to the point of fighting.

The rest of the company said, "Mr. T'ao the Third, you've won quite a lot; don't you have this much regard for your friends? We'll all go security. If you win and these two don't pay you, we'll all pay you!" T'ao the Third still refused. "I'll only go on if Hsü Liang writes a bond," he said.

Hsü Liang was so angry that he grabbed a brush and wrote a bond, making a clear statement that this was a genuine, friendly loan and not an idle scrap of paper. Only now was T'ao the Third willing to throw. He said, "Big Hsü, draw any piece you like and I'll beat you!" Hsü Liang replied, "Don't crow! Chuck down your blasted bones!" He threw, and it was a seven.

Hsü Liang took up his pieces; he had a nine of Heaven [twelve and seven]. He put them down on the table and said, "My little T'ao the Third! Look at your father's pieces!" T'ao the Third looked at them, but said nothing. He took two pieces, looked at one of them, and then slowly drew the other towards him, saying, "Earth! Earth! Earth!" The moment he picked it up he threw it down on the table, and said, "Little grandson of the Hsü Family! Look at your grandfather's pieces!" It turned out to be an Earthly Bridge, a two of Earth matching an eight of Man. He grabbed the I.O.U. and said, "Big Hsü! if you haven't got the money tomorrow, I'll see you in the Lich'enghsien yamen!"

By this time everybody's money was exhausted and it was past one o'clock, so they dispersed. Hsü and Wu went back to Little Silver's house, rapped on the door, and went in. They said, "Give us something to eat—quick! We are starving!" There was a customer in Little Gold's room, so they went into Little Silver's room. Little Gold put her cheek against Hsü Liang's and said, "How much money did you win today? How many ounces are you going to give me to spend?" Hsü Liang said, "I've lost more than a thousand!" Little Silver said to Wastrel Wu, "Did you win?" He replied, "It's still less worth asking me!"

With this the food was brought on: a bowl of fish, a bowl of mutton, two bowls of vegetables, four cold dishes, a chafing dish, two pots of wine. Hsü Liang said, "Why should it be so cold today?" Little Gold replied, "The northwest wind has been blowing all day, and it's been cloudy. It's probably going to snow."

The two of them poured down one gloomy cup after another, until, before they knew where they were, both were several parts fuddled. At this point somebody could be heard calling for the gate to be opened, and Little Gold's "mother," Big-Foot Chang, went to the gate. She came in with somebody saying, "Mr. T'ao, I'm sorry, but there is no room. Please come tomorrow." The man was heard to answer, "Dog fart! What do I care whether you've got room or not! What turtle of a guest is it? If he's got any guts, let him come out and fight T'ao the Third; if he hasn't, let him crawl out on his four legs!"

It was clearly the voice of Fat T'ao the Third. When Hsü Liang heard it, his anger overflowed, and he wanted to rush out. But Little Gold and Little Silver used all their strength to hold him back.

If you don't know what happened afterwards, then hear the next chapter tell.

CHAPTER 20

A wastrel's gold and silver is the axe to cut off his life;

A Taoist through ice and snow seeks a quickening herb.

SO LITTLE Gold and Little Silver were using all their strength to hold Hsü Liang back. Wastrel Wu, sitting near the door of the room, pulled the *lientzu* aside and peeped through the crack. He saw that T'ao the Third had walked over into the middle *chien*, his face flushed with drink, and, throwing the *lientzu* of Little Gold's room five or six feet into the air was marching in with great strides. The guest who had come into Little Gold's room earlier, hid his face with his sleeve, and rushed out like a streak. Big-Foot Chang went in with T'ao the Third. T'ao asked, "Where are the two little bastards?" Big-Foot Chang said, "Please sit down. They're coming. They're coming." She quickly ran over and said, "Don't make a noise. This T'ao the Third is a garrison officer of Lich'enghsien, and in great favor with the officials; if he says 'one' to them, no one says 'two.' Nobody dares to provoke him. Please don't you two gentlemen blame us for asking the two girls to go over to him right away." Hsü Liang said, "But we are not afraid of him! What could he do?"

After this Little Gold and Little Silver went over. As Wastrel Wu listened, he began to sweat in his heart. His I.O.U. was in that fellow's hands. What should he do? He heard Fat T'ao in the other room roaring with laughter and saying, "Little Gold, I'll give you a hundred ounces! Little Silver, I'll give you a hundred ounces too!" He then heard them say, "Thank you, Sir!" And again Fat T'ao, "Don't thank me. This is all a filial offering from my grandsons this evening. Altogether they presented me with more than three thousand ounces. Besides there is an I.O.U. from my grandson Wu the Second in my hands; my grandson Big Hsü went guarantee. If the money isn't paid by tomorrow night, see if granddaddy don't settle their fate!"

Here Hsü Liang said to Wu Erh, "This creature is certainly hateful! But I've heard he's a terrible fighter and can handle fifty or sixty men. Are we going to swallow our anger?" Wu the Second said, "Never mind about being angry, but what about this I.O.U. that has to be settled tomorrow?" "Even though I've got the money at home," Hsü Liang said, "it would take at least three days to send a man for it. 'Distant water doesn't help a present fire!'"

Then they heard T'ao the Third shouting again, "Both of you girls stay with me tonight. You're not to go to anybody else's room! If you move, I'll stick a clean knife into you and pull it out red!" Little Gold said, "We're not deceiving you; but we both have guests tonight." Then they heard Fat T'ao strike the table and throw the teacups on the ground with a clattering noise as he said, "Dog fart! Who dares to sleep with T'ao the Third's girls! Ask them if they've got any heads to spare! Who would try to kill a fly on a tiger's head? I've got plenty of money that my grandsons so dutifully gave me! I'm ready to kill one or two men and pay out a few thousand ounces and that'll be the end of it! Go on! Go and ask my two grandsons if they feel like coming over or not!"

Little Gold ran over quickly and showed her bill for a hundred ounces to Hsü Liang. It was indeed a bill that he had lost and when he saw it, it was still harder to bear. Little Silver came over too and whispered, "Put up with it for a bit, Gentlemen, and let us two 'sisters' make a couple of hundred ounces. We have never seen a whole hundred ounces in all our lives. Neither of you two have any money: let us earn a couple of hundred. We'll buy wine and fine dishes tomorrow and invite you."

Hsü Liang got very angry and said, "Get out! Get out!" Little Gold said, "Don't be angry, Sir! Please put up with it for a bit. You two can make shift on this *k'ang* for tonight. Tomorrow when he's gone you can come to my room and jump into my warm bed, and my 'sister' will come here to keep Wu Erh company. Is that all right?" Hsü Liang repeated, "Get out! Get out!" Little Gold went out of the room muttering to herself, "No silver and you still want to act the fine gentleman. Shame on you!"

Hsü Liang was white with anger. He sat stupefied for a while. Then he pulled Wastrel Wu to him and said, "Brother Wu, I've got something to discuss with you. We are both from Ch'ihohsien. We've come to the capital and received this sort of treatment from them. It's unbearable! I'm ready for anything. Just think: if you can't return that thousand ounces tomorrow you'll be taken into the yamen. You won't even see a magistrate. You'll be finished off with secret tortures. We might as well take a couple of knives and hack him to bits. They can only kill us once. What do you say?"

While Wu Erh was thinking it over, Fat T'ao could be heard shouting in the opposite *chien,* "That miserable little Wu Erh is an escaped murderer from Ch'ihohsien! But I'm going to hand him over to the Ch'ihohsien authorities tomorrow, and then we'll see whether he'll get out alive or not! And that miserable little Hsü Liang is an accomplice too. Who doesn't know it? They both ran away together!"

Hsü Liang got up as though he was going out. Wastrel Wu pulled him back and said, "I've got a way of dealing with him, but you must swear to heaven to keep it secret and then I'll tell you." Hsü Liang said, "Look here! What a suspicious fellow you are! If you've got a good way of doing it, we'll just get him out of the way. It was my idea anyhow. If we're brought to court, I'm the most guilty: you are only an accomplice. Am I likely to stir up trouble for you?"

Wu Erh thought a bit. It seemed reasonable. And besides there was that thousand ounces due tomorrow; trouble was sure to come of that. It was the only thing to do, so he said, "My blood brother! I've got a special sort of drug. When you give it to anyone, he doesn't change color, so that even a spirit can't tell that he has been poisoned." Hsü Liang, astonished, said, "I don't believe it. Is there really such a wonderful thing?" Wu Erh said, "Who would want to fool you?" Hsü Liang said, "Where do you buy it? I'll go and get some right away." Wu Erh said, "You can't buy it! I got it in the seventh month of this year from a house in a T'aishan ravine. But if I give it to you, whatever you do, don't involve me in the business!" Hsü Liang said, "That's easy." He took a piece of paper and wrote, "I, Hsü Liang, having quarreled with a certain T'ao, and wanting to kill him, have learned that a certain Wu has in his possession a powerful drug, such that whoever drinks it immediately dies. I have persuaded the said Wu to give me some of it. The said Wu has no responsibility in the matter." This written, he handed it to Wu Erh saying, "If the affair comes before the law, you have this evidence, so you will not be involved."

Wu Erh read it and decided that it was quite foolproof. Hsü Liang said, "Don't let's waste time. Where is your drug? I'll go and get it with you." Wu Erh said, "It's in my pillow box. I keep it in this room," and took a small leather case from inside the *k'ang*. He unlocked it and took out a porcelain phial sealed with wax.

Hsü Liang asked, "How did you come across it in T'aishan?" Wu Erh said, "I went up the mountain by the west path from Terraced Hill and came down by a path to the east, a very narrow track all the way. One night I was staying at a little inn where I saw a dead man wrapped up in blankets, lying on the *k'ang*. I therefore asked them, 'Why do you put a dead man on the *k'ang*?' The old woman said, 'He's not dead. That's my husband. The day before yesterday he found some sort of grass, wonderfully sweet-smelling. He picked a handful and brought it home. He steeped it in hot water and drank it. And what do you think! As soon as he'd drunk it, he was like a dead man. Of course we cried till we couldn't cry any more. But luckily help came. There is a Taoist hermit who lives in a cave deep in these mountains; his name is Green Dragon. He happened to pass through here that day, and when he heard us crying, he came to see what was the matter. He said, "What did your old man die of?" So I gave him the grass stuff to look at. He took it and laughed and said, "This isn't poison. It's called 'Thousand Days' Sleep.' He can be cured. I'll go and find some of the herb that will counteract this drug. You take care of the body. Don't let it come to any harm. In forty-nine days I'll send you the medicine, and as soon as you use it, he'll be well." More than twenty days are past now.' I asked her, 'Have you any of that herb left?' She then gave me a handful. So I brought it along with me, made an infusion, and put it in a phial to keep it for fun. It's just the thing we need today!"

Hsü Liang said, "Does it really work? If it doesn't really knock him over, then we are done for! Have you tried it?" Wu Erh said, "It 'hits the target every time.' I've already . . ." When he reached this point, he stopped. Hsü Liang asked, "You've already what? You've already tried it?" Wu Erh said, "No, I haven't tried it. But I've already seen that man drugged so that he looked like dead. If it weren't for Green Dragon's counteracting drug, he would have been buried for good long ago."

At this point, when the two of them had talked themselves into good spirits, the *lientzu* was lifted and a man came in. He grabbed Hsü Liang with one hand and pinned Wu Erh to the wall with the other, saying, "All right, all right! So you'd plot against a fellow's life to get his money, would you!"

One look showed them it was T'ao the Third. Hsü Liang held the phial firmly in his hand and struggled to get free. But how could he resist Fat T'ao's oxlike strength! How could he struggle free! As for Wu Erh, that son of drink and debauchery, it is still less necessary to speak of him. Then T'ao pursed his lips and whistled shrilly a couple of times and two or three more strapping fellows came in and tied up Hsü and Wu with cords. T'ao then sent them under guard to the gate of the Lich'enghsien yamen.

T'ao the Third went in and filed his charge with the clerk of the court. The reply was brought out that it was too late to do anything that night; for the time being they would be handed over to an attendant and brought into the hall of justice at the hour of *ch'en* [7–9 A.M.] the next morning. Then they were conducted to the quarters of the attendants. Luckily Hsü Liang still had a few ounces of silver left on him; he brought them out to prime the guard with, and in this way they were not badly treated.

Next morning the early session was held in the reception hall and presided over by a prosecuting deputy. Attendants brought the three men before him. The deputy first asked who the plaintiff was. T'ao the Third gave evidence, "Last night I lodged at the Changs' brothel. These two men, Hsü Liang and Wu Erh, saw that I was carrying bills for several hundred ounces of silver and began scheming to rob me. They decided to attack me. I happened to go outside the window to relieve myself and heard them, so I went in and grabbed them and dragged them along to the court. I beg Your Honor to examine and judge them."

The deputy asked Hsü Liang and Wu Erh, "Why were you two

men plotting against life and property?" Hsü Liang gave evidence: "I am Hsü Liang, of Ch'ihohsien. T'ao the Third kept insulting us till we couldn't endure it any longer and therefore we planned to get rid of him. Wu Erh said he had a powerful drug 'which always hits the target,' which had been tried out and found very effective. Just as we were making our plans, T'ao the Third caught us." Wu Erh then gave evidence, "I am Wu Hsing-kan, a Collegian of Ch'ihohsien. Hsü Liang was insulted by T'ao the Third. It was nothing to do with me. Hsü Liang was determined to kill T'ao. I was afraid trouble would come of it, so I used the 'strategy of delaying the enemy' and told him that I had a special kind of drug called 'Thousand Days' Sleep' which would send a man off but would not kill him. It was entirely Hsü Liang's idea. I have a written statement here to prove it." And he drew out the document and handed it up.

The deputy asked Hsü Liang, "What exactly did you say in your discussion last night? Tell me the truth, and this court can release you." Hsü Liang then told him the whole of the previous night's conversation without changing a word. The deputy said, "In this case it is only a question of 'heated talk'; there is no reason to call it 'intent to kill.' " Hsü Liang kowtowed and said, "Your Honor is truly just. Have mercy!"

The deputy then asked Wu Erh, "Is everything that Hsü Liang says true?" Wu Erh said, "Absolutely true." The deputy said, "You don't seem to have done anything very bad." He ordered a clerk to make a record of all the evidence and again asked Hsü Liang, "Where is that phial with the drug?" Hsü Liang drew it out and presented it. The deputy took off the wax cover to smell it; it was fragrant like orchids and musk, with a slight suggestion of the fumes of wine. He laughed and said, "Anybody would be glad to take this sort of poison." Then he passed it to the clerk saying, "Take good care of this drug. Have these two men conveyed separately to Ch'ihohsien and send a complete record of the case."

This word "separately" meant that Hsü Liang and Wu Erh were now led to different places. That same night Hsü Liang took the bottle of poison and went to see Lao Ts'an. Lao Ts'an poured it out to examine it. The color was like peach blossoms, the smell rich, the vapor heady. He tasted a little with the tip of his tongue: it was slightly sweet. He sighed and said, "How could this sort of poison do other than make a man drunk for a long time?" He poured the poison back into the phial through a glass funnel and handed it to Hsü Liang, saying, "The instrument of the crime and the human witness are all ready now: there is no danger of his not confessing. But, according to all he says, it would seem that these thirteen people are not dead after all and that there is a way of bringing them back to life. I have heard about that Green Dragon; he is a hermit, but he has no fixed abode and is not easy to find. You go ahead with Wang the Second and report to your superiors. Although the case is really settled, we are not ready to make a final report. Tomorrow I'll go to look for Green Dragon. If I can find him and so can save the lives of thirteen people, won't that be still better?" Hsü Liang replied, "Certainly, Sir."

The next day Wastrel Wu Erh was conducted by the authorities of Lich'enghsien to Ch'ihohsien. Hsü Liang and Wang Erh were called on as witnesses, and of course at the first hearing he confessed to everything. He was put in prison for the time being, but without fetters, to wait for news from Lao Ts'an.

The story goes on that the next day Lao Ts'an hired a donkey and threw his bedding roll over its back, and after breakfast started out for the east route to T'aishan. Suddenly he remembered that beside the Well of Shun there was a fortuneteller's booth whose sign was "An P'in-tzu: Fortuneteller." [1] This fortuneteller was a man of some education, so it might be as well to inquire of him. In any case to go out of the South Gate he had to pass this way. He went along, wrapped in thought, and soon arrived at An P'in-tzu's gate. He tied up his donkey and sat down on a plank bench.

When they had exchanged a few commonplaces, Lao Ts'an asked, "I hear you have known Green Dragon for a long time. Do you know where his cloudlike wanderings are leading him now?" An P'in-tzu said, "Ai-yah! You want to see *him?* What for?" Lao Ts'an then told An P'in-tzu all that had happened. An P'in-tzu said, "What bad luck! Yesterday he sat here with me for several hours. He said he was going back to the mountains this morning at dawn. At this moment I don't suppose he can be more than ten li out of the South Gate." "This is certainly bad luck!" Lao Ts'an agreed. "However, which part of the mountains has he gone to?" An P'in-tzu said, "The Black Pearl Grotto in the Inner Mountain. Last year he lived on The Mountain of the Spirit Cliff, but there have been more and more pilgrims lately, and he did not like the way they crowded to his thatched hut, so he has moved to the Black Pearl Grotto in the Inner Mountain. Lao Ts'an asked, "How many li is it from here to the Black Pearl Grotto?" "I haven't been there," An P'in-tzu said. "He told me a little less than fifty li. From here you go due south through Yellow Cinnabar Gap,[2] then west to Snow Valley, then south again, and you come to the Black Pearl Grotto."

"Thank you for your directions," said Lao Ts'an as he straddled his donkey, and went out of the South Gate. He followed along the foot of the Thousand Buddha Mountain toward the east, then turned south around a spur of the hills. When he had traveled about twenty li, he came to a village where he bought a few griddlecakes for a snack and asked a farmer the way to Black Pearl Grotto. The farmer said, "Not far from here you come to Yellow Cinnabar Gap, a little away from the road. Go nine li to the west past Yellow Cinnabar Gap, and you come to Snow Valley. Again eighteen li to the south, and you get to the Black Pearl Grotto. But the path is not easy. If you know the way, then it's a good level path; if you don't know it, then it's terrible! There are boulders of all sizes and no end of thorns. It would take you a lifetime to get there! I don't know how many people have lost their lives on it." Lao Ts'an laughed and said, "You don't mean it's worse than the road followed by the T'ang monk [3] when he brought back the Scriptures?" The farmer colored up, "Yes, about as bad as that!"

Lao Ts'an realized that the farmer had intended well. He couldn't be rude to him, so he said very politely, "It was a slip of the tongue that made me offend you, Sir; may I ask you again, Sir, which is the easy route, and which the difficult one? Please direct me." The farmer said, "The paths in these mountains are like the ninefold whorls of the pearl: every step or so a bend. If you go straight forward you are certain to walk into a tangle of thorns; but neither must you purposely turn aside, for if you do, you will fall into a deep pit and you will never get out. But I'll tell you the secret since you are willing to take advice. The path in front of you always grows out of the path you have already covered, so when you've gone a few steps, if you will turn round and look back along the path you have come by, you can't go wrong."

When Lao Ts'an heard this, he raised his clasped hands and said, "Thank you very much for your instructions." He then took his leave of the villager and went forward as he was told. And truly it was not long before he arrived at the mouth of the Black Pearl Grotto. There he saw an old man with a beard down to his belly. He went forward and bowed, "Surely this must be the Taoist Father, Green Dragon?" The old man quickly returned the salutation and said, "Where do you come from, Sir? What is your business here?"

Lao Ts'an then told him the story of the Ch'ihohsien affair. Green Dragon thought a while, then said, "It is fated that I should help. Well, let's sit down and talk it over at leisure." There were no tables and chairs in the cave, nothing but rocks of all sizes.

Green Dragon made Lao Ts'an take the seat of honor, then said, "This 'Thousand Days' Sleep' is very potent. If you take a little, you are intoxicated for a thousand days and then wake up; if you take a lot, you won't come to life again. There is only one kind of drug that can dispel it, called 'Quickening Incense.' It is produced among the immemorial ice and snow of Huashan, the Western Peak,[4] and is a quintessential extract from an herb. If this incense is slowly burnt over a gentle fire, you can be brought back to life, no matter to what degree you have been intoxicated. Several months ago a man in a T'aishan gully happened to drink some of the poison, so I went myself to Huashan to the house of an old friend and begged some of the incense. Fortunately I still have a little left. I think it will be about enough for your purpose." Then he took a big gourd out of a cranny in the rock wall. There were a great many miscellaneous objects in it, including a phial less than an inch high, which he gave to Lao Ts'an.

Lao Ts'an poured out some to look at it. It appeared to be rather like frankincense: a dull black in color, it had a rather bad smell. Lao Ts'an said, "What an unattractive color and smell it has!" "How do you expect a thing which will save life to have a pleasant color and smell?" Green Dragon said.

On hearing this Lao Ts'an was filled with respect. Being afraid of making a mistake, he again asked how to use it. Green Dragon said, "Shut the sick people up in a room; no fresh air must get in through the windows and doors; and then burn the incense. Its effect will depend on whether the nature of the individual is good or bad. If it is good, he will come to life as soon as it is lighted; if evil, you must go on heating it for a long time, and in the end he will revive."

When Lao Ts'an had thanked him, he followed the same route back. By the time he reached the little inn where he had eaten, it was already quite dark, so he stayed the night there and at dawn started back for the city; before the hour of *ssu* [9–11 A.M.] he was at the yamen giving Governor Chuang a full account of the affair. He also told him that he was going next day with his "family" to Ch'itungts'un.

The Governor said, "Why do you take your 'precious family'?" Lao Ts'an said, "To cure a man, a woman must burn the herb. To cure a woman, it must be a man. So unless I take my concubine, I can't do it." "In that case do as you think best," the Governor said, "but I hope that if you go now you will come back soon. Our official seals will shortly be locked up for the New Year holiday, and when I have a little leisure from my public duties, I hope to talk with you and receive much advice."

Lao Ts'an said, "Yes." Then he gave several ounces of silver to the servants in the Huang family and went off with Huan-ts'ui to Ch'ihohsien and put up at the inn in the South Suburb. He went to the *hsien* yamen to visit Tzu-chin, who was very glad to see him. Tzu-chin told him that Wastrel Wu Erh had confessed everything and said further, "The thousand ounces that Hsü Liang took has already been paid in. I have received a letter from Prefect Pai ordering it to be returned to Wei Ch'ien. Wei Ch'ien would rather die than accept it, so we let him give it to the hall of charity." [5]

Lao Ts'an said, "Two days ago I sent Hsü Liang with three hundred ounces to be returned to you. Have you received it?" Tzu-chin said, "I have not only received that, but I have become a rich man. When the Governor heard about that affair of yours [6] he sent a special messenger with three hundred ounces which I've already received. Two days later Huang Jen-jui sent another three hundred ounces to be paid on your account. After that Hsü Liang arrived with the three hundred ounces you had sent—altogether three lots. Don't you call that becoming a rich man! The Governor's three hundred can on no account be sent back. I must pay back yours to you and Jen-jui's to him."

Lao Ts'an thought a while, then said, "Jen-jui also has a girl to whom he is pledged; her name is Ts'ui-hua, and she comes from the same house as my concubine. She's a very honest girl, and Jen-jui is much too lonely when he is away from home. Having done one good deed, why stop without doing a second, and using the other two payments to strike a blow for Jen-jui." Tzu-chin clapped his hands in approval, "Since I'm going with you to Ch'itungts'un tomorrow, how shall we do it?" He thought a bit, then said, "I have it!" Immediately he called in the attendants, told them the plan, and ordered them to carry it out the next day.

The next day Wang Tzu-chin and Lao Ts'an went by sedan chair to Ch'itungts'un. The elders and the headman had long before prepared a place for them. After a midday meal in their lodging, they went on foot to visit the Chia family graveyard. There was a small temple not far from it. Lao Ts'an chose a little two-*chien* room in the temple and told the men to work day and night pasting it up so that the air could not get in. Next day at dawn the thirteen coffins were all carried into the temple. They first raised the lid of a laborer's coffin. The body had not decayed, so that put their minds at rest. They then took out all thirteen bodies and placed them carefully in the two-*chien* room, burned the "Quickening Incense," and in less than four hours there was a slight sound of breathing from all of them. Lao Ts'an planned the treatment. First they were given warm liquids, then gruel, and after seven days they were all sent home.

Wang Tzu-chin had already gone back to the city three days before. When Lao Ts'an had brought everything to a conclusion, he was ready to go back, but Wei Ch'ien had learned by now that it was Lao Ts'an who had sent the letter to the Governor. Both the Wei and Chia families came to kowtow and tried by all means in their power to keep him as a guest. Each family sent him three thousand ounces, but Lao Ts'an wouldn't accept the smallest reward. The two families could think of nothing else but to arrange a theatrical performance in his honor. They sent a man to the provincial capital to engage one of the leading troupes of actors and also to get the cook from the North Pillar Restaurant. Thus they prepared to keep Lao Ts'an over the New Year.

Who would have thought that in the middle of the next night Lao Ts'an would slip away to Ch'ihohsien? When he arrived at the *hsien* city it was only just getting light. It was not a good time to go to the *hsien* yamen, so he went first to the inn where he was staying to see Huan-ts'ui. He pushed open the door of the middle *chien* and saw Hsü Ming's wife lying there with no signs of waking up. He further opened the door of the inner room and took a look at the *k'ang*. The coverlets appeared to bulge and on the pillow were two heads, both fast asleep. He gave a jump and then looked more closely. One of them turned out to be Ts'ui-hua. He didn't like to disturb them so he went into the next *chien* and woke up Hsü Ming's wife. There was no place for him to rest, so he went into the courtyard and paced up and down. Here he saw the servant belonging to the main building on the west carrying luggage and putting it on a cart. It seemed to be a traveler from distant parts preparing to leave, so he stopped to watch. He saw a man come out and give orders to the servant.

As soon as he saw him, Lao Ts'an shouted, "Brother Te Hui-sheng! Where have you come from?" The man looked attentively and said, "Isn't that Brother Lao Ts'an? How do you happen to be here?"

Lao Ts'an then told him all the events described in the above twenty chapters and asked, "Where are you going, Brother Hui?" Te Hui-sheng said, "I'm afraid there is going to be war in the northeast next year, so I'm taking my family back to Yangchou." Lao Ts'an said, "Can't you wait one day?" Hui-sheng agreed to do so. By this time the two Ts'uis had got up and washed and the two families were introduced to each other.

At the hour of *ssu* [9–11 A.M.] Lao Ts'an went into the yamen and learned that in the Chia family case, the Governor had sentenced Wastrel Wu Erh to three years' imprisonment, and that Ts'ui-hua had been purchased for four hundred twenty ounces altogether. Tzu-chin returned three hundred to Lao Ts'an, but he would only accept one hundred eighty ounces, saying, "We'll send somebody into the provincial capital with Ts'ui-hua today."

Tzu-chin then wrote a letter giving details of all that had been done. Lao Ts'an returned to his inn and sent Hsü Ming and his wife to take Ts'ui-hua into the city. That night he told the landlord to hire a cart and also to have Huan-ts'ui's brother brought to the inn. At daybreak he took Huan-ts'ui and her brother and together with Te Hui-sheng and his wife, they formed a party going to Chiangnan.

It is further said that Hsü Ming and his wife conducted Ts'ui-hua to the home of Huang Jen-jui. Jen-jui was naturally very pleased. He opened Lao Ts'an's letter and read it. In it was written:

> *May all lovers under the sky achieve the marriage state;*
> *These things are fixed in heaven: do not miss your mate.*

Notes

ABBREVIATIONS '

Chinese Classics: The Chinese Classics, tr. by James Legge. I–II, 2nd ed. (Oxford, 1893–1895); III–V (London, 1865–1872).
    I. *The Confucian Analects, The Great Learning,* and *The Doctrine of the Mean.*
    II. *The Works of Mencius.*
    III. *The Shoo King* [*The Book of History*].
    IV. *The She King* [*The Book of Odes*].
    V. *The Ch'un Ts'ew with the Tso Chuen.*
Eminent Chinese: Eminent Chinese of the Ch'ing Period, ed. by Arthur W. Hummel (Washington, 1943–1944), 2 vols.
I Ching: The Yi King [*The Book of Changes*], tr. by James Legge (Oxford, 1822), Sacred Books of the East, XVI.
Texts of Taoism: The Texts of Taoism [the *Tao Te Ching* and the *Writings of Chuang Tzu*], tr. by James Legge (Oxford, 1891), Sacred Books of the East, XXXIX (referred to as I) and XL (referred to as II).

INTRODUCTION

[1] *Wu Shih Nien Lai Chung Kuo Chih Wen Hsüeh.* Written in 1922, and published in *Hu Shih Wen Ts'un, Erh Chi, Chuan Erh* ("Collected Writings of Hu Shih," 2d. ser., II), (Shanghai, 1924). Most of the novels mentioned in the Introduction are discussed at some length here. Hu Shih's prefaces in the Ya Tung T'u Shu Kuan (The Oriental Book Company) editions of some of the novels contain valuable material. These editions, hereafter referred to as Ya Tung, provide the best punctuated texts of thirteen of the chief novels of China. Lu

Hsün's *Chung Kuo Hsiao Shuo Shih Lüeh* ("Outline History of the Chinese Novel") (Shanghai, 1924), gives a brief treatment of these novels. Some of them are described in Ou Itai, *Le Roman Chinois* (Paris, 1933). See also T'an Cheng-pi, *Chung Kuo Hsiao Shuo Fa Ta Shih* ("History of the Development of Chinese Fiction") (Shanghai, 1935).

2 Lin Shu (*tzu* Ch'in-nan), 1852–1924, knew no foreign language but was a great stylist in Chinese, and with the help of several collaborators performed the colossal task of translating some 152 Western books into classical Chinese. These works were very uneven in quality, ranging from *David Copperfield* and the *Faerie Queene* to Florence Barclay's *The Rosary* and many books of Rider Haggard and Conan Doyle.

3 Ya Tung edition. The story revolves around the heroine Ho Yü-feng, whose father has died in prison through the intrigues of a high official. She runs away into the country where she takes the name Shih-san Mei (Thirteenth Sister) and, while waiting for an opportunity to avenge her father, goes about dressed in red as a female knight, righting wrongs, aiding the weak, and punishing the wicked. Her adventures have been popular on the Peking stage.

4 Ya Tung edition. It appeared with the title *Chung Lieh Hsia I Chuan* ("Record of Loyalty, Courage, Chivalry, and Justice"). Then it became the *San Hsia Wu I* ("Three Heroes and Five Champions") and finally the *Ch'i Hsia Wu I* ("Seven Heroes and Five Champions").

5 Ya Tung edition. Translated by Pearl S. Buck with the title *All Men Are Brothers* (New York, 1934) and by J. H. Jackson with the title *Water Margin* (Shanghai, 1937).

6 From Liang Ch'i-ch'ao, 1873–1929, *Hsin Min Shuo: Lun Chin Pu* ("The Renovation of the People: Essay on Progress") quoted by Hu Shih in *Chinese Literature of the Last Fifty Years*, pp. 131–132. *Hsin Min Shuo* is the general title under which the essays written by Liang Ch'i-ch'ao for his *Hsin Min Ts'ung Pao* (a fortnightly magazine published in Yokohama from 1901 to 1903) appear in the *Yin Ping Shih Ho Chi, Chuan Chi, Ti I Ts'e* ("Collected Works of Liang Ch'i-ch'ao," in *Chuan Chi*, I).

7 Ya Tung edition. Chapters ii and iii are translated in George Kao, *Chinese Wit and Humor* (New York, 1946), pp. 189–208.

8 Ya Tung edition. This book was the chief source of a series of abridged translations into English which appeared in the *Peking Gazette* and were published in book form by the Tientsin Press, 1922, with an air of mystery and anonymity, under the title *Reminiscences of a Chinese Official: Revelations of Official Life under the Manchus*, and reprinted in *Oriental Affairs*, X and XI (1938–1939).

9 Material for the life of Liu T'ieh-yün is to be found in a short biography by his friend Lo Chen-yü in his *Wu Shih Jih Meng Hen Lu* which is quoted almost in full by Hu Shih in his preface to the Ya Tung edition of *The Travels;* and in the prefatory material to the *Lao Ts'an Yu Chi, Erh Chi* ("Second Part of the Travels of Lao Ts'an") edited by Lin Yutang and published by the Liang Yu Shu Chü, 1935. The main source for the brief biography that follows is a detailed statement by Mr. Liu Ta-shen, the son of Liu T'ieh-yün. Mr. Liu very kindly prepared the manuscript of this statement when he heard that this translation was being made. It was then printed in the first number of a literary magazine, *Wen Yüan*, published at Fu Jen University, Peking, 1939, by members of the Fu Jen and Yenching Universities. There is a biography of Liu T'ieh-yün under the name Liu E in *Eminent Chinese*.

[10] T'ieh-yün is his *tzu* (style). His *ming* (personal name) is E. His family home was at Tant'u (now called Chinkiang) in Kiangsu.

[11] The T'ai-ku sect was named after the teacher, Chou Hsing-yüan (*hao* T'ai-ku), who flourished in the middle of the nineteenth century. According to the modern dictionaries *Tz'u Hai* and *Tz'u Yüan*, his doctrines were handed down from the patriarch, Li Chao-en, who founded the Ta Ch'eng Chiao (Teaching of Great Perfection) at the time of the Ming Emperor, Chia Ch'ing (reigned 1522–1567). Mr. Liu Ta-shen asserts that this information is incorrect and is based upon an essay by Lu Chi-yeh entitled "T'ai-Ku Hsüeh P'ai Chih Yen Ke Chi Ch'i Ssu Hsiang [The Vicissitudes of the T'ai-ku Sect and Its Doctrines]" in *Tung Fang Tsa Chih* ("The Eastern Miscellany"), XXIV, no. 13, 71 f. Mr. Liu claims that the doctrines of the T'ai-ku Sect are derived from the teachings of the great philosopher Wang Yang-ming (c. 1472–1528). The disciples of Chou T'ai-ku divided into a northern and a southern branch. The northern was led by Chang Chi-chung (*hao* Shih-ch'in) who during the T'aip'ing Rebellion went into the Huang Yai Mountains in Shantung with a great many followers. In 1867 the authorities attacked them, insisting that they were bandits and heretics. Chang and about a thousand of his followers were killed. Li Lung-ch'uan of Yangchow led the southern branch, which became known as the T'aichou Hsüeh P'ai (the T'aichou School), T'aichou near Yangchow being the home of Chou T'ai-ku. Huang Hsi-p'eng (*tzu* Kuei-ch'ün) established a lecture room at Soochow and succeeded as leader of the T'aichou branch. Mr. Liu Hou-tzu, son of Mr. Liu Ta-shen, has written two well-documented articles on the history and teachings of the T'ai-ku sect. One is entitled "T'ung Chih Wu Nien Huang Yai Chiao Fei An Chih [Discussion of the Proceedings against the Seditious Secret Society at Huang. Yai in the Fifth Year of T'ung Chih]" and was published in the *Shih Hsüeh Chi K'an, Ti Erh Ch'i* ("Historical Papers, Second Issue") by the Peking Research Institute in 1936. The other, "Chang Shih-ch'in Yü T'ai-ku Hsüeh P'ai [Chang Shih-ch'in and the T'ai-ku Sect]" appeared in 1940 in the *Fu Jen Hsüeh Chih* ("Journal of Fu Jen University"), IX, no. 1, 81–124.

[12] Biography in *Eminent Chinese.*

[13] Also known as Chang Chin-kuo. He is the original of the noble Governor Chuang in the novel. See ch. iii, n. 26.

[14] See ch. iii, n. 27 and ch. xiv, n. 1.

[15] See ch. iii, n. 34.

[16] Kang I is the original of Kang Pi, the inhuman official who appears in chs. xv, xvi, xvii, xviii. Yü Hsien is the original of the ruthless official in chs. iv, v, vi. He later became Governor of Shantung. At the time of the Boxer Rebellion he was Governor of Shansi. See ch. x, n. 12. The villainy of Kang I and Yü Hsien is described at length in Li Pao-chia's novel about the Boxer Rebellion, *Keng Tzu Kuo Pien T'an Tz'u* ("The Rebellion of 1900—A Story to be Sung and Recited"). The presence of Yüan Shih-kai, future President of the Chinese Republic, in Shantung at this time is not mentioned in his biography in *Eminent Chinese.*

[17] Mr. Liu Ta-shen, the fourth son of Liu T'ieh-yün, is married to the daughter of Lo Chen-yü.

[18] At this time Liu T'ieh-yün lived in a house rented from his friend Ma Chien-chung, author of the *Ma Shih Wen T'ung*, the first attempt by a Chinese to apply Western grammatical categories to the Chinese language.

[19] In the original manuscript, when the young official Shen Tzu-p'ing is traveling into the mountains, he is frightened by a fox. The publishers changed "fox" to "tiger" on the grounds that in China foxes are objects of superstitious belief and

thought to transform themselves into seductive maidens and old men. Since later in the episode Shen Tz'u-p'ing meets a mysterious maiden and an eccentric old gentleman, it was easy to assume some demonic connection between them and the fox. See ch. viii.

20 See Gideon Ch'en, *Tso Tsung-t'ang, Pioneer Promoter of the Modern Dockyard and the Woolen Mill in China* (Peiping, 1938). Biography in *Eminent Chinese*.

21 Quoted from H. A. Giles, *A Chinese Biographical Dictionary* (Shanghai, 1898). A fuller biography is to be found in *Eminent Chinese*.

22 The Liu family still has a copy of chs. xxvii, xxviii, and part of xxix, but they have never been reprinted. It is tantalizing to hope that a copy of chs. xxix–xxxiv may come to light sometime in the future.

23 See Chu Hsi, *Yü Lei* ("Conversations"), quoted by Feng Yu-lan in *Chung Kuo Che Hsüeh Shih* ("History of Chinese Philosophy"), II, 918.

24 See n. 8, above.

25 Pao Cheng has become a legendary Chinese Solomon. In several plays of the Mongol period (1280–1367) he is the *deus ex machina* who solves difficult law cases.

26 Published in the *Chung Kuo Kung Lun*, II, no. 3 (December 1939).

27 Some of the more obvious discrepancies in the Chinese text have been corrected in the translation.

AUTHOR'S PREFACE

1 Another version referred to as a fisherman's song is quoted in vol. 34 of the *Shui Ching Chu* ("Water Classic with Annotations") by Li Tao-yüan (d. 527):

> Of the three gorges of Eastern Pa, the Sorcerer's
> Gorge is the longest;
> Three sounds of monkeys screaming there, and tears
> drench the listener's clothes.

2 This is the wife of Ch'i Liang who was killed when the Marquis of Ch'i was attacking the city of Chu. See *Tso Chuan*, Duke Hsiang, 23rd yr. (*Chinese Classics*, V, 499). According to the *Lieh Nü Chuan* ("Records of Exemplary Women"), she was left without any relatives and slept with her head on her husband's corpse at the foot of the city wall. All the passersby were moved and wept. After ten days the city wall fell down and buried the corpse. She ran to the Tzu River and drowned herself.

3 These were the two ladies Hsiang, daughters of the mythical Emperor Yao, who became concubines of his successor Shun. When Shun died, they wept so violently that tears were sprinkled over the bamboo around them until it became mottled. There is a variety of bamboo called *Hsiang Fei Chu* (Hsiang Concubine Bamboo) or *Pan Chu* (Mottled Bamboo).

4 Lord Ch'ü is Ch'ü Yüan of the third century B.C. He was a minister of Prince Huai of the state of Ch'u. He was disgraced through the intrigues of rivals and is said to have committed suicide by jumping into the River Milo. His poem, the *Li Sao* ("Encountering Sorrow"), an allegorical autobiography, is the most important early Chinese poem outside the *Book of Odes*. It has been translated into English by Lim Boon Keng, *The Li Sao* (Shanghai, 1929). There is a version in Robert Payne, *The White Pony* (New York, 1947).

⁵ Meng Sou, the Old Man of Meng, is Chuang Tzu, the great Taoist of the fourth and third centuries B.C., who is said to have been a native of Meng in modern Anhwei. The book that goes by his name is one of the greatest imaginative works in Chinese literature.

⁶ T'ai Shih Kung ("The Grand Astrologer") was the title of the office (inherited from his father), held by Ssu-ma Ch'ien, 145–86, author of the *Shih Chi* ("Historical Records"). The first half of this history has been translated by E. Chavannes as *Les Mémoires Historiques de Se-ma Ts'ien* (Paris, 1895–1905).

⁷ See ch. ii, n. 4. The collected poems of Tu Fu are often called the *Ts'ao T'ang Shih Chi* ("Poems of the Thatched Hut") after the small house in which he lived during his years in Szechwan.

⁸ Li Hou-chu, or Li Yü, was the second and last ruler of the Southern T'ang state which lasted from 937–974. He was a vassal of the new Sung dynasty, but finally had his kingdom taken away from him and was kept under restraint at the Sung capital. He was greater as a poet and musician than as a ruler, and was one of the first writers of lyrics in the *tz'u* form. Several of his poems are translated in Ch'u Ta-kao's *Chinese Lyrics* (Cambridge, England, 1937) and in *The White Pony* by Robert Payne.

⁹ The Man of the Eight Great Mountains ("Pa Ta Shan Jen") is the *hao* of Chu Ta, a member of the house of Ming, who after the downfall of the dynasty in 1644 became a monk and devoted himself to wine, painting, and calligraphy.

¹⁰ This is Wang Shih-fu of the thirteenth century. His poetic drama, the *Hsi Hsiang Chi* ("Story of the Western Chamber"), is a development of the T'ang period story *Hui Chen Chi* by Yüan Chen 779–831 [translated by Waley in *More Translations from the Chinese* (London, 1919)] and is the most elaborate example of the so-called northern poetic drama. There is an English translation, *The Romance of the Western Chamber*, by S. I. Hsiung (London, 1935).

¹¹ Ts'ao Hsüeh-chin of the 17th century is generally accepted as author of the *Hung Lou Meng* ("Dream of the Red Chamber"). This is the greatest Chinese novel of domestic life. There is a much-abridged translation by Chi-chen Wang.

¹² The word for "hollow," *k'u* (here meaning "vessel"), has the same sound as the word for "sob," *k'u*. Similarly the word for "cup," *pei*, has the same sound as the word for "sad" or "sadness," *pei*.

¹³ The Pai Lien Scholar from Hung Tu. Pai Lien means "(iron) tempered a hundred times to make it pure." We infer a reference to Lao Ts'an's family name (which was also the *hao* of the author) T'ieh, meaning Iron. Hungtu is an old name for Nanchang in Kiangsi, but here, as the author explains in an unpublished continuation of *The Travels*, it refers to no specific place, but is used in its literal sense, "the great centers of population."

CHAPTER 1

Motto: Each chapter is prefaced by a couplet consisting of two lines of six to eight characters, strictly parallel in form. Here we have:

> *T'u pu chih shui: li nien ch'eng huan;*
> The land does not hold back the water: every year comes disaster;
> *Feng neng ku lang: tao ch'u k'o wei.*
> The wind beats up the waves: everywhere is danger.

T'u (land) corresponds to *feng* (wind); *pu chih* (does not hold back) to *neng ku* (can beat up); *shui* (water) to *lang* (waves); *li nien* (every year) to *tao ch'u* (everywhere); *ch'eng* (becomes) to *k'o* (can be); *huan* (disaster) to *wei* (danger).

The couplet is frequently unintelligible until the contents of the chapter are known. In this case the first line refers to the illness of Mr. Huang (Yellow), which symbolizes the annual floods along the Yellow River, while the second line refers to the ship in danger of being wrecked, which symbolizes the precarious condition of the Chinese ship of state. Thus the first chapter introduces in allegorical form two of the main themes of the book, flood control and political reform.

¹ Tengchoufu, now usually known as P'englai, is a city on the extreme north shore of the Shantung Peninsula. The P'englai Pavilion, originally built under the Sung dynasty, is said to be on the spot from which Ch'in Shih Huang Ti (reigned as emperor 221–209 B.C.) is reputed to have sent a Taoist sage, Hsü Fu, with three thousand men and women and a cargo of seeds to an island in the east. Tradition claims that the Japanese are the descendants of these people. The Han Emperor Wu (reigned 140–86 B.C.) is said to have seen the island of P'englai from here. The fame of the view is due to a mirage, probably caused by a group of rocky islands off the coast, which are thus the original of the Chinese Islands of the Blessed: P'englai, Fangchang, Yingchou, in which men and animals never die and where the palaces are of gold and silver. These islands are the eastern counterpart of Mount K'unlun, the home of the Western Queen Mother, another abode of immortals. Their names are still seen on banners at funerals. See Po Chü-i's poem "Magic," translated by A. Waley in *A Hundred and Seventy Chinese Poems* (London, 1918).

² A good example of the allusiveness of Chinese. This is an abridged quotation from a poem at the end of the *T'eng Wang Ko Hsü* ("Preface to Prince T'eng's Pavilion") by Wang Po (647–675). The Preface was written to introduce a set of poems commemorating a feast given by Yen Po-yü at the pavilion built by Prince T'eng on the bank of the river Kan at Nanchang in Kiangsi. The complete lines are:

> In the morning the painted roof-tree [seems to] fly
> [like] a cloud over the South Bank;
> In the evening the bead screens [seem to] roll up [like]
> rain from the Western Hills.

The whole essay has been translated into French by G. Margouliès in his *Le Kou-Wen Chinois* (Paris, 1926), p. 148.

³ *Yen yü wan chia*, lit., "smoke rain ten-thousand houses." The expression *yen yü*, "mist and rain," is common in poetry. Thus the ninth-century poet, Tu Mu, has

> Four hundred and eighty temples of the Southern Dynasties,
> So many towers and terraces among the mist and rain!

See Ts'ai T'ing-kan, *Chinese Poems in English Rhyme* (Chicago, 1932), no. 57.

⁴ The Chinese have a multiplicity of names. The most common are: the *hsing*, family name; the *ming*, personal name, given by the family, sometimes of two characters (one of which is frequently common to all of one generation in a family), sometimes, as here, of only one character; the *tzu*, a fancy name assumed on coming of age; and the *hao* or style, a fancy name chosen by the man himself or his friends. Besides this a man may have an additional *hao* or *pieh-hao*, a nickname. The author's *hsing* is Liu, his *ming*, E, and his *tzu*, T'ieh-yün. He has

used one character of it, T'ieh, meaning Iron, as his hero's family name, and added Ying, meaning Heroic or Daring as his personal name. Lan Ts'an was the nickname of a Buddhist priest of the T'ang period who started his career as a menial in a monastery on Hengshan, the sacred mountain of the south, in the T'ien Pao period (742–756). It is told of him that "he was lazy (*lan*) by nature, and fond of eating leftover scraps (*ts'an*), and was therefore called Lan Ts'an. When Li Pi, a famous statesman, visited the monastery, he went one night to see Lan Ts'an, who was poking a fire and roasting taros. Lan Ts'an pulled out half a taro and gave it to Li Pi saying, "Don't say much. Be prime minister for ten years." When he died the Emperor gave Lan Ts'an the title of Ta Ming Ch'an Shih (Illustrious Master of Meditation). The Pu in Pu-ts'an means "to mend or repair." The *hao* then means "he who mends broken things or leftovers," and probably refers to the profession of medicine.

⁵ Chiangnan (or Kiangnan), lit., "South of the River," is used sometimes for the territory south of the Yangtze River but here for the provinces of Kiangsu and Anhwei, which formed one province at the beginning of the Ch'ing period.

⁶ *Pa ku wen*, lit., "essays with eight thighs (or sections)," were essays written in the rigid, artificial style required for the official examinations. They were required to be written in eight *pi* (sections or paragraphs), and were usually limited to a total of 450, 550, or 600 characters.

⁷ Ch'iench'eng ("Thousand Chariots") was a Han-period city about one hundred miles northeast of the present Tsinanfu. Sufficient territory to support a thousand chariots was a theoretical unit in early Chinese administration.

⁸ Shen Nung, the Divine Husbandman, was a culture-hero, inventor of agriculture, and father of medicine. The connection between husbandry and herbal medicine is obvious. Huang Ti, the Yellow Ancestor, was the reputed author of the *Nei Ching* ("Classic on Internal Medicine"). Thirty-four chapters of this book have been translated by Ilza Veith in *Huang Ti Nei Ching Su Wen* (Baltimore, 1949). Yü the Great was the first institutor of flood control and reputed to have been the successor of the mythical Emperor Shun.

⁹ Wang Ching was a Han-period official who was well versed in astronomy, mathematics, and the *Book of Changes* and practiced various forms of meditation. In the time of Ming Ti, reigned 58–76, he had great success in controlling floods. He rose to be Prefect of Luchiang in the present province of Anhwei. His biography is in the *History of the Later Han Dynasty*, ch. 106.

¹⁰ A *hsi hua t'ing* ("west reception hall") is a regular part of a large Chinese house.

¹¹ Wen Chang-po means "Leader in Literary Composition." Te Hui-sheng means "Student of Morals and Wisdom."

¹² *Feng ts'an lu su*, lit., "eating in the wind and sleeping in the dew," a conventional phrase.

¹³ This refers to the famous mirage to be seen from Tengchoufu (see n. 1, above). The expression "sea market, mirage tower" occurs in a story in the *Sui T'ang I Shih* ("Material not Included in the Histories of the Sui and T'ang Periods"). Chang Ch'ang-i was a royal favorite, and people came for his patronage like crowds to a market. Li Chan said, "This is like a market in the sea and a mirage tower. How can it last long?" Su Tung-p'o (see ch. iii, n. 22) has a poem called "The Sea Market," referring to the Tengchou mirage.

¹⁴ The whole description of the boat which follows is symbolic of the Chinese ship of state. The twenty-three or twenty-four chang represent the twenty-three or twenty-four provinces into which China was divided before the revolution of

1911. The captain is the Emperor. The four helmsmen are the four Grand Secretaries or perhaps the members of the Chün Chi Ch'u or Grand Council of State. The six masts with old sails are the six boards, or government departments. Of the two new masts the one with slightly worn sails is probably the Tsungli Yamen or Foreign Office, which was created in 1861. Until the Western powers forced themselves on the Chinese there was no Foreign Office, as traditionally China was considered to be the only civilized state in the world, all other peoples being tributaries. The new mast with new sails is probably the Haichün Yamen or Board of Admiralty, created in 1890. The men looking after each mast are the two presidents of each board, one a Chinese and the other a Manchu.

¹⁵ The Peking-Tientsin railway was opened for traffic in 1900. Liu T'ieh-yün was specially interested in the building of railways (see Introd.).

¹⁶ The gash three *chang* long represents Manchuria, usually referred to in China as the Three Eastern Provinces. At the beginning of the twentieth century these were already threatened by Japan and Russia. The other "bad place to the east" is Shantung, already threatened by Germany and Great Britain.

¹⁷ *K'ao t'ien ch'ih fan*, lit., "lean on Heaven to eat rice." In Ch'üfu, the birthplace of Confucius, a stone carving illustrating this saying shows a man with a rice bowl leaning against an enlarged "Heaven" character.

¹⁸ Presumably one of the princes, uncles of the Emperor.

CHAPTER 2

¹ Ta Ming Hu, the Great Clear Lake, fed by the numerous springs of Tsinan, occupies the whole of the north of the old city, covering about a quarter of the total area within the city walls.

² Ch'üeh-hua Bridge. The magpie is a bird of good omen. See Derk Bodde, *Annual Customs and Festivals in Peking* (Peiping, 1936), p. 59.

³ The city of Tsinan was formerly known as Lihsia, which means "Beneath Li." Lishan is the old name of the mountain which rises about two miles south of the city. The district in which the city is located is called Lich'enghsien. See ch. xix, n. 7.

⁴ Tu, the *Kung Pu* ("Official of the Board of Works") better known as Tu Fu (712–770), was one of the greatest poets of the T'ang period. The lines of the poem are misquoted. The first should be: "In the west of the lake this pavilion is the oldest." Tu Fu visited Tsinan in 745, and the poem from which these lines are quoted is said to have been written to commemorate a banquet at the Lihsia Pavilion to which the three poet friends, Tu Fu, Li Po, and Kao Shih, were invited by an important dignitary called Li Yung (*hao* Pei-hai). The poem is translated in full by Florence Ayscough in her *Tu Fu, An Autobiography* (London, 1929), I, 70. For a scholarly work on Tu Fu with translations of nearly 400 poems, see William Hung, *Tu Fu* (Cambridge, 1952).

⁵ Ho Shao-chi, 1799–1873, a distinguished calligrapher, was principal of the Lo-yüan Academy at Tsinan from 1858 to 1860. See *Eminent Chinese*, p. 287.

⁶ T'ieh Kung (*ming* Hsüan) was Governor of Shantung under the second Ming Emperor, Hui Ti (reigned 1399–1403). Hui Ti was a minor when he came to the throne and antagonized his uncle, Chu Ti, who had been given control of a large area in the northeast with the title, Prince of Yen. Chu Ti rebelled against his nephew, finally defeating him and becoming Emperor with the reign title,

Yung Lo (reigned 1403–1425). T'ieh Hsüan was loyal to Hui Ti and opposed the Prince of Yen. He and his whole family were killed by the usurper.

⁷ Ch'ien Fo Shan is another name for Lishan (see n. 3). The mountain contains innumerable Buddhist grottoes. See Segalen, *Mission Archéologique en Chine* (Paris, 1923–1924).

⁸ Mr. Liu Ta-shen has a painting by this artist which belonged to his father and probably was in his mind when he wrote this sentence.

⁹ *Ku Shui Hsien Tz'u.* This is one of the few places mentioned that the translator was unable to identify on a visit to Tsinan. The term *Shui hsien* (Water spirit) is used to refer to several famous individuals who were drowned. It is also the name of the narcissus plant.

¹⁰ *Shuo Ku Shu* is a form of entertainment in which a story is sung to the accompaniment of one or more stringed instruments, the performer marking the rhythm by striking a small drum on a stand and clapping a pair of castanets. This art is still quite popular in Peking and other northern cities, most of the performers being girls (attractive for their looks as well as their singing), though the best are men. The singing is accompanied by conventionalized gestures and a great variety of facial expressions. The subjects are drawn from the common store of Chinese legend and fiction. The life of these singers is the subject of Lau Shaw's *The Drum Singers* (New York, 1952).

¹¹ *Hsi-p'i* and *erh-huang* are the two commonest types of melody used in the modern northern opera. When the two alternate in the same piece, the mixture is spoken of as *p'i-huang.* The question of the origin of these styles is highly controversial. *Hsi-p'i* is generally sharp and shrill and *erh-huang* is softer and more melodious. *Pang-tzu-ch'iang* is a style of operatic music characterized by the use of the *pang-tzu,* a piece of wood which is struck violently to emphasize the rhythm. These three types of opera music came into favor about the year 1800.

¹² These three famous actors are still frequently referred to in discussions of opera at the present day. Ch'eng Chi-hsien, grandson of Ch'eng Chang-keng, was still a popular actor in Peking in 1940.

¹³ *K'un-ch'iang* or *k'un-ch'ü,* is a style of singing, quieter and more refined than those already mentioned, but less often performed nowadays. In the Ming dynasty reign period, Chia Ch'ing (1522–1566), Liang Ch'en-yü, a poet and musician of K'unshan in Kiangsu, learned a number of folk songs from Wei Liang-fu, a noted singer of his district, and converted them into art songs which were then used in drama.

¹⁴ Named after the legendary Emperor Shun who is supposed to have farmed the land at the foot of Lishan. See the couplet at the head of the chapter. There are several other mountains in China that claim to be the scene of Shun's activities. See *Chinese Classics,* III, 66.

¹⁵ The genuflection (*ta-ch'ien-erh*) is the salutation of the Manchu, the left leg bent, the right stretched behind, the right knee and right hand almost touching the ground. The low bow (*tso-i*) is the common formal Chinese salutation consisting of a low bow with the hands hanging loosely below the knees and hidden by the sleeves, after which the clasped hands are raised to the level of the eyes.

¹⁶ *Wu yin, shih erh lü.* The five notes are those of the scale which is still in use (see ch. x, n. 5) and the twelve tones are those of the ancient bamboo pitch pipes. See *Chinese Classics,* III, 36, 48.

¹⁷ *Ya ch'iao wu sheng,* lit., "not even the sound of rooks and sparrows."

¹⁸ Lit., "the five *tsang* [heart, liver, spleen, lungs, kidneys], and the six *fu*

[gall bladder, stomach, bladder, large and small intestine, and another group of organs, probably imaginary, called the *san chiao*]."

[19] *Jen-shen-kuo*, the magic fruit which confers immortality.

[20] This and what follows is an accurate description of T'aishan in Shantung, the most famous sacred mountain in China. The South Gate of Heaven is a gateway at the head of the gorge up which the Pilgrim Way climbs, and passing through it the traveler reaches the various temples scattered over the top. It is clearly visible from the plain four thousand feet below when viewed from the south, but cannot be seen from the west approach which our author has in mind.

[21] In Anhwei Province, two hundred miles west of Hangchow.

[22] From *Lieh Tzu*, ch. 5. See ch. iii, n. 6.

[23] *Analects*, 7.13 (*Chinese Classics*, I, 199). The complete chapter is: "When the Master was in Ch'i, he heard the *Shao* (music in the style of the legendary Emperor Shun), and for three months he knew not the taste of meat. He said, 'I thought not that music could be made as excellent as this!' "

[24] In an interesting "Note to the Second Chapter of Mr. Decadent" Mr. C. S. Ch'ien has identified "Meng-hsiang" as the *hao* of Wang I-min of Wuling, Hunan, who in 1886 received an appointment in the Yellow River Conservancy under Governor Chang Yao (see ch. iii, n. 26). Mr. Ch'ien gives the text of a poem by Wang I-min describing the singing of Little Jade Wang and assumes, quite reasonably, that our author had this poem in mind when he wrote his description. See *Philobiblon*, II (Nanking, September 1948).

[25] Po Hsiang-shan (*ming* Chü-i), 772–846, built a country retreat at Hsiang-shan (Fragrant Mountain) and used this name as his *hao*. The line quoted in the text comes from a poem called the "P'i Pa Hsing [Song of the Guitar]," which is translated by Witter Bynner and Kiang Kang-hu in *The Jade Mountain* (New York, 1929), pp. 125–129.

CHAPTER 3

Motto: See ch. vi, n. 10.

[1] Lü Tsu is one of the Taoist Eight Immortals (*Pa hsien*). His name was Lü Tung-pin. He was the son of a T'ang official and was born in Shansi about 750 A.D. He learned the mystery of the elixir of life and was canonized by the Sung Emperor Hui Tsung (reigned 1101–1125). He is prayed to for prescriptions in case of sickness, is the patron of barbers, and grants noble progeny. He is represented with a sword in one hand and a fly whisk in the other, a symbol of ability to fly through the air. Temples in his honor are very common. His conversion is the theme of the *Huang Liang Meng* ("The Yellow Millet Dream"), a drama by the thirteenth-century dramatist, Ma Chih-yüan.

[2] Under the Empire there were academies at the provincial capitals in which scholars, usually *Chü-Jen*, prepared for the *Chin-Shih* degree. The grounds of the Golden Spring Academy are now occupied by a modern municipal hospital, but the academy building still stood in a garden at the back in 1936.

[3] Ch'en Tsun (d. 25 A.D.) was so hospitable that he used to detain his guests by throwing their linchpins down his well. T'ou Hsia Well means "the well in which linchpins were thrown."

[4] Pottery made in I-hsing, Kiangsu, 150 miles west of Shanghai. These red stoneware teapots are still used all over China.

[5] This descriptive name was given to a variety of pipe with two bowls. These

would be filled with different kinds of tobacco so that the smoker could take his choice.

⁶ Lieh Tzu was a Taoist philosopher about whom no facts are known. A book is attributed to him. In *Chuang Tzu,* ch. i, we read, "Lieh Tzu could ride upon the wind and pursue his way in a wonderful and admirable manner, returning after fifteen days. Among those who attain happiness, such a man is rare. Yet although he was able to dispense with walking, he still had to depend on something." See *Texts of Taoism,* I, 168–169. The opening chapters of the *Chuang Tzu* probably date from the early third century B.C.

⁷ The elaborate doctrine of the pulse is fundamental to the Chinese art of medicine. "Deep" (*ch'en*) is described as "deeply impressed like a stone thrown into water"; "quick" (*shu*) as "six beats to one cycle of respiration," i.e., while the doctor breathes in and out; "taut" (*hsien*) as "stringy, like a tremulous musical string." The deep pulse is associated with the female principle (*yin*) and indicates an external disease due to the seven passions. If the pulse is deep and quick, there is latent heat; if tense, there is colic due to chills. See K. C. Wang and Wu Lien-teh, *History of Chinese Medicine* (Tientsin, 1932).

⁸ *K'u han* medicine. Liu Shou-chen (c. 1165–1233) taught that diseases were caused by excessive heat in the body and introduced the use of cooling medicines. This was opposed by Chang Chieh-pin of the Ming period.

⁹ Lit., "the humor of the liver is easily moved." This was a doctrine developed by Ch'en Yen of the Sung period (his work was published c. 1174), who classified illnesses into those produced by internal causes: wind, heat, moisture, fire, dryness, cold, and the seven passions; and those produced by hunger, insect bites, etc.

¹⁰ *Hsin liang fa san yao,* lit., "pungent, cool, and causing-to-perspire medicine," i.e., a diaphoretic.

¹¹ *Chia wei kan chieh.* The nucleus of this prescription, the licorice and kikio root, was devised by Chang Chi (*hao* Chung-ching), the Chinese Hippocrates of the Later Han period (he received the title *Hsiao-Lien* during the reign of Ling Ti, 168–189) as a cure for diseases of the throat. The other ingredients were added to the formula in the Sung period by the court physicians of the Emperor Jen Tsung (reigned 1023–1064) who were ordered by him to annotate the old materia medica. The eight ingredients are as follows: (1) *sheng-kan-ts'ao,* licorice; (2) bitter *chieh-keng* (*Platycodon grandiflorus*), the kikio root or big bluebell; (3) *niu-pang-tzu* (*Arctium lappa*), burdock; (4) *ching-chieh* (*Nepeta japonica*), ground ivy; (5) *fang-feng* [lit., "protect from the wind"] (*Siler divaricatum*), a root resembling the carrot; (6) *po-ho,* peppermint; (7) *hsin-i* (*Magnolia kobus*); and (8) *fei-hua-shih,* talcum. The adjuvant or *yin-tzu* is an ingredient which helps to make the medicine effective.

¹² *Hsing tao,* lit., "activating the Tao or Way."

¹³ *Hou-pu-tao,* lit., "waiting to fill a *tao.*" Such a person has been placed on a waiting list and will become a *taot'ai* (intendant of circuit) when those ahead of him have filled vacancies.

¹⁴ Tso-ch'en is his *hao.* The name used later, Hsien, is his *ming.* Tso-ch'en means "Supporting Minister of the Left." This ruthless official is a transparent satire on the notorious prefect, Yü Hsien, who encouraged the Boxer rebels. The character for his family name was different, though pronounced in the same way. His other names were identical. See *Eminent Chinese,* p. 407. Cf. Introd., n. 16, and ch. x, n. 12.

¹⁵ From the "Biography of Confucius," in the *Shih Chi* of Ssu-ma Ch'ien, ch. 47. The paragraph in which the expression occurs runs as follows: "When he

[Confucius] had been State Counsellor for three months, the sellers of lambs and pigs no longer raised their prices unreasonably, men and women travelling in the roads kept themselves apart, things dropped on the road were not picked up, and when strangers arrived at the city from the four points of the compass they did not have to seek help from the magistrates, for everybody treated them as though they had come back to their own country." See Chavannes, *Les Mémoires Historiques de Se-ma Ts'ien,* V, 327; also Lin Yutang, *The Wisdom of Confucius* (New York, 1938), p. 66.

16 *Chan-lung,* lit., "standing cages." The cage was an unauthorized instrument of torture consisting of a rectangular frame of upright wood slats, so high that the victim, whose neck was held in a small orifice in a flat board which formed the top, was only able to touch the ground on tiptoe. When he could no longer remain on his toes the whole weight of his body rested on his neck and he was slowly choked to death. The cage is said to have come into use because of the difficulty local officials had in obtaining a death sentence, which had to come from Peking or the provincial capital. Technically, a man who died in the cage was not executed but merely "died."

17 Retribution in a later existence for evil committed in this is a popular Buddhist conception. The term translated "what he will reap," *kuo-pao,* means "fruit recompenses." This is opposed to the term *hua-pao* meaning "blossom recompenses" applied to suffering in this life for sins committed in the previous existence.

18 Chang Chün-fang took his *Chin-Shih* degree about 1004 A.D. The Sung Emperor Chen Tsung (reigned 998–1022) favored Taoism, and, when the northern capital was threatened by the Jurchen, sent the palace collection of Taoist books to Hangchow, where Chang was put in charge of them. He arranged the material in 4,584 volumes and submitted them to the Emperor. Then he selected over ten thousand important passages which he published in the *Yün Chi Ch'i Ch'ien,* which became a recognized compendium of Taoist literature.

19 Chi Chen-i (*hao* Ts'ang-wei) was born in 1630, took his *Chin-Shih* degree in 1647, and rose to the office of censor. He was very wealthy and bought several famous libraries, specializing in de luxe editions. A bibliography of his books, *Chi Ts'ang-wei Shu Mu,* was printed by Huang P'i-lieh in 1805. See *Eminent Chinese,* p. 118.

20 Huang P'i-lieh, 1763–1825, took his *Chü-Jen* degree in 1788. He was a great book collector, and in 1812 he possessed 187 Sung wood-block books. Between 1800 and 1824 he edited and printed a selection of works from his collection with the title *Shih Li Chü Huang Shih Ts'ung Shu. Shih Li Chü* was the fancy name of his study. See *Eminent Chinese,* p. 340.

21 T'ao Ch'ien (*tzu* Yüan-ming), 365–427, was one of the greatest pre-T'ang poets. See William Acker, *T'ao the Hermit, Sixty Poems by T'ao Ch'ien* (London, 1952).

22 Su Tung-p'o (*ming* Shih), 1036–1101, was the greatest Sung poet and also a fine calligraphist. He is the subject of a biography by Lin Yutang, *The Gay Genius* (New York, 1947).

23 Mao Tzu-chin (*ming* Chin), 1599–1659, had a rich collection of old books, and made a business of editing and reprinting them.

24 *Fu kuei fu yün.* From the *Analects,* 7.15 (*Chinese Classics,* I, 200). The complete chapter is: "The master said, 'With coarse rice to eat, with water to drink, and my bended arm for a pillow; I have still joy in the midst of these things. Riches and honors acquired by unrighteousness are to me as a floating cloud.' "

[25] Prince Ch'i was the seventh son of T'ai Tsu, the first Ming Emperor. His principality was in Shantung.

[26] Governor Chuang is modeled on Chang Yao (or Yüeh), the Governor of Shantung under whom the author served. Chang Yao held military posts and had a reputation for building dikes, roads, and factories. See Introd., n. 13.

[27] Chia Jang served under the Han Emperor Ai Ti, who reigned from 6 B.C. to 1 A.D. For his "Three Methods" see ch. xiv, n. 1.

[28] See ch. i, n. 9.

[29] See ch. i, n. 8.

[30] From *Mencius*, 3b. 11 (*Chinese Classics*, II, 283).

[31] P'an Chi-hsün took his *Chin-Shih* degree in the Chia Ch'ing period (1522–1567) of the Ming dynasty. He was an expert on surveying, built many dikes and sluices, and wrote several books on flood control.

[32] Chin Wen-hsiang (this is his posthumous title; his *ming* was Fu), 1633–1692, became an editor in the Bureau of History in 1652. In 1677 he was made Director General of the Grand Canal (*Ho Tao Tsung Tu*). He advocated deepening the river bed, raising dikes, and building water gates. He wrote *Ch'ien Ku Ho Fang Kuei Chien* ("A Mirror of River Control through Thousands of Years"). See *Eminent Chinese*, pp. 161–163.

[33] This passage from the *Book of History* is very obscure. See *Chinese Classics*, III, 134.

[34] *The History of the Later Han Dynasty* was written by Fan Yeh. Ch. 106 contains the biography of Wang Ching which is quoted here.

CHAPTER 4

[1] The button secured the tassel at the apex of the conical official hat. There were nine ranks of officials distinguished by their buttons as follows: ranks one and two (including viceroys and governors), red; three and four (including higher officers in provincial governments), blue; five (including district magistrates), crystal; six, opaque white; seven, eight, and nine, gold. "Tiger boots" (lit., "tiger-gripping-the-ground boots") had crested toecaps and were formerly worn by military officials.

[2] A military orderly officer, assistant to the adjutant in charge of the Governor's military secretariat.

[3] The term *ko-shih* is a transliteration from Manchu into Chinese of a word meaning "guard." Later it was used for a governor's messenger.

[4] This was one of the circuits of Shantung. The full names of the five places included are Tsinanfu, Tungch'angfu, T'aianfu, Wuch'enghsien, and Linch'ingchou.

[5] Before 1852 the Yellow River entered the sea south of the Shantung Peninsula. It then changed its course, running into the bed of the Tach'ing River which flowed just north of Tsinan. The former importance of Lok'ou would seem to be that it was at the head of the navigable portion of the Tach'ing River.

[6] This is a temple to Kuan Yü, one of the heroes of the wars of the Three Kingdoms in the third century A.D. The Sung Emperor Hui Tsung (reigned 1101–1126) gave him the posthumous rank of Duke and then Prince. Shen Tsung (reigned 1573–1620) of Ming honored him with the title of Emperor (Ti), Protector of the Country. He is the patron of soldiers and brings success in various undertakings. His temples are found in almost every village in China. For a description of his apotheosis see ch. 78 of the *San Kuo Chih Yen I*, which was translated by

C. H. Brewitt-Taylor as *The Romance of the Three Kingdoms* (Shanghai, 1925–1926).

⁷ Collegian (of the National Academy) was a title valued for the dignity it gave and as a starting point for an official career without taking the regular examinations. It might be awarded for merit or by purchase. In the latter case it was called *chuan-ti* (euphemistically "by contribution"). The names Yü Hsüeh-shih and Yü Hsüeh-li mean, *Yü*, Student of the Book of Poetry and *Yü*, Student of the Book of Rites.

⁸ Each of the five watches lasts about two hours. The third is the middle of the night. The fifth watch ends before dawn. The second watch would end about 11 P.M.

⁹ "Kinsman" is used loosely for lack of a better term. Strictly it should be "relation by marriage."

CHAPTER 5

¹ Lit., *san pan t'ou-erh* (head of the three bands). In a yamen there were *san pan*, three companies of more or less menial attendants, and *liu fang*, six kinds of secretarial underlings attached to the six departments.

² *Ching piao*, a posthumous testimonial of merit (originally a banner; later a memorial arch or other monument) conferred by the Emperor upon faithful widows and loyal officials.

³ *Kao an men-shang*. *Men-shang* were the superior subordinates of the magistrate (whose subordinates were his private employees) who performed no menial offices. *Men-shang* means "above the gate." The *kao an men-shang*, lit., the *men-shang* who drafts documents, was the most important person in the yamen under the magistrate. He reported all applications to the magistrate and saw to the execution of all orders.

⁴ Kuan Yin or Kuan Shih Yin, lit., "she who hears the sounds (prayers) of the world," corresponds to the Indian Buddhist bodhisattva, Avalokitesvara, and is one of the most popular Buddhist deities in China.

⁵ From Ch'aochou in Kwangtung.

⁶ Soochow and Hangchow in the provinces of Kiangsu and Chekiang respectively, are two cities famous for their beauty, much celebrated in poetry.

⁷ The King of Hell (Yen Wang) is *Yama*, the Hindu Pluto, introduced into China by Buddhism.

⁸ There are ten inches (*ts'un*) in a foot (*ch'ih*), and ten feet in a chang.

CHAPTER 6

¹ The I-Ho T'uan is also known as the Boxer Society. This secret society originated with Kao Sheng-wen of Honan who was executed for a crime in 1771. It was the organization that started the Boxer Rebellion in 1900. Its members held many superstitious beliefs as shown in the text. Cf. ch. xi, n. 30.

² Erh Lang, lit., "Second Son," was a magician variously identified as son of the Jade Emperor, a Taoist deity, and as son of Li Ping, a third-century official noted for his success in flood control. Erh Lang was given posthumous titles by several later emperors. See Arthur Waley, *Monkey* (London, 1942), ch. 6.

[3] Kuan Yeh (Old Gentleman Kuan) is another name for Kuan Ti. See ch. iv, n. 6.

[4] In the novel, *Monkey*, Sun Ta Sheng (Sun the Great Sage), the Monkey King, is the chief attendant of the monk, Hsüan Chuang (Tripitaka), who goes to the Western Heaven to obtain Buddhist scriptures. He symbolizes human potentiality and is believed to control evil spirits and to bestow health, protection, and success on mankind. Hsüan Chuang's other companions are Chu Pa Chieh (The Pig of Eight Vows), the Horse, and the Monk Sha (Sandy). Cf. ch. xi, n. 29.

[5] The Monkey King stole this staff from the Dragon King of the Eastern Sea. It had miraculous powers and had originally been buried in the bed of the ocean by the Great Yü to regulate the level of the waters. At the will of its owner it would change its size and weight from that of a needle to a pillar thousands of miles long. The Monkey King usually carried it behind his ear.

[6] This appears to be from a local song. "Ssu-shih-wu" means "four, ten, five," i.e., forty-five, but it seems to be meaningless here and to be used simply because it rhymes with Kueitefu.

[7] From a well-known anecdote told in the *Li Chi* ("Book of Rites"), halfway through the second part of the section, "T'an Kung." "Confucius was passing T'ai Shan and found a woman weeping and lamenting at a tomb. The master leaned over the front bar of his chariot and listened to her. He sent Tzu Lu who said to her, 'Your weeping is like that of one who has had successive sorrows.' She said, 'Yes, some time ago my husband's father was killed by a tiger. Then my husband was also killed. And now my son has been killed.' The Master said, 'Why do you not leave this place?' She replied, 'Because there is no harsh government here.' The Master said, 'My children, take note of this. Harsh government is fiercer than a tiger.'" See James Legge, *The Li Ki,* in Sacred Books of the East, XXVII (Oxford, 1885), 190–191.

[8] The expressions come from the *Book of Changes*. For "lofty seclusion" (*fei tun*) see Hexagram 33, particularly the expression "lofty seclusion is not without profit" (*I Ching*, 308). For "high-minded" (*kao*) see Hexagram 18, where we read "They do not serve king or nobles, but, high-minded, put their self-cultivation first" (*I Ching*, 96).

[9] Ch'ang-chü "the long rester" and Chieh-ni "the firm recluse" were two recluses who rebuffed Confucius, condemning him as a busybody. See *Analects,* 17.6 (*Chinese Classics*, I, 138).

[10] Chih Tu was a Han period Governor of Tsinan. He had a reputation as a fierce and severe official who was not even afraid of the royal family. He was nicknamed Gray Falcon (Ts'ang Ying). Cf. the couplet at the head of ch. iii.

[11] Ning Ch'eng was a Han official who imitated Chih Tu and was befriended by him. He was however not as honest as Chih Tu and made a fortune.

[12] The prefectural yamen of Ts'aochoufu was in the *hsien* city of Hotse. Here the reference is to the *hsien* yamen.

[13] The red button is worn by viceroys and governors. See ch. iv, n. 1.

[14] See ch. i, n. 5.

[15] From the "Biography of Lin Hsiang-ju," ch. 81 of the *Shih Chi* of Ssu-ma Ch'ien. Lin Hsiang-ju was an astute and daring official of the state of Chao in the third century B.C. The more powerful state of Ch'in had offered to exchange fifteen cities for a famous piece of jade belonging to Chao, and Lin was sent with the jade to effect the exchange. He soon realized that the King of Ch'in had no intention of giving up the cities so, pretending that there was a flaw in the jade

which he wanted to point out, he got it back in his own hands. "Hsiang-ju then stood near a column of the building, so angry that his hair rose, pushing up his hat." He made a daring speech imputing trickery to the king and then threatened to dash himself and the jade against the pillar. By other stratagems he managed to send the jade back safely to Chao.

16 Feich'enghsien is an actual district in Shantung. Peach Blossom Mountain is probably an invention. The name is doubtless derived from the "Story of The Peach Blossom Fountain." (See ch. ix, n. 35.) This reference to Peach Blossom Mountain anticipates the expedition of Shen Tzu-p'ing in chs. viii–xi. The peaches of Feich'enghsien are famous and are known as Fei peaches.

17 From the "Chieh Ch'ao [Answer to Ridicule]" by Yang Hsiung (53 B.C.–18 A.D.), an essay answering a personal attack and defending the wandering scholars of Chou times, especially those well read in the *Book of Changes*. The quotation cites the case of Yen Ho who escaped from the pressing invitation of the ruler of Lu (Shantung) by knocking a hole in the back wall of his house.

18 From a story in the *Kao Shih Chuan* ("Biographies of Great Scholars") by Huang-fu Mi (215–282). The early Emperor Yao invited Hsü Yu to be Lord of the Nine Territories, but he didn't wish to accept. He therefore washed his ears on the bank of the Ying River, to show that he would be sullied by accepting office. This story and the one cited in n. 17 are elaborated from anecdotes in *Chuang Tzu*, ch. 28, "Kings Who Wished to Abdicate."

19 A poem by Ch'ao Pu-chih (1053–1110) contains the lines

> When Yü-k'o painted bamboo,
> In his breast he had the completed bamboo.

Yü-k'o is the *tzu* of Wen T'ung (1018–1079), celebrated poet, calligrapher, and painter.

CHAPTER 7

Motto: "Borrowed chopsticks" means "political advice." The expression comes from the "Biography of Chang Liang" in the *History of the Former Han Dynasty*. Chang Liang one day visited Liu Pang (later Kao Tsu, the first Han Emperor, reigned 206–195 B.C.), while he was eating. Liu Pang said, "Here is a guest who will tell us how to discomfit the King of Ch'u." Chang said, "Please lend me your chopsticks to draw a plan with."

For the *Na Ying* see n. 22 below.

"A treasure house of books" is lit., "Books equivalent to a hundred cities." The expression is taken from a passage in the "Biography of Li Mi" (d. c. 512 A.D.) in the *History of the Northern Dynasties*: "A man who has gathered together ten thousand volumes of books, how is he inferior to an official who governs a hundred cities?"

1 Quoted from the *Tso Chuan*, Duke Hsi, 28th year. See *Chinese Classics*, V, 209.

2 The expression occurs in the *Classics*, e.g., Mencius, 1a. 4.5 (*Chinese Classics*, II, 133). It is later applied specifically to district magistrates who are the officials nearest to the people.

3 Shaolinssu is a temple at the foot of the sacred mountain Sungshan ("The Exalted Mountain"), near Loyang, in the province of Honan. It was reputedly

founded between 477 and 500 under the Wei dynasty. There are several rock faces in the neighborhood of the temple, one of them reputed to be that against which the Dharma meditated for nine years.

[4] Ta Mo, the Dharma, or Bodhidharma, is a legendary Indian Buddhist monk who is fabled to have arrived at Canton at the beginning of the sixth century. He was well received at Nanking by the Emperor Wu of the Liang dynasty, then crossed the Yangtze on a reed and settled at Shaolinssu under the Wei dynasty. Here he practiced meditation, sitting gazing at a rock wall for nine years. He is the reputed founder and First Patriarch (*T'aitsu*) of the mystical Buddhist sect known as Ch'an or Zen. He is credited with discovering the tea plant and with writing the *I Chin Ching* ("Canon of Changing the Sinews"), which is, however, more a system of breathing than of active exercise.

[5] Shen Kuang cut off his left arm on a snowy night in order to persuade Dharma to accept him as a disciple. Dharma was moved and accepted him, changing his name to Hui K'o (Wisdom Adequate). He received the mantle and almsbowl of the Dharma, became head of the Ch'an sect and was known as the Second or Lesser Patriarch (*Shaotsu*). He died about 593 at an age of more than a hundred years.

[6] A prefecture in the south of Shensi province.

[7] A native of Chiangning (present Nanking) who was known for strength and bravery and entered the palace as a bodyguard in the K'ang Hsi period (1662–1722). He could defeat anyone he fought with, could break hard objects, and could squeeze pewter into a fluid in his hand! He died in his bed at over eighty.

[8] Yüeh is a name for the provinces of Kwangtung and Kwangsi together. These disturbances were the beginning of the Taiping Rebellion (1850–1864).

[9] Hsiang means Hunan, from the river Hsiang that runs through the province. Huai similarly is the name of a river that runs through Anhwei. The two armies were commanded by Tseng Kuo-fan and Li Hung-chang respectively, and fought the Taiping armies.

[10] See n. 22 below.

[11] A *ch'üan-t'ieh* is an elaborate visiting "card" consisting of a sheet of pink paper folded concertina fashion five times making a sort of booklet of ten pages (plus additional narrow fold at each end) on which were written forms of salutation suitable to be presented to persons of different rank. When presented, the booklet would be open at the page which suited the occasion.

[12] The books just mentioned are neither old nor important. They appear to be collections of schoolroom models for the writing of "eight-legged essays" (see ch. i, n. 6).

[13] The *T'ang Shih San Pai Shou* ("Three Hundred T'ang Period Poems") is a standard collection which has been translated into English by Kiang K'ang-hu and Witter Bynner as *The Jade Mountain*.

[14] The *Ku Wen Shih I* by Yü Ch'eng, published in 1745, is a standard textbook of classical prose selections. Many of the selections have been translated into French by G. Margouliès in his *Le Kou-Wen Chinois* (Paris, 1925).

[15] The *Hsing Li Ching I* is a popular rehash of various writers on philosophy. It is an abridged and revised edition in twelve books (published in the eighteenth century) of the *Hsing Li Ta Ch'üan Shu* (published in 1415 in seventy volumes by Imperial order).

[16] These three books, the *Yang Chai San Yao*, the *Kuei Nieh Chiao*, and the *Yüan Hai Tzu P'ing*, are all concerned with geomancy or fortunetelling. *Yang Chai* means "[Selection of sites for] houses of the living," as opposed to *Yin Chai*

"houses of the dead," i.e., tombs. *Yüan Hai* means "Vast ocean." Tzu P'ing is the name of an ancient astrologer. Astrology is often called "the Art of Tzu P'ing."

17 The *San Tzu Ching* has been edited with English translation by H. A. Giles. It is a digest of Chinese ideas on morality and history, written entirely in lines of three characters, which was used as an elementary school text.

18 The *Pai Chia Hsing* consists of nothing but a list of the more common surnames in China. About four hundred are included. Giles gives 2,150 in his dictionary.

19 The *Ch'ien Tzu Wen* is attributed to Chou Hsing-ssu of the sixth century. It contains one thousand characters, not one repeated, and was used as an elementary school text.

20 The *Ch'ien Chia Shih* is a collection of T'ang and Sung poems for school children to memorize. "Thousand," of course, simply means a large number. The original collection was made by Liu K'e-chuang (*hao* Hou-ts'un), 1187–1269. A later modified Ming edition is more commonly used. The poems are all of the "new style" demanded in the examinations. See ch. xii, n. 5. Ts'ai T'ing-kan, *Chinese Poems in English Rhyme* is a translation of all the *chüeh-chü* in the *Ch'ien Chia Shih*.

21 The *Four Books* are *Ta Hsüeh* ("The Great Learning"), *Chung Yung* ("Doctrine of the Mean"), *Lun Yü* ("Analects of Confucius"), and *Meng Tzu* ("Book of Mencius"). The *Five Classics* are *Shih Ching* ("Book of Odes"), *Shu Ching* ("Book of History"), *I Ching* ("Book of Changes"), *Li Chi* ("Book of Rites"), and *Ch'un Ch'iu* ("Spring and Autumn Annals") with the *Tso Chuan* ("Commentary of Tso"). See *Chinese Classics, I Ching,* and Legge, *The Li Ki* (Sacred Books of the East, XXVII–XXVIII). The *Book of Rites* and the *Commentary of Tso* are much bigger than the others and are, therefore, not carried by the bookstore.

22 Liu Hsiao-hui is a name invented to disguise a reference to the family of Yang I-tseng, 1787–1856, a native of Tungch'angfu (another name of the city is Liaoch'eng) who became *Chin-Shih* in 1822. After holding many offices, he was, in 1848, appointed *Ho Tao Ts'ung Tu* ("Director General of [the Southern Portion of] the Grand Canal") with headquarters at Ch'ingchiangp'u in Kiangsu. Lao Ts'an, being a Chiangnan man, speaks of *our* Commissioner for Water Transport. Yang made a great collection of books, especially Sung editions, and erected a special building, the Hai Yüan Ko, to house them (see ch. viii, no. 2). He reprinted a number of his more valuable books in a collection called *Hai Yüan Ko Ts'ung Shu.* His son, Yang Shao-ho (1831–1876), prepared a catalogue of the family library called the *Ying Shu Yü Lu.* This, or the *Hai Yüan Ko Ts'ung Shu,* is referred to in the text in the disguise of the *Na Shu Ying.* Much of the *Hai Yüan Ko* collection is still in existence, having been purchased in January 1946 by the national government. It is now housed in the National Library of Peking. See *Eminent Chinese,* p. 888.

23 *Liang-Pang,* lit., "twice posted," is a designation of a *Chin-Shih* and presumably means that he has been posted as a successful candidate in the Metropolitan Examination and the Palace Examination. See Brunnert and Hagelstrom, *Present Day Political Organization of China* (Shanghai, 1912), art. 955.

24 Old name of present province of Hopei.

CHAPTER 8

[1] A *chüeh-chü*, lit., "cut-off lines," is a poem of four lines of five or (as in this case) seven characters, in contrast to the *lü shih* or strictly regulated verse of eight lines of five or seven characters each. Both *chüeh-chü* and *lü-shih* are "new style" verse. See ch. xii, n. 5.

[2] *Shu* is the word for "book" or "books." Here it refers to a family collection of books. The four collections assembled in the library of Liu Hsiao-hui (see n. 22, ch. vii) were:

(1) the collection of Chi Ts'ang-wei (see ch. iii, n. 19).

(2) The collection of Ch'ien Tseng (*hao* Tsun-wang), 1629—after 1699, a collector and scholar who prepared three bibliographies of his library. One of them, the *Tu Shu Min Ch'iu Chi*, is described by Teng and Biggerstaff in *An Annotated Bibliography of Selected Chinese Reference Works,* rev. ed. (Cambridge, 1950), p. 42. It gives details of 601 Sung and Yüan books. Ch'ien Tseng's collection included the books from the great library, Chiang Yün Lou, of his great-grand-uncle, Ch'ien Ch'ien-i, 1582–1664, that had survived a disastrous fire in 1650. See *Eminent Chinese,* p. 157.

(3) The Shih Li Chü collection, i.e., the collection of Huang P'i-lieh (see ch. iii, n. 20).

(4) The collection of Wang Shih-chung made during the Chia Ch'ing period, 1796–1821. The name of his library was *I Yün Ching She,* which means "The Elegant Cottage Planted with Rue" (rue being used to keep books free from insects). Wang obtained most of the books in Huang P'i-lieh's *Shih Li Chü* collection and published the *I Yün Ching She Sung Yüan Pen Shu Mu* ("Bibliography of Sung and Yüan Books in the I Yün Ching She"). On the history of these libraries, see C. S. Gardner, *Chinese Traditional Historiography* (Cambridge, 1938), fn. 49 and chart on pp. 42–43.

[3] Strictly this should be "bookworms" (*tu yü*). English-speaking people in China call them "silver fish" which is a very descriptive name. The free translation, "mildew," reproduces the jingling rhyme of the original.

[4] When a high official raised his teacup from the table, this was a signal that he wished to bring the visit to a close. The attendants would call out, "The teacup is being raised: escort the guest to the door (*tuan ch'a; sung k'o*)."

[5] Chinese geomancers interpret the undulations of mountain ranges in terms of the activity of a dragon under the ground.

[6] Lit., "rush feather nests (*p'u ts'ao mao wo*)."

[7] Lit., "they were so frightened that their superior souls (three in number), flew away, and their inferior souls (seven in number), dispersed."

[8] In a story from the *Shih Shuo Hsin Yü,* ch. 19, *Hsien Yüan* ("On Noble Ladies"), a collection of anecdotes from the Han to the Tsin dynasty by Liu I-ch'ing of the fifth century, a certain Mrs. Wang (née Hsieh) is described as being refined and natural in her manner so that she had a silvan air. The expression is intended to suggest a life of refined retirement in the country.

CHAPTER 9

[1] Western Peak (Hsi Feng) is apparently the *hao* of the girl's father. Pillar Official (*Chu Shih*) was the term for censor in the Chou period, because censors

stood beside pillars in the palace during an audience. "For correction" is a polite formula used in the dedicating of a poem or piece of writing.

² *Chi mieh hsü wu.* This is an expression used for Buddhist Nirvana, a state of mystical absorption.

³ The Taoists claimed to mix lead and mercury and refine them to make the elixir of life which is substituted for all ordinary food and confers immortality. Dragons and tigers in Taoist language symbolize water and fire, the two active opposites that produce the life of the universe.

⁴ Mr. Liu Ta-shen provided the following paraphrase of these poems. For the references to members of the T'ai-ku School, see Introd., n. 11.

(1) While I was being taught the truth of things by my teacher (Li Lung-ch'uan), I was so absorbed that I did not notice the passage of time.

(2) When my friend Huang Hsi-p'eng had started to teach, he humbly admitted that his knowledge was not great and that sometimes he still could not understand the doctrine.

(3) Many men who are filled with earthly desires, when they find a teacher to lead them, become heavenly natures.

(4) The teaching of the master (Chou T'ai-ku) is unique and incomparable like a sudden awakening after a deep sleep. The author, after studying under his teacher (Li Lung-ch'uan), felt a sudden and complete enlightenment.

(5) The universe is a confused cycle of life and death, but when you have received this teaching, from a state of calm you proceed to a state of emptiness and formlessness.

(6) When the teachers (Chiang Wen-t'ien and Huang Hsi-p'eng) were together teaching in Soochow, disciples from north and south were united and had no divisions. How commendable that was!

For detailed commentary on these poems see Appendix, page 267.

⁵ Wang Yu Chün (Wang, the General of the Right) was the official title of Wang Hsi-chih (321–379), the most famous calligrapher of China. The quotation is from his *Lan T'ing Chi Hsü* ("Preface to the Party at the Orchid Pavilion"), which was written to introduce the poems composed by Wang and his friends one spring day in 353 A.D. at the Orchid Pavilion in the mountains near Shaohsing in Chekiang. The "Preface" is translated into English by Lin Yutang in *The Importance of Living* (New York, 1937), pp. 156–158, and into French by Margouliès in his *Le Kou-Wen Chinois.* The complete sentence quoted is: "But when that which we have enjoyed fatigues us, our feelings change according to our surroundings, and melancholy follows."

⁶ *Ts'ang-t'ou* (hoary head *or* green head) is an ancient term for a manservant, popularly assumed to refer to the gray hair of an old servant. Literary sources give other derivations. See C. Martin Wilbur, *Slavery in China during the Former Han Dynasty* (Chicago, 1948), p. 448.

⁷ An imaginary place where there is a temple of the female immortal, Pi Hsia Yüan Chün (The Princess of Colored Clouds), daughter of Tung Yüeh Ta Ti (The Emperor of the Eastern Peak, T'aishan, in Shantung). Legends about this lady go back to very early times, but she was definitely canonized as a political measure by the Sung Emperor, Chen Tsung (reigned 998–1023).

⁸ I.e., he is an unconventional person.

⁹ *Kung* includes the ideas, unselfish and disinterested, unprejudiced, and public-spirited. See Waley, *The Way and Its Power* (London, 1934), p. 162.

¹⁰ See ch. vi, n. 9.

¹¹ Another recluse. See *Analects*, 18.7 (*Chinese Classics*, I, 335).

¹² See *Analects*, 2.16 (*Chinese Classics*, I, 150). The orthodox interpretation is,

"The study of strange doctrines is injurious indeed" (Legge). The ambiguity lies in the word *kung* which means "to attack" and also "to apply oneself to, to study."

[13] Han Ch'ang-li (*ming* Yü), 768–824, was a pivotal figure in the history of Chinese literature. Primarily a prose writer, he brought together various tendencies in the prose style and established a standard. He was an ardent Confucian and opposed Buddhism and Taoism. His memorial, "Protest against Honoring a Bone of Buddha," resulted in his banishment to the wild south.

[14] *Yüan Tao*, an essay upholding Confucianism with its ideas of positive virtue and social order against Taoism and Buddhism. It was translated into English by H. A. Giles in his *Gems of Chinese Literature* (Shanghai, 1923), and into French by Margouliès in his *Le Kou-Wen Chinois*.

[15] Chieh, last ruler of the Hsia dynasty, and Chou, last ruler of the Shang dynasty, are reputed to have been bloodthirsty tyrants whose crimes showed that the mandate of heaven was exhausted.

[16] When Han Yü was exiled to Ch'aochou in Kwangtung he summoned a famous monk of the locality, Ta Tien, and entertained him for ten or more days. He said that Ta Tien's mind could transcend his body and that he could overcome all his passions. Han Yü has been much criticized for his inconsistency.

[17] Chu Fu-tzu (Chu, the Teacher) is the title of honor used for Chu Hsi (1130–1200), the greatest of the Sung philosophers. His interpretation of Confucianism was considered authoritative until the twentieth century. See J. P. Bruce, *Chu Hsi and His Masters* (London, 1923).

[18] See the *Chung Yung* ("Doctrine of the Mean"), 6 (*Chinese Classics*, I, 388): "Shun loved to question others and to study their words, though they might be shallow. He concealed what was bad in them, and displayed what was good. He took hold of their two extremes, determined the Mean, and employed it in his government of the people."

[19] Lit., "with the greater there is no stepping beyond the door bar; with the lesser virtue passing in and out is allowed." See *Analects*, 19.11 (*Chinese Classics*, I, 342).

[20] Chu Hsi and Lu Hsiang-shan (*ming* Chiu-yüan) had a famous meeting in the Goose Lake Temple in Kiangsi in 1175 at which they started a philosophical controversy which their followers continued.

[21] This is from *Mencius*, 6a. 10.8 (*Chinese Classics*, II, 414). It is the conclusion of a discussion of men's inconsistencies in applying moral principles.

[22] This comes from the account in the *Book of History* of the punishments authorized by Shun. See *Chinese Classics*, III, 38, 39.

[23] From *The Great Learning*, 6.1 (*Chinese Classics*, I, 366).

[24] From *Analects*, 9.17 (*Chinese Classics*, I, 222). The complete saying is, "I have not seen one who loves virtue as he loves a beautiful woman."

[25] From *Mencius*, 6a.4 (*Chinese Classics*, II, 397). These words are put in the mouth of Kao Tzu who considers human nature to be morally indifferent. Mencius himself insists that moral tendencies are innate.

[26] From *Analects*, 1.7 (*Chinese Classics*, I, 140).

[27] The "Kuan Chü" is the first poem in the *Book of Odes*. The lines quoted are nos. 3, 4, 9 and 12. See no. 87 in Waley, *Book of Songs* (London, 1937). Cf. *Chinese Classics*, IV, 1.

[28] See Introd., n. 23.

[29] Legge's translation of the complete sentence is: "Thus it is that the *Feng* (Lessons of manners) of a state of change (expressing people's feelings when government is corrupt), though produced by the feelings, do not go beyond the

rules of propriety and righteousness." This comes from the "Great Preface" to the *Book of Odes,* par. 10. The "Great Preface" does not refer specifically to the "Kuan Chü" though it was at one time printed with it. See *Chinese Classics,* IV, Prolegomena, 36.

30 The expression is found in the "Biography of Hsü Mien" (d. A.D. 535) in the *Nan Shih* ("History of the Southern Dynasties"). During an evening party a friend asked Hsü Mien, who was in charge of government appointments, to give him a high office. Hsü Mien said, "This evening the wind and the moon are to be our only topics of conversation: it is not fitting to discuss business." "Wind and moon" is used for the delights of a moonlight excursion, especially at the time of the moon festival in the eighth month.

31 A name for the gown of a Buddhist monk.

32 Lit., "like wet cinnabar." Cinnabar (mercuric sulphide), which gives immortality, suggests a very healthy appearance in an old man. Cf. ch. xiii, n. 70.

33 T'eng Liu Kung is a playful name for "snow." T'eng Liu is the name of a snow spirit. In the *Yu Kuai Lu* ("Record of Marvels"), the following story occurs. "Hsiao Chih-chung (d. 713), a great T'ang period official, was going hunting when an old stag asked a Taoist for protection. The Taoist said, 'If T'eng Liu makes snow fall and Sun Erh causes a wind, then Hsiao Chih-chung will not come hunting.' The next day there was a heavy snow and a strong wind."

34 From *Mencius,* 7a.3 (*Chinese Classics,* II, 479). "Shu," the word translated, "Book of History," can also be used for books or writings in general.

35 The "T'ao Hua Yüan Chi," by T'ao Ch'ien (see ch. iii, n. 21), is a political allegory. A fisherman followed a certain river till he found himself in a marvelous peach orchard. At the source of the river he discovered a tunnel through the mountain, and passing through it entered a region where the people had lived happy and undisturbed since the Ch'in period tyranny (221–206 B.C). There is a clear affinity between Tzu-p'ing's visit to the Peach Blossom Mountain and the "Story of the Peach Blossom Fountain." The piece is translated in Giles, *Gems of Chinese Literature.*

36 *Hu wei.* A common expression is *hu chia hu wei* (the fox borrowed the tiger's majesty). It refers to a story in the "Ch'u Ts'e" in the *Chan Kuo Ts'e* ("Policies of the Warring States") edited by Liu Hsiang (77–76 B.C.). "The tiger hunted all animals in order to eat them. He caught a fox. The fox said, 'You don't dare eat me, for the Emperor of Heaven has set me over all animals. If you eat me, you will go contrary to the will of Heaven. If you don't believe me, I will walk in front of you, and you will see all the animals flee when I appear.' The tiger agreed and was convinced of the fox's importance, not knowing that the animals were really afraid of him."

37 See ch. vii, n. 19.

38 *Ya ku* (welcoming drum) is the name for a melody which imitated the rhythm of the drums used in a yamen. The character here pronounced *ya* means "welcoming." This character was used by mistake for another character, the *ya* in yamen.

39 The *ch'in* (lute) and *se* (zither) are two ancient stringed instruments with long sounding boards having seven and twenty-five strings respectively. The English translation is arbitrary.

CHAPTER 10

¹ Such stumps of trees supported by their gnarled roots are associated with Taoist immortals and hermits.

² In the *Shih I Chi,* a collection of stories, mostly fabulous, by Wang Chia of the fourth century, there is the following story. "When the Great Yü was cutting the Dragon Gate (cf. ch. xiv, n. 3) through the mountains he came to a chasm several tens of li deep, so dark that he could not see to go on. He therefore took a torch and went down. There he found a beast like a pig (really a dragon) holding in his mouth a night-shining pearl that shone like a candle." A round object like a pearl is regularly associated with the dragon. It is variously interpreted as the sun, the moon, an egg, a pearl, the symbol of potency.

³ I.e., a folding rule bent in a series of right angles.

⁴ The *Han Kung Ch'iu* must be a melody related to the thirteenth-century play of the same name by Ma Chih-yüan, which tells the story of the beauty Chao Chün. See ch. xiii, n. 2.

⁵ The Chinese scale consists of five notes, *kung, shang, ·chüeh, chih, yü.*

⁶ From *Analects,* 13.23, where the terms are given a moral significance. Thus Waley translates, "The true gentleman is conciliatory but not accommodating." In later writings the terms are often given an occult or philosophical interpretation. Thus, in the *Kuo Yü* ("Discourses of the States"), probably written in the third century B.C., in the "Cheng Yü," we read: "Harmony (*ho*) results in the production of things, but identity (*t'ung*) does not. When the one equalizes the other, there comes what is called harmony, so that then there can be a luxurious growth in which new things are produced. But if identity is added to identity, all that is new is finished." Quoted in Fung Yu-lan, *History of Chinese Philosophy,* tr. Bodde (Peiping, 1937), p. 34.

⁷ In *Chuang Tzu,* ch. 32, there is the following story: "There was a man who, having had an interview with the king of Sung, and having been presented by him with ten carriages, showed them boastfully to Chuang Tzu, as if the latter had been a boy. Chuang Tzu said to him, 'Near the Ho there was a poor man who supported his family by weaving rushes (to form screens). His son, when diving in a deep pool, found a pearl worth a thousand ounces of silver. The father said, "Bring a stone, and break it in pieces. A pearl of this value must have been in a pool nine *chung* deep (i.e., deeper than any nine pools), and under the chin of the Black Dragon. That you were able to get it must have been owing to your finding him asleep. Let him awake, and the consequences to you will not be small!" Now the kingdom of Sung is deeper than any pool of nine *chung,* and its king is fiercer than the Black Dragon. That you were able to get the chariots must have been owing to your finding him asleep. Let him awake, and you will be ground to powder.'" See *Texts of Taoism,* II, 211–212.

⁸ The instrument here called a harp is the *k'ung hou,* a sort of lute with twenty-three strings. It is mentioned in ch. 28 of the *Shih Chi* of Ssu-ma Ch'ien (Chavannes, *op. cit.,* III, 495) but has long been obsolete.

⁹ This is the name of one of the songs, supposedly collected by the ancient Music Bureau (*Yüeh Fu*), whose metrical patterns were employed by later poets. The story goes that a Korean ferryman, Huo Li Tzu Kao, one morning saw a white-headed madman carrying a pot rush into the river, heedless of his wife's

warning, and drown himself. The wife of the madman took up her harp and sang a heart-rending song:

> I told my man not to ford the river,
> But my man forded the river;
> He fell into the water and was drowned,
> And now what hope is there for my man?

She then threw herself into the water and was drowned. The ferryman told the story to his wife, named Li Yü, who was greatly touched, took up her harp, and made a song about it. Ts'ao Chih (192–232), son of the great general, Ts'ao Ts'ao, was one of the earliest poets to use the title "Harp Melody (*K'ung Hou Yin*)" for one of his own compositions.

[10] The *hai* period is 9 to 11 P.M. The day is divided into twelve periods of two hours named after the Twelve Terrestrial Branches (see ch. xi, n. 2), of which this is the last.

[11] Apparently the top is shaped like a plum blossom, with five serrations.

[12] The poem is of course about the Boxer Rebellion and the part played by the notorious Yü Hsien. (Cf. ch. iii, n. 14.) The Rebellion occurred in 1900, the year of the Rat (*Keng-Tzu*) in the Chinese calendar. "Eastern Mountain" (*Tung Shan*) is the name of the province of Shantung reversed. "Suckling tiger" symbolizes Yü Hsien who was Governor of Shantung from 1897 to 1899, just before the Rebellion. *Men* and *hu* are two words for the outer door of a house. Ch'i and Lu were two ancient states partly coterminous with Shantung. "To visit Heaven" means to report at court. "Western Hill" (*Hsi Shan*) is the name of Shansi reversed. Yü Hsien was made Governor of Shansi by the Empress Dowager. "Father Adam's sons" means Westerners. Yü Hsien was notoriously antiforeign, his persecution of Christians in Shantung leading up to the Boxer Rebellion. He was Governor of Shansi at the time of the Rebellion and encouraged the attacks on foreigners. "Neighbors four" refers to the foreign powers at all four directions of the compass. "Heavenly house" is the court of the Empress Dowager who fled to Sianfu in Shensi. "Blackhaired people" are the Chinese people. This type of political prophetic riddle in ballad form has been very common in Chinese history. Such songs were often sung by children.

[13] Lit., "combed into a *yün chi* (cloud coil) but modified into a *chui-ma chuang* (style of falling-off-a-horse)." A *yün chi* (cloud coil) is a definite style like the conventional cloud whorls which appear in Chinese designs. The *chui-ma chi* is another style associated with the name of Sun Shou, the wife of Liang Chi, of the later Han period. She is described as expert in the arts of seduction and wearing her hair to one side like a man falling off a horse. In a poem by Hsü Yu-jen of the Yüan period we have,

> The wind blew the willow leaves round and round like dancing phoenixes;
> The rain weighed down the lotus like a falling-from-horse coiffure.

[14] This is the beautiful leaf of the *tz'u-ku, Sagittaria sagittifolia,* a water plant whose roots are used for food. The leaf goes to a sharp point and has two long tapering lobes that lie back along the stem.

[15] Adapted from the language of the *Book of Changes,* where the comment on the first hexagram is, "the dragon lying hid: it is not the time for active doing." See *I Ching,* 58.

[16] From the *Maha prajna paramita sutra* (*Ta Pan Jo Po Lo Mi To Ching*). See D. T. Suzuki, *Manual of Zen Buddhism* (London, 1950), p. 26.

256 *The Travels of Lao Ts'an*

CHAPTER 11

Motto: The couplet refers to the Boxers in the north (plague rat) and the revolution in the south (mad dog). Cf. n. 6, below. The expression "panic-making horse" (*hai ma*) comes from *Chuang Tzu*, ch. 24, where, however, the meaning is "to injure horses." In a parable on the doctrine of inactivity in government, Huang Ti is represented as asking a boy who tends horses about the government of mankind. The boy says, "In what does the governor of the kingdom differ from him who has the tending of horses and who has only to put away whatever in him would injure the horses?" See *Texts of Taoism*, II, 96–97. *Hai ma* is subsequently used for a horse that creates a panic or disturbance in the herd.

¹ Gold lotuses (*chin lien*) are bound feet. The story is that the Marquis of Tunghun, sixth ruler of the Southern Ch'i dynasty (479–501), made his concubine, P'an Fei, dance on lotuses of gold and said, "At every step a lotus grows." *Ling-chih*, the "Plant of Long Life," is a many-colored fungus, emblem of longevity, often represented in the mouth of a deer, who is credited with the power of finding it. The Islands of the Blessed (see ch. i, n. 1) are described as covered with it. The God of Longevity is often represented riding on a deer and with the Plant of Long Life growing around him. Presumably the design is embroidered on the shoes.

² Three cycles of sixty years (*San Yüan Chia-Tzu*). From early times the Chinese have used the Cycle of Sixty as a means of naming the hours, days, months, and years. The cycle is formed by combining the series of Ten Celestial Stems, named *Chia, I, Ping, Ting, Wu, Chi, Keng, Hsin, Jen, Kuei*, with the series of Twelve Terrestrial Branches, named *Tzu, Ch'ou, Yin, Mao, Ch'en, Ssu, Wu, Wei, Shen, Yu, Hsü, Hai*. Thus the first term in the cycle is called *Chia-Tzu*, the second *I-Ch'ou*, the eleventh the *Chia-Hsü*, etc. The cycle is completed in sixty combinations, after which a new cycle begins again with *Chia-Tzu*. The recurrence of *Chia*, first of the Celestial Stems, every ten years, is thought to have special significance. The beginning of a new cycle (as in 1864 and 1924, both of which are *Chia-Tzu* years) is of course significant. Mr. Liu Ta-shen says that the cycles are named by analogy with the division of the year into two periods of three cycles of sixty days or two months. The second cycle in each case contains an equinox and the third, a solstice. The first cycle is called the Opening Cycle (*K'ai-Yüan Chia-Tzu*); the second is called the Dividing or Equinoctial Cycle (*Fen-Ch'a Chia-Tzu*); and the third the Pivotal or Solstitial Cycle (*Chuan-Kuan Chia-Tzu*). Yellow Dragon's argument seems to imply that three cycles of sixty, i.e., 180 years, again form a greater cycle, and that such a cycle beginning in 1864 is the third of a series of greater cycles of which the first began in 1504, the second in 1684. The third, beginning in 1864, is thus a Pivotal or Solstitial Cycle in which great changes are bound to occur. The sixty-year Opening Cycle (1864–1923) is thus the first phase of this greater Solstitial Cycle.

³ T'ung Chih is the *nien-hao* (name of reign period) of the Emperor Mu Tsung I, who reigned from 1862 to 1875. Before the Ming period the *nien-hao* was frequently changed during the course of one reign. In the Ming and Ch'ing periods each reign has only one *nien-hao* and this is often used by Westerners as though it were the name of the emperor. Thus T'ung Chih is loosely used as the name of the emperor. Kang Hsi is another such name.

⁴ This was when Annam finally became a protectorate of France.

⁵ Refers to a well-known story from the "Yen Ts'e" in the *Chan Kuo Ts'e* (see

ch. ix, n. 36). The state of Chao was about to attack Yen (see ch. xiv, n. 2). Su Tai, acting for Yen, said to Prince Hui of Chao, "On my way today I passed the I River. An oyster was sunning himself on the bank when a kingfisher took him in his beak. The oyster then caught the kingfisher's beak in his shell. Neither would let go and eventually a fisherman captured them both. This is a parable of what will happen if Chao and Yen fight. The powerful state of Ch'in will take them both when exhausted." The prophecy came true, for the ruler of Ch'in conquered the whole of China, taking the title Ch'in Shih Huang Ti in 221. The parable here is applied to the Sino-Japanese War of 1894. After the Treaty of Shimonoseki which concluded the war, the Western powers stepped in and strengthened their hold in China. Russia, Germany, and France forced Japan to give up the Liaotung Peninsula which had been awarded her in the treaty.

6 The successive pairs of the ten Celestial Stems are each under the influence of one of the five elements: Wood, Fire, Earth, Metal, Water; and each of the Terrestrial Branches is under one of the twelve animals of the Chinese Zodiac. *Keng-Tzu* [1900] is the year of the Rat (*Tzu* is under the Rat). *Wu* is the Branch under the influence of the Horse which is opposite the Rat in the zodiacal circle. The clash takes place under the influence of Metal (*Keng* is under Metal). *Keng-Hsü* [1910] is the year of the Dog. The clash is between the Dog and its opposite the Dragon, again under the influence of Metal. See also the couplet at the head of the chapter.

7 In the *Chung Yung* ("Doctrine of the Mean"), 10.4, we have, "to lie under arms; and meet death without regret:—this is the energy of Northern regions, and the forceful make it their study." See *Chinese Classics*, I, 390.

8 The Empress Dowager, Tz'u Hsi T'ai Hou. The novel was written well before Tz'u Hsi died at the end of 1908.

9 Yü Hsien and Kang Pi (see Introd., n. 16), Jung Lu, and others. They were all Manchus or enlisted under the Manchu Banners, and in the Boxer Rebellion aimed not only at ousting the Westerners but at strengthening the Manchu dynasty to keep the Chinese under control.

10 In the *Doctrine of the Mean*, 10.3, we have, "To show forbearance and gentleness in teaching others; and not revenge unreasonable conduct:—this is the energy of the Southern regions, and the good man makes it his study." See *Chinese Classics*, I, 389–390.

11 Wei Po-yang of the second century wrote the *Ts'an T'ung Ch'i*, a book of alchemy which purported to expound the *Book of Changes*.

12 It is difficult to find any "political changes" of importance in 1904. Proposals were being made for the abolition of the old examination system, but this reform was only carried out in 1905. Various revolutionary societies were formed which in 1905 amalgamated in the T'ung Meng Hui, which later became the Kuomintang.

13 The language is that of the *Book of Changes*, comment on hexagram 40: "When thunder and rain come, the plants and trees that produce the various fruits begin to burst their husks." See *I Ching*, 245.

14 This expression must be taken as a general reference to the Golden Age of early Chinese history. There is great confusion in the accounts of who the individuals were. According to one scheme the Three Rulers were: (1) The Celestial Ruler, T'ien Huang, (2) The Terrestrial Ruler, Ti Huang, and (3) The Human Ruler, Jen Huang; the Five Emperors: (1) Fu Hsi, (2) Shen Nung, (3) Huang Ti, (4) Yao, and (5) Shun.

15 The Ah Hsiu Lo or Asuras are one of the eight classes into which the Buddhists

divide all spirits. In the Rig Veda they were considered as deities along with the Deva, but in Buddhism they became Titans, enemies of the Gods, and then demons. They are described as being constantly at war with the Master of the Tao-li Heavens. See n. 28, below.

[16] The *Wu-Chi*, the Boundless or Unlimited (comparable to A. N. Whitehead's "creativity"), is, strictly speaking, a Taoist conception. The *T'ai-Chi* the Great Ultimate (comparable to Whitehead's "primordial nature of God"), is a conception found in the *Book of Changes*. It is the source of the Yin and Yang (comparable to Whitehead's "physical and mental poles"), the dual principles whose interaction gives rise to the multiplicity of things. The Sung philosophers systematized these conceptions.

[17] *Yao* means "to intertwine or change." The character has the form of two diagonal crosses, one above the other. The separate lines, broken or unbroken, in the trigrams and hexagrams of the *Book of Changes* are called *yao*. *Hsiang* is an image, or representation, or emblem, i.e., a hexagram of the *Book of Changes*.

[18] From *Analects*, 5.19. "Chi Wen-tzu used to think thrice before acting. The Master hearing of it said, 'Twice is quite enough.'" (tr. Waley). Cf. *Chinese Classics*, I, 180. Chi Wen-tzu (*ming* Hsing-fu) was an official of the state of Lu who died 568 B.C.

[19] The *Book of Changes* is the most venerated and least intelligible of the Chinese classics. It consists of sixty-four hexagrams (*kua*) with their explanations, and several appendices. Originally a handbook for divining with the milfoil plant, it became a book of philosophy, and the hexagrams became emblems containing the secrets of the universe. The discussion in this chapter is a good example of the jejune speculation to which the *Book of Changes* gives rise. Each hexagram is composed of two trigrams and these in turn of three whole (male) or broken (female) lines, called *yao*. There are eight trigrams as follows: (1) *Ch'ien* ☰ is Heaven, the ruler and father, (2) *K'un* ☷ is Earth, the mother, (3) *Chen* ☳ is the eldest son, or thunder, (4) *Sun* ☴ is the eldest daughter, or wood and rain, (5) *K'an* ☵ is the second son, or water (in clouds and springs), (6) *Li* ☲ is the second daughter, or fire, (7) *Ken* ☶ is the youngest son, or mountain, and (8) *Tui* ☱ is the youngest daughter, or water (in marshes or lakes). The trigrams are either auspicious or inauspicious. The hexagrams take their meaning from the component parts. The two hexagrams discussed in the text are the following: (1) no. 49, *Ke* ䷰ (*tse huo ke*), the water and fire hexagram of Change or Revolution (inauspicious). It is composed of *Tui* ☱, female water of marshes (*tse*), which is inauspicious, over *Li* ☲, fire (*huo*). (2) no. 63, *Chi Chi* ䷾ (*shui huo chi chi*), the water and fire hexagram of Completion (auspicious). It is composed of *K'an* ☵, male water of clouds and springs (*shui*), which is auspicious, over *Li* ☲, fire (*huo*).

[20] The *Kuan Tzu* is a book attributed to Kuan Chung (seventh century B.C.), but probably written in the third century B.C. It is a politico-economic text of the Five Elements School which stresses the importance of natural influences, especially water, on human life. The quotation is from ch. 30, "Chün Ch'en [Rulers and Subjects]," where subjects are said to respond to good government as the crops respond to rain.

[21] "T'uan Tz'u [Treatise on the Definitions]" is the term used for the explanatory remarks under each hexagram in the *Book of Changes*. The quotation is from the "T'uan Tz'u" explaining Hexagram 49, *Ke*. In Legge's translation the "T'uan Tz'u" appears as appendix i. See *I Ching*, p. 253.

22 Lit., "like fire, like rushes." The expression refers to a story in the "Wu Yü" in the *Kuo Yü* ("Discourses of the States"), in which the Prince of the state of Wu once impressed a rival state by ordering one wing of his army to be clad entirely "in red like fire," and the other "in white like flowering rushes." A display of military magnificence is sometimes referred to as "like fire, like rushes."

23 See ch. xii, n. 11.

24 The five vowels of the Japanese alphabet.

25 Worship of Yü Ti (the Jade Emperor), chief of the Three Pure Ones of Taoism, was instituted by the Sung Emperor, Chen Tsung, in 1012.

26 From the *Tao Te Ching*, 5. The straw dogs were used in praying for rain and after the sacrifice were thrown away. The translation is taken from Arthur Waley, *The Way and Its Power* (London, 1934). Cf. *Texts of Taoism*, I, 50.

27 From *Chuang Tzu*, ch. 14. See *Texts of Taoism*, I, 351–352. Our author gives a summary of the idea of the passage, not a direct quotation.

28 The Thirty-three Heavens are the *Tao-li* Heavens. *Tao-li* (meaning thirty-three) is a corrupt transcription of the Sanscrit *traiyastrimra*, which means the heaven established by Indra and his thirty-two brother *devas*. The Seventy-two Earths refers to the seventy-two terrestrial paradises (*fu ti*), abodes of Taoist immortals.

29 The *Hsi Yu Chi* ("Account of a Journey to the West") by Wu Ch'eng-en (c. 1510–1580) is one of the great novels of China, based on the life of the seventh-century monk Hsüan Chuang, who made a remarkable journey to India, collected Buddhist books and, returning to China, translated many of them into Chinese. He also wrote an account of his mission, the *Hsi Yü Chi* ("Account of the Western Regions"). Various interpretations of the novel have been given, one of the most elaborate being that of Chang Shu-shen (*flor.* 1736–95), whose *Hsin Shuo Hsi Yu Chi* attempts to show that the whole novel is an allegorical expansion of the Confucian classic, the *Ta Hsüeh* ("Great Learning"). Timothy Richards in his abridged translation of the novel with the title, *A Mission to Heaven*, has outdone the Chinese in fanciful interpretation. Waley has translated about a third of the book with the title, *Monkey*. The episode of the Black Chicken Country occurs in chapters 37–39 (chs. 19–21 in *Monkey*). The monk is reading late at night in a certain Paolin Temple when he is visited by the ghost of a king who says that a magician has drowned him in a palace well, taken his shape, and usurped his throne. The monk's followers, the Monkey King and the Pig of Eight Vows (see ch. vi, n. 4), with the help of the Crown Prince, succeed in deposing the usurper and restoring the rightful king. Chang Shu-shen interprets the name, Wu Chi Kuo (Black Chicken Country), as a homophone for Wu Chi Kuo (Darkened Source-of-action Country) and as symbolizing mind (in itself morally neutral) as having been darkened (morally perverted) and needing to be brought back to the light (the true path of morality). Waley takes the *wu* as equivalent to *ming* ("to crow"), and calls the country Crow-cock.

30 The Boxer Society used the stock methods of Chinese secret societies: incantations and charms were thought to make them invulnerable to arrows and bullets. The revolutionaries were mostly people educated abroad or with some foreign (scientific) ideas who denounced all traditional superstitions. Cf. ch. vi, n. 1.

31 See *Analects*, 6.20. Waley's tr., "by respect for the Spirits (propitiating them) keep them at a distance" probably gives the original intention, but the translation given is the traditional interpretation, and probably what our author intended. See *Chinese Classics*, I, 191.

CHAPTER 12

Motto: "White Snow Song" refers to the poem by Lao Ts'an about the frozen river. The name is taken from that of an ancient tune (of the type collected by the Music Bureau) for the fifty-stringed lute entitled "White Snow." It is cited as a model of refined music by Lu Chi, 261–303, in his *Wen Fu* ("Prose Poem on the Art of Literature"). See Margouliès, *Le "Fou" dans le Wen-siuan* (Paris, 1925), p. 91.

[1] Hsieh Ling-yün, 385–433, was born in the present Honan and held office under the Chin and Sung rulers.

[2] The "Imperial Enclosure" (*Tzu Wei Yüan*) is a name for the stars immediately surrounding the North Star (*Tzu Wei*), which is itself the abode of the supreme ruler of the universe, T'ai I. These stars correspond to an earthly court with its protecting walls.

[3] One of the ancient Chinese methods of determining the seasons was by the position of the Bushel or Dipper. John Chalmers (in an essay on the Astronomy of the Ancient Chinese in *Chinese Classics*, III, Prolegomena, 93 ff.) quotes Ho-kuan-tzu as saying, "When the tail of the Bear points to the east (at nightfall), it is spring to all the world."

[4] From the *Book of Odes*, the poem entitled "Ta Tung." The translation is adapted from that in Waley's *Book of Songs*, where it is no. 284. Cf. *Chinese Classics*, IV, 356. In the poem the idle aristocracy of the Chou period are likened to the various constellations which are named after useful articles but cannot be used.

[5] "New style" verse (*hsin t'i shih*) was the distinctive style of verse of the T'ang period 618–907 A.D. Written in lines of five or seven characters, in contrast to "old style" verse, it had a rather rigid tonal pattern which was later formulated in a system of rules. The evolution of this tonal pattern can be traced back to the Han period and even to the *Book of Odes*, but it first became a conscious concern of poets in the age of Shen Yüeh, 441–513, and Hsieh T'iao, 464–99. Shen Yüeh was the first writer to classify the four tones of the Chinese language and to show their value for the rhythm of verses. In his time, however, the distinction between the "old" and the "new" styles was by no means clearly established. Hence the difficulty Lao Ts'an had in understanding the principle of classification in Wang K'ai-yün's *Anthology*. The rules of "new style" verse are discussed at some length by J. R. Hightower in his *Topics in Chinese Literature* (Cambridge, 1950), pp. 61–67.

[6] Wang K'ai-yün (*tzu* Jen-ch'iu), 1833–1916, was a Hunan man who had followed Tseng Kuo-fan and wrote an account of the T'aiping Rebellion called the *Hsiang Chün Chih* ("History of the Hunan Army"). See ch. vii, n. 9. His *Pa Tai Shih Hsüan* ("Poetic Anthology of Eight Dynasties") is a valuable collection of pre-T'ang poetry.

[7] Shen Te-ch'ien (*hao* Kuei-yü), 1673–1770, was patronized by the Emperor Ch'ien Lung who enjoyed hearing him discuss ancient poetry. His *Ku Shih Yüan* ("The Spring of Ancient Poetry") is a standard collection of pre-T'ang poetry. He made several other well-known anthologies. See *Eminent Chinese*, p. 645.

[8] Wang Shih-chen (*pieh-hao* Yü Yang Shan Jen), 1634–1711, was author of a famous book of literary criticism, *Yü Yang Shih Hua*, and of the *Ku Shih Hsüan* ("Anthology of Early Poems").

⁹ Chang Ch'i (*tzu* Han-feng), 1764–1853, was a versatile scholar and poet. His *Ku Shih Lu* ("Early Poems Reprinted") is an anthology of pre-T'ang verse. See *Eminent Chinese*, p. 25.

¹⁰ The expression is vague in the original. Presumably it is material for dike-building: wood, osiers, straw, or stones.

¹¹ Lit., "Forest of Brushes Academy." Scholars who had passed the examination for the third degree, *Chin-Shih*, and then were successful at a special palace examination became members of the academy. They were expected to pursue more advanced studies.

¹² Shouchou, a city in Anhwei.

¹³ A *ch'ientzu* is an instrument, something like a metal knitting needle, on which a pellet of raw opium is picked up and roasted.

¹⁴ *Ts'ui* is the blue-green of kingfisher feathers. Ts'ui-hua means "Green Flower," suggesting a flowerlike head ornament made of pieces of kingfisher feather or jade of this color. Ts'ui-huan means "Green Jade Bracelet."

¹⁵ See ch. vi, n. 15.

CHAPTER 13

¹ Hsi Shih (or Hsi Tzu) was a famous beauty employed by Fan Li, minister of Kou Chien, Prince of Yüeh, as a decoy to debauch Fu Ch'ai the Prince of Wu, at the end of the fifth century B.C. The story is a frequent subject for poetry and drama. See n. 4, below.

² Wang Ch'iang (also known as Chao Chün) was a beauty in the harem of the Emperor Yüan Ti of Han (reigned 48–33 B.C.). According to tradition the court painter Mao Yen-shou put a blemish in her portrait because she would not give him the customary bribe. She, therefore, found no favor with the Emperor and was promised to a Tartar chieftain. The Emperor discovered her true beauty too late. See ch. x, n. 4.

³ This is a popular distortion of a passage in *Chuang Tzu*, ch. 2 (*Texts of Taoism* I, 191). Chuang Tzu is showing the relativity of knowledge and of preferences. He says, "Mao Ch'iang [a contemporary of Hsi Shih] and Li Chi were accounted by men to be most beautiful, but when fishes saw them they dived deep in the water from them; when birds, they flew from them aloft."

⁴ Early occurrences of these expressions are to be found in the following: In his "Lo Shen Fu [The Fu of the Lo River Spirit]" Ts'ao Chih (192–233) says, "Her hair was like a fleecy cloud obscuring the moon." In his "Hsi Shih Shih [Poem on Hsi Shih]," Li Po (699–763) says,

> Her beauty overshadowed the beauties of past and present;
> The lotuses were shamed by her color like jade.

⁵ The peony is one of the most prized flowers in China and is the representative flower of spring. Two kinds are mentioned in our text, the *mu tan* (tree peony with a fibrous stem) and the *shao yao* (similar blooms, but a fleshy stem).

⁶ The *tan chu yeh hua*, lit., "pale-bamboo-leaf flower," is a wild medicinal plant with leaves like bamboo.

⁷ The "heart" here is the *tan t'ien* (center of vitality; lit., "the field of cinnabar"), the region of the body where cinnabar (*tan*), the source of immortality, is secreted. This is a Taoist conception. Cf. ch. ix, n. 32.

⁸ The highest honor for a strict Confucian scholar would be to have his tablet

placed in the local Confucian temple, where pigs would be roasted at the annual sacrifice to the Sage and portions of the meat then placed in front of all the tablets.

⁹ The people's dikes are *nien;* the main dike is a *t'i.* These different dikes can still be seen, for instance, near Tsinanfu. The river is less than a mile wide and is rimmed by small dikes built and maintained by the farmers whose land they protect. The government-built dikes are massive embankments twenty feet high and are anything up to three miles away from the water. The land between the two dikes is fertile and thickly populated.

¹⁰ "Turtle's eggs." The turtle is a creature of ill repute in China. A turtle's egg is much smaller than a turtle and is therefore thoroughly contemptible.

CHAPTER 14

¹ Chia Jang's memorial on river control appears in the *History of the Former Han Dynasty,* ch. 29, "Kou Hsü Chih [Monograph on Watercourses and Ditches]." He claimed that there were three main methods of river control. The best was to give the river a wide strip of territory in which to flow at flood time, where necessary moving the population and destroying towns. The next best was to hold the river in by dikes, but to establish a system of overflow ditches with water gates which would conduct the flood water where it could be used for irrigation. The third and worst method was to repair and heighten the existing dikes thus raising the river bed precariously above the surrounding plain. Cf. ch. iii, n. 27.

² This is the period (403–221 B.C.) when the Chou dynasty had lost all power to control the feudal princes, and the seven leading states, Ch'in, Ch'u, Yen, Ch'i, Han, Chao and Wei, were constantly striving for the overlordship.

³ These labors of Yü are recorded in the *Book of History,* in the section "Yü Kung [The Tribute of Yü]." For the Dragon Gate (*Lung Men*), see *Chinese Classics,* III, 134; for the Gap of Yi (*Yi Ch'üeh*) and Whetstone Pillar (*Ti Chu*), see *Chinese Classics,* III, 128–129; for the Chieh Rock (*Chieh Shih*) see *Chinese Classics,* III, 130–131.

⁴ Ch'u T'ung-jen (*ming* Hsin) was a man of wide reading, especially classics and history, who became *Chü-Jen* at sixty in the K'ang Hsi period, 1662–1723, but failing to obtain his *Chin-Shih* degree, retired and wrote books. His pupils were very successful. He made a collection of essays by ten authors of T'ang and Sung. His collected works have the title *Tsai Lu Ts'ao T'ang Chi.*

⁵ See ch. ix, n. 34.

⁶ Cash were copper coins with holes in the middle by which they were strung together. The standard size of a string was one thousand cash. As appears in the text, the value of a string of cash in terms of silver ounces varied from time to time.

⁷ Kuei Men Kuan ("Gate of Ghosts") was originally the popular name of a narrow gap between two cliffs in Kwangsi, but it became used to describe any remote or dangerous place. During the Chin period (265–419) a Chinese army pursued the people known as the Crossed Legs (*Chiao Chih*) through this pass into the malarial regions to the south. Very few of the Chinese came back. They became ghosts; hence the name. The Chiao Chih are usually identified as Annamese and the name is thought to have phonetic origin. Popular tradition claims that they slept with their legs crossed.

⁸ "Knotted grass" (*chieh ts'ao*) is an expression of gratitude. The *Tso Chuan,*

Duke Hsüan, yr. 15, has the following story. Wei Wu-tzu, a great officer of the state of Chin in the sixth century B.C., became ill and said that his concubine, who had no children, was to marry again when he died. Later when he became worse, he said she was to be buried with him. His son Wei K'o followed his father's first injunction. Some time later he was fighting against the Ch'in army at Fu Shih, beat them, and captured a great Ch'in warrior, Tu Hui. This was achieved by the help of an old man who tied the grass into knots and tripped up Tu Hui. That night the old man came to Wei K'o in a dream and said that he was the father of the concubine he had saved. See *Chinese Classics*, V, 328.

⁹ "Bracelets carried in the beak" (*hsien huan*) is another expression of gratitude. Yang Pao of the Han period, when he was nine, went to the north of the Hua Yin Mountain and saw a yellow bird which had been caught and dropped by an owl and was in danger from ants. Pao picked it up, took it home, and fed in on "yellow flowers" for a hundred days. When its wings had grown, it flew away. That night the bird came in the form of a boy dressed in yellow and holding four white jade bracelets in his beak, and said, "I am sent by the Western Queen Mother (Hsi Wang Mu). You have been kind and helpful to me. I want to thank you," and gave him the four white-jade rings. Then it said, "Your sons and grandsons will be white and pure like this jade, and will occupy great offices." The prophecy was fulfilled. Four generations of Yang's sons were high officials. The story is told in the commentary to the "Biography of Yang Chen (son of Yang Pao)" in the *History of the Later Han Dynasty*, ch. 84.

¹⁰ This was said by the merchant prince, Lü Pu-wei (d. 235 B.C.), at Hantan, capital of the state of Chao, when he found Tzu Ch'u, later Prince Chuang Hsiang of Ch'in, being badly treated as a hostage. Seeing a chance to advance his interests —Ch'in was the rising power—he attached himself to the prince, secured his release, and had his succession to the throne recognized. He later gave up a beautiful concubine to the prince, and she became the mother of Ch'in Shih Huang Ti, the great unifier of China. It is possible that Lü Pu-wei was really the father. The story is told in the *Shih Chi* of Ssu-ma Ch'ien, ch. 85, "Biography of Lü Pu-wei." This biography has been translated by Derk Bodde in *Statesman, Patriot, and General in Ancient China* (New Haven, 1940).

¹¹ The Yu Jung T'ang ("Hall of Great Capacity") was a bank in Tsinan.

CHAPTER 15

¹ *Ch'itung yeh jen.* The reference is to *Mencius*, 5a.4 (*Chinese Classics*, II, 351), where a certain opinion is condemned as being not that of a superior man, but of an uncultivated person of the east of Ch'i. The identification of Ch'itungts'un with the home of the famous "uncultivated" person may be a local tradition, or may be pure invention on the part of our author.

² Chia T'an-ch'un is the name of an efficient and masterful girl in the *Hung Lou Meng* ("Dream of the Red Chamber"). See author's Preface, n. 11. Her character appears in ch. 26 of the translation by Chi-chen Wang (ch. 55 of the original), where she is called Quest-Spring. There is a play on the name "Chia" which has the same pronunciation as *chia* meaning "false" or "to feign."

³ This is the Mid-Autumn (Chung Ch'iu) festival celebrated on the fifteenth of the eighth month. Offerings are made to the moon, which is full at this time, and families make each other presents of moon cakes. These are white and round and flat with a sweet filling of fruit and sugar.

⁴ Cf. ch. 1, n. 4.

⁵ So evil that Heaven punishes him by not giving him children.

⁶ An invocation of Amida Buddha, a common exclamation.

⁷ The names are ironical. Sheng-mu means "Beloved of the Sages." Pi means "Assistant in Government," while Kang, the family name, means "Hard." Kang Pi is a caricature of Kang I, the reactionary official who encouraged the Boxers and was a personal enemy of Liu T'ieh-yün. See Introd., n. 16, and *Eminent Chinese*, p. 407.

CHAPTER 16

¹ Lit., "a regular custom of the wharves (where there are always many whores)."

² The expression is reversed from a line in a poem by Lu Yu, 1125–1210.

> I reach the end of the mountains and the source
>   of the stream and there seems to be no path.
> But here the willows are thick and the flowers bright
>   —there is still another village.

³ The expression is *t'ung yin*, which means "showing a common reverence." It comes from the *Book of History;* see *Chinese Classics*, III, 73.

⁴ Made in Huchoufu in Chekiang.

⁵ Purple (*tzu*) is a term used to describe an official seal. In ancient times a special kind of purple clay from Wutu in southern Kansu was used for the seals of men of high rank, and especially for those of the Emperor.

⁶ From the *Tso Chuan*, Duke Huan, 15th yr. See *Chinese Classics*, V, 64.

⁷ The *nuan ke* is the heated upper part of the hall.

⁸ To the right of the table, i.e., the west, since the hall always faces south.

CHAPTER 17

Motto "Iron cannon" (*T'ieh p'ao*) is a play on the name "Iron" of Lao Ts'an. See ch. i, n. 4. For "jade-bracelet reward" see ch. xiv, n. 9.

¹ This is probably an echo of the second incident recorded in the "Chou Yü" section of the *Kuo Yü* ("Discourses of the States") in which Duke Chao admonishes the Emperor Li to refrain from suppressing the complaints of his subjects lest their pent-up rage should result in his overthrow.

² From *Chuang Tzu*, 3, where the principle of following the Tao or Nature is illustrated by the skill of a certain prince's cook who followed the interstices between the bones of the animals so accurately that he did not need to sharpen his knife for nineteen years. See *Texts of Taoism*, I, 199–200.

³ Lit., "your strength sufficient to carry a bronze tripod." The expression comes from the description of Hsiang Chi (or Hsiang Yü), the great rival of Liu Pang, founder of the Han dynasty. See "Biography of Hsiang Chi" in the *Shih Chi* of Ssu-ma Ch'ien (Chavannes, *op. cit.*, II, 249).

⁴ Lit., "table skirt." This is a hanging (usually embroidered) that covers the top, front, and sometimes the sides of a table at weddings, funerals, and formal occasions.

⁵ Red is the wedding color.

⁶ This is the shrine of Yüeh Lao (The Old Man of the Moon, who with an invisible red thread joins people who are destined to marry) at West Lake, Hangchow.

7 Ts'ui Huan means "a green bracelet"; Huan Ts'ui (using the same characters reversed) means "[a landscape] surrounded with greenery."

CHAPTER 18

1 The name, Fu-t'ing, means "helper of the court."

2 From the "Hou Ch'ih Pi Fu [The Second Fu (Prose poem) of the Red Cliff]." See Drummond Le Gros Clark, *The Prose Poems of Su Tung-p'o* (Shanghai, 1935); and Lin Yutang, *The Gay Genius* (New York, 1947), p. 231.

3 *K'ou pei*, lit., "mouth stone-steles," i.e., the mouths of the people were like tablets recording the good deeds of the just official.

4 Fu-erh-mo-ssu is a very rough transliteration of Holmes.

5 *Hsing ling*, lit., "to impose forfeits." A guest who fails in a scholarly competition is compelled to drink a cup of wine.

6 I.e., the Governor.

CHAPTER 19

1 I.e., opium.

2 *Liang fu* was a salutation made by Manchu women.

3 A stereotyped expression meaning "to take leave." The old post roads had shelters or pavilions built at every ten li. In poems of parting the host often goes with his guest to the first pavilion on the road.

4 K'e-ch'e-ssu. Apparently a foreign missionary.

5 I.e., the third, eighth, thirteenth, eighteenth, etc. of the month, in other words every fifth day.

6 I.e., two *chien* forming one light room and the other separated off by a partition. The outside door would be in the larger room.

7 The prefectural city of Tsinan, seat of the provincial government of Shantung, is in the *hsien* of Lich'eng. The local administration is the responsibility of the magistrate of Lich'enghsien. Cf. ch. vi, n. 12.

8 *P'ai-chiu* is a gambling game played with thirty-two dominoes and a pair of dice. The dominoes have from two to twelve pips. There are four places at the table: (1) that of the banker, (2) the place opposite the banker, called the Gate of Heaven, (3) the Upper Place, to the right of the banker, and (4) the Lower Place, to the left of the banker. Any number of players can stake their money on (2), (3), or (4). The banker first throws the dice to determine where he should start. A one indicates the Banker; a two, the Upper Place, to his right; a three, the Gate of Heaven, etc. Thus when a seven is thrown, Hsü Liang, who is playing Gate of Heaven, is entitled to start. Then the banker moves two dominoes to each of the four places. He compares his score with that of the players at the other three places and payment is made accordingly. This is done four times, and then the dominoes are shuffled. When the sum of the pips on two dominoes is less than ten, that counts as the score. When it is ten or twenty, it is called a dead ten and counts nothing (except where a player gets two matching tens or when one domino is a twelve, two, or eight). When it is more than ten, ten is first subtracted. Thus eleven counts as one. The four highest scores are (1) an Emperor—a six and a three, (2) a pair of Heavens—two dominoes with twelve pips each, (3) a pair of Earths—two with two pips each, (4) a pair of Men—two with eight pips each. Below these come such combinations as a Bridge of

Heaven—a twelve of Heaven with an eight of Man; and a Bridge of Earth—a two of Earth with an eight of Man. Then come combinations of twelve, two, or eight with other numbers. Finally groupings without twelve, two, or eight.

In addition to an ordinary stake on one of the three places a special stake can be put on a corner, for instance between the Gate of Heaven and the Upper Place. In this case the player only wins or loses if both the neighboring places win or lose.

CHAPTER 20

[1] Lit., "Satisfied with my poverty, I know the Decrees of Heaven."

[2] Huang Ya Tsui. *Huang Ya* is the yellow powder produced when cinnabar (see ch. ix, n. 32) is burned. The *Yün Chi Ch'i Ch'ien* (see ch. iii, n. 18) says: "*Huang ya* is the most potent drug for prolonging life; *ya* (which can mean either 'tooth' or 'sprout') is the beginning of all things, and from the fact that it is turned yellow by fire we have the term *huang ya*, yellow *ya*." The place name is probably fictitious and implies the presence of Taoist hermits in the mountain.

[3] This is the commonest way of referring to Hsüan Chuang, hero of the *Hsi Yu Chi*. See ch. xi, n. 29.

[4] Hsi Yüeh Huashan in Shensi is one of the five sacred mountains of China. There are Northern, Southern, Eastern, Western, Middle Peaks. The Eastern Peak (Tung Yüeh) is T'aishan in Shantung.

[5] Before the advent of modernized charities there were many privately organized orphanages and free porridge kitchens in China, often under Buddhist patronage.

[6] I.e., Lao Ts'an's taking Ts'ui-huan as his concubine and Wang Tzu-chin's having advanced the three hundred ounces for her purchase. Apparently Huang Jen-jui had not returned it to him when he said he would in ch. xvii.

Dupuis —

Explore of Red R.

in 1867

Appendix

ELUCIDATION OF THE POEMS
AT THE BEGINNING OF CHAPTER IX

(1) "The nine lotus-enthroned" are nine ranks of Buddhas. "The Jasper Pool" (Yao Ch'ih) is a pool in the palace of Hsi Wang Mu, the Western Queen Mother. Cf. ch. I, n. 1. Her cult is rather Taoist than Buddhist, but here the Jasper Pool is apparently identified with the sacred lake in the Western Paradise of the Pure Land (Ching T'u) sect of Buddhists.

Hsi-i, lit., "Inaudible and Invisible" (taken from the *Tao Te Ching*, 14, see *Texts of Taoism*, I. 57 where, however, "i" is translated, "Equable") is the name by which the Sung Emperor, T'ai Tsung (reigned 976–998) honored the Taoist recluse, Ch'en T'uan, who practised the arts of breath-control and abstention from food, and is said to have slept for a hundred days at a time. His *Chih Yüan P'ien* is a book of Taoist techniques.

"The ocean now rolls where mulberries grew [*ts'ang sang*, lit., "blue, mulberry"]" comes from the *Shen Hsien Chuan* ("Lives of the Immortals") by Ko Hung, 4th century. A female spirit Ma Ku (2nd century) said to Wang Fang-p'ing, "I have seen the eastern sea become mulberry fields three times. When I went to the island of P'englai (see ch. I, n. 2), the water had become twice as shallow as it was before. I wonder when it will be dry land again." Ma Ku is credited with having reclaimed a coastal region of Kiangsu for mulberry growing. A more complete form of the expression is *ts'ang hai sang t'ien*, "blue sea, mulberry fields." The meaning is, "ages have passed in a short time."

(2) (Chang) Tzu-yang was a Taoist recluse of the Sung period, named after a famous cave in Shansi, the Tzu Yang Tung, which was his hermitage.

"Ts'ui Hsü Yin" is the name of a Taoist song, "The Song of Verdant Vacuity."

"Thunderclap Lute (*P'i Li Ch'in*)." There was a withered *t'ung* tree growing on a rock. One night it was struck by lightning, and the part that was not burned fell across a path. A Taoist named Ch'ao made a lute out of it. See Liu Tsung-yüan, 773–819, "P'i Li Ch'in Tsan Yin."

"Heaven-sent flowers clung to the encircling cloud." This refers to ch. 7 of the *Wei Mo Chieh Ching* ("Vimalakirti Sutra"), which is translated in the Eastern Buddhist, v. 2 to 4. When Vimalakirti, in answer to questions by the bodhisattva Manjusri, had given a correct exposition of the Buddhist doctrine of transcending all distinctions of "self" and "others," a heavenly maid scattered flowers over the assembled company. These flowers could not touch the bodhisattvas but attached themselves to lesser disciples who were unable to brush them off. The sutra goes on to show that the flowers only existed for the lesser disciples because they had not eliminated all distinctions from their minds.

(3) "Sky of lust" (*ch'ing t'ien*), "sea of sense" (*yü hai*), and "river of desire" (*ai ho*) are all Buddhist expressions.

"River of Righteousness" (*kung te shui*, lit. "water of [eight] excellencies") is the water in the seven pools of the Pure Land Paradise.

"Man T'o Lo flowers" are lotuses. The lotus is a Buddhist symbol of religious perfection. The dazzling purity of its blossoms grows out of the mud at the bottom of a pool.

(4) "With cracking of rock and trembling of heaven" (*Shih p'o t'ien ching*). From the "Li P'ing K'ung Hou Yin [A Poem on Li P'ing Playing the Harp]" by Li Ho (791–817). The lines run:

At the place where Nü Kua melted rock to repair heaven,
The rock cracked, heaven trembled, and called forth autumn rain.

This is a metaphorical description of the effect of the harp music. See Robert Payne, *The White Pony*, p. 308.

"Three nights under one mulberry tree." In a memorial submitted to the throne in A.D. 166 condemning licentiousness in the palace, Hsiang K'ai pointed out that according to the Buddhist ideal theoretically accepted at court one should never stay long enough in one place to develop attachments of any kind. This is expressed in the words, "a monk does not sleep three nights under the (same) mulberry tree, not wishing to develop a strong liking for it. This is the perfection of purity." See *History of the Later Han Dynasty*, ch. 60b, "Biography of Hsiang K'ai."

(5) "'Wild horses' gallop night and day with clouds of dust" (lit., "wilderness horses, fine dust, night and day, ride fast"). Adapted from *Chuang Tzu*, 1 (*Texts of Taoism*, I, 165), where, after the fabulous gigantic bird called P'eng has been described, we read: "(But similar to this is the movement of the breezes which we call) the horses of the fields, of the dust (which quivers in the sunbeams), and of living things as they are blown against one another by the air." The chapter aims at showing that greatness and smallness are purely relative. Our author uses the expression to build up his picture of the swarming life of the universe.

"Life teams, plants throng [lit., "The five creatures and hundred plants are blown against each other (or respire together)]" is a development of the latter part of the above quotation from *Chuang Tzu*.

Condor Peak (Ch'iu Ling or Ling Ch'iu), is a mountain in India where there were many vultures and where the Buddha is reputed to have preached.

"Seize from Hu Kung his life-suspending power." In *Chuang Tzu*, 7, there is a story of a wizard who is brought by Lieh Tzu to visit his master, Hu Tzu. Hu Tzu shows his superior power by appearing to the wizard in several transformations. In the first he appears to be dead—"with the springs of his (vital) power closed up." See *Texts of Taoism*, I, 263–265.

(6) "The Peepul (or Pipul) leaf is old." *P'u t'i* is a transliteration of the Sanscrit word, *bodhi*, which means "wisdom" or "enlightenment." The *p'u t'i* tree or peepul, or *bo* tree is the *ficus religiosa* under which Sakyamuni became enlightened. The point of the first two lines would

seem to be that just as the teaching of the Lotus Sutra, a late Maha-yana scripture, is essentially the same as that of the historical Buddha, so the two branches of the *T'ai-ku* School held to the same princi-ples.

The second two lines refer to an Indian Buddhist story which is given in the *Fa Hsien Chuan* (translated by James Legge with the title *The Travels of Fa Hsien*). In this book the monk Fa Hsien, the first Chinese pilgrim to the sacred places of Buddhism, describes his journey to India, A.D. 399–415. The story is quoted, with minor varia-tions, in the first volume of the *Shui Ching Chu* ("The Water Classic with Annotations") by Li Tao-yüan (d. 527).

"Three li northwest of the city of Vaisati, north of Patna, there is a tope called, 'Bows and weapons laid down.' The reason why it got that name was this:—The inferior wife [*hsiao fujen*] of a king, whose coun-try lay along the river Ganges, brought forth from her womb a ball of flesh. The superior wife, jealous of the other, said, 'You have brought forth a thing of evil omen,' and immediately it was put into a box of wood and thrown into the river. Farther down the stream another king was walking and looking about, when he saw the wooden box (float-ing) in the water. (He had it brought to him), opened it, and found a thousand little boys, upright and complete, and each one different from the others. He took them and had them brought up. They grew tall and large, and very daring and strong, crushing all opposition in every expedition which they undertook. By and by they attacked the kingdom of their real father, who became in consequence greatly dis-tressed and sad. His inferior wife asked what it was that made him so, and he replied, 'That king has a thousand sons, daring and strong be-yond compare, and he wishes with them to attack my kingdom; this is what makes me sad.' The wife said, 'You need not be sad and sorrow-ful. Only make a high gallery on the wall of the city on the east; and when the thieves come, I shall be able to make them retire.' The king did as she said; and when the enemies came, she said to them from the tower, 'You are my sons; why are you acting so unnaturally and re-belliously?' They replied, 'Who are you that say you are our mother?' 'If you do not believe me,' she said, 'look, all of you, towards me, and open your mouths.' She then pressed her breasts with her two hands, and each sent forth 500 jets of milk, which fell into the mouths of the thousand sons. The thieves (thus) knew that she was their mother, and laid down their bows and weapons. The two kings, the fathers, hereupon fell into reflection, and both got to be Pratyeka Buddhas. The tope of the two Pratyeka Buddhas is still existing.

"In a subsequent age, when the World-honoured one had attained to perfect Wisdom (and become Buddha), he said to his disciples, 'This is the place where I in a former age laid down my bow and weapons.' It was thus that subsequently men got to know (the fact), and raised the tope on this spot, which in this way received its name. The thousand little boys were the thousand Buddhas of this Bhadra-kalpa." *The Travels of Fa Hsien*, ch. xxv, pp. 73–74.

Glossary

chan-lung See ch. iii, n. 16.

chang Ten Chinese feet. A Chinese foot is about fourteen inches.

chien A standard unit in Chinese buildings, about nine by twelve feet in a humble home, but much larger in a wealthy family, being the space contained by four wooden columns that support the roof. In the case of buildings of more than one *chien,* the individual *chien* may be partitioned off into separate rooms or several *chien* may constitute one large room.

ch'ientzu An instrument for roasting opium. See ch. xii, n. 13.

chin A catty, equal to about one and one-half pounds.

Chin-Shih The third and highest literary degree, awarded as a result of the triennial *Hui Shih* (Metropolitan Examination) at the capital, followed by the *Tien Shih* (Palace Examination). *Chin-Shih* is sometimes translated as "Metropolitan Graduate" or "Doctor of Letters."

ch'ing A measure of area equal to a hundred *mou,* i.e., about 15.3 acres.

chou or *chow* A department, an administrative unit larger than a *hsien* and smaller than a *fu. Chou* is sometimes added to the name of the seat of government in a department, e.g., Ts'aochou.

ch'üan-t'ieh A sort of visiting card. See ch. vii, n. 11.

chüeh-chü A poem of four lines. See ch. viii, n. 1.

Chü-Jen The second literary degree, awarded as a result of the triennial *Hsiang Shih* (Examination at the Provincial Capital). *Chü-Jen* is sometimes translated "Provincial Graduate" or "Master-of-Arts."

fu A prefecture, the largest administrative unit under a provincial government. *Fu* is sometimes added to the name of the seat of government in a prefecture, e.g. Ts'aochoufu.

hao Additional name assumed by a man himself, or given by his friends. See ch. i, n. 4.

hou-pu Lit., "waiting to fill." An expectant official who has been approved for a certain office when it falls vacant. See ch. iii, n. 13.

hsien A district, the smallest administrative unit. There were 1,381 *hsien* in the empire. *Hsien* is sometimes added to the name of the seat of government in a district, e.g. Ch'engwuhsien.

Hsiu-Ts'ai The lowest literary degree, awarded as a result of biennial examinations in the prefectural cities. Sometimes translated as "Licentiate" or "Bachelor-of-Arts."

hu A lake.

k'ang A built-in brick bed with flues under it for heating.

lao Old.

li A measure of distance, about one-third of a mile.

lientzu A curtain of cloth, reeds, or other material (according to the season) hung in a doorway in place of a door. It is usually stiffened with wooden cross pieces.

lo A silk fabric with a row of small holes separating every five or more threads in the weave, producing an effect of stripes.

men-shang. A nonmenial employee of a magistrate. See ch. v, n. 3.

ming Personal name. See ch. i, n. 4.

mou A measure of area, about one-seventh of an acre.

pieh-hao A nickname. See ch. i, n. 4.

pien A horizontal plaque, usually of lacquered wood, on which is an inscription, such as the name of a building.

shan A mountain or hill.

taot'ai Intendant. Officials with this title were charged with different sections of the provincial administration. In the text the title refers to a *fen hsün tao* or military *taot'ai* or intendant of circuit who had authority over several prefectures (*fu*) and departments (*chou*). See ch. iv, n. 4.

ts'un A village.

tui-lien A pair of parallel verses written sometimes on paper or silk scrolls and hung in a room, sometimes on wood or lacquer plaques and hung outside a building.

tzu A fancy name additional to the *ming*, also given by the family. See ch. i, n. 4.

wu-hsün-pu A military orderly officer. See ch. iv, n. 2.

yamen A general name for the headquarters of an official, from a district magistrate up. A yamen usually included a hall of justice, administrative offices, and living quarters.

yu-t'iao Lit., "oil-strips." Long strips of dough fried in deep fat.

Key to Chinese Pronunciation

Most Chinese "words" or names consist of from one to three syllables. The generally accepted system of transliterating Chinese used in the English-speaking world is the Wade-Giles system. Most of the syllables are represented in this system as consisting of two parts, an initial consonant and a final vowel or vowel group (sometimes ending in *n* or *ng*). Ten finals (*a, ai, an, ang, ao, e* or *o, en, ou, i, erh*) can form syllables without initials. The following tables show approximately how the Wade-Giles symbols should be pronounced.

INITIALS

Wade-Giles Symbol	Pronounced	Wade-Giles Symbol	Pronounced
ch	j in jay	p'	p in spill
ch'	ch in charm	s	s
f	f	sh	sh
h	h (slightly guttural)	ss or sz (only used before u)	s
hs	sh	t	d
j	r	t'	t
k	g in gay	ts	dz
k'	k in skill	ts'	ts
l	l	tz (only before u)	dz
m	m	tz' (only before u)	ts
n	n	w	w in way
p	b in bait	y	y in you

FINALS

Wade-Giles Symbol	Pronounced	Wade-Giles Symbol	Pronounced
a	ah	ia	yah
ai	eye	iang	yahng
an	on in yon, or ann in mann (German)	iao	yow (ow in how)
		ieh	yeah
ang	in lang (German)	ien	yen
		ih	rr (not trilled)
ao	ow in how		
e or ê	u in cup	in	in
ei	ay in say		
en or ên	un in bun	ing	ing
eng or êng	ung in bung	iu	ew in mew
		iung	ee + ung, or jung (German)
erh or êrh	er in ermine		
i (sometimes written yi when there is no other initial)	ee		
		o (after initials other than h and k)	aw in law

Wade-Giles Symbol	Pronounced	Wade-Giles Symbol	Pronounced
o (after h and k or without initial)	u in cup	uang	oo + ang in lang (German)
		ui (wei)	way
ou (ow)	ow in low	un	un in und (German)
u (after initials other than ss or sz, tz, tz')	oo	ung	ung in bung (German)
u or ŭ or e (after ss or sz, tz, tz')	indicates prolonged buzz produced by voicing the consonant	uo	uaw in squaw
		ü	ü in über (German)
		üan	ü + ann in mann (German)
ua	wa in wand, or ua in guava		
		üeh (io)	ü + eah in yeah, or ue in luette (French)
uai	wi in wine		
uan	wan, or uan in Don Juan (Spanish)	ün	une (French)

A FEW EXAMPLES OF COMPLETE SYLLABLES

Wade-Giles	Components	Complete Syllable as in
so	s + o	saw
lao	l + ao	(al)low
tao	t + ao	Dow
t'eng	t' + eng	tongue
T'ieh	t + ieh	(twen)ty hei(rs)
Liu	l + iu	(loca)l u(nion) or lieu
Ts'an	ts' + an	(i)t's Hon(duras)
ying	y + ing	(pla)ying
yün	y + ün	(cit)y un(ion)

Other Works in the Columbia Asian Studies Series

MODERN ASIAN LITERATURE SERIES

Modern Japanese Drama: An Anthology, ed. and tr. Ted Takaya. Also in
paperback ed.   1979
Mask and Sword: Two Plays for the Contemporary Japanese Theater, by
Yamazaki Masakazu, tr. J. Thomas Rimer   1980
Yokomitsu Riichi, Modernist, by Dennis Keene   1980
Nepali Visions, Nepali Dreams: The Poetry of Laxmiprasad Devkota, tr.
David Rubin   1980
Literature of the Hundred Flowers, vol. 1: *Criticism and Polemics*, ed.
Hualing Nieh   1981
Literature of the Hundred Flowers, vol 2: *Poetry and Fiction*, ed.
Hauling Nieh   1981
Modern Chinese Stories and Novellas, 1919–1949, ed. Joseph S. M.
Lau, C. T. Hsia, and Leo Ou-fan Lee. Also in paperback ed.   1984
A View by the Sea, by Yasuoka Shōtarō, tr. Kären Wigen Lewis   1984
*Other Worlds: Arishima Takeo and the Bounds of Modern Japanese
Fiction*, by Paul Anderer   1984
Selected Poems of Sŏ Chŏngju, tr. with intro. by David R. McCann   1989
The Sting of Life: Four Contemporary Japanese Novelists, by Van C.
Gessel   1989
Stories of Osaka Life, by Oda Sakunosuke, tr. Burton Watson   1990
The Bodhisattva, or Samantabhadra, by Ishikawa Jun, tr. with intro. by
William Jefferson Tyler   1990

The Travels of Lao Ts'an, by Liu T'ieh-yün, tr. Harold Shadick.
   Morningside ed.   1990

TRANSLATIONS FROM THE ORIENTAL CLASSICS

Major Plays of Chikamatsu, tr. Donald Keene. Also in paperback.   1961
Four Major Plays of Chikamatsu, tr. Donald Keene. Paperback text
   edition   1961
*Records of the Grand Historian of China, translated from the Shih chi
   of Ssu-ma Ch'ien,* tr. Burton Watson, 2 vols.   1961
*Instructions for Practical Living and Other Neo-Confucian Writings by
   Wang Yang-ming,* tr. Wing-tsit Chan   1963
Chuang Tzu: Basic Writings, tr. Burton Watson, paperback ed. only   1964
The Mahābhārata, tr. Chakravarthi V. Narasimhan. Also in paperback
   ed.   1965
The Manyōshū, Nippon Gakujutsu Shinkōkai edition   1965
Su Tung-p'o: Selections from a Sung Dynasty Poet, tr. Burton Watson.
   Also in paperback ed.   1965
Bhartrihari: Poems, tr. Barbara Stoler Miller. Also in paperback ed.   1967
Basic Writings of Mo Tzu, Hsün Tzu, and Han Fei Tzu, tr. Burton
   Watson. Also in separate paperback eds.   1967
The Awakening of Faith, Attributed to Aśvaghosha, tr. Yoshito S.
   Hakeda. Also in paperback ed.   1967
Reflections on Things at Hand: The Neo-Confucian Anthology, comp.
   Chu Hsi and Lü Tsu-ch'ien, tr. Wing-tsit Chan   1967
The Platform Sutra of the Sixth Patriarch, tr. Philip B. Yampolsky. Also
   in paperback ed.   1967
Essays in Idleness: The Tsurezuregusa of Kenkō, tr. Donald Keene. Also
   in paperback ed.   1967
The Pillow Book of Sei Shōnagon, tr. Ivan Morris, 2 vols.   1967
Two Plays of Ancient India: The Little Clay Cart and the Minister's Seal,
   tr. J. A. B. van Buitenen   1968
The Complete Works of Chuang Tzu, tr. Burton Watson   1968
The Romance of the Western Chamber (Hsi Hsiang chi), tr. S. I. Hsiung.
   Also in paperback ed.   1968
The Manyōshū, Nippon Gakujutsu Shinkōkai edition. Paperback text
   edition
Records of the Historian: Chapters from the Shih chi of Ssu-ma Ch'ien.
   Paperback text edition, tr. Burton Watson   1969
Cold Mountain: 100 Poems by the T'ang Poet Han-shan, tr. Burton
   Watson. Also in paperback ed.   1970
Twenty Plays of the Nō Theatre, ed. Donald Keene. also in paperback
   ed.   1970
Chūshingura: The Treasury of Loyal Retainers, tr. Donald Keene. Also
   in paperback ed.   1971
The Zen Master Hakuin: Selected Writings, tr. Philip B. Yampolsky   1971
*Chinese Rhyme-Prose: Poems in the Fu Form from the Han and Six
   Dynasties Periods,* tr. Burton Watson. Also in paperback ed.   1971
Kūkai: Major Works, tr. Yoshito S. Hakeda. Also in paperback ed.   1972
*The Old Man Who Does as He Pleases: Selections from the Poetry and
   Prose of Lu Yu,* tr. Burton Watson   1973

STUDIES IN ASIAN CULTURE

NEO-CONFUCIAN STUDIES

COMPANIONS TO ASIAN STUDIES

A Guide to Oriental Classics, ed. Wm. Theodore de Bary and Ainslie T.
   Embree; third edition ed. Amy Vladeck Heinrich, 2 vols.   1989

INTRODUCTION TO ASIAN CIVILIZATIONS
Wm. Theodore de Bary, Editor

Sources of Japanese Tradition, 1958; paperback ed., 2 vols., 1964
Sources of Indian Tradition, 1958; paperback ed., 2 vols., 1964; 2d ed., 1988
Sources of Chinese Tradition, 1960; paperback ed., 2 vols., 1964